ANCHORED

BRIDGET E. BAKER

For my brother Jesse

Oh, how I miss my anchor.

Every.
Single.
Day.

Nothing can make it right. Nothing can heal my heart. Nothing can replace you.

PROLOGUE

The human brain interprets an image in thirteen milliseconds. At any given time, more than a hundred billion neurons are firing in the gray matter of an average kid. I learned that on my very last day of school.

The day before I escaped.

In spite of all those speedy, hard-working neurons, humans frequently make very poor split-second decisions. I'm kind of the expert on the consequences of bad calls.

If the semi-truck driver had serviced his brakes properly, my parents might still be alive. If I'd just lied about my bizarre dreams of Terra, Aunt Trina might not have surrendered us to the state. If I'd dealt with things better at the group home, well. There probably isn't any reality where that would have happened. But if I hadn't freaked out and screamed at my caseworker when he suggested separating me from my big brother Jesse, he might never have fixated on me.

If so many tiny details in my life had played out just a smidge better, someone else could be stuck making this decision instead of me. Someone else could be responsible for saving the world, and that would probably be way better for, well, for everyone.

Because if I'm being honest, I'm not sure the world deserves to be saved.

TERRA

A few years ago, Abraham decided to add a chicken to the performing animals in the troupe's show. We all laughed. I mean, who's heard of a trained chicken?

Except the audiences went wild for her.

That chicken jumped up for treats. She pecked the poodle on the nose when he got too close. She fluffed up and strutted around on command.

A year later, Abraham's poodle caught a duck, and we ate it for dinner. We didn't find the honking little duckling until the next day.

It was all alone—doomed, really.

Or so we thought.

But our chicken adopted that duckling, ushering it around, feeding it, and grooming it. They were entirely different animals, but the chicken didn't care. Sometimes the duckling would hop into a puddle to splash around while the hen looked on with horror, but otherwise, they were inseparable.

I'm exactly like that duckling.

Although, at seventeen, I guess I'm technically a duck.

Either way, after Mom died, the troupe took care of me. Only, unlike the duck, I can't ever float or quack or honk. I have to pretend to be a chicken, and everyone outside of my troupe needs to believe my act.

When the first rays of the sun warm my face, I slide out of bed and dress. The first hour or two of every day are the very best—because there aren't any other ducks around to notice me.

I can be myself.

"Alora," Betty calls from outside. "Are you awake yet?"

"Mornings are the worst." My best friend Rosalinde pulls a blanket over her head. Her words are so muffled that if she didn't say the same thing every morning, I might not understand her. "And they just happen over and over."

"The alternative is probably worse."

"Too early for jokes." Rosalinde throws a pillow at me.

I duck and escape out the door of our wagon.

"Wait," Rosalinde mumbles. "Raisins!"

As if I'd forget.

I *love* our troupe's cook, Betty, but her porridge is disgusting. To be fair, it's not like anyone makes great porridge. It's essentially mush, after all. Sugar is too expensive for regular use, but raisins make the tasteless slop almost bearable. Unfortunately, they're usually gone by the time Rosalinde finally drags herself out of bed. Or, they would be, if I didn't fill my pockets for her.

"I need water from the stream for washing the pots and pans," Betty says. "And—"

"You need more firewood," I say.

"Exactly." Her mouth snaps shut, her hands drop to her belly, and her eyes look off into the distance. She's not paying attention to me anymore.

"Is the baby kicking?"

She nods. "He or she is a feisty little thing. Kicks like a mule."

"Do mules kick harder than horses?" I lift one eyebrow.

Betty rolls her eyes. "No idea, but that's the saying, Miss Sassy. Now get to Lifting."

I could physically reach down and stack the enormous empty buckets and then lug them down to the stream with my capable bare hands, but it's so much easier to reach out with my duckling senses until I feel each bucket, and then Lift them into the air.

With the sun barely rising, it's dark enough that it's still enormously apparent when I do, because every time I Lift, light spills from my eyes—like a warning beacon that I'm a duckling to anyone close enough to see.

"At least you don't need a candle to keep from tripping." Betty laughs. "Now hurry along. I need water for the coffee right away—you've seen Martin without it. No one wants that."

The six large buckets float through the air next to me as I skip down the path to the stream. They're easy to Lift when they're empty, but even once I fill them up, it's not so bad to Lift them back to the wagon circle. I set them down carefully in their proper places around the makeshift kitchen—one on the table near the breakfast pots. One near the fire for coffee. The rest near the washrack. Betty can't lift anything heavy right now with her baby due any day, so I make her job as easy as possible.

By the time I come back with several dozen logs and stack them in a neat pile by the fire, Betty's porridge is almost ready and everyone else is turning out of their wagons, bleary eyed and stiff.

"I'm starving." I pick up a bowl and ladle it to the

brim with porridge. Lifting works up an appetite, almost as much as if I had actually hauled everything myself.

"Don't be taking a double helping of raisins," Betty says. "If Rosalinde wants them, she can roll out of bed early enough to get them herself."

"Yes ma'am," I say.

But when Betty turns her back, I Lift a handful of raisins and tuck them into my pocket. We've been playing this game for years.

Betty looks at the raisins in my bowl and narrows her eyes at me.

I've never been caught, but she *knows* I'm doing it. She's mostly only pretending to be annoyed. Rosalinde isn't Betty's daughter, but we're all part of the same flock in this troupe. Which is why I can Lift here—safely. Without fear. At least until the citizens show up, the ones who would be appalled that a *woman* can do what only men can.

Everyone always says they want to be special, but in actuality they want fancy feathers or a shiny beak. They want to stand out. . .while fitting in perfectly.

If they really were different, they'd hate having to hide all the time. I scarf down the last few bites of my breakfast, carefully allocating one raisin to each bite, and head for the arena, dropping Rosalinde's raisins in her bowl with a wink.

"You better hurry, Alora. I hear the citizens of Spurlock wake up early," Martin says.

I can't allow any of them to see my eyes light up, or they'll know. I trot the rest of the way to the clearing where we'll be performing before too long.

The framework for the set is stacked against a thick copse of trees. I Lift each piece of wood quickly and, almost without thinking, assemble the risers and fix them in place. I'm careful to loop rope around each of my corners so they don't look anomalous, but I Bind it all nice and tight. Can't have anything falling apart mid-show. Once the risers are done, I move to the arena floor, the wooden support pieces flying through the air.

I've never talked to anyone else who can Lift, and I've certainly never been trained properly, but it comes as easily as breathing, as naturally as running or jumping or riding a horse. Maybe even more so.

Finally, I finish by setting up the tightrope across the top of the entire arena, with a rope ladder dangling from either side. Just after I Bind the last cords and cables in place, I notice little specks moving upward from far downhill—from Spurlock castle. They're people, trekking up the hill toward us.

Martin wasn't wrong—they *do* wake up early here. Luckily, Dolores is already standing at the ticket booth, ready to take their money. Healers may not own any arable land, and they may rely on the patronage of citizens to support themselves, but at least they're able to travel from place to place. Since they've taken me in, I can sleep under the stars and see all the sights Terra has to offer. Citizens may look down on Healers, but this life's not so bad. Not so bad at all.

By the time I walk back to the wagon ring to check in, Abraham has the animals ready in their pens. The horses stomp their hooves and toss their heads, their feather headdresses shaking. Ironsides the elephant sprays the monkeys, and they shriek and throw clumps of what I really hope is dirt at Abraham. He should've moved her water bucket once the elephant finished drinking. I Lift it and shove it a few feet back. Abraham salutes by way of thanks.

Martin walks away from our circle and toward the arena, resplendent in his finest suit, the red lapels freshly pressed, his teeth gleaming when he smiles. Rosalinde's stretching to prepare for her contortionist act in the center of the circle, alarmingly close to Betty's banked fire. All around me the troupe's finalizing last-minute details for our performance, but there's still no sign of Thomas, my partner.

When a rock flies past my head, I whirl around, smiling. He's headed for the clearing, ready to warm up. I jog after him, excitement filling me along with big, heaving lungfuls of air.

We always warm up as the stands start filling to give people a little taste of what's to come. Citizens have been known to march all the way out here and balk at the ticket price without something to lure them into the show. Sometimes I Lift Thomas up to the wire for our warm up, but not today. The stands are already filling. My lovely fear-free morning is gone. Now it's time to follow my one cardinal rule.

No one outside of our troupe must ever discover that I can Lift.

Mom's been gone for a long time and my memories of her fade more every day, but I can still hear her voice in my head, repeating the same thing over and over. "Keep your ability hidden, Alora. It's the only way to stay safe."

Healers can't Lift like citizens—they can only Heal.

And among the Healers and citizens, only men have powers. Women can't Lift *or* Heal. They've never been able to do either. A woman's main purpose in life is to bring Mother Terra's new children into being.

Except for me.

Martin says if anyone finds out what I can do, the citizens will take me away, ripping me from the people and the life that I love. Or worse, they could decide that I'm dangerous. . .and destroy me.

I'd rather avoid both alternatives.

Thomas climbs up the ladder closest to us, one rung

at a time, and I follow after him, a little impatient. Once we finally reach the top, I grab the rods sitting on the platform. Thomas snatches both of his staffs out of my right hand, clearly ready to begin, and maybe a bit annoyed that I've been following so close on his heels.

He lifts both sticks over his head immediately, but I land the first strike, our poles thwacking loudly, and we're off. Our routine has changed over the years as we've grown older and bolder. Last month I added the second wire, and that has been my favorite addition yet. We race up one side and down the other, striking and blocking slowly, and then a bit faster. We've just started when Martin waves at us, signaling that we're nearly ready to begin. Indeed, the stands below us are nearly full—which means we've accomplished our task.

Healers are allowed to camp near citizen settlements because of the service they provide—Healing for the injured. They pay for that, and it's enough to buy necessary provisions.

Most of the time.

But if citizens get lucky and avoid injury, or if there's a lean year, things get dicey.

More than fifty years ago, Martin's grandfather worked with several other wagon trains of Healers and came up with a plan. They needed another revenue stream, another way to earn money and purchase food and textiles from the citizens. Now pretty much every troupe of Healers performs as they travel. Our shows usually only draw a decent crowd for the first few days in a new place, but it's enough to cover what we need and set a bit aside. Plus, the performances alert the citizens in each area to our presence, and they bring anyone who's injured after the shows. It's a win all around.

When Martin stands up and begins talking to the crowd, the usual expectant buzzing begins in my arms and spreads through my body. It's always like this prior to a performance. Before my very first show, years ago now, I was terrified, worried that I would completely screw up. I thought the buzzing might make my hands shake, or worse, that I might fall.

Today, I watch, high on buzzy anticipation as Gibby the monkey rides Fuzz the donkey. Biff, Boff, and Buff, our three poodles, jump through hoops, and Ironsides stands on her hind feet, her massive trunk held straight up in the air. The buzzing amplifies when Martin announces Betty's singing and again when he brags about Rosalinde's incredible bending abilities. When Martin announces Roland's strength, the buzzing disappears, because I finally have something to do, some way to contribute. I hide behind the barricade while Roland starts off by lifting small objects. A heavy iron barbell. An enormous barrel with liquid in a chamber at the very top, so it sloshes out. That makes it look full when it really isn't, and then finally, it's my cue.

I help Roland by Lifting an empty wagon for his grand finale. The crowd gasps and cheers, absolutely stunned that he's a Healer, yet he's lifting an entire wagon. It's magical precisely because there's no way he could possibly do it other than using his own brute strength. His eyes aren't lit up, which is the first piece of evidence for the crowd that he's a Healer, not a citizen Lifting. But the second piece is that if he *could* Lift a wagon, he'd be powerful enough to join a Unit, the leaders of the citizen's standing army. No one strong enough to Lift a wagon would forego that kind of honor.

Unless they weren't supposed to Lift at all.

Martin announces Thomas and me next. We stroll out from opposite sides of the stage and climb the ladder up to the tightropes, our poles now tucked into the back of our waistbands. The key with any performance like this is to hold their attention while simultaneously building their anticipation. The beginning is actually the hardest part for me, although it's not at all tricky. It's the panache, the presentation aspect of it that stresses me out, because to prepare them for the second half, I have to make them believe I'm in danger, which means making intentional mistakes and fumbles.

I walk the wire slowly, inching forward, wiping my brow, glancing down at the ground below and wobbling. Thomas walks toward me slowly, steadily, holding out one hand to reassure me. When he finally reaches me, he feints at me threateningly, and we both whip out our sticks. That's when the fighting begins. He and I have practiced pole fighting on a tightrope since shortly after Mom and I joined the troupe. It comes easily to me, mostly because I sense the wire and have a natural understanding of rhythm. Moving fifty feet in the air feels almost as natural as it does on the ground.

After a moment of our sticks clacking as we turn, dodge, and duck, I leap across the three-foot gap to the cable that runs parallel to the one on which we began. No ladders connect it to the ground—it looks as though it hangs from two tall, thin poles. This crowd gasps, exactly as they always do. Thomas leaps across after me. While we jump back and forth, sticks still clacking, Rosalinde climbs up the ladder on my side. She's carrying a black sash in her hand. It's thick and dark and quite substantial. It has to be, or it won't work. Even with my eyes closed, light leaks through when I Lift.

Martin stops us with his booming voice. "This delightful audience is *bored*! We demand more." The audience leans forward in their seats, hooting and shouting, clearly agreeing with him wholeheartedly. They clutch snacks in their greedy hands, their mouths drop open, and their eyes widen.

Martin motions to Rosalinde, and I twirl my way down the wire until I'm standing in front of her. She makes a show of grabbing my wrist. I struggle, but she refuses to release me. Finally I relent, and she ties the sash around my eyes. Not once, not twice, but three times around, and then she knots the back. I can't see anything anymore, but I know that on the other end of the wire, Abraham's trading Thomas' sticks for two shiny, whip-thin long swords. They're blunt, but the crowd can't tell from so far away. They gasp and sigh and exclaim all around.

One woman, bless her, actually cries out. "Watch out! He has swords!"

Now that my eyes are covered, my other senses rush to fill the void. The wash of cool autumn air flows over my body, and the sun's rays lick the bare skin of my arms. People shift and murmur in the stands. Thomas dances across the wire to face me, but I stay still, fixed in place, while Rosalinde and Abraham climb back down the ladder. The smell of popcorn and apple pies wafts toward me from Betty's food stand. Based on the smacking of lips, the jangle of coins, and the crinkle of the pie's wrapping paper, she's doing brisk business for this early in the day.

The thin wire flexes beneath my feet, and I sense the parallel cord as well, Thomas moving toward me along it. Nearly three hundred people are watching down below. It's the perfect time to perform here, really. It's too early in the season for the fall harvest, and too late for watering to be necessary anymore. While the citizens wait for their crops to dry out enough to be cut, they have very little to do, so a troupe in the area is welcomed with giddy glee.

It's strange to think that I used to need my abilities to handle anything up here at all. After so many years,

I'm completely comfortable standing blindfolded on a wire, high in the sky. I rush Thomas, leaning forward as I sprint along the cable. Just as I reach him, I leap into the air, grab a pivot point I've Bound with sand, and spin over his head. I smack him in the back and he stumbles forward. He spins around and comes after me with his swords. I block him easily with my sticks and leap to the parallel wire.

The crowd cheers as we hop back and forth again, much like we did at the beginning, except now I'm blindfolded and defending against Thomas' swords with my sticks. Eventually, we wind up near the platform on Thomas' side of the wire and I stumble backward and drop one stick. The same woman from before cries out again, and a young child sobs. Poor thing.

I hold up my remaining stick to block his sword strike and when he hits the stick with the dull blade, I release a Binding and the top of the stick falls to the ground below as though he sliced it off.

I may never tire of the crowd's reaction.

The remaining piece of my stick falls from my hands, and I wobble in what I hope looks like fright, and fall, grabbing the wire with my bare hands, dangling pathetically from it. I swing back and forth a few times to get some momentum before I jump out and grab the parallel wire. I swing hand over hand the entire length of the cord until I reach the far end. Finally, I shimmy down the pole holding the wire up and land on the ground. I take a bow to pretty impressive applause for a morning show.

A startled yell from far above me and to the right can only be from Thomas. There's no time to try and sense what's happening that far away. I yank off my blindfold and spin toward the sound. Thomas's wire has broken and he's holding on to the end, swinging downward. I have a split second before he lands on the hard ground with a splat. I close my eyes as tightly as I can and slow his descent to the ground so that he lands more softly, probably only breaking his arm. I probably shouldn't have done anything, but I couldn't just watch and hope he wouldn't break his neck and die instantly.

You can't Heal dead.

Hopefully no one was watching me. I *was* facing away from the crowd, and my eyes were closed, so not much light would leak. I doubt anyone would notice the split second slowing of his fall.

But if they did. . . .

The trouble is, very few people alive can Lift a person. Every single one of them has been born into or drafted for military service, and they're probably all ranked in a unit somewhere, commanding officers for either Isis or Amun. My eyes flaring to light while my friend's descent miraculously slowed could be a beacon for anyone who's looking.

I finally take a huge breath, let it out, and turn around.

Not a soul is looking at me—all eyes and attention are focused on Thomas. My heart rate gradually slows, and my breathing evens out.

"Alora," Martin says, his voice urgent and low.

"Yeah?" I brace myself for a monumental scolding.

"Betty's having her baby." Martin points. "That means—"

"I'll take care of her chores too," I say. "I know."

He winds his way back to the front of the ring and closes out the show. Even after the performance is over, he doesn't miss a beat. Not with Thomas falling—he heals his broken arm in front of the gathered audience as some kind of bonus—and not when Betty's baby decides to come early.

I race to complete all my tasks so that I can be there

when the baby's born. I've never seen a Naming, and I'm desperate to be at my first. After all, if I'm ever blessed with a baby of my own, I'd like to know a little more about what's coming.

I race toward Betty's bright blue wagon, elbowing my way past my friends who are lined up outside. "She told me I could watch," I say.

"She told everyone that," Thomas says.

"You owe me," I hiss.

He rolls his eyes and shoves Roland back so that I can squeeze past and up the stairs. "Now we're even."

"Hardly," I say. I try to push past Sara, Betty's oldest daughter, who's standing on the top step.

"Um, family trumps friends." Sara crosses her arms. "I can barely see from here as it is."

I can't even argue with that, but I'm desperate to finally see a baby be born—and the magic that happens afterward, when Mother Terra names it. Then I notice the window off to the left. No one can see through the window, with it being almost ten feet off the ground. But. . .I Bind some dust in two places and leap across to it, dangling from my newly created handholds and peering through the window and into Abraham's wagon.

Betty's lying on her back on the bed, her head leaned back against the wagon wall, her hands braced on either side of her belly. Her face is bright red and her mouth is wide open. She's in obvious distress and possible pain. I blink. This is nothing like I was led to expect. I release my hold and drop to the ground.

Thomas throws his head back and laughs. "Serves you right."

"No one mentioned it would be so. . .disturbing." I frown.

"That's the birth." Sara smiles at me. "The birth is

always hard. It's the Naming that people love to see. Give her a moment. The birth is nearly done."

"Will you tell me when it is?"

Sara nods with a half smile. "I will."

It doesn't feel like a moment. It feels like I'm pacing for an hour. Two. But finally, Sara points at the window. "The baby's born, and she's wrapped."

I Bind handholds again and leap upward, dragging my face up and into the window.

Sara's right. Betty no longer looks upset, or angry. She looks peaceful, and the tiny child wrapped in her arms looks pinker than I expected, but she looks healthy and strong, one arm waving back and forth next to her head.

And then a golden glow begins around Betty and the child. I rub my eyes, but everything looks the same. It really is otherworldly, just like I've heard, as if they're somehow lit from within. Then I notice that Abraham's glowing, too.

"Her name is Sheena," Betty whispers.

Abraham bows his head. "Her name is Sheena. Welcome to the world."

"Does he hear it too?" I hiss. "Or just the mother?"

Sara rolls her eyes. "Both mother and father hear the name when a child is born."

But sometimes there is no father—or no father who will claim a child, anyway. Like with me. I had only a mother, and when she Wasted. . .

I release my handholds and drop to the ground.

And not a moment too soon. Seconds later, a thundering of hooves sounds just past the ring—coming up the hill from the castle below. Most citizens who need Healing come by foot or in the back of a wagon.

A dozen mounted riders? That's nothing good.

I think back to the risk I took, Lifting Thomas to slow his fall. . .without the blindfold. No one did anything at the time, but what if someone noticed. . .and took the information back to Spurlock Castle? It would take them some time to determine what to do, and then to return here. My heart hammers, and my mouth goes dry. I consider hiding, but it's likely already too late for that.

The riders are already here. Eleven horses, by my count, each of them ridden by a soldier in a bright red livery, halt just past our wagon ring.

That's far too many soldiers for me to do anything other than lift my chin and wait . . . and offer a silent prayer to Mother Terra that they aren't here for me.

❀ 2 ❀

TERRA

Martin must have heard the commotion, because he quickly emerges from Abraham's wagon and jogs down the stairs. The riders have just stopped, their horses nervous and jittery. They chomp on their bits and stomp their hooves. The men mounted on them appear much calmer.

"Where's the troupe leader?" a dark-haired man with a gravelly voice asks.

"I'm here." Martin swells up, his chest expanding. "Do you need Healing?"

"None of us," the man says, his expression grim. "But our Unit Leader's son requires your assistance."

I shouldn't breathe a sigh of relief at hearing a child is injured, but I do. I'm a bad person.

"Your leader is the Lord of Spurlock Castle?" Martin glances in the direction of the largest settlement on this side of the Flashing Forest.

The soldier nods brusquely.

Martin closes his eyes. "Is his son Wasting?"

The man shrugs. "He says no. You're bid come to evaluate him."

The citizens almost always insist on having Healers come when a young person is Wasting, though there's nothing anyone can do about that. Abraham would normally accompany him as part of the Healing pair—his size and strength are usually a slight deterrent to grief-induced rage. Even Lifters don't want to mess with two good-sized men, but Martin won't ask him to leave his baby, and he won't take Roland and leave the troupe utterly defenseless either.

"I'm ready." Martin jerks his head at Thomas. "Bring my horse."

"And mine, too," Thomas says.

Martin shrugs. Thomas isn't very skilled yet, but Healers work in pairs.

Unfortunately, Thomas is so small, no one would think twice about him being around. Not much protection for Martin in a possibly hostile situation. While Thomas prepares Francis and Sunshine near the front of camp, I lead Wind over to the big oak tree on the side of the camp and throw his bridle on—with my balance, I don't need a saddle. I'm hoping if I leave near the back of the group, Martin won't even notice I'm going until we're almost there.

I won't allow him to treat someone who's doomed to die without anyone to watch his back.

My plan works perfectly. Martin's so busy talking to the gravelly-voiced man that he never even turns around. Thomas is such a nervous rider that he focuses all his attention on keeping Sunshine from jumping six feet in the air over every rain puddle. Any horse dumb enough to be terrified of water should go into the cookpot, but Thomas unreasonably loves his stupid mare—probably for her gorgeous butter-colored coat.

The guys are going to kill me when they realize I'm behind them. Every time Martin glances over his shoulder on the side I'm on, I pull Wind back or urge him forward so there's another horse and rider between me and him.

As we draw closer to the castle looming ahead, I urge Wind to put on a little more speed.

"Whoa," a tenor voice next to me says. "Why aren't you up by the other two Healers?" His eyes narrow. "And why would they bring a *woman*?"

Because we can't Heal, so what's the point? "I'm an assistant."

His frown deepens, probably because I don't have a bag or supplies, so how can I possibly be planning to assist? Luckily, like most citizens, he knows very little about Healing, so he doesn't bother to argue further.

He does mutter something rather rude about women and racing around and Healers not keeping us in line. Then he shakes his head and spits. He doesn't shift over at all, forcing me to ride along the weedy hedge instead of making room for me on the well-packed and worn road.

Not that I'm surprised. Most of the Followers of Amun treat women like trash. It's one of the many reasons Martin would have objected to me coming, had I given him the chance.

As if he heard my voice, Martin turns around, his eyes widening in alarm when they meet mine. His lips flatten into a thin line. I knew he'd be upset, but what can he say? They won't let him take me back home. He's stuck with my help, whether he wants it or not. I may not look as impressive as Abraham or Roland, but I pack a bigger punch, and it's one that none of these idiots will ever see coming.

Not that I want to chance it. Martin has been so severe about keeping my abilities hidden—he'd probably rather go home on a stretcher than have me stop them from harming him.

The second we reach the wall that surrounds the settlement around Spurlock Castle, the large wooden doors swing open. The men on horses urge their mounts through, and we follow. Racing through the streets of an actual city isn't something I imagined I'd be doing anytime soon. My heart hammers against my ribcage and my thoughts rattle around in my head like dice in a cup. It's so big, so grand, and so overwhelming.

I force myself to focus on why we're here.

A little boy is probably dying.

There's nothing on Terra that Healers hate more than Wasting. It's the one thing they can't Heal, the one injury for which they can't puzzle out a fix. One day you're fine, and the next you're burning up with fever. Three days later, you die.

I wonder how many days this little boy has been struggling.

I hope against hope it's not the Wasting. Maybe it's something else. Maybe it's an unidentified injury.

When we reach the next set of enormous wooden doors, the last defense around the castle proper, the men begin swinging off their horses and tossing reins to stable boys. I'm not sure what to do with Wind, so I lead him over near Martin and Thomas. They're tying Francis and Sunshine to a fence post. Since Wind doesn't get along with others very well, I move down one section and tie him alone.

"I know you're going to say—"

"You should not have come," Martin hisses, his eyes flinty.

"Abraham wasn't coming," I argue, "and I didn't want you here alone."

"Hello." Thomas waves with a small scowl. "I'm right here."

"You know what I mean," I say as kindly as I can manage. "It's not like you know what to do with a real sword."

"Well, I can't tell you how pleased I am that instead of being alone, I've got two of you to babysit." Martin glares.

Does Martin really see *me* as a liability? Still? After my mother Wasted, I know I was a burden, but I was only six. I feel like I've grown and become much stronger— I've proven myself since then. Abraham knows how to punch someone in the nose, but I can Lift an entire wagon.

"Joshua, our leader's son, has been like this for two days," the gravelly-voiced man says. Now that he's dismounted, it's clear that he's tall. Like, ridiculously tall. He towers over even Martin. "Come this way."

I bow my head out of habit, and possibly as a result of the ingrained respect and fear that everyone on Terra has for members of the units, the thirteen men at each castle who command the rest of the soldiers. This man isn't only large—for him to be wearing the livery and running errands for the Spurlock unit leader, he's likely a member of the unit himself. That means he's one of the most powerful and well-trained Lifters in this entire region.

He could very likely squash me like a bug. Maybe Martin was right. Maybe I shouldn't have come. I force my hands to stop shaking. My fear's natural, but hardly helpful.

I expect Martin to explain to this huge man that he can't Heal someone who is Wasting. I expect him to prepare this leader of soldiers for the inevitable. But instead, Martin merely walks alongside the tall man, tight-lipped, his movements jerky.

He's scared.

Even if I'm no match for one of these military trained men, much less thirteen, I'm still glad I came. Family sticks together, no matter what. Martin may not have been Named my father with some kind of golden glowing light, but he's the father of my heart, and that's what matters.

We finally enter a dark room, the curtains pulled firmly closed, blocking nearly every bit of sunlight that would otherwise stream through. The only light comes from a handful of candles strewn around—two on the bedside table. Two on a desk. A lone candle on the wooden beam at the foot of the bed.

It appears they aren't worried about the bedding catching fire, but I certainly would be.

Focus, Alora. That is *so* not the issue right now.

"My lord, the Healers are here." The tall soldier stands entirely still and stares at the man by the bed.

The broad-shouldered man by the bed rises from his chair. I assume he's the Lord of Spurlock Castle— currently their Unit Leader. "You're Healers?"

Martin nods.

"Good. Joshua's injured." Even in the dim light, I can see that his hands are clenched at his sides.

"He's injured?" Martin's eyes are kind. "Or he's Wasting?"

The lord's brow furrows and his lips twist. "It's not the Wasting. If it was, there would be no reason to bring you, would there?"

Oh, no. He's already this aggressive?

"Why don't you tell me what happened, exactly?" Martin walks slowly toward the bed, Thomas tripping along at his heels. I stand against the wall. "What kind of injury is it?"

"A few nights ago he fell off his bed. Joshua told us

about it the next morning," Lord Spurlock says. "Then later that day, he started feeling poorly. I'm sure it's related."

The kid fell a few feet. . .and got up and told his parents about it. They think that caused this? He's lying prone, utterly unmoving. I'm not even a Healer, but I can tell he's Wasting. The father's delusional. A Unit Leader would be completely capable of ending Martin and me, and no one would stop him. But the Lord of Spurlock Castle, who also happens to be their Unit Leader?

He could stab us in the heart and no one would even bother to reprimand him.

Based on the slump in Martin's shoulder, he knows that as well as I do. He rubs his hands together. "Let's check the little fellow out." He steps toward the bed and places his hands on Joshua's small shoulders.

"Can you make me better?" His voice is tiny, desperate.

"I sure hope so," Martin says.

Thomas glances back at me, his eyes downcast. We've been partners on the tightrope for years. I always save him when he stumbles or falls. I always keep him safe.

But I have no idea whether I can catch any of us today, after this.

Martin releases the boy and straightens. "I've delved him." He clears his throat. "I can find no injury."

Lord Spurlock growls. "Try again."

"There isn't anything—"

"Try again!"

Martin flinches and turns back toward the boy.

"Dad." The boy's voice is tiny. "No one can Heal this."

"He hasn't even tried." The father steps closer. "He will do his very best. He'll try all night, if that's what it takes."

So Martin delves the boy again, and then he keeps

right on trying. I've asked so many questions about Healing over the years that I already know it's a total waste of time. I can sense objects that surround me—their weight, their structure. I'm assuming all citizens can—or at least the male ones who can Lift. I've never asked, since apparently females can't Lift, just as they can't Heal. I can sense anything that I Lift or Bind—although luckily I can't sense the Bindings of others. Similarly, Martin and Thomas can sense the internal organs when they delve. I've tried, and all the inner organs feel like a big mushy mess to me, like one mass of gooey juice. Like the inside of an orange.

But to a Healer, every part of the human body is distinct and different.

And when someone is Wasting, everything is working perfectly. The body simply heats up. . .and then gives out. Which means there's nothing for Martin to fix, nothing to adjust, nothing to correct. All he can do is sense the shape and feel and functionality of perfectly working body parts over and over. . .until the boy dies.

An agonizing hour after we arrive, a woman I assume is the boy's mother enters. "Oh, Joshua."

Martin gratefully shifts backward so that his mother can embrace him.

"Is this the Healer?" Her bright eyes are hopeful in her round face. "Does he know what's wrong?"

Lord Spurlock's tone is flat. "Not yet."

"Kyle said he's been here an hour." She frowns. "Just tell me."

"There's nothing to tell," the father says. "Nothing."

"He's Wasting," she whispers, her face turning up toward Martin. "Isn't he?"

Martin nods.

"He's not," Lord Spurlock practically shouts.

She places a hand on her husband's arm. "Hush,

Leonard. Yelling at these people won't help Joshua." Her voice drops to the barest of whispers. "And it won't help me, either. You can't frighten this away, dear. Not this."

Lord Spurlock's shoulders droop first, and then his entire body slumps, like a puppet with sliced strings. He collapses into the chair, and his wife sits down on the edge of the bed, next to Joshua. Both of them talk softly to their son.

Martin and Thomas inch backward toward me slowly, trying not to draw any more ire. We stand by the wall for three more hours, almost forgotten.

Until the boy dies.

His mother sobs quietly. Lord Spurlock picks the little boy up and clutches him to his chest, rocking back and forth. It's an extremely private moment, and I'm uncomfortable witnessing it. I scoot quietly toward the door and crack it a bit.

The gravelly-voiced man, probably Kyle, stands outside, his eyes widening when he sees me. "Is Joshua alright?"

I shake my head tightly.

His face falls. "Oh, no."

"We probably ought to leave," I whisper. "I think they need some privacy."

"It was the Wasting, then," he whispers, his voice surprisingly gentle.

I nod.

"Yes, you probably ought to be shown out." He widens the door and motions silently for Thomas and Martin to come. They don't waste any time following Kyle's directions. We're halfway down the hall to the main corridor when someone calls for us.

"Wait. Healers, wait."

I freeze, dread pooling at the bottom of my stomach.

We were so close to escaping. I turn slowly, Martin and Thomas turning stiffly at my side.

"Yes?" Martin asks.

It's Joshua's mother. Tear tracks streak her face. "You haven't been paid."

Martin shakes his head. "No payment is necessary."

She walks toward us, her soft slippers barely making a sound on the plush carpet. "You came to try and save my boy in his last moments. You knew what was happening, and you came anyway. And when my husband frightened you, you were still kind." She unclasps a golden pendant from around her neck and extends it. "I don't have money with me, but please. Take this."

Martin's eyes widen. "I couldn't possibly."

"If you don't, I'll be forced to leave and hunt down our clerk to obtain payment."

She'll have to leave the bedside of her deceased child and his mourning father. Martin sighs and extends his hand, reluctantly taking the ornate pendant, a symbol of a Ram's head. It represents Amun, the foretold God whom the Followers of Amun believe will one day return.

"I know Healers don't believe in Amun, but you can melt it down or sell it to one of his followers." She forces a sad smile. "Thank you for your kindness and your willingness to help." Her eyes well with tears.

"Our thoughts are with you, Lady." I try to curtsy. I have no idea what I'm doing, but I manage not to fall on my face.

She wipes her eyes and turns around, jogging back to her husband and departed son.

And then we walk out, mercilessly safe. Unchallenged. Alive. I shouldn't be, but I'm startled to find that when we emerge, the sun has already set. There's a chill in the air, and I shiver. Most concerning of all, Francis, Sunshine, and Wind aren't where we left them. Martin looks at me, and then we all turn to the soldier who brought us.

Kyle grunts. "I trust you can find your way back to your wagon ring."

"What about our horses?" Martin asks. "We tied them to this post in our haste." He points to the conspicuous lack of mounts anywhere.

"Ah." The man nods. "They'd have been taken to the stable. Look for Robert and tell him you're the Healers whom Lord Leonard bid come."

We follow his directions to the stable and locate Robert pretty easily. He has the reddest face of any man I've ever met, and he's even surlier than Lord Spurlock. . .which is moderately impressive. His nearly black hair is streaked with silver, almost the exact color of his eyes. "They're here." Robert points, and I follow the direction of his arm and find our horses. Thank goodness.

The guy's saddles are slung over the side walls of the stall doors. The bridles are slung next to them.

I didn't expect them to take such good care of our horses, honestly. I lift the latch to enter Wind's stall and he whuffles against my hand, searching for a treat. "The second we get home, boy, I promise." I bridle him and lead him out while I wait for Martin and Thomas to saddle Sunshine and Francis. They lead their horses out, and Thomas gives me a boost up onto Wind. After all, I can't exactly Bind handholds to hop up right here in the Unit stable.

I breathe a heavy sigh of relief as we all head for the exit. Wind is nervous, as are Sunshine and Francis. They can probably pick up on our nerves, but soon we'll be gone. Robert's leaning against the front doors of the stable, glaring. We can't escape this place fast enough.

"Your saddle is canted sideways," Thomas says.

I glance over at Martin and realize that his is. Every

horse holds in some air, but Francis is the absolute worst about it. It would be just our luck for it to slide around sideways and have Martin fall off now that we're finally heading home. He groans and swings off, bending a little to tighten the girth.

The necklace hardly makes a sound when it slides out and lands on the cobblestone floor of the front of the stable. Only a tiny clink, really. But Robert notices it immediately, his eyes narrowing and his lip curling. He straightens and strides toward us. His fingers dart downward and pick it up. "You trashy thieves. This is her ladyship's pendant."

I shake my head. "No, you don't understand. She gave it to us, as payment."

He sneers. "She would never—she wears it everywhere. You stole it, and you won't get away with it." His eyes glow, silver light spilling outward, and I realize he's Lifting something. I reach out with my senses, *feeling* for any threat.

The dagger isn't large, but even something small can do a lot of damage when it's aimed at a man's heart. I don't have time to think, to argue, or to be rational. It's why I came—to protect Martin.

I Lift the dagger and send it flying into the side wall. Then I Lift Robert from the ground by his throat, his eyes bulging, and fling him against the front of the stable. His head makes a thump as it connects with solid wood, and I shudder.

"Run," Martin shouts. "Run, now." He leaps to the back of Frances and gallops out of the stable. Thomas and I follow without argument. The guards aren't accustomed to blocking people from exiting, and they simply move aside as we thunder past the gates to the main castle. By the time we reach the entrance to the surrounding town, someone is sprinting after us, shouting.

"Faster," Martin screams.

Wind could outpace both the other horses without a thought, but I don't let him. I stick to their sides, and as our horses exit the main city gate and cobblestones give way to packed dirt, we accelerate yet again. We reach the wagon wing of the troupe in record time, all three horses winded and huffing.

"Hitch up the wagons," Martin yells. "We leave immediately."

"I don't understand," I say. "You didn't actually steal anything. Surely the lady will clear that misunderstanding up."

Martin doesn't even look at me. He's staring at the other members of the troupe who are all goggling at us wide-eyed and open-mouthed. "Alora Lifted in the camp. They'll be coming for her any moment."

They pack faster than I imagined possible. Moments after we arrive, the wagons are hitched, the horses are hooked up, and we're on the road.

"Tie Wind to the back of my wagon," Martin says. "Next to Francis. He'll need a break."

"But then where will I—"

Martin pats the bench seat beside him. "I have some things to tell you, and they aren't good."

"What do you have to tell me?" The hard ball forming in my stomach isn't patient. I shouldn't have Lifted or harmed Robert, but he tried to kill Martin. It was self defense. Surely Lady Spurlock will see that.

"I've always stressed the importance of keeping your ability hidden." Martin's voice is gruff, angry even.

"He would have killed you," I say. "He sent a dagger—"

"Thomas could have Healed that," he says. "And as

you say, the lady would have cleared up the misunderstanding."

"You can't Heal dead." I set my jaw. That dagger was
headed for his heart.

Martin's strong hands cover mine where they're
knotted on my lap. "I love you, Alora. You know that."

"I'm sorry." My voice is small, broken. "Did I ruin
everything?"

He turns toward me then, his hands squeezing mine.
"I'm not angry with you. I'm worried about you."

"But why?" I wail. "Everyone knows women can't Lift.
It's not a crime to abandon life as a citizen and join a
troupe, they just think it's a fate worse than death so
none of them do it. They'll assume you Lifted to stop his
dagger, or that Thomas did. No one will suspect what
they know cannot be."

Martin shakes his head slowly. "Robert was staring
right at you. He saw your eyes light up."

"So they'll finally know the world isn't as simple as
they thought," I say. "It was the Followers of Amun. They
hate women. They probably won't even care."

"Wrong," Martin says. "They do hate women, but
they have a prophecy about a woman who will one day be
born who will be able to Lift. They call her the Warden,
and they believe she will destroy Terra."

I swallow. "They can't possibly—"

"They've all taken an oath, every last member of the
Followers of Amun." Martin stares straight ahead. His
knuckles grip the reins of the wagon so tightly that
they're entirely white.

"What kind of oath?"

"To kill you, Alora." His voice trembles. "Now they
know you're real and not some empty threat made up by
their forefathers. They'll never stop coming for you." He
turns to face me. "You'll never be safe again."

❧ 3 ❧

EARTH

The obnoxious bleating of my alarm clock drags me back to reality, and I force my eyes open. My eyes burn, but it can't be helped. I've got to get up, shower, and get moving. There are dollars to be made, because we've got bills to be paid. It doesn't keep me from groaning as I roll off my mattress and stand.

My brother Jesse yawns as he exits the bathroom ahead of me, his hair managing to stick up in four different directions in spite of being wet. "Morning."

I grunt.

He stops and leans against the doorframe. "You okay?"

I shrug. "*I'm* fine. Tired, but fine. But over on Terra. . ."

He tilts his head sideways. "Twist an ankle on the tightrope again?"

I roll my eyes. "Martin would Heal that immediately." I shake my head. "Other than, you know, being tele-kinetic, my dreams of Terra are pretty mundane. But not last night."

"What does that mean?"

I fill Jesse in on the bizarre happenings. "And Martin loaded everyone up and took off." I drop my voice, which is completely ridiculous given that not a soul can hear us in this tiny apartment, alone. "He said the Followers of Amun want me *dead*. He said that's why my mom brought me to live with them in the first place."

Jesse blinks. "Your imagination's running wild today."

"Maybe."

"Do you think you're really in danger?" For all his teasing, my brother looks uncomfortable.

"I mean, that's the question, I suppose. *Is* Terra real, and can I be permanently injured there?" I shake my head. "I don't know."

"You've been Healed there." He bites his lip. "You go to bed here with bruises and wake up completely fine. Sprained ankles. Scrapes and cuts."

I sniff. "I know."

"I'm worried."

"Me too."

"I'll think about it today," he says. "You do the same."

It hardly seems like a solution, if I really do live on two different worlds, Earth and Terra, and if dying on one means dying on both. But I don't know what more we could possibly do. I don't even remember that Earth exists when I'm on Terra. I've been dreaming of Terra as long as I can remember, and it's still confusing. I consider my situation on Terra while I shower, dress, and eat. Every time I close my eyes, I hear the dull thunk Robert's head made as I flung him against the stable wall.

I may be in danger, but that doesn't feel too real, not yet anyway. No, what bothers me the most is that I may have killed someone.

The doors on the city bus hiss as I step down to the sidewalk. Ah, the muggy embrace of Houston in September. I walk as quickly as I can toward my place of employment: Perry's Steakhouse. I'd love to walk through the front door and order a thick, juicy steak with risotto, or the grilled swordfish that's flown in from the coast. Sitting down to eat that might get my mind off of Terra, at least momentarily.

But that's not on the menu for me. Ever.

As a dishwasher who takes her payment in cash under the table, I'm sort of Exhibit A of a cautionary tale. I'm a good warning to kids who want to drop out of school. By the time I reach the staff entrance, I've only been outside of the air-conditioned bus for a moment, but my shirt's already clinging to my skin. Thanks to a substantial wine delivery, the staff door's blocked by crates stacked up on a cart. I don't want to be late, so I circle to the front of the restaurant warily. If I'm quick, maybe no one will notice I broke a small rule—sometimes that's what life demands. Break a little rule to avoid running afoul of a large one.

I duck through the front door quickly, pausing for a moment while my eyes adjust to the light inside the restaurant. Perry's employs mood lighting expertly, even at lunch, but it's always a bit of a shock when you push past the front door. Small lights wink from the wine display. The low fixtures throughout the main dining area are bright enough to read the menu, but dark enough that your meal remains private. As I walk past the doorway into the dining room, I notice that some of the guests here for an early lunch ordered my favorite dishes. The chateaubriand they carve at your table, usually enough for two. Perry's famous pork chop, so moist and delicious it melts in your mouth. I pause and breathe in the scent of the very best of all: the southwest filet mignon wrapped in applewood-smoked bacon. It's served with a corn and fig relish so amazing that I'd almost trade one of my kidneys to get it. I do have two, after all. My mouth waters involuntarily, but I swallow and keep walking.

I always come to work hungry. It would be an insult to do otherwise.

Of course, I've only ever had a few bites of the relish. By the time the plates reach me, there usually isn't any left over. The administration would definitely fire me if they knew, but when the bus boys bring the plates back to be washed and they're covered in delicious food, I just can't scrape it all in the garbage. So I eat it—or I dump it in a to-go box and take it home.

The assistant manager, Ramon, who knows nothing of my pilfering, scowls at me when I reach the sinks in the back. "What are you smiling about?"

I can hardly tell him that I doubt the emaciated woman in the blue backless dress will finish her filet, much less the relish on top. So instead, I force a smile. "It's nothing. I'm fine. Just excited for another wonderful day at work."

His scowl softens to a frown. "You're ten minutes late."

I glance at the clock, which even after my wine delivery detour reads eleven thirty-two a.m. I don't bother arguing with him—that's what got me stuck on lunch shifts in the first place. Doing both lunch and dinner shifts gives us overtime hours, so they don't allow that, but being stuck on lunch shifts isn't really enough to be full time. I need to make Ramon happy or I'll never get my full time hours back.

The problem is, he gets mad at people for nothing at all and becomes downright enraged if you disagree with him over anything. My best path is to politely acknowledge his displeasure and get right to work. I dive right in on the enormous pile of plates waiting for me in the second sink. Of course Henry, my co-worker who was supposed to come in at ten-thirty to clean up all the prep work dishes, isn't here yet either. He's far more than two minutes late.

If I were Ramon, I might be cranky too. If I'd come an hour late like Henry regularly does, the assistant manager might have been elbow deep in sudsy water himself. That image brings an unbidden smile to my face.

After a few minutes of huffing and stomping around behind me on the pristine, porcelain tile floors, Ramon curses. "Is Henry ever coming?" He fumes. "When he does, I'm firing him. He's been late too many times."

Henry's tardiness is so consistent that it's nearly his hallmark. "Don't fire him. He loses track of time some-times, but he always works hard once he gets here." Jesse's always reminding me that most people are oper-ating at capacity. If Henry loses this job, where else could he work? What's less skilled than washing dishes?

Ramon raises one eyebrow. "You're pulling double duty because he didn't show. You should be brandishing a pitchfork."

I shrug. "So if I don't mind. . ."

Ramon's face turns bright red, as if defending Henry was a terrible offense. "I don't like noble gestures. If he's not here in the next hour, I'm firing you both."

Who hates noble gestures? That's why they're noble! Ugh. Ramon is the worst. And Henry better not be more than two hours late. Without this job, I won't make rent.

Pretty soon my shoulders ache and my skin smarts from the hot water, and thanks to Henry's absence I'm barely keeping up. The pile isn't diminishing at all, no matter how much elbow grease I expend.

But on the flip side, working alone makes it much easier to scrounge for leftovers. My belly and the to-go box I shoved into the drawer next to my sink are both entirely full in less than forty-five minutes, which I know because I'm watching the clock like a pot that's never going to boil.

I may be about to lose my job, thanks to my big mouth and a stupidly loyal streak, but the new mushroom risotto is even better than the garlic potatoes. And in a rare stroke of luck, someone, probably that bony woman on what was clearly a first date, actually left an entire filet (minus one or two token bites) on her plate. I can't very well eat it here, gnawing on it like a dog over the sink, but I stuff it into my box for Jesse.

Thanks, skinny rich lady. Don't worry, you're better off not eating that fifty-dollar hunk of meat. Yes, your bony clavicle looks absolutely gorgeous protruding from your body at that awkward angle.

I'm so full I might pop when Henry finally shows, five minutes before Ramon said he'd fire us. "You're nearly two hours late." I lift my eyebrows. "That's bad, even for you."

Henry's hair is wet, and his dark curls stick to his forehead.

My eyes are drawn to a shining drop of water—or perspiration—rolling down his neck. "You're dripping."

He hasn't even glanced up yet. He's too busy taking his soccer bag to the back and replying to a text. His t-shirt clings to his abs. Not for the first time, I glance appreciatively at the outline of Henry's washboard stomach. Maybe I'm not as loyal as I am flirty.

"My soccer game got delayed." He glances up at me absently. "Whoa, look at that pile of dishes. I'm so sorry."

I throw a towel at his head. "Just start working." It would be just like Ramon to fire us even though Henry squeaked in before the deadline. . .because he wasn't washing anything yet.

"Alice, I'm sorry."

After more than a year, I'm used to people calling me

by my fake name—Alice—instead of Alora, but some-times it still strikes me funny. Even on Earth, I'm stuck pretending to be a chicken.

"Don't frown—I really am sorry. I forgot I was even working today until I was in the shower after practice, but I threw on my clothes the minute I realized it and ran over here."

"You forgot?" I sigh. "I've been doing my best, but as you noticed, I'm way behind, and I'll warn you, Ramon is not pleased."

"Is Ramon ever in a good mood? If I was an assistant manager at forty, I'd probably yell at everybody I could too. His paunch isn't helping his mood, either."

I don't bother pointing out that being a dishwasher in his early twenties doesn't exactly set Henry on a different trajectory than Ramon. That kind of insight probably wouldn't be appreciated. Henry may talk trash, but at least he dives right in to help me catch up. Ramon comes by a few minutes later, but instead of chewing Henry out, he just glares at him for a moment, glances at me with narrowed eyes, and spins on his heel.

Right after Ramon stalks away, my favorite server plonks an enormous pot down next to Henry. "Bunch of stuff is piling up over there." Chris gestures to the corner where the bus boys usually stack things. "If you hadn't been so late, we wouldn't be behind."

I shake my head at Chris. "It's fine. I'll grab them." I wipe my hands on my apron and jog across the kitchen. I'm loading up a tray when a phrase in the dining room catches my attention. I've heard it before—but not here.

Never on Earth.

"—Followers of Isis. But apparently they're preparing for something big."

My head snaps sideways.

"Who cares?" An overweight man slices a bite off his

ribeye and pops it into his mouth. His designer suit can't do anything about his double chin. "Look, until Holden says we should be concerned, I'm not worried what they're doing, and you shouldn't be either."

Without thinking this through, my feet start moving. I'm not allowed to leave the kitchen, but in this moment, I'm not getting caught up on rules. It's the first time in my entire life that I've heard someone talk about Isis or Amun as anything other than some kind of joke about ancient Egyptian history. As I approach, the heavy man looks up at me. The other gentleman he's eating with makes eye contact with me as well. Silvery eyes that just match the silvery accents in his dark, short-cropped hair, and a ruddy, red face.

My heart practically stops dead in my chest. Because the companion, the one who mentioned the Followers of Isis, other than the length of his hair, looks *exactly* like Robert—the man I flung into the stable wall on Terra. I choke and cover it with a cough.

"Are you alright?" the heavy man asks. "Can we help you with something?"

I'm not on Terra. And clearly I did not think this through. Here on Earth, I have no reason in the world to be walking to their table—I'm a dishwasher. I tilt my head, searching the lookalike's eyes for any kind of recognition. "Robert?"

The man's silvery eyes widen. "Yes. My name is Robert." He glances at his companion for guidance. Then, apparently not getting any, he turns back to me. "I'm sorry, have we met?"

I swallow. "I'm positive I know you from somewhere, but I can't place where."

"Do you work here?" the heavyset man asks, glancing pointedly at my white staff polo shirt with the word 'Perry's' embroidered on it.

"I do, right. I was coming to see whether you have any dishes you're finished using. I can take them to the back and get them out of your way." I glance down at the full plates of food that clearly just arrived. I'm such an idiot.

"We don't yet." Robert smiles at me, but his brow furrows. "But give us a few moments and I'm sure we will."

I gulp. "I overheard you mention the Followers of Isis."

The overweight man flinches, and Robert's eyes widen.

"It's just that I have a project due for my Egyptian Antiquities class, and it's on Isis and Amun-Ra. I figured maybe you were, like, specialists on him or something. I'd love to interview you."

The heavy man pulls a card out of the inside pocket of his suit. "I'm not an expert *per se*, but I'd be happy to teach you everything I know." The gleam in his eye makes me nervous. His smile broadens. "Call me, whenever."

My stomach turns.

"Alice!" Ramon's urgent whisper yanks my head back more effectively than a punch to the nose.

"I'd better go. I apologize for interrupting your meal."

"You can interrupt my meal anytime," the heavy man says.

Ugh. I spin around and race back for the kitchen, but a strange look on Robert's face sets my teeth on edge. He's still staring at me intently while I gather up the dishes on the tray and take them back to the sink.

"What was that?" Ramon barks.

"I thought I knew someone," I mutter.

Ramon's scowl scorches me from across the kitchen, and I know one of his rants is coming. The other employees freeze as if they can feel it, too. "If the Queen of frigging England comes to eat here, and it turns out she changed your diapers as a baby, you will stand in front of that sink and wash dishes. And under no circumstance, *ever,* are you to *leave this kitchen.* Do you understand me?"

I don't think the Queen of England even changed the diapers for her own children, but I keep my lowly serf mouth shut about it. "Yes, sir."

A commotion from the dining room draws my eye. When the kitchen staff congregate at the door to the dining room, Henry and I follow suit, staying carefully near the back of the rubberneckers.

"What's going on?" I ask.

Ramon disappears to address the issue, whatever it is. Manager and all.

"Someone has passed out," Chris says. "One of the guests. He's on the floor, unresponsive."

I jostle past Jenny until I can barely make out the dining room. There's a man on the floor, mouth and eyes open, not moving at all. His eyes are vacant.

It's Robert.

Ramon storms through the door and orders us back to our positions. I obey, but I wash dishes without thinking, my mind spinning a million miles a minute.

I flung Robert into the side wall of that stable. It likely caused damage to his skull, and maybe a brain bleed. Martin could have Healed him, if we hadn't run. But then the man surely would have told everyone I could Lift. Martin fled. . .to save me. To keep my secret hidden. Now on Terra, we don't know whether he survived to tell people about me. . .or died.

What if he bled and bled and bled into his brain. . .and then finally died?

And now, a seemingly healthy Robert here, a mirror image of Robert from my dream world, just. . .collapses?

The ambulance comes a few moments later, and I listen for the rumors. Finally Chris drops off a tray of dishes. "Heart attack, the medic said. They couldn't revive him on site. They're taking him to the hospital, but it doesn't look promising. They think he's—" He drops his voice to a whisper. "—dead."

My shift is nearly over when Robert's dinner companion, the heavyset man, pokes his head into the kitchen. "Is there a manager I can speak to?"

"Mr. Sinclair, of course." Paul, the general manager of the entire restaurant, has materialized as if by magic. "I am so sorry about your friend. What more can we do? Anything at all."

"I'd love to speak to you privately, if possible." The man glances my direction and our eyes lock. He doesn't frown. He doesn't smile. Then he turns and ducks into Paul's office.

The skin across my shoulder blades crawls. What is he asking? Why does he need privacy to do it? Is he asking about me? I live by three rules: take care of Jesse, avoid being noticed, and don't trust anyone. Robert dying, and then this guy coming back here to talk to Paul, put me on high alert for both the second and the third.

I need to know what this guy is saying and whether it's about me. Pronto.

"Hey, I'll go grab another tray of plates," I say.

"I can go." Henry wipes his hands.

I leap in front of him and put both hands against his chest. "No, it's fine."

Henry's eyes widen and he meets my eyes. "Okay. You're being really weird today. What's up?"

I don't have time to deal with him, not right now. "We can talk later." *Now let me go*, I plead with my eyes.

Henry raises one eyebrow and then shrugs. "Okay.

I've been meaning to talk to you about something anyway."

Huh? "Uh, great."

Henry smiles and goes back to washing. I breathe a sigh of relief before jogging across the kitchen to the bus boy's cart. It happens to be right around the corner from Paul's office. This time I stack the plates as slowly as I can, one ear turned toward the closed door.

It's hard to make out anything over the clangs and bangs from the kitchen, but I catch isolated phrases, mostly from Paul. I inch a little closer, inspecting a dirty plate as if it needs evaluation for some reason.

"Warum brauchen sie diese Informationen?" Paul asks in German.

Paul asked the man why he needs the information. Paul has no reason to know that I speak German, so perhaps they switched languages to prevent eavesdropping. But they could switch to Spanish, Russian, Mandarin, Czech or Swahili, and I'd still understand. I have no idea how, but I've always been able to speak any language I hear. I've learned the hard way to keep this ability to myself. My French teacher thought it was cool right up until she got freaked out and called the school counselor, who only relaxed when I lied and said I learned to speak French fluently from a childhood nanny.

The man's reply is too soft to hear, but I make out the words *Freund* and *Familie*, which means family friend. But who is he claiming as a family friend? Paul? Robert? Me?

"Ich darf keine Namen von Mitarbeitern nennen." Bless Paul for speaking so loudly. "Ich kann dir ihre Adresse sicher nicht geben."

The man asked Paul for my name and address, apparently, but he won't give it to him.

"I wish I could help you more," Paul says, inexplicably switching to English. "Today has been harrowing all around, and I offer my greatest condolences to you again that this took place in our restaurant. I can certainly ask Alice whether she'll speak with you. Would that suffice?"

I practically sprint across the kitchen and plunge the entire tray of dishes into my side of the sink.

"Whoa there, Speedy Gonzales. What's going on with you?"

I glance behind me one last time and then turn back to Henry. "I thought I saw someone I knew in the dining room."

"So that's why you went in there." Henry shakes his head. "Ramon's still steamed about it."

"I know, but I was wrong. I didn't know him. But in a bizarre twist, that's the man who died. And now the old man who was sitting across from him is in Paul's office, asking about me."

Henry's eyes widen. "Are you serious? Wait, does he think you, I don't know, had something to do with it?"

I shrug. "I hope not. I didn't even touch them or their food or anything. I couldn't have."

"Of course not." Henry scowls, suddenly. "Paul didn't tell him anything about you, right?" Something about the intensity in Henry's expression surprises me.

"Yeah, I mean, no, of course he didn't. But he said he'd ask me if I would talk to him."

"You'll obviously refuse." Henry's still scowling. "That guy may be upset about his friend, but there's no reason to drag you into this, just because you thought you knew him. It was a coincidence."

I don't mention that I knew his *name*. And I certainly don't mention that he was talking about the Followers of Isis. The only place I've ever heard anyone mention the Followers of Isis or Amun is on Terra. Can I really afford *not* to talk to him? He's the first person on Earth who might know something about my bizarre dreams.

Dreams in which I'm now in danger, it seems.

My hands tremble and my heart races. I want to run, immediately, as fast and as far as I can. I wish I had a circle of wagons to ride with me over the nearest mountain range, or through an eerily lightning-laced forest. But here on Earth, I don't have an adopted family that stands behind me. I'm all alone, me and Jesse, and for transportation, a city bus is pretty much my only option.

A moment later, Paul and his guest emerge from his office. I brace myself for him to approach and ask my permission to speak to the customer, but they just shake hands. The heavy man leaves without a backward glance.

It's a relief. . .and it's also the saddest part of my day, honestly.

Or, at least, right up until I'm packing up to leave it is. Because for the first time since I started working here, Ramon notices when I stick my to-go box into my shoulder bag.

And he fires me for it.

4

EARTH

Henry argues with Ramon about his decision, but between meeting someone I saw on Terra, and the heavy guy asking Paul to share my info, I can't handle any more stress.

"It's fine," I say. "I'll go."

Henry pivots on his heel, turning to face me. "What?"

I shake my head. "I'll find something else. It's okay." I sling my bag over my shoulder, lighter without a takeout box inside. I find it ironic that only this morning, I argued with Ramon for *Henry's* job, and now he's trying to save mine.

"Don't have them call here for a reference." Ramon glares at me and crosses his arms.

As if I would dare to list a job where I'd been fired. Luckily, I'm young enough that experience usually isn't necessary. I duck out the staff exit, no wine crates blocking my way this time, and jog through the sweltering, muggy air toward the bus station.

Most of the city buses run erratically, but Frank's OCD keeps him on time, and his bus should arrive in two minutes. I don't slow down in the parking lot—after the horrible day I've had, I just want to get away from here. I reach the curb and keep moving, desperate to reach the right street corner in time.

But someone grabs my hand and yanks me backward.

At first I'm incensed. Who grabbed me? Was it the man from the restaurant? Before I can spin around to see who it was, a red Mazda careens through the red light and crashes into an older navy Suburban a few feet ahead of me. The driver and passenger of the Mazda are flung toward the windshield until their seatbelts pull them short. I watch their heads jerk forward and then fly back.

I've seen this exact encounter play out before, but instead of a pedestrian, I was in one of the vehicles. As if the accident in front of me dislodged a memory, it plays out in my mind all over again. Except in the accident I just witnessed, unlike when my parents died, the back seat is empty of two young children. And this time, the driver and front seat passenger don't fly through the windshield headfirst like Mom and Dad did.

Why did the car's seatbelts save these people and not my parents? Has technology improved that much in eleven years?

"Hey, are you okay? I'm sorry if I scared you, but if I hadn't grabbed you, you'd have. . ." Henry still hasn't let go of my hand. I glance at the cars again, their front ends crumpled down so much that the people in the Mazda could almost reach out and touch the windshield of the other car.

Henry didn't finish saying it, but I know what he means. He's right. If he hadn't stopped me, I'd have been squished into human jelly between a few tons of metal.

"Thanks."

Frank's bus is rounding the corner up ahead, and I'm still on the wrong side of the road. If I don't get over there right now, before this accident blocks the entire road, it'll be a half an hour or more before the next bus. I yank my hand away. "Today has been awful all around. I really appreciate your support in there and your save out here, and I'll miss working with you, Henry, but I've got to go."

Henry frowns and drops his hands to his sides. "You never would give me your phone number, and after you left, Ramon mentioned he doesn't have an updated address on file for you. He said you usually get paid in cash, so he's not sure how to get you your last paycheck." Henry's voice drops to a whisper. "Look, I know you would never steal. I don't think taking leftovers people were tossing is a big deal. They shouldn't have fired you." Henry shakes his head. "I don't know what's going on with you, obviously, but I'd like to help if you'll let me." He hands me a piece of paper.

I unfold it.

Henry. 832-535-0363.

He ran after me to give me his phone number. Another dishwasher, and a chronically late one at that, wants to help me. Knowing what he makes, I have no idea how he can afford to repair whatever junker car he surely drives and gasoline to and from his soccer games, but it's still a kind offer.

The bus pulls up and the doors open, so I turn and dart across the street. When I glance back at Henry, his kicked puppy eyes stare back at me. I exhale heavily, and holler, "I'll be okay. I promise."

He shrugs and I can barely hear him when he responds. "Payday's tomorrow."

I do need that money. "I'll text you."

Henry smiles.

The bus driver grunts impatiently, and I climb into the bus. I take my seat and look down at the slip of paper with Henry's phone number. I should toss it out the window, but it would save me an awkward trip back to Perry's if he's willing to bring me what I'm due. I whip out my phone and save his number, and then I stuff the paper back in my pocket anyway.

I don't even have to change buses to reach Jesse. He works near Rice University, and after I reach that stop, I stroll toward our favorite bench in the Village. An ancient live oak tree shades it pretty much all year, and it's far enough from the shopping traffic that you can still hear yourself think. I sit down, breathe a sigh of relief and glance at the time on my phone. Four-forty p.m. Jesse should have a break soon. I text him. AT OUR BENCH.

He replies immediately. EVERYTHING OKAY?

LONG STORY.

BE THERE IN FIVE.

I lean back against the bench, reviewing the last day in my mind. I need Jesse—I'm starting to spiral a bit. Four minutes later, my big brother barrels around a shrub. His jeans are torn and filthy and his shirt is mud-streaked, but my heart lifts when I see his warm eyes, his unkempt hair, and his prominent nose. He's here and he's safe, so my world is okay. His eyes scan me for injuries as he jogs over. "You look alright. Well, as good as you ever do." His eyes squint up when he smiles. Which means they squint up a lot.

"Funny, very funny."

He sits down next to me. "I've got about ten or fifteen minutes, and then we've got a bunch of flower bed perimeter stone to finish."

"So last night on Terra, we all had to run."

"I know."

I swallow. "Because I was worried I might have killed someone."

Jesse frowns. "You didn't mention that tidbit."

I explain about how I tossed the guy who attacked Martin into the side wall of the stable. "And today, for the first time ever, I saw someone. At the restaurant."

"You've never seen anyone at the restaurant?" Jesse lifts both eyebrows.

I roll my eyes. "No, I mean I saw someone from Terra. . .on Earth. The guy I almost killed, or I might have killed. I'm not sure. His name was Robert," I say.

Jesse's always making jokes, about everything. They never stop. But his face blanks alarmingly, and his mouth gapes open. "And?"

"And I barged into the dining area and talked to him." I look at my hands. Now that I mention it, it sounds stupid. "He and the guy he was with were talking about the Followers of Isis." My voice has dropped to a whisper.

"Are you sure this guy was the same person?" Jesse asks. "I mean, presumably he wasn't dressed quite the same at Perry's. He didn't arrive on a horse, did he?" The corner of his mouth quirks. As his brain processes my news, he's already turning it into a joke.

"I asked him about Amun-Ra."

"Wait, what?" Jesse asks. "What did he say?"

I shake my head. "Nothing, but his buddy offered to talk to me and gave me a card." I pull it out of my pocket. "And then a few minutes later. . .Robert died."

"He *died?*"

"I mean, I don't know that for sure, but the paramedics couldn't revive him. One minute he was eating a steak, and the next, unconscious on the floor, unresponsive."

"You knocked him out back on Terra," Jesse says. "And then today, he died on Earth. Are you *positive* it's the same guy?"

My gaze drops to my hands.

"Alora, what's wrong?"

I shudder. "I think so." I look at my fingernails—so normal, so regular. It's hard to believe any of what I'm saying may be true while I'm sitting on a bench, looking at my perfectly regular hands. "I've never seen the same person on Earth and Terra. Never."

"That you recall." His stomach growls. "Hey, where's my food?"

I always give my pilfered leftovers to Jesse when I finish with my shift.

I open my mouth to explain, but before I can, some guy stops on the path in front of us, yelling loudly into his phone. "I don't know how to do that! And I need to get this thing submitted by five, or I get a zero. If I get a zero, I fail." He's wearing a blue Astros shirt and an Astros hat turned backwards. He walks past us and sits on another bench ten feet away.

Jesse meets my eye, and I know just what he's asking without him saying a word. Computer problems are kind of his forte. I shake my head. If today reinforced anything for me, it's that you should never get involved.

"I don't have time to drive over there, man. I've got. . ." The world's biggest Astros fan looks at his watch. "Twelve minutes." He curses. "No. I don't even see that option." He clicks on his laptop. "No." He sighs and balls one hand into a fist.

My brother starts to stand up. I grab Jesse's arm and shake my head again.

"Okay, but hurry. I'm not even sure whether I can submit it after five."

Jesse shakes me off and walks over to Mr. Astros, who's probably a student at Rice. "Can I help? I'm pretty good with tech issues."

They start talking computer stuff, and I swear, I have no idea what they're saying. A few minutes later, though, he's beaming at Jesse and thanking him profusely. "That was awesome. I have no idea how you did that, but thank you so much." He pulls out his wallet.

Jesse puts up his hand. "No way. I was happy to help."

The kid looks at Jesse. "No, seriously, you look like you work pretty hard." He hands Jesse a wad of bills. "And look, my buddy John is on his way over here. He works at a computer company. He's going to be impressed that you fixed it."

Jesse smirks. "Doubtful."

"I'm serious. He's super smart and he has a startup company. He told me last week that they're hiring."

"My break's almost over," Jesse says, "which is too bad. I would've loved to meet him."

"Maybe I could text him," Mr. Astros says.

"Text who?" A tall guy with black hair that falls into his eyes walks toward us from Rice Village. "You don't look nearly as panicked as I expected to find you, Landon." When he shoves the hair back from his face, I realize he's got stunning golden irises.

"John!" Landon waves. "This guy saved me, just in time."

John's forehead furrows. "So I didn't need to drive eighty miles an hour to get here."

Landon laughs. "Do you ever go any other speed?"

"What was the problem?" John asks.

"It was simple," Jesse says. Then he starts speaking the one language I've never understood. RAM. Data. Caches.

Blerg. "Hey J," I say. "I think your boss is looking for you."

Jesse freezes and looks over his shoulder. Frank's waving his direction. "Darn, yeah. It was nice to meet you John, but I've got to run. Good luck, Landon."

I love that Jesse cares about people, I do. But I wish

I'd been able to talk to him a little more. Now it'll be an hour or two until he's done with his shift and I can confess that I was fired. After he leaves, I expect John and Landon to buzz off. Landon high fives John and heads back the way he came, but John sits down next to me.

Why?

"I didn't catch your name, or your brother's for that matter. Jay, maybe?"

"I'm Alice," I say stiffly, accustomed to giving everyone my fake name. "Nice to meet you."

"Now go away," he says.

"Excuse me?"

He laughs. "You said nice to meet you, but you were channeling some pretty strong 'go away' vibes."

I bite my lip. This guy is sitting too close, and interpreting my tone far too well—but he's not actually leaving. It's disconcerting. "I'm sorry. It's been a long day."

"Already?" He looks at the Perry's logo on my polo shirt. "I'd have figured life would be rougher for you right around the dinner rush."

I groan. "Not for me. Not anymore, anyway. I got fired today."

"That is rough."

I sigh, but don't explain more. He needs no encouragement, and I don't handle small talk well.

John shakes his head. "Alright. Well, believe it or not, I do know when to back off. Look, Landon might have mentioned this already, but I've got a startup, and I'm looking for programmers. Good ones. Your brother seems way too bright to be cutting hedges."

"So you think landscapers aren't smart?"

"Are you always this prickly?" He leans back and looks over my face. "Or have I upset you in some specific way?"

Rich guys who drive eighty miles per hour in their

posh cars. Guys with perfect hair and two hundred dollar shoes who have startups at the age of, what? Twenty? Yeah. I hate him, but no, it's not specific. "I just get cranky on days when I get fired."

"Right, right. You don't happen to know as much as your brother does about computers, do you? I probably should have started there." He winces. "Sorry."

I snort. "I can usually turn my brother's computer on and off. That's about the extent of my tech-related skillset."

"Usually?" He laughs. "Yeah, my company's probably not a great fit for you." He holds out his hand.

What does he want to do, shake? I glance down and realize he's holding a card. What's with people and giving me their number today?

I take it, our fingers brushing as I do. I don't expect the jolt when we touch. My eyes meet his and he smiles. He must know he has a killer smile. Perfect teeth, a dimple on the right side, and the brightest, tawny gold eyes I've ever seen. I drag my gaze down to the card. "CEO of Game Theory. Cute name."

"Thanks."

"So you want me to give this to my brother."

"I'd love to have him come interview for my last programmer spot. I mean, if you hate me, or if he would rather plant petunias, that's fine. But I am looking for good people, and I offer benefits. I doubt he's getting that here." John points at Jesse, shoving a wheelbarrow full of stones around the hedge.

"No, he's not."

"So maybe pass the opportunity along, even if my smell offends you."

"I will." I pause, ignoring his jest, and uncomfortable at the silence. Hopefully it's awkward enough that he'll finally go.

"And since you won't be working for me." He stands up. "I'd love to take you to dinner sometime. Maybe I can convince you I'm not as horrendous as you seem to think I am."

I chuckle.

"Unlikely, I realize," he says. "But I'd like to try."

I sigh. "I don't think you're awful, but—"

"So you're saying I've got a chance."

This guy is determined. I'll give him that. "I have a boyfriend, okay?" I have no idea why I lie, except that he makes me shaky in a way I can't explain.

"Oh. You do? And what's this mysterious boyfriend's name?"

"He's not mysterious," I say. "His name is Henry. He plays club soccer, and until today, we worked at the same place." There. That ought to shut him up.

"Alright, alright. Sometimes I'm way off base. I'll leave you alone, I swear. But pass that card along to your brother."

"I will."

"And maybe tell me your brother's name so that when he calls, I'll know who I'm talking to."

"Right," I say. "It's Jordan Walker."

"But you call him J."

"Siblings and their nicknames," I say with a half grin. "I've called him J for years."

"You're lucky, Alice. I'm an only child, and it sucks to always be alone."

For the first time all day, I realize that he's right. My life may suck in most ways, but in the ways that matter more than anything else, I am lucky. Not everyone has a Jesse in their life, but I do.

It's enough. It's more than enough.

5

EARTH

John finally stands up and brushes off his jeans, even though they're already immaculate. "Well, see you around, I hope."

I roll my eyes, but I can't stop the smile. "Maybe so."

After he's gone from my line of sight, I walk to the bus stop, waving at Jesse as I pass his crew.

"See you soon." He wipes his forehead before he waves, smearing dirt from his eyebrow to his hairline.

While I wait for the bus, I consider throwing John's business card in the trashcan right next to me. We've got enough weird things going on. If Paul relents and gives that guy my information. . . well. The address on my fake ID isn't correct in any case. But it still makes me nervous. For instance, our lease was taken under our fake names: Alice and Jordan Walker. If someone was resourceful enough, they might put our name with our address.

Plus, Jesse's almost nineteen, but his ID says he's twenty-seven. He could maybe pass for a young twenty, but there's no way anyone will believe he's twenty-seven.

They don't check that stuff for a yard crew, but a real office job would be different. He'd need a better ID, and I just gave John his assumed name, making any sort of upgrade like that. . .complicated.

Ultimately, though, I hang on to the card. We've had enough of our dreams crushed by other people—enough of our choices taken away. I won't make my brother's decisions for him, even if I think it might be for our own good. Jesse can puzzle over the possible solutions to this stuff himself. I stick the card in my bag.

The worst thing about this particular bus stop at this time of day is that it's in full sun—no shade at all. Unsurprising with my luck, but I wait for more than half an hour for the dumb bus I need to show up. By the time it rumbles around the corner, I've pitted out the armpits on my shirt. Ah, the indignity of public transit in Houston. People complain that the bus smells funny, as if it's the fault of the unwashed masses who use them. I often wonder whether any funky smell is a function of patrons being stuck waiting on buses in the heat. I'm walking up the steps when Jesse jogs up behind me.

"Hey!" I say.

"We finished early."

"That's good," I say.

"Which means I won't get quite as many hours." Jesse shrugs. "But that's fine."

I sit down on a bench and slide all the way over. Jesse drops in next to me. "Speaking of hours, I tried to tell you earlier, before you white-knighted on me."

"What?" He turns toward me, his eyes calm.

I grit my teeth. "I got fired."

"Wait, so some guy you saw in Terra last night croaks at your restaurant, and then you get fired? Why? For talking to him?" The righteous indignation in Jesse's voice warms my heart.

I shake my head. "Ramon caught me leaving with a box of food I didn't pay for."

Jesse's eyes widen. "So that's why you didn't bring me anything to eat today."

"Sorry."

He laughs and something inside my chest eases. If he's laughing, he's not mad, and if he's not mad, I'm okay.

"And." I whip John's card out of my bag. "Here. That tech guy wanted me to give you this. He wants to have Jordan Walker in for an interview."

Jesse's eyes light up in a way I haven't seen in a very, very long time.

My heart constricts. "I'm not sure that it's a good idea."

"Why not?"

"You'd have to give him your ID," I whisper. "And it's a real desk job. You do not look older than twenty."

Jesse rubs the scruff on his chin that's still awkwardly irregular. "I may have a work-around for that."

My eyebrows climb.

"I've been playing around with this for a while. I think I can change the date."

I hiss, "Are you talking about hacking into the DMV?"

He shrugs. "It's not like government systems are super high tech. Their encryption—"

"That's a felony!"

"So is using fake IDs," Jesse points out.

"Except if you take a job you care about, you're stuck. You can't just change out your entire *identity* at some future date, and you may be eighteen, but I'm not yet."

"If you think that's true—if you believe that you have a record back home—then you can't ever go back to your real name."

"But you can."

"You stole a thousand bucks when we ran. If you can't be Alora Benson again, then I can't be Jesse Benson, either. Not in a year, not ever. Unless."

"Unless what?" I shouldn't be so desperate to get my name back, but for some reason, I am. Maybe when you have almost nothing, your name feels like a lot.

He shakes his head. "You were never tried, much less convicted. Maybe they dropped those charges years ago. I really doubt they're still looking for you. But if we're worried, that's even more reason for us to make these IDs into something we can use forever."

I want to believe that everything is fine. I want my life to be normal now, or in six months when I turn eighteen, or even in a year or two. Heck, I'd be fine if I knew things would be normal in five years. At least that's a timeframe, and I can count down patiently. But it's not that simple. "He found us in California," I say.

Jesse leans back against the bench and sighs. "It was too expensive to live there, anyway."

I snort. "It really was. We could barely afford a hot dog, much less an apartment. Arizona was cheaper."

"It shouldn't cost anything to live on the surface of the sun. They should've paid us to live there."

"He found us there, too, J." I shiver. It's almost ninety degrees outside today, and the bus air conditioner can't keep up. I'm not shivering because I'm cold. "We can't take any chances."

"I never saw him in California. Or Phoenix."

I huff. "Well, I did."

He nods. "And when you saw him, we ran. Every time."

"Which is the only reason he didn't haul us back to Washington by our ears and toss me in juvie and you in another group home."

"Maybe." Jesse shrugs. "But I can't be hauled back anymore. I'm an adult."

"I'm not, and Declan Rosenbaum is still looking for us, Jesse. He never stopped. You know that."

"It's been almost three years, Alora. That's a long time. I doubt Washington's still paying a social worker to hunt us down that long after we ran—they aren't bounty hunters. Besides, if they do find you, I can tell any judge in America that I'll be your guardian. The worst is past us."

"You think they'd let the kid who ran away with me be my *guardian*?" I shoot off the bench. "I saw him, Jesse, and he saw me, too, only a year ago. Two years after we left, two years after I stole that money. I think it's wishful thinking that he'd drop it between then and now, after coming so close to catching us."

Jesse's blue eyes hold my gaze for a moment. "I agreed with you at the time, and I've never complained about having to run. But I'm eighteen, and you will be soon. Plus, I like it here. We haven't seen any evidence of Declan, and I'm confident that we won't. We're safe." He puts his hand over mine. "*Alice Walker* is safe."

"That's probably true. I'm just stressed, okay?"

"I know you are." Jesse pats my hand. "I know."

I lean back against the bus bench and close my eyes. "The problem with assuming we're fine is that by the time we find out we aren't, it's too late to do anything." I close my eyes and think about the day we escaped three years ago. We had no plan, no idea what we were doing, and I was only fourteen. We shouldn't have stolen that cash, but I didn't know how else we'd be able to afford to go anywhere.

I can't be stupid and risk getting caught, not again. Stupid makes you desperate. Terra may not be real—it may all be a dream—but my danger here on Earth *is* most definitely real.

"You know," Jesse says. "I could look into it. I can poke around until I find out what charges were ever brought against you."

"So you're suddenly a skilled computer criminal?" My heart flips. "That's not a good idea. Hacking into government websites sounds significantly worse than stealing petty cash."

Jesse snorts. "Most of what I'd be looking for could be located in public records."

"Not the DMV," I whisper.

"Why are you whispering?" Jesse leans closer to me, his voice the barest of whispers. "No one's tapping the conversation of a gardener and a recently laid off dishwasher." He chuckles.

"Oh, shut up."

"Look, I'm not an idiot, okay? I know what I'm doing."

Maybe it would be good to know what exactly *is* out there on me—and something Jesse said sticks with me. Why would a social worker continue to search for us? They aren't bounty hunters. But why else would someone come after me and Jesse?

Unless.

I think about the car accident that killed Mom and Dad. "Something happened that got me thinking."

"Uh-oh." Jesse sighs heavily. "And you've strained your brain again. Is it bad this time?"

I shove him. "I was running to the bus stop, and I almost stepped into the road. . .right in front of a car. I almost became roadkill."

No quip this time. "Whoa, and?"

"My buddy Henry yanked me backward, which saved my life. There was this wreck, right in front of me, that I would have walked right into. One car ran a light and there was a head-on collision, just like—"

"Like Mom and Dad." The corners of his mouth turn down.

"Except for a few differences. First, it was two cars that collided, not a semi truck and a car. But most importantly, no one flew through the windshield."

"Okay," Jesse says.

"Do you ever wonder why Mom and Dad did?"

He shakes his head. "Did what?"

"Why didn't their seat belts stop them? Or the air bags? I'm sure they had them, even back then, right?" I shrug. "I don't know. But I have this clear memory of the accident and you and I were fine, because our seatbelts held us in place." When I close my eyes, I can still feel the *wham* from the seatbelt where it blocked my movement. "Mom and Dad went shooting through the front windshield. Were they not wearing seatbelts?"

Jesse frowns. "They were. They always clicked them in place. Always."

"Maybe we should look into that, while we're nosing around. It just feels, I don't know, strange."

"What exactly did you want me to look into?" Jesse's brow furrows. "Seat belt malfunction?"

I don't know. My brain's spinning. Maybe I did pull a muscle in my gray matter. "Maybe hack the Washington police server, and if there's a file on their death, that means it wasn't just an accident, right?"

"Hack the Washington police server?" He rolls his eyes. "Weren't you just flipping out about me changing a date of birth on a driver's license? Now you want me to hack a *police network*?"

"I don't know what you can do. If you can't, then whatever, but I was just thinking about them dying.

That's what set everything else off, and it feels weird, that's all."

"Our life has sucked," Jesse says.

"I know."

He sighs. "It's not your fault we had to run. Not the first time, and not the next two times. We're in this together. We always have been." He leans against the side of the bus, and I lean my head against his shoulder. We sit like that until we reach our stop. My life sucks, but at least I've got Jesse.

I insist on stopping on the way home to grab a gallon of milk and a loaf of bread. And when we reach the register, I toss a bag of peanut butter M&Ms on the counter. Jesse shakes his head but doesn't argue.

Once we're outside, I hand him the bag. No one loves M&Ms as much as Jesse does, and peanut butter more than any other. He tosses each and every one up in the air while we walk, catching one at a time in his open mouth. We don't have a ton of money, but we don't need a lot. Life's greatest joys aren't that pricey.

Once we reach our apartment, I sigh in relief. I'm glad to be done walking in the heat, and it's good to be home, even if home is simple. A wooden spool someone around the corner was throwing away that we repurposed as a table, spray painted red, white, and blue. Metal stools from Wal-Mart, and two huge beanbag chairs for the family room. Our only big-ticket items are Jesse's laptop, which rests on an old desk we found by the dumpster, and a used television we bought from some guy down the hall in a moving sale. Thirty-six inches might not be an impressive size anymore, but it's bigger than anything we had growing up.

While Jesse showers and changes clothes—he gets really dirty at work—I start to make ramen noodles. While I wait for the water to boil, I turn on the TV, sit down on a stool, and pull out my phone. No messages, which is no surprise. We both use burner phones and change them monthly. It's an extra $20 a month, and the phones aren't smart, but it seemed like the best move. I never give out my phone number, so really they just keep us connected with each other.

Something stiff in my pocket pokes my leg, and I pull out the scrap of paper with Henry's phone number on it. Since we're due to change phones in a week and a half, I could call him. It's not like he'd be able to find me forever, or track me. Or send that heavy gentleman my way.

Jesse sits down next to me and plonks a salad bowl full of ramen in front of me. He's eating a single package, but I eat about five times as much as he does. We think it's somehow part of the Lifting I do on Terra, like I have to fuel the telekinetics somehow, whether I'm here or there, but I'm always famished, and I never gain any weight.

"Thanks for finishing up dinner." I was distracted enough thinking about Henry that I forgot about it entirely. Good thing Jesse showers fast.

"What's that?" He eyes the paper in my hands.

"Nothing." I fold the paper in half again and stuff it back in my pocket.

"It looked like a phone number. Do you have a boyfriend you're hiding from me?" He arches one eyebrow.

Heat rises in my cheeks.

"Whoa-ho-ho! Why are you hiding him?" He pauses, but not for long. "There's something wrong with him, isn't there?" He rubs his hands together in front of his beaming face. "Is he hairy? Does he smell? Oh, wait, I know." He slaps his thighs. "He's got a lazy eye."

"You shouldn't make fun of people for having a lazy eye."

He frowns. "Wait, does he have one? Because I was kidding—I don't care."

I shake my head. "No, of course not."

"So he smells."

"No, he doesn't smell. Geez."

Jesse's eyebrows climb.

"And he's not my boyfriend! It's the phone number of my only friend from work."

"You have been holding out on me." Jesse beams.

"What about you?" I deflect. "It's not like you've told me about anyone from work."

"I work with eleven other guys." His voice is flat.

"You could be gay."

"I could be," he says. "But I'm not."

"Fine. Look, it's Henry, the other dishwasher at work who yanked me back from that wreck. He had followed me out to give me his number, because he offered to *help* me. Henry, the flaky, always-late dishwasher, is going to help me." I snort. "It was a kind offer, but not one I'll be taking."

"Umm, let's review. He saved your life today. He makes you blush and sputter defensively. And he sprinted out to make sure he'd hear from you again. On top of all that, he's always late, but *he* didn't get fired. Maybe he does have connections he could use to find you a new job. Or am I missing anything?"

"He might be a little bit cute."

"Oh my goodness." Jesse bats his eyes and smirks. "Well, if you don't call him I'm, like, totally going to do it for you."

"Whatever."

Jesse snatches my phone and flips it open. When he speaks, it's in falsetto. "Why hello, Henry! Yes, of course

I called." He pauses. "Well, only because I love you, and I can't live without you. Why yes, I did notice your huge muscles when you rescued me from certain death today." He giggles. "Oh, I *do* think I owe you something for that." He shimmies at me.

I lunge forward and grab my phone. "Knock it off. I need to think about it before I call him."

"Why? What is there to think about? Are you worried he's an undercover agent for Washington Social Services? He's probably not the first agent they've sent undercover across state lines to haul you home."

I frown. "Stop making fun of me."

"I'm sorry, but what started out as a healthy amount of caution has turned into an excuse to hide from the world. You may not *like* like this guy Henry, but it's time we each found some friends. Maybe even someone who knows, I don't know, our *real* name. Or, if we're feeling über crazy, our actual age."

"Friends?" I can barely process the word. People to whom we don't owe anything and with whom we spend time. . . for fun.

"Call Henry, and if the most you get out of it is a work referral you can use and your last chunk of cash, you're still better off than if you don't call."

"You haven't called that John guy yet." I cross my arms. "I guess we're both chicken."

He raises one eyebrow at me. "Maybe we are."

I think about what he said while I finish my ramen, and then I hold up my phone. "I'll call Henry in my room, and you stay here and call John. Deal?"

There's no hint of laughter in Jesse's eyes when he says, "Deal."

We can't afford more than a one-bedroom place. For a while Jesse and I shared the bedroom, but eventually we both wanted somewhere we could go to be alone for a few minutes. Jesse got stuck with the family room, and I got the bedroom. Sometimes I feel a little guilty, but Jesse doesn't seem to mind changing clothes in the bathroom, so I try not to feel too bad.

I look down at my phone. I hear Jesse talking in the other room. Guess I'd better hold up my end of our bargain. I dial Henry's number.

"Hello?"

"Henry, it's Alice."

"You actually called. I didn't think you would."

"Yep." And this is why I hate talking on the phone. I have no idea what to say, so the awkward pause stretches, like a limo. Like taffy. And now it's sagging like off-brand yoga pants. Blerg.

"Are you still there?" Henry asks.

Good idea. Let's blame the cell phone reception. "Yeah, can you hear me now?"

"So I talked to Paul. I told him firing you for taking home a few things that no one was eating anyway was ridiculous."

"You did?"

Henry grunts. "He insists you were *stealing*. Like you stole a steak, cooked it, popped it into a box, and were going to sneak that out."

"That would break fewer health codes," I say.

"Why did you take it?" Henry asks. "I mean, I've seen you eating things now and again. Not to my taste, but taking home other people's leftovers? Really?"

Great. I'm a charity case. Any thoughts I had of turning Henry into a friend evacuate the building. "So can you bring me what they owe me? Or do I need to go steal it from Paul?"

"He tried to say you don't get your pay, since you were fired."

What? My eyes sting. I gulp in air to keep from crying on the phone. We need that money.

"I told him he'd better cut you a check, or pull it out of petty cash, or something, or I'd talk to his superior." Henry's a better guy than I thought, not that his threats will help much. It'll probably just get him fired, too, if he keeps pushing.

"It's okay—"

"It worked. He gave me your pay." He pauses. "Alice Walker. I didn't realize it, but I never knew your last name until he told me."

Wait, what?

"I've got class and then soccer in the morning, but I can bring it by your place tonight or tomorrow. Just text me the address."

Uh, that's not going to happen. "Well, the thing is," I say.

"Or I'm happy to meet you somewhere. I can even buy you dinner. Think of it as like, the farewell dinner you didn't get, but deserved."

"I'd rather you not invite Paul and Ramon."

Henry laughs. "Yeah, that would be awkward."

I smile, but of course I'm on the phone so Henry can't see me. "Where did you want to meet?"

"Since I have no idea where you live, and it feels like you want to keep it that way, why don't you choose a place?"

"Can I just text you?" I ask.

"That's fine. I'm working lunch shift again tomorrow. Want to meet me around six?"

"Sounds good," I say. "See you tomorrow."

Jesse pokes his head into my room after I hang up. "And?"

"I'm meeting him for dinner tomorrow. I just have to pick a place."

"Maybe pick something over in the Katy area," he says, "because then you could come with me. You can apply for jobs. . . while I interview."

I beam. "That's great!" I jump off my bed, which is really just a mattress resting on plywood and concrete blocks, and run over to give him a hug. "I'm so proud of you, J."

He shoves me. "A simple interview has nothing on you."

Huh?

"You just called Alice Walker's future husband for the first time."

I roll my eyes. "Please."

We watch television for a while, but Jesse keeps checking his phone.

"Waiting for a text?" I ask.

He grins. "It's more pathetic than that. I keep rereading the one where he sent me the address. I just can't believe I'm interviewing for a real IT job." He shakes his head. "It feels. . .unreal."

I yawn.

"Whoa, are you tired?"

I shrug. "Always."

"You'd better get your beauty sleep, then." He shuts off the television. "You've got interviewing to look good for tomorrow." He bites his lip. "And a date."

"Shaddup." I stand up. "I'm going to shower, then I'll head to bed."

"Didn't you shower this morning?" Jesse laughs.

"You shower twice a day, too."

"I work outside all day long."

"I walk outside. . .in Houston."

He bobs his head. "Good point."

I grab my pajamas and try to forget how long and miserable today has been while the hot water pours down my back. I'm toweling off my hair as I step out of the tub into a puddle of water on the floor.

I slip and land on the heel of my right hand, which makes a loud crack. "Ow!"

Jesse bangs on the door. "What's wrong?"

I groan. "Oh, man. Nothing, I guess. I fell and landed on my hand. My wrist is throbbing. I think I might have broken it."

"Can you dress yourself?"

"Of course, dummy. I'm not three years old."

"I'm trying to be considerate. Sheesh."

The throbbing in my wrist increases as I fumble through dressing. I can barely bend it by the time I reach for the door handle with my left hand.

Jesse's hovering when I emerge. "Let's see."

I yank my arm back. "Doesn't matter."

He sighs. "If you can go to sleep, it doesn't."

"I can, and I know it'll be fine once I get to Terra. Martin will Heal it. Although I do feel a little bad dumping more stuff on my plate right now."

Jesse tilts his head sideways. "You feel bad for dumping stuff. . .on yourself?"

"It's just that I don't remember anything about Earth when I'm there, so I always feel guilty leaving myself inexplicable problems to resolve."

"What do you think about all the injuries that randomly pop up?"

"The troupe thinks I sleep walk."

Jesse snorts. "Are you serious?"

I shrug. "It's not so different from the truth. I am walking around here the whole time I'm sleeping there."

He crosses his arms. "It still bugs me that the times don't add up. You're awake here for like fifteen, sixteen hours, and the same there, right?"

"We're talking two different dimensions," I say. "And you're worried their clocks don't line up with ours?"

Jesse frowns. "I was thinking about something. You saw someone there, someone who got injured. You were worried he might die there. Then you saw him here. . .and he died. Your injuries from here cross over there, and. . ." He frowns. "If you die there. . ."

"You can't worry about that."

"Says the queen of worrying."

He has me there.

Jesse steps closer and drops his voice. "For the first time that we know of, you're in actual danger on Terra. You want me not to worry about it?"

I push past him to my bedroom. "Maybe that guy died here because he died there. Maybe these worlds are connected somehow, and as bad as I feel about causing his death, he did try to kill Martin, and if he died. . .he probably couldn't tell anyone that *I* Lifted. Which means I'm safe over there. My secret isn't out."

"I know you have to go to sleep and find out. But. . .just don't die, okay?" He frowns. "I know we may not completely agree on our situation right now, but you're the only person who matters to me. You know that."

I do. "I love you, J."

He hugs me. "Love you too."

My throbbing wrist doesn't make it easy to fall asleep. Every time I shift, I bump it and pain screams up my arm. But that's not the only reason I struggle. When I close my eyes, I either see Robert, lying on the floor lifeless, or my parents flying through the windshield. The year we've spent in Houston has been pretty peaceful, boring almost. Until last night—when I kicked the hornet's nest on Terra—and then today when I lost my job, and now that Jesse's decided to try for a new one.

At the end of the day, I'm not afraid of dying, but what will happen to Jesse if I do?

It's a hard truth to accept that he might actually be better off without me. He could go back to using his real name. He wouldn't need to worry about a criminal record —he doesn't have one—or being underage—because he's not. All in all, I'm sort of a millstone around his neck, dragging him down, down, down. If I'm honest about it, I always have been.

That thought keeps me up far too long.

❧ 6 ❧

TERRA

I wake up with another unexplained injury, this time in my wrist.

"I swear, one of these days, I'm going to tie you to the bed." Martin grimaces as he Heals me, his wrist swelling as mine is repaired.

A moment later, Thomas takes the injury from him. He closes and uncloses his fist without trouble, which tells me the injury has faded significantly.

"Have you ever wondered why Healers become injured themselves when they Heal someone?" I ask. "It feels unfair. It's not like someone who Lifts is, I don't know, floated around themselves."

Martin shrugs. "You Lifters expend all the energy as if you moved things yourself—maybe it's something like that. Energy in motion, or cost and consequence." He shakes his head. "We may never know, but that's why we work in pairs."

"Speaking of." Thomas holds up his wrist. He'd clearly like Martin to take the injury back—it becomes smaller each time it's Healed.

Martin rolls his eyes. "Your body heals quickly, son.

Whatever tiny injury yet remains will quickly be gone. It's time for us to get back on the road."

Thomas grumbles on his way to his wagon, but he smiles at me so I know he's not upset.

You'll never be safe again.

Martin's words run through my head over and over. If he's right, and if Robert survived long enough to tell anyone what he saw, which of course I mostly hope he did, then I'm not the only one who will be in danger.

Every single person in my family will be at risk. I thought about it in the wagon last night as we rode through most of the night. I've thought about it every second since I woke up late morning.

The Warden.

What does that word even mean? I've never heard it before. How can I be the fulfillment of some kind of prophecy? I'm just me. I don't even have parents.

I haul pots and pans to the river and clean them quickly, Lifting without a second thought out here in the wilderness where no one can see me. By the time I return, everyone's ready to go again, desperate to put distance between us and the Followers of Amun, who might know my secret.

Wind stomps his hoof, clearly ready to be untied and moving under his own initiative again. I Bind dust in place and walk up to his back, swinging my boot over. Up ahead, everyone else appears to have been waiting on me. "Martin?"

He's already sitting on top of his wagon, reins in hand. "Yes?"

I bring Wind up alongside him. "I've been thinking about all this."

"I figured you would."

"I have some questions."

He smiles. "Maybe you tie Wind up again."

So he has more to tell me. I'm not sure how many more surprises I can handle. "Okay."

Wind wants to run—he's not excited to be stuck behind a lumbering wagon now that he's no longer tired, but he's a good sport. After a few head tosses, he settles down. "Good boy." I rub his nose and jog around to climb up onto the bench seat on the front of the wagon.

"You slept alright?"

"Other than the wrist, you mean?" I ask.

Martin shakes his head. "You've been getting those bumps and bangs since you were a baby, your mother said."

My mother. At first, I was devastated that she died. But now I hardly remember anything about her. I'm too ashamed to admit it, but she's more of a vague memory than anything else. "I'm sorry you've always had to Heal them."

Martin clucks and his horses move forward quickly. "I never minded."

Healers don't complain much. "Here's what I've been thinking about," I say. "You told me that I'd never be safe."

He exhales dramatically. "I realized the second I said it that you'd fixate on it."

"You wouldn't need to run if—"

"I've never told you the truth about your mother." His words fall like rocks in a pond, plonk, plonk, PLONK.

The truth. He's never told me the truth? "What?"

"You were Named, you know."

My heart skips a beat. "Everyone is Named."

"Your name was revealed to your mother. . .and your father." Martin's voice is tight, small. He feels guilty for keeping that from me, for allowing me to believe that, like many others, I only ever had a mother.

"You never told me that." Why? Why would he keep that a secret? "He didn't want me?"

Martin sighs. "Your mother and your father had a falling out after you were born. You see, they realized quickly that you were different. Your mother insisted that you needed to leave, that your father couldn't keep you safe."

"From the Followers of Amun?" It's a lot to process. "They knew I was the Warden?"

"You weren't quite two the first time you Lifted, your mother said. And you grew more powerful every day. They knew they couldn't hide it for long. And they were wealthy—they had servants who were bound to notice and talk."

"So my father kicked me out?" I try to imagine my mother, protecting me from a monster.

Martin shakes his head. "You have it all wrong. Just listen for a moment."

My mouth snaps closed.

"Your mother and father both loved you—and they were Followers of Isis. Your father was a powerful warrior, and he wanted to keep you. He felt that he could protect you, himself, but also that he could convince his supporters to help keep you safe."

The Followers of Isis, unlike the Followers of Amun, cherish and protect women. They don't see them as something to be used, but something to be cared for—it makes sense they might see the Warden differently as well.

"But your mother was too afraid. When he wouldn't listen to her fears, when he wouldn't run. . .she made a difficult choice."

"A difficult choice?" A knot forms in my stomach.

"She left your father."

I close my eyes.

"And she found us. She explained your story to me, including all the particulars, and she asked me what the Healers believed."

I realize that I don't know. "I've never heard of the Warden."

He shrugs. "We don't believe in her or not believe in her. She's not really part of our doctrine. But we do believe that men and women have equal value. Unlike Amun, we don't believe mothers and sisters and daughters must serve us, or that you have no value of your own other than as vessels of Mother Terra to continue our species. Unlike Isis, we believe you're as capable of protecting yourselves as we are—but all Healers are weak when compared to Lifters, more focused on service and care."

"There was no upside to taking me in," I say.

"I had lost my own child," Martin says softly. "He Wasted a few years before your mother arrived."

"What about your wife?" I've never been able to bring myself to ask what happened to her. Anytime she comes up, adults talk in hushed tones or leave the area.

"She left." His lips flatten into a hard line. "Losing a child is. . .fraught. Losing a child to the Wasting, well. You feel utterly powerless."

He sat in that room with Joshua and his parents, consoling them—and he'd already been through the same thing himself. Martin's stronger than I realized.

We wind through thick stands of pine trees, the horses hooves clomping softly ahead of and behind us. The Flashing Forest is quiet during the day. I hope we're beyond it by nightfall. The bright flickers and splashes of light at erratic times freak me out—and the horses hate them too. The trees form the divide between Amun and Isis—and I realize we're headed away from Amun territory, where they want the Warden destroyed, and toward

Isis land, where my father holds sway. Or where he used to. . .

"Who is my father?"

"Your mother made me swear never to tell you who you were, and when she Wasted. . ." Martin closes his eyes.

I don't really recall details about Mom passing. I remember being sad and hugging her for a long time, and that she felt very, very hot to the touch. Not much else.

"She never relented, you know. She insisted that knowing who you were would help no one. She said she didn't want me to take you to your father." He closes his eyes. "Not until you were in grave danger."

Until. Not *if* I'm in danger. When. Mom knew it would come to this, that someday I'd be discovered.

Another realization dawns on the heels of the first. I've been so accustomed to having no parents that I sort of assumed my father had also died. "Wait. My father's alive?" I turn to glare at Martin. "All this time I've had a parent and you kept it from me?"

"You have a brother too—apparently you were quite close. You missed him more than anything when you left."

How can this be? I wrack my brain for any recollection of a father or brother and come up blank. Nothing at all. We left when I was quite young, but still. "We're headed toward them?"

"We're headed away from Amun," Martin says. "That is all."

"But if I'm in danger. . ." I finally force myself to say it. "Then I'm putting you all at risk. I can't do that, not now that I know."

"We talked it over last night," Martin says simply. "After you went to sleep."

"What?"

"Everyone agrees that you should stay with us. There's every chance that Amun doesn't know a thing, and even if Robert talked, that no one believes him. But if there is danger, you're safest with us, hiding in plain sight. We'll tell anyone that asks that you're my daughter, and we'll insist that you're a Healer. They can't *force* you to Lift, so they can't prove you did anything."

If Robert and the dozen other people who saw me clearly that day give an accurate description, they'll spot me immediately. I could definitely see Lord Spurlock killing anyone who tries to protect me. I open my mouth to argue and realize that Martin knows the same thing I do—and they discussed it.

I want to be angry, but how can I? The entire troupe's willing to risk their lives for mine. "At least tell me my father's name." My throat's scratchy and my voice rough.

"Your mother didn't want—"

"I don't even have a last name." I hate how broken I sound.

Martin wraps an arm around me. "You can have mine."

Which means the world to me, but it won't quench my thirst for the truth, now I know it's out there. "But you do know it."

He's quiet for a long time. I've pushed him too far. "Duncan Sterling," he says unexpectedly. "He's the—"

"The leader of Sterling Castle." He's the ruler of all of Isis—which is almost unbelievable. "Are you saying *Duncan Sterling* is my father?"

Martin doesn't reply, and that's my answer. If my mother was right, and if my father hasn't changed his mind about protecting me, reaching him is my best hope at keeping the troupe from harm. Last night they decided to risk everything for me.

So tonight, while Rosalinde is busy cleaning up after

dinner, I pack my few belongings in a satchel. After she's asleep, I slip out of the wagon and down the steps. I untie Wind, halter him, and swing up onto his back. "We have to be quiet, boy. Very quiet."

He whuffles, as if he might understand. I pause at the edge of the wagon ring, my heart climbing into my throat. I look around at the brightly painted wagons. Yellow, Martin's. Blue, Betty and Abraham's, their new baby probably snoozing inside. Green, Thomas and Wayne's. Purple, Andrea and Steve's. Red, Roland and Danica's. Orange, mine and Rosalinde's. I continue around the circle, thinking of everyone I'll miss—everyone who means everything to me.

Martin and Thomas and Rosalinde won't understand, I know. But arguing with them in the morning would only make it harder. I walk quietly past the animal pens, and Biff, Boff, and Buff whine and whimper softly.

"It's okay, boys. I'll be fine."

"Will you?" Abraham's deep voice startles me.

I tug on Wind's reins, and he stops. "I will."

I'm lucky it's Abraham on guard, and not Steve, who always follows Martin's orders to the letter. Worst of all would be Thomas. He'd raise the alarm immediately.

Abraham only grunts.

"You have a new baby, so more than anyone, you get it. I can't stay here and ask you all to risk everything for me. I can't."

"Who better to protect you than us, Alora?" With only moonlight to go by, his eyes are hard to see, but I know the expression he's wearing well. Disappointed resignation, which means he accepts my decision.

"You have no idea how much it means that you all love me enough to risk it, but I can't let you make that choice."

"Not a single person disagreed with Martin's request,

you know. Not me, not Betty. Certainly not Thomas or Rosalinde." Abraham smiles. "Not even my Sara, and you know how pragmatic she is."

That's an understatement. "Not even Sara, huh?"

Abraham nods. "And who else can help me manage all the animals?"

"I think you'll do alright," I say. "And please don't be heroes if Amun does follow. Tell them I left, and tell them where I went. I don't want any of you punished for me. Promise."

"I promise." His eyes are sad. That much I can see, even in the dim light.

Sad eyes or not, Abraham doesn't try to stop me as I urge Wind forward and race down the smooth, well-trodden path. I'm not an expert at maps and roads like Martin, but this route is fairly simple. Sterling Castle is the very first fortress on the main road once you exit the Flashing Forest—the barricade that protects all of the land of Isis from the land of Amun. Like Spurlock and most of the other castles, it's a city that formed around a fortress, but the entire settlement is much, much bigger than Spurlock. I've never been inside, but we travel past Sterling once a year, at least, so I've seen it from afar many times.

My general knowledge of the area notwithstanding, I'm not sure how much farther I need to go. I can't even make out the moon up ahead, so I can't tell where it is in the sky or what time the sun will rise. My eyes are burning, my shoulders are complaining, and Wind is tired, even though I've kept him to a controlled gait to cover the most ground possible.

When the road widens ahead and the trees thin, I'm a little surprised. I was dreading sleeping on the ground, but I didn't think I'd have a choice. Wind and I need a break. The cool ocean breeze gusts against my face, and I close my eyes for a second, trusting Wind to remain steady. I had almost forgotten that Sterling sits just past where the Flashing Forest meets the ocean. It makes it one of the most easily defensible spots on Terra. Ocean waves crash into boulders on one side, and the forest lies ahead of it.

The sun's rays are just peeking over the horizon when Wind and I leave the forest behind us. As the ground slopes upward toward Sterling City, Wind begins to wheeze. I slide off his back and lead him along. I'm more likely to be allowed through the main gate if I don't look threatening.

Hopefully all they'll see is a girl, leading her horse after a long journey, with a small bedroll strapped to his back.

I stop a moment later to allow Wind to graze. I locate a rock with a shallow dish shape in the top and give him some of my water. I'm not sure what sort of reception I'll find at Sterling and for a moment, I consider releasing Wind. Maybe he'll head back down the road and Martin will find him. Or he could be found and taken by someone who needs a plow horse. Wind would hate that.

Ultimately, I'm too selfish to let him go. It might be better for him, especially if Martin's wrong and the leader of Sterling Castle isn't my father. Or if they also think I need to be destroyed.

Ugh.

It's such a gamble either way. But eventually Wind has recovered, and I don't have a good excuse for delaying the final portion of my trip. Wind and I walk up the rather steep path toward Sterling City quietly, if not very quickly. Homesteads appear, farmers already out tending to crops and animals. They lift their hands in acknowledgement as I pass, and I return the motion as if I belong.

My heart races when I imagine introducing myself to my father, and apparently a brother. My worries and fears distract my focus. . .until a nearby farmer doesn't wave. Instead, he takes one look at me and his entire family turns out of their cottage and rushes toward the fence, looking behind me, toward the Flashing Forest.

That's when I finally notice the sound I ought to have heard right away.

The pounding of hooves—a great many hooves.

I spin around, Wind skittishly dancing to the side, toward a vast group of men in blood-red livery. Mounted cavalry.

The Followers of Amun.

They're likely members of Units, which means their strength and skill should be significant. And racing into Sterling like this, mounted and armed, is practically an act of war. I can only think of one reason they'd do it.

To destroy the Warden.

Stupid Robert must have lived long enough to tell at least one person—and they believed him. I swing back up onto Wind's back. My sweet boy's desperate to escape the pounding mass of horses below us, his prey instinct kicking into full force. I don't even make a kissing sound before he's off, the wind flying through his mane and my hair as we race for the gates of Sterling City. It's hard to tell with any precision, but it seems that they're about as far from me as I am from the entrance.

I'm not sure whether we'll make it before my pursuers close the gap.

Soldiers in blue livery on the wall call out loudly. "Amun riders approaching!" The city gates swing closed.

Even if I make it—will the Isis guards let me in?

The pounding of hooves grows louder. I glance behind me.

My heart hammers and blood rushes through my ears.

Chunks of dirt and rock fly into the air behind Wind as we race toward the gates, but the riders are gaining on us. We aren't going to make it in time.

Unless.

They already know I'm a woman who can Lift. They've sent at least a hundred men after me because of it. Why shouldn't I use whatever I can to slow them down? For nearly fifteen years, my mantra has been *keep hidden, keep safe.* But it's too late for that now—I'm not hidden, and I'm definitely not safe.

My hands tremble on the reins as Wind pounds the path toward the gate. I reach out with my senses for anything I might use—and settle on the most substantial thing that won't resist Lifting. The gravel along the road beneath me.

I Lift great fistfuls of it and Bind all the tiny rocks into place just behind me with as much force and strength as I can manage, blocking the path between me and the Followers of Amun. They're going to have to slow or stop and do some fancy maneuvering to avoid it. The farmer I'm passing stares at me with shock, but I don't stop.

I watch over my shoulder to see what happens. Wind's energy is flagging—he's beyond tired. I need this plan to buy me some time.

The riders practically fly—their mounts clearly accustomed to long, hard rides. Their heads are low, because they're also exhausted. I counted on that not changing, and so far, it appears I'm right. I Bound the gravel at the height of a person on horseback—not wanting to risk injuring innocent animals.

As the first row of riders, five wide, rides into the gravel, men scream and fall from their horses, writhing. Their horses keep running for a bit, veering off the path, confused and scared. The row of men behind them also hits the remaining gravel, two of four falling from their horses, the other two slumping forward.

The entire mass of them slows, shouting and arguing.

I Bind another row while they descend into chaos, and then I urge Wind forward again. I'm nearly to the gates, but I turn to see if my second attempt was as effective as the first.

The racing soldiers stop before the Bound rocks this time, touching them and milling around. After a bit of yelling and confusion, they circle around, heading toward me with renewed fervor.

They're spread out and many are trailing, but the bulk of their force is still headed for me, faster now, with even grimmer expressions. With only a few hundred yards to go, the soldiers of Amun draw bows and nock arrows.

They let them fly.

I'm barely able to Lift all fifteen arrows, halting them before they reach me, and then flipping them the opposite direction. Then I send them right back at the attackers with as much force as I can muster.

Quite a few soldiers repel my attempt, but almost as many hit my intended targets. The soldiers cry out and those who blocked howl with rage.

Like they didn't already hate me enough.

I finally reach the gate, which has by now been well and truly barred.

I bang on the heavy wood. "Let me in! Open the gate!"

"Who are you?" a man's voice asks.

"Alora Sterling. Daughter of your Lord." I really, really hope that's true, or at least that they'll let me in while they look into it.

Silence.

Almost a hundred riders pound toward me—and I Lift every tiny rock and pebble I can sense and fling them as hard as I can at the oncoming soldiers. Perhaps because they're so much smaller than the arrows, the soldiers don't manage to defend against these as well. Dozens of my projectiles find their targets. Men shout, fall, and flail. Horses rear and buck.

I bang on the door again.

Even with my attempts to slow them, most of the soldiers are fine—and now they're nearly upon me.

"Open the gate! Hurry!"

The mounted men's eyes gleam as they draw their swords.

A small side door I hadn't noticed swings opens a dozen feet away, and a short, bald soldier in a bright blue tunic beckons. "Over here."

I rush toward him, tugging hard on Wind's reins. He barely clears the opening before the soldier slams the door with a thunk. He drops several wooden bars behind it.

"You're really *Alora Sterling*?" His eyes widen.

I bob my head. "That's what my mother said."

The soldier swallows, his Adam's apple bobbing. "That's impossible."

"It is?"

"Alora Sterling and her mother died in a fire," he says.

My eyes widen. "That's news to me."

"I guess so. Alora was just a baby when it happened."

Did I escape Amun only to be attacked by Isis? "If you believe me dead, why did you open the gate?" At least the guard isn't shouting for anyone—or pointing any weapons at me.

Yet.

"You look a lot like her, your mother I mean, but still didn't open the gate."

"But you did."

"I only let you in because *he* ordered it."

TERRA

"Alora? Is it really you?" A man steps out from behind an alcove near the main gate. The voice is inexplicably familiar. I turn toward the speaker slowly, my grip on my reins tightening.

He ordered them to let me in—he saved my life. But why? Who is he?

I don't recognize him—I still have no idea who he is —and yet, somehow I *know* him and his presence calms my terror.

Deep blue eyes. Dark brown hair, mostly straight, but with a few slight curls around his face. When he smiles, his teeth are flawless and white. But his grin is a little lopsided, and his eyes squint up until I almost can't see the color of his irises anymore.

"Alora?" His voice is barely a whisper this time, and it's full of wonder. "We never stopped looking for you."

He knows who I am. . .does he remember me? He's so young. Maybe he's just heard about me. But from whom? "You never stopped? I only found out I still have living family last night."

He frowns. "*Living* family?" He swallows, his Adam's apple shifting slightly. "So Mom's not. . ."

I flinch. "Mom." My memories of her have faded so much that it doesn't hurt as badly as it did anymore, but I hate talking about it. "She Wasted."

And.

If he's calling her Mom, that means. . .he's. . .Martin did say I had a brother. "Are you. . ." I can't force the words out. They feel too strange.

"I'm Jesse—your older brother. Don't you remember?" He steps toward me, his black boots shiny, his ice-blue uniform pristine. "Dad's been worried that Mom might have passed away. The letter she left for him said she'd bring you back when you turned sixteen."

Clearly that never happened.

"We redoubled our search efforts a year and a half ago, when you never. . ."

I'm not the only one having trouble processing this, at least.

Jesse inhales and exhales. "Dad was worried that Amun had executed you both, but we couldn't look into it without revealing your existence." He shakes his head. "You see the conundrum. If we looked too hard, we ruined Mom's efforts to keep you safe. But we couldn't know whether you were safe unless we looked."

I stumble backward, bumping into Wind, whose sides are still heaving slightly from our run. Which reminds me. "There's an army of the Followers of Amun right behind me."

As if my words summon them, there's a banging on the gate right behind us. "Release her." More banging. "By order of Lord Devlin Rochester."

Jesse laughs, apparently completely unconcerned by the mob of angry soldiers a few feet away. "As if we'd hand over the Warden now that she's finally here." He steps toward me again, and this time I have nowhere left to go. "Welcome home." He slings an arm around my shoulder. "Gregory, tell the gate guards to fire a few volleys to make them give us some space."

"You're not. . ."

"Not what?" He tilts his head.

"I don't know. Worried about them?" I ask. "Or angry that I led them here?"

"Am I worried about a few dozen Amun soldiers?" He shakes his head. "They'd need a few hundred times that to take Sterling. Clearly they didn't think you'd reach our gates—or that you'd find shelter when you did." He squeezes my shoulder with his hand. "It's unfortunate they saw you enter, because that means they know you're here, and who you are. With that information confirmed, Rochester may yet raise the kind of force they'll need, but not in the next day. For now, come with me. I *have* to be there to see Dad's face when I tell him you're home."

I ought to throw his arm off.

Every bit of my upbringing demands that I shout that he's a stranger and protect myself accordingly. But my instincts tell me he's genuine. I may have no memories of a brother, or a father either, but he feels. . .familiar. It's a stupid thing to think about someone I've never before seen, but I can't shake the feeling.

Even so, when Wind whinnies, I use the excuse to slip out from under his arm and soothe my sweet boy. "It's alright." I clear my throat. "Can someone take Wind somewhere he can relax? He's been traveling hard for a long time. All day, and then all night, and now into another day, in fact."

Jesse leans in close and whispers to Wind. "You're a good boy, and we will pamper you. Thank you for bringing Alora here safely." He kisses my gelding's nose, and then calls one of the men we pass and asks him to walk Wind to the stable.

It makes me uneasy to watch my horse disappear, but I don't have much choice. I'm in it now, right up to my neck. As if he can sense my discomfort, Jesse pauses. Men and women walk briskly past us on the busy streets of Sterling, far less concerned by the aggressive Followers of Amun outside than I would expect. Or perhaps they're rushing around in order to perform tasks to prepare for an assault.

I really don't know much about citizens or city life.

It does take forever for us to walk through the warren of criss-crossing streets. Sterling is much larger than I realized. It's far, far larger than Spurlock. Now that the immediate danger is past, my back aches, my hands tremble, my belly rumbles, and my eyes burn. An entire night without sleep and very little the night before is catching up to me. "Is it much farther?"

Jesse stops, his brow furrowing. "You're exhausted. Of course you are—I'm an idiot. You must've ridden all night along with your horse." He frowns. "I'm so sorry. I should've gotten us new horses instead of making you walk. We're nearly to the castle gate. Can you make it, or would you like to sit down for a bit?"

I shake my head. "I'll be alright. I was just curious."

"It's no more than a mile."

"It's fine," I say. "Actually, I'm just glad you were near the gate, or I'd have had more trouble getting through." I try not to think what would have happened if I'd been stuck outside.

His eyes widen. "It's lucky that I pulled perimeter duty."

"Perimeter duty? What's that?"

Jesse nods. "I'm in Dad's Unit—one of the leaders of

the military force for the Followers of Isis." He pauses and looks a little worried. "Do you know anything about how the chain of command works?"

"A little," I say. "Each Lord among the Followers of Isis has a Unit, which is comprised of the thirteen best Lifters. They lead groupings of men as well—train them, drill them, order them around. The Units comprise the standing army of the Followers of Isis. Right?"

"The Lords do technically preside over the castle, but they aren't always the head of the Unit. They have to earn that—or be satisfied with an empty title. Still, that's close enough for now." A massive stone wall looms up ahead, even larger than the wooden city perimeter wall. Jesse waves at the guards on either side. "Jacob. Lloyd. Is Dad close?"

"He's waiting just inside," the man on the left says. "Discussing how to deal with the cavalry."

Jesse grins conspiratorially at me and whispers, "He doesn't know you're here—no one paid much attention to the person those idiots were chasing until Gregory said you were Lifting. It's lucky I was close."

I'm breathing a little too fast.

"Hey, are you nervous?" Jesse's eyes soften. "Trust me, he's going to be delighted you're here."

"And the cavalry at the gate?"

Jesse shakes his head. "The only question there is whether we kill them all so Devlin won't get confirmation —which would be confirmation in its own way—or whether we let them muck about and return home. Not much difference at the end of the day, honestly. And when Amun does send a huge army, Dad will deal with it, like he always deals with everything." He touches my arm. "I'm telling you, we've been searching for you because he wants you safe. Where were you hiding?"

"With the Healers," I say.

He chuckles. "We searched among them, but there were *so many* groups and they're always moving. It was impossible to ask too many questions or pin them down —without giving away what we were looking for, which we couldn't risk. Mom's brilliant." He freezes. "Was brilliant." His nostrils flare. Clearly he's struggling with grieving for her and welcoming me.

Poor Jesse. I gained a brother and a father. . .and he regained his sister. . .and lost his mother at the same time.

After a quick pause, he shakes it off. "It's a good day, I promise. Let's go." The mischievous glint in his eye is so familiar I knew how it would look before I saw it. Which still makes no sense.

I follow him through the gate with my shoulders wide and my head up. Even my confident brother stumbles a bit when we walk through. Thirteen men stand in front of thirteen columns of soldiers, all dressed in sky blue uniforms. Every eye fixes on us as walk through.

"Oh." Jesse turns toward the man in the center, a man who looks an awful lot like him. A prominent nose, dark hair with silver at the temples, deep blue eyes, and a troubled look on his face.

"What were you doing?" The man in the center addresses Jesse without even so much as glancing at me. "We're under attack and you're, what? Strolling through the city, flirting?" He pivots on his heel and turns toward me, his eyes flashing. "And you've brought a woman back here—"

"Flirting?" Jesse splutters.

The man freezes in place. Not even his eyes shift in the slightest. "You're here. You're alive."

"That's what I was trying to tell you. I know why Amun was thundering toward us. They were chasing her —your daughter. The *Warden*."

The man in the center—my father, presumably—steps toward me. He clears his throat. "Alora." He inhales deeply. "You look exactly like your mother did. Where is she?"

Oh, Mom. The second I meet my new family, I'm stuck breaking the news of your death.

"We can talk about that later," Jesse says, "when there aren't as many soldiers waiting on us." He glances backward meaningfully.

"Right." The wrinkles at the corners of the man's eyes deepen. His unfocused eyes refocus as if he knows what we'll be discussing and he's already dragging himself into the present. "Of course, you're right. Later."

"Alora Sterling," Jesse says, "allow me to introduce you to your father, Duncan Sterling, Lord Protector of the Followers of Isis, and the Lord of Sterling Castle."

Duncan walks toward me, his movements choppy and stiff. I wonder whether his disappointed concern for Mom's absence has entirely overshadowed any joy he feels at my return. "Alora."

My fists clench at my side. Every day for eleven years, ever since Mom Wasted, I've wished for a family of my own. I've dreamed of exactly this scenario hundreds of times, and yet now that it's here, I feel none of the *rightness* I felt when I saw Jesse. I have no sense of affection and familiarity, and no instinctual trust swelling in my chest as I look at this man, like when I saw my brother.

No, instead, I'm afraid of Duncan Sterling.

And I kind of hate him on sight.

Jesse may say he was searching for me, but I saw no evidence of that. None of the Healers mentioned it to me. As far as I can tell, he sat here in his cushy castle, ordering men around while Mom begged the Healers to take us in. He did nothing to take care of his daughter, or to prepare me for being attacked because of how *Mother*

Terra made me. And now that I'm here, he appears to have no idea what to say or do.

"Welcome," he finally says, his voice heavy with emotion. "Welcome back home."

Someone grunts to our right, and I turn to see who it was.

"Welcome home? You told us your daughter *burned alive* in a fire. Now we're just supposed to accept that she didn't? Oh, and by the way, Amun's attacking us because of her?"

The man who grunted, the man who's yelling at my father, is tall, even for a soldier. His shoulders are broad and his long blond hair is pulled back into a queue at the base of his neck. Unlike the others, he's not wearing a helmet and his hair gleams in the sunlight. His eyes, ice blue, lock on mine and a pulse passes through my entire body like I've been delved, but different.

Heat instead of ice.

The man shudders at the exact same time, and I'm positive it's because he feels the same thing as me. He can't look away, either. His eyes travel from my face downward, taking in my dark pants and bright green blouse, and then returning to my face. His hands ball into fists at his side.

I shake my head, but it does no good. The golden haze that surrounds the most handsome man I've ever seen doesn't fade. My heart lurches, and I'm overwhelmed with a desire to run toward him, leap up in his arms, and kiss him squarely on the mouth. My breath hitches, my palms sweat, and my brain blanks of all rational thought.

In the midst of my body's betrayal, my mind screams in horror. Because I know just what this is.

The exordium.

I should be giddy. I should dance with delight. Very

few Terrans meet their soulmates. Forging a bond blessed by Mother Terra, a bond that exists outside of rational thought or reason, a pull that cannot be ignored—it's supposed to be the most transcendent thing that can happen to anyone, Healer or Lifter, man or woman. I've just found the man I'm supposed to spend the rest of my life with. I should be beaming uncontrollably, leaping into his powerful arms, and pledging to love him forever.

But a simmering fury bubbles up from somewhere inside of me instead, a rage I can't fully explain.

From the time I was born, an unseen hand has made every single decision for me. I Lift when no females can. I'm a citizen, but my mother ran and hid among the Healers. To save my life, she ruined her own—my parents fought and split over me. I've always hidden every aspect of who and what I am, just to carve out a safe place for myself and the family I had to fashion out of the path I was shoved upon. Now, thanks to one mistake, made in an attempt to keep my adoptive father safe, that family has also been ripped away.

Every life I wrap around myself is shredded by forces outside of my control.

And now, I'm plonked down in a place I don't know and the very first warrior I meet is what?

My soulmate?

Hard pass. I'm finished with fate. I'm done with being forced to hide because of stupid prophecies I never agreed to fulfill. I'm done with people pushing me around. I'm not letting fate control who I am, what I do, or in this final indignity, who I love. The fury rises inside of me, so thick and so strong that it knocks back the warm, glowy joy of the exordium. I forcefully replace the dopey adoration that must have been suffusing my features with a purposeful scowl.

The hunky warrior frowns and clears his throat. He

tilts his head sideways, trying to understand what's wrong, what might be spoiling this unbelievable moment.

Good luck, Hunky. The world around me does not make sense, and now that you've been thrown in next to me, yours won't either.

"Are you complaining that my daughter didn't die?" Duncan crosses powerful arms across his chest. I can't help noticing the scars that are visible on his hands. Clearly he doesn't run to a Healer for every little thing.

A swarthy solider next to Hunky bumps him. "Go on, Kahn. Tell him it's not fair."

Kahn shakes his head and refocuses on Duncan, only glancing my way occasionally. "You told us your daughter died, and now we find out it was a lie—that you hid her existence because she's the *Warden*? Did you really think that wasn't relevant information?"

Duncan's eyes flash. "The last time I checked, I didn't answer to any of you. You answer to me. Knowing why the Followers of Amun are here changes nothing about how we handle their aggression. We must show them we won't tolerate their attacks, no matter the reason."

"You've been lying to us." Kahn's not the only one who scowls. Heads are bobbing all around him. "Amun has long sought to destroy the Warden, and now she's here, among us. You knew she had been born." Kahn meets my eye then, and the half smile he offers me sort of ruins the effect of his righteously indignant tone.

Ha. Take that. The exordium's making you look idiotic, too.

Duncan lifts his chin. "As your ruler, it's my right to keep confidential any information I deem necessary."

"Perhaps you're not a fit ruler." Kahn's full lips press into a flat line. "Maybe I should challenge your right to lead us."

Troops behind and to the side of Kahn cheer.

He inhales. "It doesn't feel like I have any other choice. You've taken our voice away from us."

What does this entitled citizen know about having no choice? He's a Unit Leader, surely born strong and celebrated as a success every step of the way. He's probably been given everything his entire life on a silver platter. My arrogant soulmate has the audacity to challenge my father for the egregious sin of *keeping me alive?*

My eyes scan Duncan again—I'm drawn to the gray streaks in his hair, the wrinkles around his eyes, and the small, faint age spots on his forearms. My heart pulses. This isn't a trick of the universe, or a feeling forced upon me. I may not know much about challenges within units, but I know there's no way that Hunky, er, Kahn won't defeat the much older Duncan, and then how will I ever get to know my father? He might die during this challenge for all I know, and then another member of my family would be gone forever.

And this time, it'll be all my fault.

Well, my stupid, gorgeous soulmate may not understand the true depth of choice or of agency, but I do. I've fought against destiny my entire life, perhaps to prepare me for this moment. With an army headed toward us, thanks to my bad split-second decision in that stable, Duncan may lose the army at his back. "We all have choices, Kahn." I smile at him and he smiles back, probably compelled by a bond I don't understand and don't want. "And today, I choose to challenge you on Duncan Sterling's behalf."

Duncan groans beside me.

I spin around. "No one needs to fight my battles for me. Not your men, not your armies, and not you. Mom didn't have your protection, and I don't need it either."

Jesse clears his throat. "Maybe we should've spent a

few more minutes going over basic Unit laws. See, you're not a member of the Unit, so issuing a challenge to a Unit Leader, Dad's First in Command no less, well. . ."

"You've just sparked an Ascension," Duncan says. He raises his voice so everyone can hear. "My daughter has challenged Kahn Brantley. The Ascension commences tomorrow at dawn."

I really should learn to keep my mouth shut.

"No way," Kahn says. "I'm not fighting you."

"You don't have a choice," Jesse says. "She issued the challenge."

Kahn glances my way, clearly torn between annoyance and pining.

"She'll never reach you," a soldier behind Kahn says.

"You might be surprised," Jesse says. "Based on what I saw her doing on her way to the city, she's far, far stronger than anyone else I've seen."

What did he see? I deflected a few arrows and Bound some rocks in place. Is that what he's talking about? Or maybe he's just trying to defend me with big, empty talk. I'm too tired to know anymore.

My eyes are drawn to Kahn, and once I look at him, I can't look away. Sharp cheekbones, a strong jaw covered faintly with blond stubble. Bright, icy, almost haunting eyes. And he's *still* bathed in that glow I can't even begin to describe. Like the halo of light around a lamp, but without a central source.

"Don't worry overmuch." Jesse's voice near my ear is soft, calm.

I tear my eyes away from Kahn. "I just started some kind of tournament that might overturn your dad's position here. Oh, and half of Terra wants me dead."

Jesse laughs. "Some of that's true, but look at it this way. It'll be awesome for everyone to see what you can do. It'll give us a perfect chance to get everyone won over to your cause. Plus, with Dad working to win them over, it'll happen quick."

A chill runs down my spine. The men aren't on board now? Do the Followers of Isis want to hand me over to Amun?

"Wait. . . I thought Isis wanted to protect the Warden?" I choke. "Not that I'm saying I'm actually her."

"Have you heard the prophecy?" Duncan's voice surprises me.

There's an actual written prophecy? "Uh, maybe?"

Duncan frowns. "We have a lot to discuss."

"Alora's pretty exhausted," Jesse says. "We might need to let her rest first."

"I agree that a nap might be in order," Duncan says. "And some food, too."

"I'll walk her up," Jesse says.

"To keep anyone from knifing me on the way?" I ask. "Or to make sure I don't steal the family silver?"

Jesse laughs and my head fuzzes, like I've heard that sound over and over in my life, even though I don't have a single memory of it. I stumble on a loose cobblestone and nearly fall.

A strong hand catches my right forearm and every hair on my body stands on end. My heart sprints. I draw in a deep breath, knowing without looking who has steadied me.

Kahn.

I shake his arm off like it burns me. "Let go."

The hurt in Kahn's eyes spears me, but I ignore it and stomp away, forcing Jesse to jog to catch up to me.

"He's not that bad a guy, actually. Although I'd be lying if I said it didn't make me happy to watch you spurn him."

I stop abruptly. "Spurn him?"

Jesse splutters. "Uh, you know, glare at him? Storm off without a backward glance. Whatever. Most of the women I know fawn all over him."

I glance over my shoulder. Kahn's still staring at me, dumbstruck almost. If he's seeing some ridiculous golden halo around me too, I don't blame him. "He's your dad's first in command?"

Jesse shrugs. "And the Lord of Brantley Castle. He's a pretty big deal."

Fantastic.

Behind Kahn, Duncan's practically shouting at a small group of men. "She's my daughter, and I never even agreed to hide her, but her mother didn't wait for my permission. What would you have done differently?"

"Should we wait for him?"

Jesse shakes his head. "Dad's fine. He permits a wide amount of latitude with his commanders. He feels that open dialogue helps foster trust." Jesse smiles. "I think he just misses Mom. They used to argue all the time, loudly, and now no one really fights with him anymore."

"You remember Mom?"

Jesse's face falls. "Just stories Dad shared, mostly. I struggle to parse out what's a memory of her, and what's a memory of what Dad told me about her. Do you remember Dad at all?"

I shake my head.

Jesse nods. "Well, we'd better get you settled. Big day tomorrow." He starts walking, weaving in and out of groups of men, and I follow, keeping my head down. Once we've passed the majority of the men, I begin to look around.

I point at a tall, wide, red brick building. "What's that?"

"The closest barracks for the squadrons." Where the rank and file soldiers live.

"And the smaller gray building?"

Jesse follows my hand. "That's where the Unit lives."

"Is that where you sleep, too?" I'm assuming Jesse's part of the Unit. He's probably one of the squadron leaders, since Dad's the leader of all of Isis. I don't know much about how the lives of citizens work, but from what I understand, strength is usually passed from fathers to their sons.

He shakes his head. "I live in the main castle with Dad. There are a few perks to being the boss's son, I guess."

Jesse finally stops on steps leading up to massive walnut doors. The vast castle that rises in front of us is black, as if the stone itself has been burned. I wonder whether it ever has.

"I'll take you to your room and introduce you to your lady's maid," my brother says. "Since you already missed breakfast, she can bring food to your room."

"I have a room?" And a maid?? To what? Clean?

Jesse pauses and our eyes meet. "Of course you do."

He leads me up and to the left of a double staircase so wide that Ironsides the elephant could march up it with room for another beside her. Sconces line the hallway, and the floor's covered in plush, ornately woven rugs. We turn down a side hallway, and walk on and on. Eventually we do stop. "This is it. It'll need some updating." He squirms. "Dad wouldn't let anyone touch it after you left. I think he kept hoping you and Mom would waltz back in, like you'd been on holiday."

I should open the wooden door in front of me, but I'm afraid. It feels like the hits never stop coming. A blue bird is carved into the front of the solid oak panel at eye level, and I trace the shape with my fingers. A memory surfaces, my delight in seeing a bird on my door. Mom's smile. How she clapped her hands and spun me in a circle.

"Are you going inside?" Jesse's voice is tentative.

I shake my head. "I remember it, I think. The door. And maybe Mom, too, showing it to me."

"I don't recall much about Mom, but I remember you. I thought about you every single day after you left. We were close, you know, inseparable really. My room's next door. I used to come inside your room whenever you would cry and fall asleep in your bed."

"Really?"

He nods.

"I had a father figure in the troupe. Martin."

"You did?"

"You sound surprised."

"Are you saying he and Mom. . ."

I shake my head. "Oh, no. Nothing like that."

Jesse sighs. "That makes more sense."

"He took care of me, but he and Mom didn't—"

"Mom and Dad were soulmates, according to Dad," Jesse says. "That's why I was shocked."

I don't recall Mom mentioning it, but then, why would she? Talking to a six-year-old about the exordium would be. . . I can't talk about it and I'm almost eighteen. "What I meant was that thinking of Duncan as my dad, well, it's weird."

"It feels like a betrayal."

"I guess so, even if I'm mad at Martin for hiding things from me."

"I understand, and I think, if you explain it to him, Dad would get it too. But you need to sleep now, so I'll leave you."

"Wait," I say. "I wanted to tell you something." He

turns toward me, his eyes earnest but also sparkling. My heart expands. "I can't explain it. This may not make sense, but I didn't have a brother back in the troupe. I had a friend, Thomas, but he never felt. . . Even if I can't pinpoint a single memory with you, I must have them because being with you, it kind of feels like, well, like I've known you and missed you all this time. Do I sound crazy?"

Jesse laughs. "Does it matter?"

I guess not. "You're the only thing that feels right in my life anymore. I'm sorry if that makes me a clingy, erratic mess. I'm sorry if I've ruined everything, what with leading an army to your doorstep and issuing challenges that cause Dad problems." I wonder whether everyone wishes I had Wasted instead of Mom. Probably.

"I'm glad you're here." Before I can stop him, Jesse hugs me. Surprisingly, it's not stiff and uncomfortable like I thought it might be. It feels as if I've done this every day of my life, and I never want to miss another day.

When he pulls back, I look up into his face. "Thank you."

I reach for the doorknob and pull it open. This room is almost fifty times the size of the interior of my wagon. The ceiling soars overhead, and the walls are lined with tapestries of small woodland creatures frolicking. My feet sink into a thick pink rug covered in blossoms and butterflies. A canopy bed sits in the center of the room, flanked by small wooden chairs on one side and a huge bookcase full of toys and dolls on the other. Two other doors open out of my room, and I remember where they lead. One holds my old clothes, and the other leads to a water closet. No more peeing in a pot and dumping it into bushes.

Even though Jesse warned me that someone would

bring me food, I jump when a small woman carrying a large tray appears in the doorway.

My brother smirks at my shock.

"Hello," I finally say.

My stomach growls. The woman glances around, unsure where to place the food tray. Without thinking, I Lift the dolls and books from the table near the window and point. "Here. Let me help."

The tiny woman screams loudly and drops the tray.

I Lift it before it can hit the ground, steadying the bowls, plates, and the glass pitcher without a thought. I place them all carefully on the table. "Sorry for startling you."

But I'm not sure whether she can hear me since she's still screaming, and now she's backing toward the door.

"Whoa," I say. "I mean you no harm."

She throws her hands up in front of her as if fending off an attack.

Jesse's laughing almost as loudly as she's screaming.

"It's fine, Natalie. She's my sister." Jesse points at the door. "You can go back to the kitchen. I promise she has no plans to destroy you, or Terra, tonight."

The woman finally stops howling, although she's now hiccupping and gasping for breath.

"Maybe you can take a moment to prepare the other staff so they don't all melt down when they see her." Jesse shoos her away. "Go."

She practically runs from the room.

I sink into a chair. "That could've gone better."

Jesse shrugs. "Everyone will know who you are and what you can do by tomorrow morning. Don't worry about it. Even now, the members of the Unit are sending word to their families of the Ascension, and they're surely sharing what they know of your return."

My return. "Do you mean me, Alora Sterling? Or me, the Warden?"

Jesse points at the wall. "That's the prophecy, there."

I spin around and stare. At a flowery needlepoint. "Excuse me?"

"Mom had one of the castle seamstresses do it, the second she discovered you could Lift."

I blink and force myself to read the words.

With the Warden it began, and with the Warden it ends. When the female Lifter returns, she will end Terra. She will reunite the divided, bring augmented strength to all men, and restore women to their rightful power. She will birth the end of all things, and create the beginning of all endings. Terra was not the beginning, but it was a beginning, and like all things, it must end. As Terra crumbles, the world will begin anew for those who are worthy.

That's not at all obtuse. "What does that even mean?"

Jesse shrugs. "Prophecies are stupid. But it did give a name to people's fear of anything different. You're the only woman on Terra who can Lift—they'd have feared you with or without that dumb, confusing pile of words."

He's probably right, but I hate the confusing prediction all the same.

"You were only a year old the first time you Lifted, you know. Not quite two." Jesse's voice is light, casual, like he's telling me a story about something ridiculous, not addressing the reason mounted cavalry are outside the walls of the city, bent on destroying me. "Apparently Mom was tired of you drinking out of bottles—she insisted you drink from a cup."

"What?" That makes no sense.

"She put your bottle on the counter, and you screamed bloody murder."

"I sound like a real peach."

Jesse laughs. "From what I hear, that's every toddler.

But, most toddlers, even male ones, can't Lift their bottle off the counter and float it right into their hand."

"I did?"

He nods. "You got your bottle, and Mom and Dad started preparing for the world as they knew it to end."

"Seems like I just cause bad things wherever I go."

Jesse frowns.

"What exactly is an Ascension?"

He chuckles. "Oh, that's what you mean. Well, usually once a year, the members of the Unit fight one another to determine rank. It's always one on one, and you can only move up or down, one place at a time. No Healing in between, and no outside interference. Aside from the annual rank determinations, an outsider eligible for entrance into a Unit—"

"Slow down! Annual rank determinations, interference, eligible what?"

Jesse laughs. "Most citizens grow up knowing these things. I'm sorry."

I grew up in hiding, without any parents at all for most of my life.

As if he's just remembering that, Jesse's eyes soften. "Once a year we duke it out to determine who's the boss within the Unit. Your rank will set your squad assignment, your pay scale, and your place in the social pecking order. Any citizen who can Lift a human twelve years of age or older is eligible to challenge into a Unit."

"I thought the members of Units had to be noble."

"It's not an official law, but it usually works out that way. Strength at Lifting usually follows family lines, so it's rare for it to manifest outside of noble lines. It can happen, though."

Huh.

"The strongest Lifters generally have children who become the strongest Lifters."

"So my challenge is valid because. . ."

"No one has questioned your right to challenge formally, although Kahn might. Could you Lift me if you had to?"

I frown. And then I Lift Jesse and float him over toward the window. I set him down by the tray. Then I cross the room and sit down to eat. He's not wrong that I'm ravenous.

"Right. Okay, so I was right about that." He brushes his uniform down.

He looks rattled. "Is that hard for most citizens?" I ask. "To Lift a person?"

Jesse swallows. "Uh, yeah. The Unit can all do it, but not as elegantly as you, and it drains us."

My jaw drops. "Drains you? Lifting one person?" I think about what I do in a normal day, how many things I Lift. No wonder the citizens didn't suspect me of Lifting the wagon, or any of the other items when we did our show. Apparently that's extremely hard to do.

"Because you issued that challenge, but you don't hold a position within Dad's Unit, your challenge sparked an Ascension. If you were to win, it would reshuffle the lineup anyway, and also, it keeps challenges to the upper ranking Unit members down. See, in order to fight one of them, you'd have to work your way through everyone else first."

"This sounds like a much bigger deal than I expected."

"Don't stress. We were due to have one in a few weeks anyway. You just sped up the timeline."

"What would have happened if I hadn't interfered?"

Jesse shrugs. "Kahn and Dad would have fought. If Kahn won, he would've taken control of all of us, including the entire Isis force until the next time we all gathered to vote."

That was a serious challenge.

Jesse shrugs. "I doubt Kahn could beat Dad, but you never know. If that happened, Dad would've fought his number two and taken Kahn's place. Unless Dad lost again, I guess, and then Dad would keep fighting until he won. If Kahn lost to Dad, he'd lose his position entirely, as the challenger, and head home. He should be thanking you, really. Although, whoever comes in last place tomorrow won't be pleased. They'll be headed home."

"Oh, no."

"It is what it is. Tomorrow you'll fight the members of the Unit from the bottom up, and every person you defeat will have to fight those below." Jesse tilts his head. "Speaking of. . .do you know how to fight? Other than freakishly strong abilities, have you had any training at all?"

"Not really, no."

"And I'm guessing your ability to Lift is essentially depleted, between your race to reach the city walls, and Lifting me and that tray."

I snort. "Uh, no."

Jesse lifts his eyebrows. "No?"

I look around the room. The four-poster canopy bed looks like the heaviest thing present. I feel for the heft of each major beam, and then I Lift it.

Jesse chokes. "Put that down. You should be conserving strength for tomorrow."

I set the bed back down. "I've never conserved my strength a day in my life. I don't think it really works like that."

Jesse frowns. "Of course it does. If I were to demonstrate my maximum strength right now, I'd be utterly drained for tomorrow."

I pick up a loaf of crusty bread. "I hope this isn't rude, but I'm starving."

Jesse shakes his head. "Go ahead."

"When you use your arms and legs to lift something heavy regularly, your muscles grow." I rip into a piece of bread and begin to chew. "It's like that. The more I use it, the stronger my powers become. I've been limited mostly by my inability to Lift around any outsiders who might see."

Jesse grabs a darker loaf of bread off the tray, and I force myself not to growl at him for taking my food. "We talk about our power as a well that depletes with use. Over time it refills."

"Well, you're the expert, but if Lifting that bed impresses you, I like my chances tomorrow. I've never been around anyone else who can Lift. The Healers had no expectations, and no way to teach me a thing, but maybe that worked in my favor."

"Some men in the squadrons can't Lift more than a blade of grass." Jesse sits on the edge of the bed. "We train them to the best of their abilities, but there are other ways to fight."

"But the Unit must be able to—"

"The men in the Unit vary in their abilities. All of them can Lift at least the weight of another human, but you'd be surprised how creative they get to conserve that strength. Not a single one of us could do what you just did with that bed, and if any man in the last hundred years did that, it would have wiped him out for days. And what you did with those rocks—Binding them in place, and hurling fistfuls of stones behind you?" He shakes his head and licks his lips. "None of us could have done that. Our abilities weaken proportionately with distance."

I'm not quite sure how to respond. I've done the majority of the grunt work for our troupe since I turned six. Transportation of pots and pans to and from the river for washing. Assembly of sets for our performances.

Wagon Lifting for the show or whenever someone needs to make repairs. What he's saying. . .it's shocking.

"Either way," Jesse says. "You should eat and then rest. But humor me? No more Lifting until tomorrow at dawn."

I don't bother arguing, and after I eat, I pass out.

❧ 8 ❧

EARTH

As soon as I smell eggs and toast, my mouth begins to water. Surely that's the reason there's drool on my pillow. Jesse almost always starts cooking breakfast before I'm up. When I stretch, I give thanks to whatever maker watches over us that my wrist has healed. Not even a faint bruise mars the perfection of the place where my hand meets my arm. Most days I mourn my lack of normal dreams. In fact, nearly every bad thing that has happened in my life, at least since my parents' death, has been a direct result of my Terran dreams.

But today, it's a blessing.

Although, I may be singing a different tune tomorrow. The Followers of Amun want to kill me, I've left my family to rejoin my birth father and brother whom I don't really know, and I've introduced myself by challenging my bio dad's first-in-command, who also happens to be my Terran soulmate?

Ugh.

Kahn has a hundred pounds on me at least, and he

looked like he was born swinging a sword with his perfectly sculpted arms. I flop back and pull the covers over my head. If I met Kahn on Earth? Oh man, I wouldn't fight that warm, suffuse golden glow. I'd run and leap into his arms. But of course, on Terra, I basically spit in his gorgeous face.

Although. If I'm honest with myself, John's nearly as hot as Kahn, and I shut *him* down just as fast.

What's wrong with me?

I slide out of bed and quickly dress in my typical workout clothing: one of Jesse's hand-me-down t-shirts and cropped yoga pants.

Jesse's already dressed for his interview when I come out, even though it's several hours away. His blue button-down shirt has a small stain on the collar, and his khakis are a little too short, but they're the best clothes he's got. I feel a pang of guilt. If I weren't such a whack job, he'd probably have much nicer things. He wouldn't be hoping desperately for an adult job at the age of eighteen—he'd be enrolled in college courses somewhere, probably on scholarship.

I look around our apartment and try to see it as a stranger might: the patched beanbag chairs, the wooden spool table and cheap metal stools. Shoved into the far corner, Jesse's cinderblock bed really is the misshaped cherry on a pathetic family room sundae. I recall how much pride swelled within me as we spray-painted and duct-taped the things that other people threw away. . .making our own safe space in an uncertain world. Even last night I was proud of how it looked.

But this morning, guilt overwhelms me. What kind of life have I doomed Jesse to endure?

"I'm sorry, J," I say.

He puts a plate of eggs in front of me, and raises both eyebrows. "For what?"

I sigh. "We're in this terrible apartment, working as dishwashers and cutting grass instead of learning about math and science and English because—" I choke. "Because I'm a nut, I guess."

He grins. "I've always loved nuts. Almonds, walnuts, and don't even get me started on peanut butter, which, little-known fact. . .comes from pea*nuts*."

"That's not a little-known fact. It's a well-known fact." I shake my head at his dumb joke.

"I can't be expected to know what plebeians do and don't know. I'm a high school drop out, remember?" He tilts his head, his lopsided smile returning.

Tears well in my eyes.

His face falls and his mocking tone evaporates. "Alora, we're here, building a home in the middle of a world that attacks and destroys and ruins, and I'm proud of us for it. We aren't here because of anything you did." He shakes his head. "We're here because our aunt sucks. Because Killian was so twisted he attacked you. Because a sadistic caseworker, instead of protecting you, targeted us. The world dealt us such a miserable hand, it would have broken me if I'd been alone. I'm only who I am, a knower of well-known facts, a lover of peanut butter M&Ms, because of you." He sits down. "None of our problems are your fault."

"You have no idea how much I want to believe that." I sink onto the other stool and lean one elbow against the makeshift table. "But if I hadn't told Aunt Trina about Terra, if I hadn't insisted it was real, she would have kept us." My voice cracks. "She wanted to keep you."

He sits down next to me and puts his hand over mine. "I'm your brother, your better half if we're being brutally honest, and because of my good nature, I'll never leave you." He squeezes my hand and then releases me. "But seriously, I'll say it one last time. Try to listen. None of that was your fault, and like it or not, you're stuck with me and this crappy little apartment."

I nod and start to shovel eggs into my mouth.

"Your wrist looks fine, at least."

"Good as new," I say.

"So no one came after you? On Terra, I mean?"

I swallow a huge bite of toast. "Not exactly. You'll never believe who I met."

"Was it the Easter bunny? I've always wondered where he came from."

"Hilarious. No."

"Don't tell me." He taps his lip and smiles. "Santa Claus? Jack Frost? Oh, oh, I know. Our parents. Terra's really the underworld, and they told you how much they love and miss us both, but me a little more because I'm generally awesome."

"Umm, no, no, and yes." I huff. "And why would you go right to underworld? You think our parents were evil?"

"The underworld is for anyone who dies. It's not like heaven or hell." The smile slides off Jesse's face. "Wait, did you say yes to the last one?"

His brain amazes me. "Yep. Because last night, I met our dad, only it's not like, our real dad. And." I cross my arms and make him wait for it. "I met you."

"What??" Jesse braces his arms, palms down, against the spool table. "First you see the guy who died at Perry's. Then you saw our dad?" He pauses. "Who somehow isn't our dad. You'll need to explain that." He shakes his head. "And then way to bury the lead. *I'm* over there now?" He bites his lip. "*In Terra*? Finally??"

"I met our dad over there, but he looks nothing like our real dad here looked. It's like he's a totally different person. And even though I recall nothing about Earth when I'm there, I *knew* he felt wrong. Which is strange."

"Whoa, if this is an underworld—people who you see over there die—then maybe I'm doomed now. Marked for death."

I slug his arm. "I'm not dead, idiot, and our dad over there wasn't the same as our actual dad, so this guy's probably not dead either. He called himself Duncan Sterling, the leader of the Isis forces, actually, and he's some kind of ripped, amazing old man who looked, like, way better than our real dad ever did."

"Hey, then, what about me? Am I super buff? Can I throw an apple a few feet into the air and core, slice, and peel it with a sword before it hits the ground? Am I a ninja?" He stands up. "Tell me I'm a ninja!"

I snort. "Actually, you kind of are. You're like Jesse 2.0 on Terra."

He whistles. "Awesome. And you're my sister over there too, right? Please tell me I didn't hit on you or something totally disgusting. Because if you didn't know we're related, and I'm like a Greek god and all, I'm just saying. That could get gross in a hurry."

"Jesse! You're so twisted. Yes, you're my brother there, too. A little older than me—just like here."

"Thank goodness. Hey, that's a legitimate concern. Lots of girls have trouble knowing how to deal with all this." He tries to smolder, which is laughable.

"You didn't hit on me—you knew right away I was your sister."

"Of course I did." He pauses. "So I'm your older brother in both places, but dad's not really our dad? That's strange, right? You said from what you recall of your mom, or I guess, our mom, she wasn't the same either. Don't you think it's strange that you've got the same sibling but not the same parents?"

"Honestly, it is odd, but that's like the tip of the iceberg to all the bizarre stuff going down right now."

He shrugs. "True. Extreme sexism, telekinetics, and healing, a tiny planet that consists of two warring factions, with no guns or major tech. Oh, and women don't get pregnant from having sex—a baby just starts growing in there. The dad finds out he's a father by some glowing golden name in his head. Does that about sum it up?"

I gulp. "And the exordium."

He sighs. "Soulmates, so drawn to one another that neither of them can ignore the feelings? You said most of the Terrans don't even believe it's real."

"Except it is."

Jesse lifts one eyebrow. "Excuse me?"

"I met you, and my Terran Dad... and I also sort of met my soulmate last night."

"You didn't." His smile is so very lopsided that I can tell he's suppressing a laugh in an attempt to be polite.

"Met him, and challenged him to a fight. With swords, I think."

He laughs. "Now *that* sounds like you."

"I know all of it sounds ridiculous. It's hard to explain. I saw this guy there, my dad's little assistant soldier, and I don't know. He was *glowing*, Jesse."

"How does your brain even come up with this stuff?" Jesse asks.

Come up with this stuff? I frown. "I don't think I *come up with* any of it. Terra's real, J. I'm not telling some kind of dream-based soap opera."

"No, I mean, I know. I do believe that." Jesse nods. "What I meant was, did he look more like Ryan Gosling or Liam Hemsworth?"

I roll my eyes. "A young Chris Hemsworth, maybe. Like Thor, pre-haircut. Or like a really young version of the guy who played Ragnar in *Vikings*, before he got all old and nasty."

Jesse's jaw drops. "Well, you are a lucky girl. I bet you squealed like a happy little piglet."

"Actually, I challenged him, remember?"

"Like, 'hey hot stuff, you can't catch me, neener neener?' But like, actually you were shimmying and batting your eyes?"

I snort. "No, more like, 'choke on my sword, you stupid glowing jerk.'"

Jesse's eyes widen. "Seriously? You didn't just blow him off?"

I shrug. "What can I say? Even in Terra, I'm alternative."

"I guess so." Jesse dumps his uneaten eggs onto my plate. "Speaking of being a freak of nature, even with the buckets of food you consume, you're looking too skinny again. You need to eat more." He starts to clean up dishes. His voice is almost too soft to hear over the water of the sink. "I wonder sometimes whether Terra's like a puzzle, and if we could just see all the pieces, the ones we have would click into place."

"Maybe," I say. "I wish it made more sense."

"Take yesterday for instance. I haven't thought about the car accident in years. Maybe because I sort of block that whole thing—losing Mom and Dad—then being abandoned by Aunt Trina. It was terrible. But you had that near miss with the car, and you asked me about it."

"What about it?"

He swivels his laptop around on our wooden spool table, and points at the screen. "I got bored after you went to bed early with your wrist."

I'm about to put a bite of eggs in my mouth, but the fork slips from my fingers and clatters against my plate. "You did it." I glance at the document on the screen. It's the file on our parent's death. The police did investigate the car accident.

He shakes his head. "It doesn't say much. I imagine they do reports on all motor vehicle accidents with a resulting death as a matter of course."

"Then what did I stumble on, exactly?"

He points down at the bottom of a form. "The interesting part is here."

"Where it says, 'Case Closed: vehicle accident resulting in two deaths'?"

"No, dummy, right above that."

I lift my eyes. The last sentence of the report says, "Forensic evidence shows seatbelts were sliced high on spool prior to accident." My jaw drops. "Why would they close the case if there was evidence the seatbelts were tampered with?"

He shrugs. "Obviously I don't know, but our parents never should have gone through that windshield. It sure looks like the cops dropped the ball." He sighs. "Or someone paid them to look the other way."

"We need to call that detective." I glance at the name on the form. Officer Gregory Stanton.

Jesse shakes his head. "They closed out the investigation years ago. They either couldn't turn up anything else and the case went cold, or they closed it for a reason. I doubt calling him will do anything but stir up more trouble for us. But that got me thinking. I still doubt anyone in Washington is looking for us, but if we call them and start poking around. . ."

"Why'd you show it to me, then?"

"I knew if I didn't, you'd badger me about it over and over, and knowing you, you'd find this report yourself. You were right. Mom and Dad's seatbelts *were* cut. That happened ten years ago, though. I agree we should look into it, but at this point, I think we should wait until we're both adults to do it, when the court has no power to shuttle you around and call it 'your best interest.' Any clues are so cold now, it's not like waiting another six or eight months will hurt."

"I'll still be a felon in a year."

He tosses his hands up. "True. So if you want me to poke around at more files, let me know. But I think it's a mistake, and it's only going to turn up more bad stuff that ruins our lives."

"Your suggestion is that we should stick our heads in the sand? That's worked super well for us before."

"When have you *ever* left anything alone for five minutes together?" Jesse smirks. "Ostriches always seem pretty happy to me."

I roll my eyes. "We can talk more about it after your interview. How's that?"

Jesse smiles. "It's as good as I'm going to get, I'm sure."

I head to Krav Maga at the YMCA while Jesse does our laundry. He's a pretty decent brother. When I get back, Jesse's still downstairs in the laundry room. When I reach our room, his laptop is open on the table. I reach to close it as I walk past, and then an idea occurs to me.

Before I can stop myself, I pull up a web browser and search 'Duncan Sterling.' If I can pull up a photo of him, and he looks just like Duncan Sterling on Terra. . .I don't know what it would prove, but it would be bizarre. I'm gripped with a desperate desire to know.

Unfortunately, it's a popular name. A very proud real estate agent, a school teacher, a minor league baseball player, the list goes on and on. I log in to Jesse's fake fb account that he uses to research people and things and poke around more. I'm not sure how long I scroll through images—none of which even somewhat resemble Duncan Sterling in Terra—before Jesse walks in the door, his arms full of a stuffed basket.

"What are you doing?"

"Nothing." I close out the browser and shut the laptop. "I just need to shower and we can go." By the time I've dried my hair, it's almost time to head to Katy for Jesse's interview.

"Whoa," Jesse says. "Look who put on her nicest outfit."

Heat rises in my cheeks. "I'm interviewing." Besides. It's not like my Wal-Mart special sun dress is that nice.

"You're also meeting the Future Mr. Alice Walker." He wiggles his eyebrows.

"Shut up."

When we reach La Centerra, I send Jesse off with a hug and a smile and watch him walk into the office building where he's interviewing. I really hope this goes okay for him. It would be nice to have some good luck for a change. I text Henry the second Jesse goes inside.

CAN YOU MEET ME IN KATY?

SURE, he texts. WHICH PART?

LA CENTERRA.

ABSOLUTELY. WHERE DID YOU WANT TO EAT?

ANYTHING IS FINE WITH ME.

I HEAR THERE'S A PERRY'S. . .

HILARIOUS, BUT DON'T QUIT YOUR DAY JOB. I'm surrounded by comedians, but I'm occasionally funny myself.

THAT STINGS. HOW ABOUT PELI PELI?

WHAT KIND OF FOOD IS THAT? I text back.

AFRICAN. IT'S GOOD THOUGH, I PROMISE.

It sounds weird, honestly, but what do I know? SURE.

I spend the next two hours walking from restaurant to restaurant in La Centerra. I carefully avoid the Perry's Steakhouse—I didn't even realize the local chain had a location here until Henry made his joke. They're looking for dishwashers at Peli Peli, and I make the mistake of glancing at the menu when I apply.

It's far nicer than I expected. I'm actually worried about whether Henry can afford it. I know I can't.

Maybe he's on scholarship for school and washes dishes for extra money. The thought of ultra-jock, ultra-flaky Henry being on scholarship makes me laugh. The woman bringing me a job application looks at me funny, but she hands it to me all the same.

Unfortunately, the application has a huge section for references, with four distinct lines. After a moment's deliberation, I write down Henry's name, with an illegible scrawl as his last name, since I don't know it. Torchy's, Bernie's, and Baker Street Pub and Grill are all hiring for dishwashers, busboys, and hostesses respectively. I use Henry as my reference for each one. I decide I should warn him. WROTE YOU DOWN AS A REFERENCE FOR MY WORK AT PERRY'S. HOPE THAT'S OKAY.

He doesn't reply, but I figure he's either still working or he's headed home to shower, so I don't fret.

When I finish, I find a bench at the base of the building where Jesse's interviewing. It's hot, but I don't figure I can hang inside any stores without spending at least a little money, and I'm as broke as I've ever been. I put in headphones, even though my crappy burner phone doesn't play music, because passersby are less likely to try talking to me.

I glance at my watch. I've been sitting in the shade for almost an hour in the late afternoon. Every part of my body is sweaty, in spite of the breeziness of my Wal-Mart sundress. But when the fountain in the shopping square begins to look like an inviting wading pool, I glance at my watch. Five-thirty-four p.m. Maybe I could just dip my toes. . .

My phone buzzes.

DONE. HEADED DOWN.

Jesse emerges a moment later. I pull out my headphones and stand, trying to tell from Jesse's face whether he got the job. I beeline toward him, pulling up short when John shoots out of the building behind him.

John's handsome face lights up when he sees me. "Alice, how nice that you came to support your brother."

"Uh, well, I'm looking for a job, too. Remember?"

Jesse beams at me. "I'm sure you'll be seeing a lot more of one another. Alice and I are kind of a package deal. She follows me around like a puppy dog."

I cock one eyebrow. "Pretty sure it's the other way around."

Jesse fakes panting and makes a slobbering sound. "I do smell worse. Maybe that does make me the dog. Dang it."

"Congratulations," I say. "Now you can quit your landscaping gig, and your smell might finally improve."

"I can't believe this brain was being wasted on mind-numbing yard work. What started as an interview turned into a strategy session." John chuckles. "Remind me to tack a few hours onto your first paycheck."

"You're not about to descend into techno-babble are you?" I ask. "Because I'm meeting Henry in like twenty minutes, so I don't have time to politely feign interest for very long."

John perks up. "Ah, the boyfriend."

Crap. I forgot I told him Henry was my boyfriend when he asked me out.

Jesse laughs. "Be careful teasing her. She's snippy enough with me and we're related."

But. . . I didn't warn Jesse that I used Henry as an

excuse. Probably because I didn't want to have to explain that John asked me out in the first place. . .because I didn't want him to blame me if he didn't get the job.

"Where are you two eating?" Jesse asks.

"Peli Peli." I scrunch my nose.

"You've never been," John says.

I want to like Jesse's new boss, truly. But he's insufferable. "I haven't, no."

John smiles. "After tonight, you won't make that face. Peli Peli's amazing."

Of course Richy McMoneyBags has been. He probably has a regular table.

"So, tell us more about Henry." John's dark eyebrows wiggle up and down, which only draws attention to the surprising, almost honey color of his eyes. "What does he do to set your heart aflutter?"

"Yes, do tell," Jesse says. "Because last night, I could hardly get you to call him. And now you're going on a date at a nice place."

"Whoa, trouble in paradise?" John asks.

Jesse turns toward him with as confuzzled a look as I've ever seen.

"He's a soccer player," I say quickly.

"You said that already," John says. "But in my experience, soccer players develop unfashionably large calves. What else you got?"

Jesse snickers. "Maybe Alice likes big calves."

I scowl at him. "I do not like large calves."

"And how are Henry's?" Jesse asks. "Maybe I should walk you over to your date so I can meet him."

John's mouth drops open slightly. He clicks it closed. "Wait, your brother hasn't met your boyfriend?"

Oh, good grief. "He's not my boyfriend, okay? This is our first date. Actually, it's not even a date. I told you I lost my job." I cross my arms and huff. "He's bringing me my last paycheck."

"You found me so detestable that you *made up a boyfriend*." John closes his eyes and shakes his head slowly. "Wow, I knew I didn't have much game, but this is a new low."

Didn't have much game? In the last five minutes, ten different girls have practically tripped over their own feet while trying to get his attention.

"Don't take it personally," Jesse says. "Alice shoots everyone down. Sometimes she even resorts to physical violence."

My jaw drops. I can't believe he's poking fun at me using Terra. Actually, I totally can. Freaking Jesse.

"I wish I could follow you to Peli Peli and watch this non-date," John says. "I almost feel bad for poor, fat-calf Henry."

"His calves are fine." I stomp. Sadly, stomping in sandals isn't very satisfying.

"Well, you won't mind if I walk over with you," Jesse says. "Just to meet the guy, right?"

I shrug. "You can crash the dinner, as far as I'm concerned. Now that you have a new job, we might even be able to afford an appetizer to split."

"As tempting as that sounds," Jesse says, "I don't think I'll do that to poor Henry. The world is already stacked against him, after all."

I shake my head. "I swear, his calves are fine!"

"Actually, I offered to take your brother to Torchy's Tacos to celebrate," John says. "You'd be welcome, but maybe we'll have to take a rain check, since you're booked up." Even when he's suppressing a smile, John has a dimple. Some things in life are monstrously unfair.

I don't know what to say at this point, so I look down

at my feet, wishing I'd had the foresight to paint my toenails.

"If we do have to hang out in the future, I can just find a bag to wear over my face," John says. "You know, so you won't be stuck looking at me."

I snort. "Oh please. Your face is gorgeous. That's not the problem."

"Not the problem?" Jesse puts his hand over his mouth. "I told you she's a handful."

"Gorgeous huh? Well, I'd like to take the compliment, but ouch. Apparently it's *who I am* that makes me so vile." John winks, and I realize he's mostly teasing.

"I'm done sticking my foot in my mouth for the evening, I hope," I say. "So I better head over there to meet Henry."

"Good luck," Jesse says. "And make sure you grab that paycheck first thing. If things get awkward, you at least want to leave with what you went to get."

I roll my eyes as I hug Jesse. "Congrats on the new job. I'm excited." I step back. "Thanks, John, for taking a chance on this big nerd. He won't let you down."

"I can already tell that's true," John says.

I step off the curb and begin walking toward Peli Peli.

Jesse and John start walking too. . . three steps behind me.

I turn around, ready to complain, when I remember. Peli Peli's across the street from Torchy's. We're walking the same way. I'm the idiot who made a big production of heading out. Maybe I'm not done being awkward for the night.

"Care to join us on the walk over?" John's lip twitches with humor and his eyes sparkle.

"Uh, I'm not used to this area yet."

"No worries," John says. "Can I recommend the bobotie? And the peppadews are amazing. They aren't on the menu alone anymore, but if you ask, they'll bring you some."

"Wow, you're quite the expert," I say. "You must eat there often."

John shrugs. "There are quite a few restaurants close to our office, but lunch comes around every day, and if I work late, dinner rolls around too. You get to know all the menus pretty quickly."

"I completely understand," Jesse says. "In fact, I don't mean to brag, but at my last job I developed an impressive proficiency with Cup'o'Noodles *and* Pizza Pockets. I can make eight—no, wait, nine—different things with them in the microwave, including a combo meal that's surprisingly disgusting."

"Spoiler alert," I say. "All nine of his 'recipes' taste disgusting."

Jesse hisses out of the side of his mouth. "Dude, don't embarrass me in front of my boss."

"Too late," I hiss back. "You just used the word 'dude' non-sarcastically." I look up, smiling in spite of myself, and realize we're not alone anymore.

Henry's two dozen feet ahead, leaning against the hood of a white Range Rover. He smiles when he sees me and waves. He looks kind of amazing, cleaned up and not elbow-deep in soap bubbles. I guess I'm so accustomed to looking at him sideways in the kitchen that I didn't give much thought to what he might look like in the real world. He's a pretty well-built guy and he's wearing shorts, which showcase his perfectly normal calves. Ha!

His shaggy brown hair and huge, rich chocolaty eyes create a California Skater/Boy Next Door hybrid that I never fully appreciated. All in all, at least Henry's not an embarrassment. Plus, as a bonus, John and Jesse will probably assume it's Henry's Land Rover, with the way he's casually waiting beside it.

"This is Henry, I presume," John says. "Listen, Alice, if this gets too awkward, just tell him your brother texted you 911 and needs your help with his new job. We'll be right across the street, and in my experience, tacos can fix most anything."

"I think I'll be fine, but thanks." I peel away from them and cross the street toward Henry. "Hey, thanks for meeting me out here. You hungry?"

Henry stares at my face. "Wow, you look amazing."

"Uh, thanks," I say.

He beams at me, which only strengthens the California surfer charm. "I'm so glad we're finally getting together away from work."

I cough. "I'm starving. You?"

"Only all the time."

My kind of guy.

He glances behind me and raises one eyebrow. "Who are those guys? They're kind of staring."

"The one with brown hair is my brother. The black-haired guy is his new boss. That's actually why I picked La Centerra. My brother had an interview here, and I figured I'd come along for moral support. And, you know, to look for a new job."

Henry slouches farther against the hood of the pristine Range Rover. "They both look pretty young."

I glance around nervously, hoping there's not an angry rich guy around the corner glaring at Henry for draping all over his car. Henry's not a small guy. If it were my car, I'd be worried he'd dent it or scratch it or something.

"My brother's only a year older than I am, and his boss *is* pretty young, but it's a startup. You know how that goes. I hope the business stays around long enough that it wasn't a mistake to quit his other job." I look pointedly at Henry's elbows, squeaking against the perfect paint job. "Hey, here's a thought. Maybe we better go inside before the owner of that SUV sees you leaning on it and freaks out."

Henry's rich brown eyes lock on mine and he quirks one eyebrow. "I think it'll be fine."

I put one hand on his arm and tug. "I'm sure you're right, but rich people are weird about their cars, especially on this side of town. You probably don't know this, but that car costs as much as a small house. I've had a rough couple of days, and I really don't want any more drama."

Henry covers my hand with his. "No drama tonight, I promise." He straightens up, and I reluctantly pull my hand back.

I think again about Peli Peli. It would be awful if Henry couldn't pay, since I can't afford anything on the menu myself. "Are you sure you want to eat at Peli Peli? I went by there today looking for a job, and it's pricey. Like, really pricey. Plus, there are a lot of places around here that are more reasonable." I don't tell him I can't pay for my meal, but I bite my lip and hope he understands the subtext.

Henry reaches into his back pocket and pulls out an envelope. He passes it to me. "It's fine, I swear. Here's your back pay, by the way. Paul says you always take it in cash."

I bob my head, my cheeks flushing. "Oh, right. I do. Thanks."

"Why do you take your pay in cash?" He tilts his head.

A million excuses pile up on my tongue, but a wave of exhaustion rolls over me. I'm sick of lying to everyone about everything. He doesn't even know my real name. Jesse and I have exactly zero friends. I'm so afraid of anyone getting close that I've created an airtight bubble around me and Jesse. A very lonely bubble, sometimes.

The lies. The stories. I've gotten *so* used to lying that I lied to John without even thinking about it. Maybe I lied to John about Henry being my boyfriend to get out of a date, but why? He's a good-looking guy, and as far as I know he's not mean to puppies or old ladies. I should have been jumping at the chance to get a free meal.

Suddenly, I can't do it anymore.

"Alice isn't my real name." I suppress the shudder that runs through me at peeling back a tiny layer of my habitual armor.

"It's not?" His eyebrows pull together. "Are you secretly a spy?"

"It's a nickname," I say. "My real name is Alora. And I get paid in cash because I don't want my income reported to anyone."

"Well, I like Alora better than Alice anyway. And look, since you're confessing things, I will too. You don't need to worry about anyone yelling at us." He holds up a key fob and the Range Rover he's been leaning on chimes. Then he presses another button and it beeps. "This car's mine, okay? And I swear I can afford to pay for dinner."

"You're a dishwasher, Henry. How can you afford a car like this and a restaurant that has fifty dollar entrees?"

Henry sighs. "Can I explain inside?"

"If you can promise me that I won't get stuck washing dishes tonight to pay for a bunch of peppadews, then sure."

"You like those too? They're my favorite."

"Focus, Henry."

"Okay, my name really is Henry—I've been honest about that. Just like yours is Alora."

"What are you talking about?"

"It's just that my last name is Perry."

He stares at me like that should mean something.

"It's stupid right? Henry Perry. It's a terrible first name for someone whose last name is Perry. At least my parents seem to be better at running restaurants than naming kids."

And it hits me. Perry's is owned by a family. . .apparently Henry's family.

❊ 9 ❊

EARTH

"**Y**ou expect me to believe that your family owns all the Perry's restaurants?" I put my hands on my hips. "I stood next to you for months, degreasing broiling pans and scraping people's leftovers into the garbage."

"Well, technically, *I* scraped leftovers into the garbage. *You* dumped them into to-go boxes."

Henry's funnier than I gave him credit for being, but it doesn't mean I buy his story. "There's no way the heir of the entire Perry's empire has been washing dishes for the past six months."

Henry grins and slides his driver's license out. He passes it to me. Henry Perry. He's twenty years old. He pulls out another piece of paper and hands it to me as well. It's the registration on a two-year-old Range Rover in his name.

"Can we go eat now?"

"It does explain why you were always late, but you never got fired." My eyebrows draw together. "Why didn't your parents get mad at you for that? They had to be the ones keeping Ramon from firing you."

"My dad's the one who insisted I do soccer," Henry says. "That's why I was always late—practices and games."

Speaking of him being late. "I put my job on the line for you that last day. When you were late, Ramon said he was going to fire you, and I begged him not to do it. He said if you didn't show up within an hour, he'd fire us both." I can't believe it. I stood up for the one person in the place that Ramon couldn't possibly fire.

Henry pats my shoulder. "Chris mentioned that. It's one of the things that impressed me about you."

"So what? You're undercover over there? Who else knows?"

His tone turns pleading. "Food, please? I'm dying of hunger. I'll explain while we eat."

I'm hungry too, and at least now I know he can afford it. We both walk toward the door, which he reaches around to grab for me when we arrive, but a host beats him to it. It's exhilarating to be here as a customer. The guy in the suit who opens the door doesn't meet my eyes, and someone else entirely whisks a chair back and then pushes it in for me. A menu appears as if by magic in my hands.

Henry orders peppadews as an appetizer, and I ask for the bobotie. The waiter disappears. "Isn't it kind of. . .I don't know, disrespectful for you to come eat here when there's a Perry's like a block away?"

Henry laughs. "I like all kinds of food, and if I'm being honest, I'm a little sick of our menu. I prefer the Taste of Texas."

I feign horror, but I'm only sort of kidding. "Seriously? The chateaubriand? How could you ever be sick of that?"

"I also figured you'd be uncomfortable eating there, especially once I told you."

"You were definitely right." I arch one eyebrow. "You meant to tell me all along?"

"I've tried to ask you out like ten times. You never even let me start, and every time I asked for your number, you'd change the subject. So yeah, I've been planning to tell you. Obviously you're too good to date a dishwasher."

"Henry! I'm a dishwasher."

"When they fired you, at first I was really upset. I almost told Ramon who I was and demanded he bring you back. But then I thought—"

"They were right to fire me."

"Because you were taking home leftovers instead of throwing them away?"

"It's a health code violation," I say. "I knew that. But things have been a little tight lately and it seemed like such a waste to throw away amazing food when. . ." I shake my head. "It was stupid."

He runs one hand through his hair. "The thing I don't get is, why do you have a fake ID? I pulled your file. There's no way you're in your mid twenties, *Alice Walker*."

I open my mouth, but I have no idea what to say. So when the appetizers show up, and the waiter takes our orders, I breathe a sigh of relief. I'm glad Henry's rich, because I could probably clear out the entire menu. I order a center cut filet with Huguenot sauce, a soup, and a sampler. Henry's eyebrows rise, but he doesn't comment. Even with the temptation of the delicious food coming my way and a rumbling stomach, I want to stand up and walk out the door, grab Jesse, and drag him home. Which reminds me of what Jesse called me last night: paranoid. I want to prove him wrong, but. . .

Henry's asking about my fake ID and I'm gripped with an overwhelming desire to bolt.

"Are you an immigrant?" he asks. "Maybe I can help you get a work visa."

I shake my head. "Worse. I'm a minor."

Henry laughs.

"I'm serious. I won't be eighteen for six more months. My brother and I had to run away from home."

My heart pounds. I twist my hands in my lap. Jesse told me we needed friends, but this—waiting to see how he'll respond? It's agonizing. I want to get up from the table and sprint to the corner. Get on the bus and head straight for our apartment. Then I want to pack our stuff and keep on moving. Maybe we can try Boston. I bet it's not sweltering there.

He hunches forward, and his eyes sparkle. "Seriously? Who are you running from? Did you see something you shouldn't have seen? Is it the mob? I can help—like, do more than just buy you dinner."

"The *mob*? There's something wrong with you, Henry."

He sits back. "I like mysteries, okay? So if it's not criminal or something, what's the deal then?"

I sigh. "I shouldn't tell you this. People always get weird once they know." Which is why I haven't told anyone in three years. "My parents died when I was little, and they ended up putting us in a group home. I didn't fit in, and things got. . . ugly."

"That really sucks."

"The social worker they assigned to us only made it all worse. Eventually we couldn't take it anymore." *I'm* the one who couldn't take it, but I hate sounding like a victim. 'We' is non-specific, but it feels a little disloyal to Jesse. I plow ahead. "I'm not old enough to live alone, and if I use my real identity, they could find me and drag me back." I left out a few relevant details, but there's trusting and then there's stupid. I'm trying to balance between the two.

Henry reaches across the table and takes my hand. Even more surprising, I let him. It feels nice to tell someone and not have them glare or mock or pull away. Although, there's plenty of time for that later.

"Look, when Paul wouldn't agree to hire you back, it made me so angry that I couldn't handle standing by and watching anymore. I firmed up my resolve and demanded that my parents promote me. I said I was sick of washing dishes while the management made bad decisions that harmed peoples' lives."

Henry? I can't even imagine it. Which means it was likely a lot less of a demand and a lot more of a wheedle.

Either way. "What did they say?" I'm surprised how curious I am.

"They started laughing." His frown is too cute for words.

"Laughing?" I don't understand.

"Apparently they were going to start me out as an assistant manager, but Dad was worried I didn't have the gumption to manage people. He said until I demanded they promote me, I should be doing scut."

Henry's dad sounds like a hoot—and like he knows his son.

I got fired, and. . . "So you're going to be working with Ramon?"

He shakes his head. "They're letting me pick the location. If I choose Katy, would you want to come work with me here? You did say you were applying for jobs."

Danger, danger! I should leap up and sprint away. Henry knows too much. I should never have told him anything.

"You don't have to give me any info you don't want to, okay? The file can just say Alice Walker. But if this feels like too much pressure, or it makes you uncomfortable, I'm fine with being your reference."

I shouldn't have shared my first name. Ever. I mentally curse Jesse for pressuring me to make friends. Friends are fair weather, isn't that what they say? They're overrated.

"I think you'd be a great waitress."

Wait. Waitress? "Really?" Not a dishwasher?

"I bet you'd get great tips, and of course, all of those are totally untraceable."

I bite my lip. I would love to be a waitress, and I'd have no stress over being outed, since my boss already knows I'm a fraud. I want the job, and I like Henry well enough.

I think about the alternative—waiting around for who knows how long for an interview to be a busboy or hostess. And that's my best-case scenario. "It might be worth a try."

Henry beams. "That's great. Can you meet me at Perry's tomorrow to fill out the paperwork?"

We agree on ten a.m. the next day and spend the rest of the meal talking about how Henry's last day went. Apparently he quit today.

"So wait, Paul fired Jeremy too? And you quit? That means they went from seven dishwashers to four in only two days." I snort. "Double shifts really suck."

"Yep. I hope they find replacements fast, or I don't know what they'll do."

"You should suggest to Ramon that they try some paper plates."

"He might pass out," Henry says. "I've always thought that pulsing vein in his neck signaled the existence of a bigger problem."

"I'd love to see him pass out." I gulp. "I'm not saying I want him to really be sick. But one good faint would be amazing, especially if it happened in, like, the dining room."

Henry laughs.

The rest of dinner is pleasant and the food—I had no idea South Africans ate so well.

"This was fun, thanks."

"I know you don't want me to know where you live," Henry jokes, but his eyes actually look wounded. "But I'm happy to give you a ride if you want one, to any corner you name."

My phone buzzes. READY TO GO?

"That's a sweet offer, and I would like to rub my hands over the leather seats in your car some time, but my brother's waiting on me."

"Oh, so he has a car?"

I shake my head. "Nah, but we both have a bus pass."

"I can give you both a ride, you know."

"That's so kind, but we really are fine on the bus."

"I get it. You don't trust me."

I flush, but I don't contradict him. "I also have no idea how far out of the way it is for you."

"If you play your cards right, I might one day reveal to you where I live. Probably not," Henry says, "but maybe."

"A girl can dream."

Henry tosses money into the black check holder and stands up. "Walk you to the bus station?"

"I think my brother's waiting outside."

"Maybe I'll get to meet him, then."

When the host opens the door and we step outside, I don't see Jesse anywhere. I look right and then left. "Maybe he's still in Torchy's. Let's walk that way."

Henry shrugs. "My car's parked over there anyhow."

"Right." We walk across the street together and I still don't see J.

"I'll text him, but you don't need to wait. I'll walk inside."

"Are you sure?" Henry looks around, dubious.

"Absolutely. And thanks so much for dinner and for bringing my last week's pay. And thanks for the new job. Wow, you've done a lot for me."

"It was honestly nothing." He shrugs. "See you tomorrow."

I edge away from him as breezily as I can, but some part of me is nervous. What's wrong with me? Henry's shaping up to be the world's nicest guy, and I'm bolting like he's a predator.

I stumble on a reflective pavement marker, of all things, and almost fall. Strong arms catch me. I look up at Jesse's new boss, John. "Oh, thanks."

I straighten and look into Jesse's silently laughing face. "Wow, that guy really likes you. And did I hear him say you got a job? Or did you agree to a second date?"

"You were listening?" I shove him. "Where were you? I was dying over there. Plus, he wanted to meet you."

Jesse points at a bench between the two restaurants. They must've been waiting for me to come out. "The only bad part was that we couldn't hear every single word. The wind is a real buzz kill."

I scowl. "I like Henry. He's nice, and his parents own Perry's, and yes, I'm going to be a waitress at the Katy location. Starting tomorrow."

Jesse smiles at me. "That's great news. Good for you."

"Congratulations. I love Perry's, too. I'll be sure to ask for you whenever I head over," John says, "but be careful. That puppy dog really likes you. And I'm guessing here, but I think you might need someone who's already housebroken."

I roll my eyes, but I wonder whether he's right.

❧ 10 ❧

TERRA

Someone banging on my door wakes me before sunrise the next morning, and I realize I slept all day and the rest of the night. Jesse meets me at the door, his arms full of gray and black clothing.

"Is there a funeral?" I rub my bleary eyes.

He shakes his head. "We wear training gear for Ascensions. I brought a few sizes. I wasn't sure what would fit you the best." He tosses me the clothing and then his brow furrows and he steps closer. "What exactly are you wearing?"

I glance down at my makeshift nightgown. "Clothing's expensive, so usually I Bind fabric in place however I want. I made this from a few blankets I found in the closet."

Jesse's eyes bulge. "What happened to not Lifting until the Ascension like we discussed?"

"This isn't Lifting. It barely took a trickle. Besides, none of the clothes in the drawers fit." I can't believe Duncan kept my clothes in the drawers—clothing made for a very small child.

He sighs. "You badly need an education on how this

works. I feel like I've handed a toddler a bucket of water and now I'm stuck watching him slosh it all over the place. Bindings pull continuously from your ability. They'll tire you out more quickly than anything else. You wore that all night long?"

I nod.

He shakes his head. "Don't do that anymore. We have loads of clothes, I just didn't think to bring any. Ask next time, okay?"

"Uh, sure. Sorry."

"It's okay, I hope. I don't want to stress you out, but if you lose the first fight against Flynn, you can never join the Unit. Which is fine I guess, but it'll look pretty bad."

"Wait, I must have missed something. Why do I have to start at the bottom again? I'm Duncan's daughter, and I challenged Kahn, not Flynn."

"Well, at some point a long time ago, presumably during a time of great talent, it became annoying for the leaders to deal with so many challenges—the limitation on challengers being able to Lift a person wasn't enough of a barrier. They changed the law so that any challenger had to work his way up the line in order to face someone higher up in the Unit."

"That seems monstrously unfair. In order to actually fight Kahn, I have to defeat how many people?" Twelve? "Whereas he only has to fight me?"

Jesse shrugs. "That's how it works."

"I better get dressed."

"Yeah," he says, "I told Dad we could have breakfast together." He steps outside the door.

Once I'm alone, I release the Bindings on my fabric pieces and they slide to the floor in a heap. I pull several shirts down over my head before I find one that doesn't drown me. I don't know where Jesse found clothing this small, since women aren't ever a part of the Unit, but the last gray button down shirt I try and the smallest pair of black pants fit fairly well.

My brother's waiting for me in the hall when I emerge. He gestures for me to follow him and heads down the interminable hallway. Eventually, we reach a long banquet hall that Jesse calls a dining room. Duncan's standing near the massive wooden table at its center. "Alora." He blinks several times, like he's blinking away tears.

"Hello." I'm not sure quite what to say to a man I don't know, who's acting like he's happy to see me—but is the person from whom my mother ran.

"Uh, I'm sorry I slept so long," I say. "I meant to wake up and see how your discussions were going."

"Not at all," he says. "I'm sure you needed the rest. We're happy you're here, and I might have made more progress yesterday without you there for them to fixate on."

Jesse glances from Duncan to me, his look pained. He can tell I don't know what to say. "We certainly are happy you're here. We've missed you."

I try not to snort or laugh or cry.

"Dad did look for you over the years, you know," Jesse continues, as if he can't handle me blaming Duncan. "He had to be quiet about it or it would have ruined Mom's ruse. She faked your death before you disappeared, for your own good."

Hence the gate guard thinking I died in that fire. Ugh. I can't believe everyone thought I burned to death.

Still lost for words, I look down the length of the polished wooden table. It's covered with platters and bowls and pitchers, all filled to the brim with fruit, breads, meats, and cheese. My eyes bulge a bit in what I'm sure is an unattractive manner. I've never been allowed to eat whatever I want with the troupe—food was limited and had to be doled out carefully—but Jesse's piling his plate high, so I do the same. Marvelously, no one seems to care much what I grab.

Are we the only people eating all of this? I can hardly believe it.

"How did the discussions yesterday go?" Jesse asks. When my eyes widen—he doesn't know?—he explains. "Dad was still arguing with Flynn and Stefan when I went to bed."

"The men are coming around slowly," Duncan says. "Your arrival was a shock to pretty much everyone, myself included. But I think most of them assumed as I did before your birth—that the prophecy would never really be fulfilled."

"The Followers of Amun believed in it quickly enough." I think about the volley of arrows they aimed my direction—twice—and I shudder. "Are they still threatening me outside the city?"

Duncan shakes his head. "We managed to kill a dozen or two from the wall, and the rest of them retreated. It's only a matter of time before we hear something else. Devlin will either attack us in force, or he'll send an envoy to negotiate for your release. It'll depend, of course."

Devlin? He uses the man's name like they're friends. "It'll depend on what?" An envoy doesn't sound too bad, but an attack *in force*? I close my eyes.

"Devlin's hotheaded," Duncan says. "But as the leader of the Followers of Amun, he almost always takes the time to think things through."

"Do you. . .know him?" I ask. "Sounds like you were close."

Duncan frowns. "We trained together. For quite some time, Isis and Amun repaired tensions between us, you know. But we. . .fell out."

"Dad stole his girlfriend." Jesse's trying not to smile, but clearly he knows some story.

Which perversely upsets me. Clearly there's a whole family history here from which I've been excluded.

"The exordium hardly lets you choose," Duncan says. "To say I stole her is unfair."

I don't even want to think about the stupid exordium. Ugh. Time to change the subject back to the real issue. "You said it depends—how Devlin will respond? Invasion or diplomacy? Depends on what?"

"On whether they believed you when you shouted that you're Alora Sterling," Jesse says. "Because Devlin will surely know that Dad would never surrender you—so sending an envoy would be a monumental waste of time."

"You've seen the prophecy at this point," Duncan says. "Jesse told me he pointed it out in your room."

I nod. "It's pretty confusing, though."

"That it is, which is exactly why the Followers of Isis have always advocated prudence. Wait and see what it may mean before taking any hasty action. Terra and all its people matter to us, clearly, but we aren't convinced that augmented strength for the men and restoring women to their former power, whatever that is, would be bad."

"But what about the beginning of the end and the creation of the endings? Or whatever that said," I mutter. "That part was bizarre."

"Like any prediction of the future made thousands of years ago, it's not especially clear." Duncan shrugs. "I'm hardly unbiased, however, as I certainly care less about the dumb prophecy and more about keeping you safe."

The rest of breakfast with Duncan is weird, but Jesse keeps the conversation going. They both go into great detail about different men and their fighting preferences, which would mean more if any of the fighting methods or the names of men they use mean anything to me. We've finished eating when I realize my hair's still hanging loose around my face.

"Can I get a tie or strap to pull my hair back?"

"What do you usually do to keep it away from your face?" Duncan asks. "It looked. . . complicated yesterday."

"I usually Bind it in place, but Jesse said I shouldn't waste my strength on things like that."

Duncan smiles at Jesse. "I think if she's accustomed to doing it, it should be okay. But maybe wait to do it until I introduce you in the arena."

"Okay," I say. "But why?"

"Smart," Jesse says. "To maximize the intimidation factor."

They think that Binding my hair back will scare trained fighters? Then again, Lifting the tray yesterday freaked the maid right out. Citizens' rules are odd—and I clearly have no idea what to expect around them. I follow Duncan and Jesse out of the castle and back to the courtyard.

The columns of soldiers awaiting my arrival yesterday seemed imposing and large, but more than five times as many people are milling around now, vying for positions near the raised arena. The sun still hasn't come up, but lights flicker in huge sconces along the stone walls at the edges of the courtyard. Large posts at intermittent intervals around the courtyard also provide light from lanterns hung from hooks.

I grab Jesse's arm and tug him down low enough that I can whisper in his ear. "Who are all these people?"

"Mostly they're nobles from the areas surrounding Sterling, as well as their family and friends, but some Unit Leaders have traveled from farther out."

"Every single person here is noble?" I ask.

"Everyone here is related in some way to a Unit

member or leader with Isis. Dad wanted to open it to the public, but far, far too many people gathered. We had to limit things somehow, and it's common for Unit Leaders to observe other Ascensions. They say they're scoping ideas, but really, they're spying on their competition. In this case, Dad's hoping your performance will generate some additional support for defending you from whatever force Amun brings."

"I thought everyone within Isis was on the same side."

Jesse laughs. "Sure, in theory, but we have a series of contests each year and all the Units are invited, from both Amun and Isis. We haven't had a real war with the Followers of Amun in decades, so it's easy to forget how strongly we disagree on some fundamentals."

Fundamentals. Like whether women have value, and whether I should be killed, for instance.

We beeline toward the three raised, circular arenas in the center of the courtyard, each of them ringed with several rows of suspended cords, each with two sets of steps—on opposite sides from one another. Hopefully the rope has some give to it, or it'll be hard to get in, even with the steps.

One of them is larger and raised slightly higher than the others. We reach the base of it just as the first rays of the sun peek over the horizon. It baffles me that so many citizens have traveled through the night just to see a sequence of fights.

I wonder at the reason behind the three different arenas, but before I can ask Jesse, Duncan walks up the steps of the largest platform, swings between the middle and top rope, and stands up straight. The crowd quickly falls silent.

"It's my pleasure to welcome you to the Sterling Unit Ascension. We weren't planning to host this for several more weeks, but I'm sure you'll all join me in welcoming my recently returned daughter, Alora Sterling."

Murmurs rise from the crowd, and heads turn sharply in my direction. My father gestures and I climb up onto the dais, shifting the flexible cord to stand next to him. Jesse follows me up, taking a place on my other side. Even here on this platform, they're placing themselves in protective positions. Their message is clear.

In spite of their show of family support, there are at least as many scowls as welcoming smiles directed at me.

"I imagine most of you were as surprised as I was to hear that Alora's alive—and perhaps more shocked to discover that she can Lift. My wife apparently felt that the best way to keep Alora safe from the radical position taken by the Followers of Amun was to hide her existence entirely."

He pauses for a moment, allowing the gathered citizens to murmur.

"As you all know, Amun would have murdered my daughter outright when I discovered she could Lift at the age of one. I couldn't stand by and let that happen, and I won't deny that I wanted to prevent the confrontation as long as possible. But my wife took my reticence one step further—and sacrificed her own life to hide Alora. From Amun. From Isis. And even from me." His face is open, and his sorrow is clear for any to see.

He allows them another moment or two for murmuring.

"I'm sorry I didn't tell you all about Alora's abilities— but I thought them well and truly gone. I won't lie and say I'm not delighted to discover she's not only alive, but that she's home. The time has now come for her to rejoin her family, and that means that I expect all of you to defend her." His eyes are sad. "I don't make this request of you lightly. It has always been the position of the

Followers of Isis that women deserve our protection, our devotion, and our dedication. We believe that their inability to Lift makes them more vulnerable and therefore more in need of our help. It does not, however, mean they are less valuable."

Duncan pauses.

"I'm sure many of you would protect Alora with no other reason or incentive, but my daughter, as you will see shortly, is fierce in her own right. She is strong, as you might expect of the Warden foretold by our oldest prophecy. Her return was a promise given to all of us by Mother Terra herself, and now that she's here, Alora will not cower or hide. Yesterday, exhausted from a long journey, she nevertheless challenged my first in command when he threatened me, unwittingly sparking this Ascension. She did that to defend a father she doesn't even know, and now, today, she stands before you, prepared to show that she is ready to fight *with* us against any of our mutual foes."

My dad's eyes dart to my hair, his eyes widening as if he's signaling me. It must be time. I Lift my hair into a dozen small sections, braiding each one together at the same time. I do this every day, so it moves along quickly. I braid those braids together and then wrap it all into a bun on the back of my head before Binding it in place. The early morning light is dim enough that the light spilling outward from my eyes makes it obvious that I'm Lifting.

After a few seconds, cheers erupt from small patches around the courtyard, and unless I'm mistaken, many of the people shouting are women. The men gathered, the soldiers, may not know what to think about me, but it's clear they respect my dad. His idea to show them I can Bind adeptly was a good one. Which means that Jesse was right, too. This very public fight matters.

No matter my total lack of experience and training, I can't lose entirely, not if I want their support.

"Today's first match will be between our newest applicant, Alora Sterling, and the Unit Leader in position thirteen, Flynn Preston."

Duncan steps out of the ring, and Jesse reaches over and pats me on the shoulder before he swings out, too. When I turn back to face the center of the ring, unsure what to expect, a tall, almost grizzled man swings into the ring. He spits, and it lands on the ground just outside of the ring. He wipes his mouth on the back of his hand and looks at me questioningly. I'm at a loss. I have no idea what this man wants, but he looks nothing like any nobleman I've seen. Every man in Martin's troupe had better manners than he does.

"Are you going to choose a weapon, or were you waiting for them to bring you a selection on a platter, adorned with little bows?"

"Right." I need to choose a weapon, because I'm the challenger. I really should've listened a little closer to what Duncan and Jesse were saying at breakfast. I do recall something about selecting a category of weapon.

I glance at Jesse, who tosses his head toward a rack a few feet from the arena. Weapons are arranged on it into sections, with a variety of bladed options available like knives, swords, axes, and machetes. Next to that is an entirely separate section of stick-shaped objects. Bows, staffs, rods, and the like. Finally, there's also an array of projectile weapons like slingshots, bows and arrows, throwing stars etcetera. I have no idea how I'd possibly use these weapons in a small arena.

Something Jesse mentioned floats to the surface. Flynn. Flynn. I focus—he said staffs, I think. He said to choose staffs with him? I think. Gosh, you'd think he'd have been more clear on what I should choose for the very first fight. The bladed weapons glimmer in their cases and I imagine them slicing through flesh and bone. The very idea of using a sharpened blade turns my stomach. "I'll choose staffs and rods."

"Non-bladed, close combat weapons." Flynn smiles.

Jesse groans.

Whoops. As if his groan calls it to mind, I recall my brother warning me that this guy handles a staff with skill and ease. Flynn holds a hand out over the ropes of the ring and a delicate woman in a beautiful yellow dress hands him an ornately carved staff. He tosses it from hand to hand and rolls his shoulders.

Jesse hops back into the ring with a fairly thick rod in hand. He passes it to me and whispers, "I said anything *but* the staff. Flynn grew up in a rough neighborhood and couldn't afford a nice weapon until he joined the Unit. He's tough, and he's getting older, but he's still fast. Really fast."

"I don't know how to use a sword, either. And I'm good with a staff." I refuse to give up before I start.

Jesse sighs. "Try to stay out of his reach. He'll wear himself out if you defend long enough. Then go for it."

I nod, trying to listen better this time. Wear him out. Defend defend defend. Then attack. As if I know how to do any of that.

"Wait!" I spin around to face Jesse as he exits the arena. "What ends the match? I don't have to kill him, right?" How did this not come up before?

He smacks his forehead with his palm. "I told you that if someone loses, they go home, implying they're alive. Please don't kill anyone!" He grits his teeth. "Hold him against the mat for a count of three and you win."

I look right into his dark blue eyes and whisper, "I can't do this."

He grins and swings down to the ground without

missing a beat. "Yes, you can." He pats my ankle from under the wire. "You're a Sterling. You were born to do this." I turn just in time for Duncan to Lift a flag.

"On my mark," Duncan says. "Three, two, one." The flag falls and Flynn raises his staff, and then he's spinning toward me, and I'm out of time.

I throw up my staff to block, expecting it to be similar to my performance with Thomas.

But I'm clearly an idiot—this is nothing like a rehearsed performance.

Flynn's staff moves faster than Thomas' staff ever did, much faster, so fast I almost can't follow the movements. I block him once, twice, but each blow sends shock waves through my arms. I try to block a third time, but I'm too slow. His staff, which seems to slow down right before it hits me so I can see that it's carved with the faces of angry animals, slams into my right shoulder and my right hand goes numb. I drop the staff Jesse gave me and it rolls nearly to the edge of the platform. Flynn doesn't waste any time. He sweeps his angry animal stick under my feet. I try to leap over it, but again, I'm too slow. Before I process what has happened, my head's cracking against the ground and my eyes are looking upward into the clear, early-morning sky.

A few remaining stars twinkle at me as if to say good morning.

It's a terrible morning. Stupid stars.

The fall knocks the breath from me and in that space when I believe I might never be able to breathe again, my brain churns furiously. Jesse believed in me, my dad believed in me, and I believed in my abilities, and here I am, flat on my back. I need to show the crowd that I'm worth fighting for, and convince them that I'm worth saving. Instead, I've perfectly showcased how pathetic I am. I hear someone above me say "One." I have until three to get up. Except I can't make my arms and legs move.

Even my lungs seem to have quit.

Somehow, in the absence of control over my body, something else takes over. It feels like it does in the show, when the blindfold has been placed on my face. I *feel* Flynn, his staff pressed down over my chest, his frame bending over me. Except there's no blindfold. I shift my eyes to Flynn's and hate the triumph I see written in them.

His eyes are mean, and I hate him.

I Lift his staff first and fling it a dozen feet up in the air, Binding it in place far out of reach.

He stumbles backward, startled by the light shining from my eyes. I try to sit up, but my right shoulder screams and my legs throb across the backs of my calves. I force myself up just as someone says "Three." I look around to see whether I've already lost.

Am I too late?

Jesse smiles at me, and I breathe a sigh of relief. I must not have lost quite yet. I turn back toward Flynn just in time to see the staff I dropped, the one Jesse gave me, arcing toward my face. Without thinking, I Bind it in place, too. Flynn's body jerks at my abrupt halt to his momentum.

He drops the staff and comes at me with his bare hands. His fist is less than an inch from my face when it occurs to me to Bind that into place as well. His eyes bug out from his head when he realizes what I've done. To his credit, he doesn't give in. I should be hitting him, slamming him, or better yet, I could grab Jesse's staff and repay some of the damage he's done to me. I can barely move my right arm, and my legs send a pulse of pain upward with every heartbeat.

I've never hit anyone before, other than Thomas, and

every time I struck him, it was an accident, an error in executing our choreography. I've never intentionally damaged another person, other than the men who were chasing me yesterday and Robert, who was hurtling a dagger at Martin.

But when Flynn brings his other fist up to punch me, I forget that I don't want to hurt him. I forget my guilt over harming another person. I release the Binding on Jesse's staff and Lift it into my hand. I slam it squarely against Flynn's chest with all the force I can muster. With his right hand Bound in place, there isn't much he can do about it. That's when I feel it. Flynn's eyes light up with gold and he shoves. I feel a push, as though someone's pushing against a door I'm holding shut. I may be untrained, but I know Flynn's trying to undo my Binding on his fist.

I laugh. I feel the shove, but it's pitiful, a half-hearted effort at best, like a kitten pawing at a ball of yarn. There's no chance he'll break through. He tries to swing at me with his free hand.

So I Bind it in place, too.

Flynn's face falls, and his eyes change. They dart back and forth, and then turn to me, and I recognize what I see. Fear. I release the Bindings on his hands and slam the staff into his right shoulder as hard as I can. I sense him perfectly, so my blow lands with precision. When he reels back, it occurs to me that I have the means to simply end this now. Easily.

I kick him in the chest and he falls backward. I Lift his feet, and this time he slams into the mat. I barely use any force at all when I Bind him into place. Slowly, so slowly, the seconds pass and the man who was counting earlier makes it to three. And I've won.

Easy peasy.

The crowd pauses for a moment, unsure how to

react, but Jesse leaps onto the platform and puts his arm around me. "Well done, Alora. Well done indeed." Scattered groups of people erupt into applause. It's hardly a ringing endorsement, but I'm just getting started.

"You have a five-minute break before the next fight." He frowns. "And it looks like you dislocated that shoulder."

"I can't move it—that's for sure."

He cringes. "I've been trained in basic first aid—I can reduce it for you, but it's going to hurt."

I nod, and he positions his arms around me. . . .and then wrenches it into place. The pain is sharp, but it's quick and then it's done. Other than the dull throbbing, obviously. I cradle my right arm in my left.

Jesse waves for a blonde woman with a tray of wine glasses to come closer.

"I'd prefer water," I say.

"You're sure?" he asks.

I nod.

He looks doubtful, but doesn't argue. Once I have a glass of water in my hand, Jesse starts talking in a low voice. "You fight Henry next. He's a good guy, only a few years older than I am."

I glance over while I sip and notice Flynn standing in the corner, talking to the woman in the yellow gown. "What happens to Flynn now?"

Jesse glances over at him. "You need to focus on your next fight."

That doesn't reassure me. Actions have consequences, and I'd like to know the result of mine. "Yeah, but what happens to him? You said he came from nothing, and now I've beaten him. His emotion shifted up there, from angry to afraid. I need to know why."

"Well, it depends on what you do next. If you defeat

Henry, then Henry will get a five-minute break and then fight Flynn."

"And the loser?" I ask.

"The loser goes back to his family."

"So I may have ended Flynn's career. . .and his livelihood?" I whisper.

Jesse looks away and then back to me, but he doesn't meet my eye. "Look, it's not your fault, okay? Yes, someone will have to leave now that you've Ascended, but that's the way it works. Not everyone can be a leader, and you defeated him, so you advance and he doesn't. You can't start feeling bad for the men you're fighting. All of the men's strategies will change at some point during your match, because if you know you're going to lose, you want to minimize injury and conserve your strength for the next fight. If you use up everything you've got on one you lose, you won't win the next one. Flynn still has a chance. . . if you win. He's probably your biggest fan right now."

But no matter what, someone is going home thanks to me. I can't quite help my guilt. I know every action has consequences, but I don't like causing someone pain or suffering.

Duncan climbs up in the ring behind me.

"Time's up already? I didn't even tell you anything yet. Okay, so Henry's a classic fighter, but he lacks creativity. He's—"

"It's okay." I stop Jesse. "I have a plan for this match already."

I limp toward the ring, and Jesse grabs my left arm. "You're limping. How badly are you injured?" My shoulder's definitely dislocated, and the backs of my legs have begun to swell.

I try to shrug, but that motion sends shooting pains down my arm. "Does it matter?"

"Not really. There's no Healing until after the Ascension ends, but in your next break we can wrap your legs, at least, or get you a sling if you need one."

I snort. "Fear me, the bandaged warrior."

His face turns serious. "I think they're plenty afraid of you."

I glance into the ring, where a man who must be Henry is already standing. He's young, like Jesse said, and he's tall. Jesse helps me climb up so I don't tweak my shoulder. Henry has dark hair that's pulled back into a queue, but a few tendrils escape and fall in soft curls around his face. I bet he has good luck with the women in Sterling, with his chocolate brown eyes and his well-defined muscles. Even his calves are perfectly turned. I know he's part of the Unit, so presumably he can fight, but he reminds me of a puppy.

A cute, overeager puppy.

And I'm the monster who's going to kick this sweet little puppy out of a job. Ugh.

As the challenger, I apparently always choose the weapon. When I choose to forgo a weapon in favor of a hand-to-hand fight, people seem surprised, but this time, when the flag falls, I have a plan. I Lift Henry and then shove him down on the mat. I Bind his entire body down. He struggles, physically, and he Lifts against the Binding, so it takes a lot more effort than I expected. Nothing has ever pushed back against one of my Bindings. I wasn't even aware it could be done. Henry's eyes flash and he clenches his fists and growls.

But it's not enough.

I'm much, much stronger than he is, poor little muscled puppy.

After the count of three, I glance around at the crowd. There's no applause this time, just shuffling and nervous whispers.

During my second break, Jesse calls for bandages. He wraps both my calves tightly, over my pants, to minimize the swelling, but I decline his offer of a sling.

"You have the Sterling pride." My brother smirks.

"That doesn't sound like a compliment." I can't imagine wearing a sling will help people to fear me—or see me as an asset.

Jesse glances over at Duncan. "Actually, it kind of is. Look at Dad. He's proud of you—one manifestation of our pride in a positive manner. He just can't be seen to interfere during an Ascension, not as the Leader of all the Followers of Isis."

Duncan Sterling's not even looking our direction—he's talking to someone who looks important, but as if he can sense my gaze, he glances over at me several times. When he notices I'm facing him, he smiles broadly.

Maybe Jesse's right. Not that it matters, of course.

There's no pride in Duncan's voice when he announces the next round of fights a moment later. "In Ring One, we have Alora and Adaniel. In Ring Two, we have Flynn and Henry." When the flags drop, I repeat the process I developed with Henry. I Lift Adaniel, a tall, lanky guy who looks around thirty, into the air, and slam him into the mat. I Bind him in place until the count of three. His eyes flash bright blue and I feel a real shove against my Binding, but it holds.

This time, the crowd is less surprised. The scattered cheers resume, mostly from women again, but I feel a little better about my win nonetheless.

"Do you even want to hear my tips for fighting Adaniel's twin brother?" Jesse asks. "Or were you planning to just shove Nathaniel down to the mat and Bind him with brute strength too?"

"Here's the thing," I tell Jesse. "Back home, I Lifted things all day long. I Bound things into place, sometimes permanently. One of the wagon wheels is still held together by one of my Bindings."

Jesse scoffs. "Doubtful. You might not feel it, what with all your vast power or whatever, but even though Binding something requires less maintenance than Lifting and holding, it's still pulling on your power. I can't Bind something for very long, and if someone else is shoving back, I usually drop pretty quickly. Once you rode far enough away from your encampment, your Bindings failed."

"You're saying everything I fix in place, everything I Bind, is drawing strength from me without me even realizing it?"

Jesse nods. "Without a doubt. It's staggering that you don't even feel it."

"I felt them push against my Binding, but I just pushed back." My eyes widen as something occurs to me. "Why didn't any of the citizens ever realize I could Lift? If these warriors can push on my Bindings?"

"It doesn't work like that. You never Lifted any of them—or Bound them in place. You can't sense someone else's work unless it's shoved against you."

That was lucky. I'm beginning to see just how vulnerable I was in hiding—without any real knowledge of what I could do or how it worked.

A man climbs into the ring.

Jesse looks up at him pointedly.

He's much larger than his twin was.

"Well, if it's working, I guess you can keep doing it. Are you tired yet?"

I shrug. "Sure. If my fight with Flynn is any indication, I don't stand a chance once my strength runs out, so I may as well climb as high as I can doing what I feel comfortable doing, right?"

He nods. "Take that sucker down."

My method works for Nathaniel and to varying degrees of success with four more men: Francis, Beren, Quincey, and Seth. Although, with Seth, it's a lot less graceful. It feels like I'm fighting an octopus, with all the wriggling and pressing on my Bindings he does.

The length of my breaks increase, because the other fights triggered by my Ascension take a lot longer to complete than mine do, and the next round can't begin until they all have five minutes from the end of their match to rest. I might be imagining it, but it feels like the swelling in my legs diminishes, and my shoulder seems less tender, too.

"How are you holding up?" Jesse asks.

I gulp. "That last one was harder."

"I noticed you were struggling."

I'm reaching my limit.

Through it all, Jesse has had my back: bringing me ice, food, drinks, and anything else I need. The gathered men may look at me like I'm a bug, but not him. My whole world may have fallen apart in the last day and a half, but I've gained one thing—something I already value more than anything else in the world. A big brother —a real, blood family member who seems to care about me just for who I am.

"Who's next?" I ask.

Jesse compresses his lips. "Actually, your next fight is against me."

❊ II ❊

TERRA

"I can't fight you." I practically fling the words at him.

"You have to," Jesse says. "It's in the rules."

I shake my head. "They aren't my rules."

"Are you scared?" Jesse asks.

"No," I lie.

I finally meet my brother, and now I'm supposed to what? Punch him in the face?

"It'll be fine, you'll see." He leans close and whispers. "Whether you win or lose, I don't care. I'm impressed you've come so far. It's even more amazing, because as far as I can tell, you can't even throw a decent punch." It's like he can read my thoughts.

The thought of punching anyone makes me want to curl up in a ball and hide, but the idea of punching Jesse turns my stomach.

I can't shoot the breeze with him while I wait for the match between Beren and Quincey—which hasn't started yet—to end. I need to get away and think of some kind of solution. I walk to the edge of the courtyard and look out through an arrow slit toward the vast forest below.

The air blowing through the gap in the rock is cool and sweet. I close my eyes and inhale deeply.

The sound of a man clearing his throat startles me, and I whirl around.

"I wanted to introduce myself." His deep voice would be compelling on its own. The tugging feeling around my heart and the stupidly warm glow that surrounds him are horrible overkill.

"I know who you are," I snap. Apparently being confronted with evidence that I have a soulmate makes my bad mood even worse.

"I'm Kahn Brantley."

"The Lord of Brantley Castle, I know."

"Right," he says. "But—"

I'm not sure how I know he's going to mention the exordium, but I do, and I can't handle it. I cannot. "I'm about to have to fight a brother I just met. Could we not do. . ." I gesture between him and me. ". . .this. Whatever this is. Could we please not do it right now?"

He frowns. "I'm not sure it's something we can choose to ignore."

"You can ignore anything. Trust me on that." I need him to stop talking to me. It's like every word he says makes my stomach flip. And then flop. Why couldn't he have a high, squeaky voice? Or a snaggle tooth? I could really get behind that. "Look, unless you have some kind of advice for me on how to deal with my current problem, I don't have much to talk about."

"It's simple. Pretend he's not your brother, because in that ring, he's not. He's an opponent, nothing more. Your task is to defeat him, so you do it. You're actually lucky that you don't know any of us. Almost every Ascension is like that for the participants—you're fighting against friends, brothers, or long-time acquaintances at the very least."

Why can't he be a jerk? Or say something mean? That would make it easier for me to hang on to my anger around him. "I don't know how you do it."

"It's not personal," he says. "It's part of our job. And that's critical—most of us know the noble families among the Followers of Amun. But we also know that we could be sent to war against them at any point."

"I think this system is broken," I say, frankly.

"You weren't raised in it."

It hits me then, that my parents' fear may be the very thing that sets me apart from the system that exists. It may be the reason I don't worry about ending it. I shake my head.

"Are you alright?" He steps closer, his eyes concerned.

"Back up there, Mr. Eager. I'm perfectly fine as long as you keep your distance."

"A spitfire," Kahn says. "That's what my mother would have called you, if she were alive."

I square my shoulders. "And would she have wanted you to defend me? Or would she have advocated for attacking me to preserve the status quo?"

"Excuse me?"

"You disliked me so much at first sight that you challenged my father's position. You were going to fight him and take it away, before you'd let him protect his own daughter." I don't realize how angry it made me until this very moment. I have a soulmate, apparently, and he wants me tossed out in the street.

Kahn's eyes widen. "I hadn't met you when I said that."

"But it had already happened." I cross my arms. "The exordium." My words hang in the air between us, repelling and compelling.

"I thought it was a lie until yesterday," he whispers. "I didn't believe it was real."

I shake my head. "Betty—a close friend—insisted it was. She experienced it with her husband Abraham."

"My father said it was a lie for people who wanted to feel special."

I shrug. "Its reality doesn't change anything."

"How can you say that?" He steps toward me again, both his hands clenched at his side. "You must not feel what I—"

"I'm sure it's the same," I say. "But it doesn't *change* anything. Not for me. I didn't choose this."

"I had a fiancée, you know," he says. "I broke things off with her yesterday, while you slept. I could barely look at her."

"Well, that was stupid, because I don't even know you." I refuse to meet his eyes. "And I won't let some unexplained, unwelcome, ridiculous feeling—"

"Unexplained? Yes. Ridiculous? Perhaps. But unwelcome?"

I look up at his face. I can't help it.

His eyes are such a light shade of blue that they're practically white. "I'd give up everything to feel this way forever." The muscles in his jaw work soundlessly. "You hate me so much. Why? What did I do?"

My mouth is so dry I can barely breathe, much less speak.

"Do I truly repulse you?" He steps closer still, his chest mere inches from mine, his breath misting across my face.

"No," I whisper.

He inhales deeply. "Then what?"

"I don't want to be this stupid Warden. I don't want to end or begin anything. I didn't want to lose my mom, or my dad, or my brother. I want. . . I want what everyone else on Terra already has: an acceptable place in this world, and the opportunity to choose my own path.

And now—" I shake my head and a single tear rolls down my cheek. "I'm sure you're wonderful. Jesse seems to like you, and I—I trust him. But I can't eliminate my ability to Lift. It's part of me, like my eyes, or my nose, or my hands." I back up until my back bumps into the cold stone of the wall.

"I like your eyes, and your nose, and your hands." He's staring down at me, transfixed. "And like you, I haven't been able to choose my life's path. I was trained to take over from my first breaths. I was sent here, and the expectations." He shakes his head. "All I'm saying is that I *understand*. If not everything, at least in part."

His words send chills down my spine that shoot outward to my fingers, to my toes. My hands move to touch him, but I force them to stop. "You can't possibly understand." My words come out as barely more than a whisper. I clear my throat and take a deep breath. "I *can* choose to ignore this, and I don't want to hurt you, but I can't—" I drop my face into my hands, unable to watch his face as I say the rest. "I can't have anything else shoved on me and not be angry about it—which is why the more I feel for you, the more I *hate* you."

The silence is too much for my shaky resolve. I peek through my fingers.

Kahn's lips part slightly, and I want, desperately, to close the space between us. I want to touch his mouth with my fingers. I want to press my lips against his, to run my hands down the sharp planes of his chest, and brush against the rough skin on his jaw.

I want my first kiss to be with him.

Right now.

I want to grab the front of his shirt and pull his head down to mine. I want so many, many things. Things I've never wanted, never longed for, never even imagined.

Until now.

But even more than all of that, I want these feelings, these desires, to be based on something real, not something shoved upon me. I want to choose what I want, not have it forced like everything else.

I shake my head and spin on my heel. Marching away rips my heart in half and it hurts, Mother Terra it hurts. It's unfair, it's miserable, and yes, it's unwelcome. I glance back over my shoulder, desperate for one last look. Does he understand, even a little bit, what I'm struggling with?

"The exordium isn't a curse," Kahn says. "It's not forcing us into anything."

Something about his low, urgent voice sends those same jolts down my spine and out to my fingers and toes. The thrill that races through me—I despise how much I enjoy it.

"To me, the way I feel about you, around you, it's the greatest blessing I could imagine. But I never want anything to hurt you, so if my presence causes you pain." He pauses. "I'll do my best to stay away." His eyelids flutter. "I'll maintain my distance. Anything you need. If I could rescind my challenge, I would. Ignorance is the most dangerous enemy. I didn't know you, so I didn't understand."

It's almost impossible to turn away from him, from his fraught eyes, from his impossibly broad shoulders, from his full mouth, twisted into regret. I want to spin back around and race into his arms. I want him to wrap me up and take me home with him—to keep.

Which is exactly the problem.

Every step I take toward the arena is agony. I need to think about something else. Someone else. The sun shines directly overhead now, and a drop of sweat rolls down the back of my neck and slides underneath the collar of my shirt. Duncan signals for me—time for my next fight. At least my struggle in being around Kahn helped me forget one thing.

I'm facing off against my brother.

I'm more aware of my movements than I ever have been, every step, every stair, another chunk of distance that separates me from Kahn. Another increment of space nearer to my brother.

I can do this. I can do this—ignore my soulmate. Fight my family. Not because I don't have a choice—we always have a choice.

No, I can do this precisely because I have a choice.

All we are in this world is a sequence of choices. Mother Terra may have made me who I am. I may even be this Warden. I may be marching down a path she set me upon in a body she gave me. I may be hurtling like an arrow toward a target she set in place.

But I can choose.

I have to believe that. Whatever comes, I won't destroy the world or end things.

Just like, when the flag drops, I can fight my brother. I can Lift him and slam him to the mat as I have with every warrior before him. I can punch him in the nose, and kick him in the stomach. I can scratch his eyes and scream defiance in his face.

But I won't.

Again, like with Kahn, I choose not to do this thing I've been told I must.

Before I can explain, before I can protest, before I can refuse to participate in this exercise, the very second the flag drops, Jesse lies down on the dusty, blood-spattered floor of the raised arena and crosses his arms over his chest. His voice is loud and clear when he counts. "One, two, three." He stands up and looks out at the gathered crowd. "I won't fight my sister, not now, not ever. But I will lay down my life for her, because I love her, and because it's the right thing to do. Mother Terra set us on this path, and it's our job to see it through."

He looks from one end of the audience to the other. "But even if she hadn't, I trust Alora. She's the Warden for a reason. We have already defended the weak and helpless, the disenfranchised. I know it's scary to think of another all-out war against Amun. And I bet it's scarier to contemplate what the existence of the Warden signifies, but we're not stronger hiding, acting like cowards. We're stronger united, swords in hands, our purpose clear."

What just happened?

People around me murmur, but I can't make out any words clearly.

I walk down the steps.

Jesse joins me at the bottom.

"I thought we were trying to intimidate them," I say.

Jesse's half smile is already familiar to me. "Maybe some siblings fight, but I'll never stand in your way. More than anything else, we need to get them on your side." He bumps my arm. "On *our* side."

When we hug, the gathered crowd goes wild.

I sit by my brother on one side of the ring. "Not to pressure you, but I can only rise if you keep defeating the guys ahead of me, which means I need you to pummel Pratt."

"I hear you." I unwind the bandage on my leg and slide my pants up above my knees. The purple has already faded into green.

"Are you sure you aren't a Healer?" Jesse asks. "Or did you pick up some tricks while you lived with them, maybe?"

I shake my head. "Does it matter?"

"It's just that I've never seen anyone heal that fast."

"Eh, it wasn't so bad to begin with." Now that he

mentions it, my shoulder barely twinges when I roll it. "My shoulder feels better, too. Just in time."

Jesse looks concerned. "What do you mean, just in time?"

"I'd welcome any advice you have on beating Pratt. I'm not sure how many more times I can use my winning strategy—it's a little exhausting with people fighting against me. But maybe I can try some new tricks now that I can move my arm."

Jesse looks nervous. "I'd stick with what works as long as you can. Pratt's the strongest Lifter we have, other than maybe Kahn. He could Lift you easily, for instance."

"And he's been watching me for the past eight fights, so he knows my strategy."

Jesse smirks. "I think most of Sterling has figured out your complicated and confusing strategy. The Followers of Amun will have it tattooed on their shoulders by tomorrow."

I shove him. "Shut up. What I mean is, he's going to have been thinking of ways to counter me if I just do the same thing."

"It's going to come down to who's stronger, or at least, what you've got left in you."

I hadn't counted on how hard it would be to hold someone down when he's both physically fighting it and shoving against my Bindings with any significant strength. There's a definite difference between the work involved in assembling an inanimate set for the troupe and fighting trained Lifters.

Jesse points out Pratt to me. He's big, which is nothing new. He's muscular, but it's lean. Long. Almost understated. His dark brown skin and eyes are nearly the exact same color.

He never takes those intense eyes off me. Not on our

climb into the ring, and not while Duncan counts us off. When the flag waves, he flexes, defined muscles rippling. It's distracting, but that's not why I stand still, doing nothing. I have a plan, albeit a rough one. If he's strong and I've been wearing myself out all day, I should let him be the one who's struggling and straining, at least for a bit.

He Lifts me in the air and shoves downward, releasing me so that he can conserve his strength, I presume. After all, gravity should slam me against the mat well enough. Jesse says it's harder to break a Binding than to create one, so instead of allowing myself to drop downward, I Bind some dust into two handholds. I grab both and pull myself up. Now I'm dangling from the air and. . . I'm out of ideas.

I swing back and forth and then flip over the holds and fling myself into Pratt. He tumbles to the mat, too surprised to do much else, I think. I Bind his wrists to the ground. "One," I hear someone count.

My eyes fly wide when Pratt lifts his shoulders off the ground, and shoves against the Binding. I hold it, barely. The counting stops. At the same time, I feel him push against the Binding, harder this time. This pushing isn't pitiful. It's like a fist to the face, but I hold. His next slam is a kick from an angry horse, but I hold again, barely. Finally, he slumps. After they reach three, I breathe a sigh of relief. I've moved up another place.

Three to go.

I turn to face Jesse. "What happens if I defeat Kahn?"

He jabs Duncan in the side, looking for all the world like a naughty toddler. "If you beat Kahn, then you fight Dad."

"Seriously?" I ask.

"Yep, that's how you become Unit Leader. Then you'd be eligible to take over the entire thing. Dad rules Isis because he defeated every other Unit Leader in a kind of boss of the bosses Ascension. So if you defeat Dad, then you could fight in the Gathering to take over for all of it."

"You're saying the entire government is run by whoever fights the best in one-on-one combat?"

Jesse nods.

"What a stupid way to pick a leader."

"Thank you for your vote of confidence," Duncan says. "I don't just make unilateral decisions, however. I work with each Unit Leader to build a consensus. And we do train every member of the Unit on a broad range of topics that prepare them to rule competently. Strategy, politics, warfare, and diplomacy."

I look pointedly at Flynn, my first defeat. "That guy's a diplomat?"

Duncan snorts, but before he can answer, someone pulls him away.

"No one excels in every subject," Jesse says.

"Guess not," I say.

"Think you'll make it to Kahn?"

I've been avoiding looking in his direction, but I can't help it when Jesse mentions him. It's like my eyes swing around to face him of their own accord. He's standing on the edge of the crowd. A gorgeous redhead in a perfectly fitted sky blue dress is talking to him. He's not looking at me, which is exactly what he promised.

But I wish he was.

As if he hears my thoughts, his head turns slowly toward me. The redhead scowls and puts one hand on her hip.

Kahn doesn't notice, too intent on me. Heat rises in my cheeks.

He caught me staring. I offer a half smile. I wonder whether it looks like Jesse's.

Who is still talking to me.

"What?" I ask.

"What distracted you?" He follows my gaze. "Uh, what's going on with you? Are you trying to stare him into submission?"

I shake my head. "I need to use the restroom."

"Oh," Jesse says. "Okay, well, there are public restrooms installed for this type of event. They're at the edge of the—I can just show you."

I notice people streaming toward the edge of the squadron barracks. "There?" I point.

"Right."

"It's okay. I can make it."

"Okay, but hurry," Jesse says. "If you're late—"

"I forfeit. I know."

Kahn walks away from the redhead without an explanation when he sees me moving and falls into step beside me.

"What are you doing?" I ask.

"I—" He swallows.

"You're supposed to leave me alone."

"I was."

"You're hounding me."

"You were undressing me with your eyes. I can't ignore you when you're imagining me without my shirt on."

My jaw drops. An image of Kahn without a shirt floods my brain, unbidden, and I can't unsee it. Which is ridiculous, because I *haven't* seen it.

I start walking again.

"You're not even denying it."

"I can't control what this stupid, non-consensual exordium shoves onto me. I can't stop my body from reacting, or whatever this is." When I finally turn toward him, he's smiling.

Double dimples. Perfect teeth. Full lips. And his eyes.

Mother Terra, his eyes. "Can't? Or don't want to anymore?"

"Nothing has changed, okay?"

"So when you're standing across from me?" He steps closer, too close.

He's inside my personal space, and I can't think. I can't breathe. I can't even see straight. His face, his chest, his shoulders fill my entire world. Everything else drops away.

His lips lower toward me.

My heart sprints away, blood pounding in my ears. "What?"

"You're telling me you don't have any trouble?" His breath is warm on my face.

The hairs on my arms rise. My hands tremble, and I clench my fists to make them stop. "Trouble how?"

"You don't want me to put my hands on you?"

I stifle a groan, because now that he says the words, I do. I absolutely *do* want his hands on me. Running up my forearms, his fingers closing on my upper arms and dragging me closer. Until there's no space between us at all.

I'm sweating. I'm breathing heavily. I can't do this. "I want you to treat me exactly like you'd treat Jesse."

"Pah, can you please *not*?"

"Please not what?"

"I've known your brother for a long time. Just, please don't say to think of you like that."

"Jesse's wonderful."

"He eats skin off of his toes. He bites it off with his teeth and swallows it."

"He doesn't." I laugh and slap his arm. "Stop—" My breath catches in my throat. My hand on his tricep. My world narrows to that one point. My fingers curl around his muscle, marveling. Perfection. My heart leaps into my throat, and I step closer.

"Kahn," a high voice behind him says. "I thought you said you'd get me something to eat. I'm terribly hungry."

"Alora, your next match." The tension in Duncan's tone tells me I'm nearly out of time. So much for the restroom.

I release Kahn's arm and step backward. He shakes himself, like a wet dog.

"Who is that?" I hate that my question comes out husky and soft. Like I'm asking him about her because I have a claim on him.

But at the thought, my heart says *mine*.

No, I remind myself. *He's not mine.*

"I'm Vanessa Houghton," the redhead says. "Kahn and I are getting married next month."

He scowls darkly. "No, we aren't."

She smiles at me, but it doesn't touch her eyes. "We had a disagreement, and we're working on the date, but we're engaged."

"We broke the engagement off last night." Kahn's voice is flat, but his eyes soften. He drops his volume down substantially. I have to strain to hear him. "We've been through this, Vanessa. We were always a political match, and we're no longer a good fit."

She scowls at me. "Because of her?"

Yeah, because of me? I can't keep my eyebrows from drawing together.

Kahn shakes his head and points behind me. "You're out of time."

Duncan's climbing into the arena. I sprint through the crowd and up the stairs just in time.

My opponent, Titan, is the largest citizen I've ever seen.

The sun has dropped a little in the sky, and it casts shadows across his face. I'm not petite or dainty—in fact, I'm pretty tall—and he's still more than a hundred pounds heavier than I am. His arms could wrap around two of me. Every part of me is drenched in sweat. I expected the crowd to thin out a bit as the day grew hotter, but if anything, the audience has grown. In the corner of the courtyard, I even spot a few men I recognize as Healers. I raise my hand to them, and they beam. They clearly recognize me, too—at least by the rumors. Lord Sterling's daughter, hidden among the Healers for a decade and then some.

This time, for the first time since my disastrous selection of staffs, I choose something other than hand to hand.

I choose swords.

The crowd murmurs, probably wondering why, though to me it seems obvious. I could never compete against Titan at hand-to-hand. He'd squash me like a bug.

When the flag drops, I dart to the right to evade Titan's first swing. A single hard parry from him, and I'll crumple. Adding a blade to the mix is my only hope to balance the scales with someone this size, but he's still going to pack a depressingly hard wallop. I Lift a handful of dust and use it in various places to block his jabs and strikes. It works well enough that it gives me an idea.

With his next swing, I Lift a pile of sand and fling it into his eyes. He cries out and rubs at them, and I run around behind him, moving rapidly. But once I'm in place, I hesitate.

I saw the Healers behind us. There are Healers here, I remind myself. If I think about it much more, I won't be able to do it. And it needs to be done if I want to win.

I slice my blade across the backs of his legs, dropping him to the ground.

My stomach flip flops, but after he falls backward, I shove my blade against Titan's throat and force him to the ground. Then I Bind his hands enough to hold him down. Jesse said he's a weak Lifter, but when he pushes against my Binding, it almost snaps. I manage to hold him for the count of three, barely.

Bile threatens as I climb out of the ring. I sliced his hamstrings. I shudder. How can Titan fight any more, given the state of his legs? I wish I had any other ideas of ways to take him down. At least I know the Healers can step in once this is over. They'll bandage him up until then.

"That was awesome," Jesse says the very second he finishes his match. My brother has defeated Quincey and Pratt, moving up two places against the one he lost to me.

I can't think of a single thing to say. 'Congratulations' feels wrong.

Every time I close my eyes, I see my blade shearing through the flesh on the backs of poor Titan's legs. Blood spills out, drenching the mat. I'm gripped with a terrible fear that there's no point to any of this. "I shouldn't have done it. I should have accepted defeat."

"Alora," Jesse says. "He will be fine. They'll Heal him, and he'll walk again."

I nod.

Jesse's voice is urgent. "This may feel pointless to you, but the higher you rise, the more people will rally to Dad's standard. This matters. It may be the only Ascension that has ever really mattered. Without enough support. . ."

He doesn't say it, but I know.

When Amun comes for me, we'll lose. My life is literally on the line. I drop my head into my hands.

"How are you?" Jesse crouches next to me. "It's a lot of violence for someone who spends her days performing."

"Too much."

Jesse's hand on my shoulder is a balm.

"Physically I'm fine, but I've never been this. . . worn out. And every time I close my eyes." I shake my head.

Jesse tries to tuck a few stray hairs back into place, his fingers unable to shove them past my Binding.

"That's not good." I tug on the stray hairs that should never have escaped. "This has never happened." I close my eyes and realize that I can feel it, the tiny drain on my abilities that's coming from the Binding on my hair.

They're right. Bindings do pull energy.

Jesse frowns. "At least you only have Stefan and Kahn left, although Stefan's an amazing fighter. Wickedly good, really."

And I'm so tired that my hair Binding is fraying, literally and figuratively. "Wonderful."

"But I think you've done enough. Truly. You're not a trained fighter, not yet, and what you've done is nothing short of tremendous. You've shown them your great strength and your ingenuity."

Without Kahn around to shred my brain, I actually hear Duncan call us for the next round. "Stefan," I say.

Jesse nods.

I climb into the ring, checking out my opponent. He looks a lot like every other Unit Leader, but his eyes concern me. They dart left and right, not nervous like prey, but confidently like a hawk choosing between a squirrel and a rabbit for his dinner.

I ask for swords again. I select a small, light sword that has almost no embellishments. Unlike the troupe's performance swords, this blade is wicked sharp. The second the flag lifts, Stefan comes for me. He spins, darts, and swipes. I'm so tired that I forget to think. I'm back on a tight rope, performing a dance. I leap over his blade and drop below it. I may have no strength left to Lift, but I still sense his body and blade clearly. I close my eyes and for some reason that helps. I block each strike and begin to jab and swing offensively, too. People are talking and shouting all around me, but I tune it all out and focus on Stefan.

I want desperately to defeat him with just a blade. These people think I'm beneath them—uneducated and untrained. To them, I'm a nobody worth nothing who still poses a tremendous threat.

I burn with a desire to prove them wrong.

But my shoulder isn't totally healed, and my legs have improved, but they're throbbing. I've been fighting in the sunshine all day long. My arms are tired, my legs ache, and my back cries. My blocks slow. My attacks wane. When I open my eyes, it's clear that Stefan sees it, too, my total exhaustion. He launches a series of lightning quick blows I'm too drained to counter.

I only spare my forearm from a deep slice from his blade by Binding air just in front of it. I've always Bound objects in the past, like dust, dirt, fabric, or rocks. I never realized air would work. No doubt every one of my opponents knew.

I'm an uneducated dope, in way over my head, thrashing around with sheer dumb strength.

And Binding that spot of air felt as challenging as Lifting a wagon.

The Bindings holding my hair in place slip, and my head aches with the effort of pulling it back away from my face.

Stefan's next strike is too fast—I can't stop it. I can't move in time, either. I try to Bind air in front of me, but I'm too weak and the sword shoves through it, slicing through my shirt and into the skin of my stomach. Blood pours out of the wound. The sharp pain energizes me enough to jump backward. I need to Lift his blade and get it away from me. I narrow my focus until all I see is his sword and I pull.

Nothing happens.

I try harder to feel Stefan's blade, but I can't seem to focus. The harder I try to focus on the blade, the more I feel things around me. Stefan himself, the ring surrounding us, the ropes, the ground, and even beyond. Flagstones, millions of blades of grass, hundreds and hundreds of people standing shoulder to shoulder. When Stefan's blade arcs toward me again, this time flying toward my heart, I'm desperate to stop it.

I reach down deep and pull as hard as I've ever pulled. The world vibrates all around me—the ring floor, the flagstones, the people, even the individual blades of grass all tremble, the grass and people bowing backward, the ring and cobblestones lifting in the air.

And then everything drops.

I only feel one thing, the thing I can't stop. Stefan's blade enters my body, headed for my heart. One voice cries out in anger as pain consumes me.

Surprisingly, it's not my shiny new father, Duncan.

It's not Jesse, either.

The voice of fury is Kahn's.

I meet his eyes for a moment, frozen in time, before the blade pierces my heart and the pain—it eclipses everything else.

Until the world, blessedly, goes black.

EARTH

I cry out, both hands clutching involuntary at my heart. Hardly any light streams through my window. When my door opens and Jesse's head pokes through, his hair is flying in all directions. Still early morning, then.

"What's wrong?"

My chest is unharmed, my heart beating steadily underneath perfectly smooth skin, but I can't seem to form words. Jesse looks me over, and then climbs into bed beside me, pulling my head against his chest.

"Bad one, huh?"

I shake my head against him. "I thought I died."

Jesse stills. "What?"

I tell him about the Ascension, and my last memory, of being stabbed in the heart.

His eyebrows rise. "Is that something Terrans can survive?"

"I don't know. I have a heart there, so our physiology seems to be the same. At least there were Healers present, standing near the outer edge of the courtyard."

"I thought you said I was there," Jesse says. "I'd never

have let something like that happen to you on Earth. What's wrong with Terran me? Sounds like Jesse 2.0 sucks."

"You were fighting your own match. You couldn't have done anything anyway," I say. "It's like a ritual or something."

He swears. "You need to be more careful. We need to figure out how to get the Terran version of you a message."

"Can't be done. How many times have we tried?" I swing out of bed and walk into the kitchen, Jesse on my heels.

"Yeah, but your dreams are growing more dangerous," he says. "I don't like it."

"And, people I know are popping up more. I fought Henry there last night."

"Wait, lover boy Henry?" He pulls out a bag of generic Corn Pops.

"Yep. He's in the Unit." A chill creeps up my spine. In seventeen years, I never encountered another single person on Terra who I knew on Earth, not even my own mom. But now Robert, then Jesse, and a few days later, Henry.

"You said they have some kind of freaky ritual or something when a baby is born, right?" Jesse asks. "Where like, the mom and dad just *know* the name."

"The mom—always the mom. Sometimes there's a dad. And actually, I even saw it happen not that long ago," I say. "Betty had another baby, and I got a peek." I shudder. "Kind of the same as here—she pushes the baby out. But then Betty and Abraham both kind of acted flabbergasted and then, bam. They looked at each other and Betty said, 'her name is Sheena.'"

"What if?" Jesse taps his lip. "What if they're connected to Earth somehow—and that's why they don't have sex to make the baby. The babies are being made *here*. The Naming thing is, like, I don't know. Somehow the name of the person on Earth, where the mom and dad made the child, just gets, like, passed over."

I frown.

"And that exordium thing is like the Naming thing. You fall in love here, you just *become* in love on Terra."

"That doesn't add up," I say.

"Why not?" Jesse tilts his head. "It seems to, to me."

"I met my soulmate," I say softly. "And I'm definitely not in love here."

Jesse swears under his breath. "Every time I think it might make sense." He spreads his arms. "Nothing."

"I know you want me to make friends and open up, but J." I gulp. He's not going to like this. "I think we need to prepare to run. It may come to that. Something isn't right on Terra, and it worries me. It seems more and more connected to Earth, and, I don't know." I shiver.

Jesse pours himself a big bowl of cereal and passes the bag to me. "But as you and I have just proven, it's not the same. You're seeing people you know, which is new, and you're in danger there, but you got *stabbed in the heart*, and then you woke up here, completely fine."

Because Healers fixed me there before I ever woke up here—I'm sure of it.

I've always been surrounded by Healers—and they've always fixed me right away.

"I can't shake the feeling that we aren't safe." I can't explain it, but as things heat up on Terra, it's like a noose is tightening around my neck. "They think I'm the *Warden*," I say. "Some prophesied female Lifter who will destroy and remake the world." I pour the rest of the nearly full bag of cereal into a salad bowl, and Jesse hands me the milk carton. I dump the rest of it in.

He shakes his head. "I know it's scary." He sits down

at the table and sighs. "But let's review. You saw some villain on Terra, and then he supposedly had a heart attack in your restaurant."

"Supposedly?" I nearly drop my spoon. "You think I'm making it up?"

"Not at all, but we weren't in the hospital. We don't know what happened to him."

"He died on Earth because I *killed* him on Terra."

"But you killed him the night before. Why wouldn't he just drop dead immediately?"

"It was a head wound," I say. "He could have gone into a coma on Terra, and then died later—at the same time as he died on Earth."

Jesse sighs. "And are you *sure* that was the same person? I mean, could it just have been someone who looked a lot like the Robert person from your dream? You did feel guilty for possibly injuring him, right?"

I freeze with a bite almost to my mouth, milk dripping back into my bowl below.

He doesn't believe me.

"And I'm your brother in both places, for heaven's sake. No threat there." He chews and swallows. "Clearly Henry's trying to help you here on Earth. He's not nefarious." He sets his spoon down and straightens. "Things are finally settling for us—I have a new job. You do, too. You've made a friend."

"Doesn't it bother you that you and Henry popped up in Terra? And that Dad didn't? Or Mom? You know, our real mom." My heart lurches.

Jesse's eyebrows draw together. "But who are you afraid of *here*?"

I don't even need to think about it. "Declan Rosenbaum."

"Right, but you haven't seen or heard from him in more than eighteen months."

"But if I had, I'd have packed you up and put you on a bus no matter what you said."

"I really do wonder what it means, that you're encountering people you know."

I narrow my eyes and shift so I'm sitting directly across from him. "What do you mean, *what it means?*"

"You're seeing people you know, all of a sudden. I mean, every time I sleep, I dream about people and things I know, mixed with a lot of fantastical nonsense. I'm never healed while I'm sleeping of course, but it does make me wonder."

"Wonder about what?"

"Hear me out here—you know I love you. You know that you're everything to me, and always have been. Without you in my life, I have nothing. You know I'm here for you, no matter what."

No matter what? That sounds ominous. My stomach twists.

"You believe you speak other languages—"

"I *believe?*" I clench my hands into fists. "You've heard me speak other languages."

Jesse's eyes are open, calm. "I have. But I only speak English."

Realization dawns, dark and terrible. "You think I'm making it up."

He shakes his head. "I think you believe you are speaking other languages."

"I heard Paul speaking in German the other day. How do you explain that?"

"Did you?" Jesse asks. "Or did you think you knew what he was saying, so it *felt* like you understood him? Did anyone else hear him? Someone we know really speaks German?"

I gulp.

"Alora, no one in the world loves you as much as me. But—"

"What about the healing?" I ask. "You saw my wrist. And last year, there was my broken arm."

"I saw a swollen wrist," he says. "And your arm was puffy and it hurt."

"You think they weren't actually broken and a good night's rest was more than enough to fix whatever was wrong."

Jesse shrugs. "I don't know what I think. I've always assumed that every single thing you told me was true and was actually happening. And that may very well be the case, but at least consider the alternative. What if your very vivid, very consistent dreams are *not* real? What if, now that life is finally good for us, your brain is conjuring up issues? Or hurdles, call them whatever you like. But what if you're scared that by branching out, by making friends, and by trusting people, you'll put us back in danger? That would be normal for someone who has gone through what we have."

I can't meet his eye.

"Our parents died, Alora. They left us when we were *so* young. And then Aunt Trina gave us to social services. Then the people who were supposed to care for you betrayed you—betrayed us both." He takes my hand. "These dreams you have are atypical for sure, and they're a problem. But I just want you to consider that it's possible that the dreams are telling us something about what's going on inside your brain, and maybe they aren't actually something that's happening on another world."

"It's not fake," I whisper. I'm not making this all up, and then cutting myself in the middle of the night, or whatever he thinks.

"I don't think you're crazy."

"Just delusional, and maybe paranoid."

He exhales. "Look, all I'm saying is, maybe we've been looking at this wrong. We can't get a message to Terran Alora in any way we've figured out, but we can look into things here on Earth. You wanted to contact the detective from Mom and Dad's police file. I can dig around to find out about him today after work. We can look into what happened to them. Maybe some resolution there will help you feel better, here and on Terra. I'll even look up your court files and our foster files."

"What will any of that prove?"

"That I'm on your side. Let's see what we can find out about what happened to us and our family. Maybe someone is following us, but it could be for other reasons than we think." He leans back. "Or maybe not."

"You don't think Declan's after us?"

Jesse goes back to eating what is almost certainly soggy cereal by now. "I don't know. I've never even spoken to the man—heck, I only met him once, when he was leaving after a meeting with you. The social worker I talked to was a woman named Denise or something."

My heart cracks a little at his words. "Do you think I'm making him up?"

"I believe there was someone scary, ominous, and threatening. I believe he might even have told you he was a caseworker, but caseworkers don't cross state lines— they don't have that kind of latitude, or those kinds of resources. Maybe he was a child predator or something and he did search for you. Or maybe you saw someone you thought was him, but really he just looked similar."

My entire life people have told me I was crazy. Mom and Dad. Aunt Trina. Social workers—including a shrink at the group home—and Declan Rosenbaum. But one person always believed me—believed in me.

And now he thinks I'm losing my mind, too.

I choke on a sob.

"Look, Alora, I don't know anything. I'm just saying, we should look into it a little more before packing our bags again."

"Any digging we do could lead them to us. You said that yourself."

His eyes are sad, and I realize that he doesn't believe there's anyone to lead anywhere. He's hoping it's all in my head. "If they're still looking for us, that's right. But I think we're safe here, and I'm willing to gamble I can prove it."

"What about Henry? Now that I've seen him on Terra, I feel like I shouldn't be working for him here. Right?"

Jesse leans toward me, his eyes intent. "I'm on Terra, too. Will you cut me out next?"

Tears well up in my eyes. "You're the only person who matters. You anchor me—you keep me safe and sane."

"I love you, Alora, more than anyone or anything. You're my sister, my favorite person in the world, but people need more than one person they care about in their life. We need friends, we need acquaintances, we need mentors." He sets his spoon down and places his hand over mine on the spool table. "Humans need connection to anchor them, like you said, and right now, I've got a job that pays ten times what I've ever made before. If we save that money and someone does show up, we can repay what you stole. We can hire a lawyer to defend us. Even one month at this new job could completely transform our circumstances. My health insurance starts in four days. It allows me to include one member of my household. I've already filled out the paperwork to add you."

"Did you give them our actual address?" I pull away. "I don't need health insurance, and I don't care about connecting with anyone else. I don't trust anyone else, not for the next six months, anyway, not until I'm considered old enough to live without someone else controlling me."

"We've never let anyone in, but that doesn't mean we shouldn't try." Jesse's shoulders droop. "Can you at least try?"

"People suck, J. They always do."

"You have friends and family on Terra."

"I ran away to keep them alive, and now I'm down to one person I care about, even there. You."

He stares at me a long time.

I wonder whether he's thinking that's just more evidence that Terra is only a reflection of my fears on Earth.

"I need to shower and go to work. Let me look into some things tonight, and we can talk about this more. At least give me a day. Can you do that?"

I set my jaw and look out the window. The sun is up, and somehow that makes me sad. The day is here—and this conversation really happened.

Jesse takes my silence as consent and goes to shower. He leaves for work, and I head for Krav Maga. I feel much better after an hour and a half of punching and kicking things. I shower afterward, dress in one of my old Perry's uniforms: a white button down shirt with a Perry's logo above my heart and black pants. I take the bus over to my new job. I'm a little early, but I didn't want to be late on my first day, and buses are notoriously unpredictable. It's only 9:33 a.m. when I reach the restaurant, but the front door's already open. I breathe a sigh of relief.

A woman's voice calls out when I enter. "We're closed."

"Oh, I know. My name is Alice," I say. "I'm here to work."

"What exactly do you do here?" A short woman in a business suit walks around the corner. "We certainly don't need dishes washed yet, and you aren't dressed like a janitor."

"I'm here for a new waitress position."

She eyes me like I'm a mouse. Eating her dessert.

"I'm a little early, but I'm supposed to meet Henry here for some training and to fill out paperwork." What if Henry's parents didn't let him choose the Katy location? Or what if he didn't actually have the authority to hire me? I want to dart into a hole and hide, like the mouse she clearly thinks I am.

The woman pins me with a stare. "Henry mentioned hiring someone, but he said her name was Alora." Thank goodness. She knows Henry, and she knew I was coming.

He told her my real name? "Uh, I'm sorry. The confusion's my fault. Alice is my legal name," I say. "It's also my aunt's name, so I've always gone by a nickname—Alora. I forgot to tell Henry that my legal name is Alice."

I expect recognition to roll over her, so we can start over. That doesn't happen. If anything, her frown deepens. "How do you know my son, *Alice*?"

Why isn't Henry here yet? I can't believe I'm having to deal with his very unfriendly mother alone. I can't exactly tell her I know him from Perry's. If she looks into it, she'll find out I was fired. Actually, since I'm already wearing a Perry's shirt, she may figure that out anyway. My job may be gone before it ever existed. This is what happens when you trust someone else, when you rely on someone else.

Before I think what to say, the door opens. Henry blows into the room with a grin on his face. "Alora! I'm so glad you came."

His mother raises one eyebrow. "Were you worried she wouldn't come? Is she unreliable?"

Henry raises one eyebrow and looks from his mother to me and back again. "You sound crazy, Mom. Please tell me you aren't interrogating my friend and my first hire as an assistant manager."

"You hired a friend?" Now she's frowning at Henry, but he doesn't look nearly as withered as I felt.

"Please, Mom. I hired her to be a waitress, not to take over the restaurant. Like you've never given a job to a friend you trust."

She rolls her eyes. "It's been a long morning, that's all."

"Ease up, alright? Geez." Henry shakes his head at me, as if to say his mother's bonkers.

That might be what irritates her again. "Where did you say you met her?"

"I didn't say," he says. "Because I didn't think you'd care, but she's a friend of a friend at school."

"You go to Rice?" his mother asks. "Why didn't you just say so?"

I shrug.

"Because you're terrifying." Henry tilts his head sideways. "Ease up, Mom. It's not the Spanish Inquisition."

Mrs. Perry puts one hand on her hip, glares at me one more time, and spins on her heel. She marches back into the kitchen. Henry rolls his eyes. "Sorry about that. My mom's a little overprotective and when I told my parents I was hiring a girl, well. I should've been here earlier to make sure you didn't bump into her alone. I did come early—I just didn't realize you'd be quite so early."

"It's fine," I say.

In spite of his reassurance, I'm skittish as a colt when we fill out the paperwork in the office. "Why did you tell her you met me at school?" I ask. "I don't have a college ID. I didn't even know where you were going until your mom said Rice."

"Sorry," he says. "But honestly, it's not a big deal. She's just having a bad day."

"For the record, I'd never go to Rice."

"Why not?" Henry scowls. "It's a good school."

I laugh. "Because I could never afford it, goof."

"Sorry. Maybe if you'd tell me more, I could lie better for you." He rolls his eyes, but he's smiling. "Look, I had to explain where I knew you. I couldn't say Perry's, and you don't play soccer. It's not like she can look up school records."

I glance at the door.

"If the whole thing is too upsetting and you want to leave, that's fine. I swear, my mom's protective of me, but she'll back off, and she's almost never here. Seriously."

I am nervous, but what if Jesse's right? What if I'm scared for no reason? "Okay," I say. "I'm sorry I over-reacted."

"So, day one. Do you want to try a table or two today?"

My jaw drops, but I nod my head. I could really use some tips. Waitressing could be really good, since I'll essentially get paid daily.

He walks me through the basics—how to place the order, where to pick it up, and the typical process. He shows me how to ring someone up—pretty simple, but it's a new Henry I'm watching. One who knows the ins and outs of how Perry's works and has confidence in showing someone else. I can hardly reconcile him with the chronically late dishwasher I knew for months.

Finally, he hands me an iPad.

"Uh, what's this?"

"You need to study the entire menu. Before you can wait tables, you need it memorized, that way you can answer questions and gracefully accommodate substitutions."

He's a completely different person. "Where was this Henry hiding?"

His goofy smile is familiar, at least. "I think sometimes people expand to fit their role." He shrugs. "When I was a dishwasher, I washed dishes."

"And now that you're a manager?"

"I've been watching the managers here my entire life, and my mom and dad." His eyes widen. "You've met my mom. My life has been one big long training course on restaurant management."

Interesting—Henry is like one of those little green lizards that are almost a plague here in Houston—anoles. They can change colors to blend in. I just didn't expect him to blend into his job upgrade quite so well. "Where should I go to study?" I lift the iPad to remind him what I'm talking about.

"Up to you." He shrugs. "You can stay in here. I have some paperwork to do, but I won't be noisy. Or you can sit outside on a bench, or wherever you want."

The thought of sitting in here with Henry doesn't worry me, but with his mom in the next room. . .I stand up. "It's not too hot outside today. I'll be on that bench by the fountain if you need me."

"Be back before eleven, okay?"

I nod.

It isn't too hot, but I'm still sweating a little as I scroll through the menu—humidity is a miserable, miserable thing. I'm surprised to find that I already know most of it. My months of scraping plates and sampling leftovers might have been helpful after all. On my third time looking over the menu, I've got most everything down. My mind wanders, and when it does, I can't help but think about what Jesse said.

Is it all in my head?

The accident wasn't in my head—and neither was the

detail I just remembered about the seatbelts. I was right. Mom and Dad's belts were cut. And that detective from the report Jesse hacked would know *why* the police just dropped it.

Gregory Stanton.

Before I can talk myself out of doing it, I open up a browser and search up the number for the police station. Then I dial it on my phone.

"Spokane Major Crimes Unit, Bethany speaking. How may I direct your call?"

"Uh, hi, my name's Alice." I can't think of anything else to say.

"Okay. Hi, Alice. Who did you call to speak with?"

"I'm looking for detective. . . uh, it says Gregory Stanton. I'm sorry, I was looking at a chart. I have a message from, er, from his doctor. Is he available?"

"Can you hold for a moment?"

"Sure," I say.

A series of beeps and clicks follow, but before too long, Bethany picks back up. "Yes, he's here. Let me patch you through."

"Thanks." My heart begins to pound—I wasn't sure if he'd still be working there, or whether they'd push through calls from random people. And. . .now I'm panicking that I claimed to be calling from his doctor. Idiot.

I wait for a moment, and then the line rings again. "Gregory Stanton."

"Hello, yes, this is Alice."

"You're from Dr. Jet's office?"

"Uh, no," I say, trying to sound confused. "I'm not sure why you thought that. I'm calling about an old case you worked. I'm not sure if you'll remember it."

"So this isn't about my recent labs?"

Oh, man. Now I feel terrible. "No, it's not. I'm sorry,

I have no idea how. . .I mean, maybe the calls got crossed."

"Are you calling for me? Gregory Stanton?"

"Er, yes, I am. But again, I was hoping to talk to you about my parents' case."

"I handle homicides, young lady."

"I'm aware of that."

He's quiet for a little too long. Finally, he grunts. "Alright then, why don't you tell me your parents' names."

My throat is suddenly tight, but I manage to squeak out, "Debra and Peter Benson."

When he makes no sound for more than ten seconds, I wonder whether I've lost him. But then he sighs gustily. "That was quite a few years back."

"Yes," I say. "It was, but I finally saw a copy of the file."

"And you're wondering why we didn't do a more thorough job."

"Something like that."

"Can you give me your number?" he asks. "I need to run to the restroom, but I'll call you right back."

I read my number off and he hangs up. I wait more than ten minutes, a little depressed. Looks like he was blowing me off, and I ought to get back into Perry's.

Then my phone rings, and the screen reads UKNOWN NUMBER.

I press talk. "Hello?"

"This is Gregory."

"Thanks for calling me back. Is everything okay?"

"Not exactly," he says. "I left the precinct to call you from a secure line."

❧ 13 ❧

EARTH

I feel like I've stepped onto the set of some television show. It would be ridiculous, except I've come to expect the utterly unbelievable to happen in my life.

"You deserve to know the truth, but I couldn't risk talking at the station. I have a wife and kids."

My stomach drops.

"I had only begun looking into your parents' murder when I got called into the police chief's office. He told me to close the case and focus on the rest of my case load."

"Wait, so you just dropped it?"

He pauses. "I was young. The Chief was commanding."

"So you did. You got handed a case with two orphans whose parents had their seatbelts cut, and you dropped it."

He clears his throat. "Yes."

"Why?"

"We have a lot of cases now, and we had a lot then. We don't have unlimited resources. A case like that usually takes priority. A young couple with two children die in a suspicious way? Typically we'd have diverted several detectives and any other resources necessary to close it. I don't know why we didn't. Maybe the Chief was feeling pressure to solve another case we had—an older woman was my next case, a single schoolteacher. But we ended up finding the culprit on that one pretty quickly, and we never went back to your parents. I don't know why we dropped the Bensons, but I know I never felt good about it, not for all these years."

"Then why'd you do it?" My voice has gotten heated, and people walking by turn to look at me. I force my hands to unfold and lay flat on my thighs and I drag a few breaths in and out of my nose.

"I follow orders, little miss, even when they don't make perfect sense." He sighs. "I'm sorry and that's why I called you back, but like I said. I got a family of my own to think about."

He hangs up.

I understand he didn't want to risk the safety of his family just to get answers for two kids he'd never met, but it's depressing to hear that the police gave up so easily. Maybe nothing could bring my parents back, but for the first time I wonder whether all the crap I've been through since they died might not be entirely my fault. Maybe there's something or someone else pulling the strings.

Maybe Jesse was right about one big thing—I'm beginning to doubt whether Declan Rosenbaum is a social worker at all.

Henry waves at me from the staff entrance. "Alora! You ready? Lunch hits are rolling in."

I jump to my feet. "Sure, yes. I think so."

The next three hours fly past. One guy yells at me for bringing him a cold steak, which was definitely not cold, but otherwise it goes pretty well. I enjoy waiting tables more than I expected, and the tips aren't bad either, especially given the limited number of tables I took. I still cleared almost a hundred bucks for three hours' work, not including my paltry hourly wage.

When I reach the office, Henry smiles at me. "How'd it go? Frank said you did fine."

The head chef at lunch, Frank, didn't say two words to me, so I'm happy to hear he didn't hate me. "I liked it," I say. "It's more interesting than washing dishes, that's for sure."

"But harder to snack." Henry cocks his head sideways.

My stomach rumbles, and heat rises in my cheeks. "True."

"Want some lunch? Manager perk, I get whatever I want. Judging by how you ate last night, I'd say you're probably hungry."

I wonder whether it's a manager perk, or a son of the owner perk, but I don't argue. "Your mom's not still here, right?"

He shakes his head. "Nah, she took off when lunch got started. She's not so awful though, I swear. If you give her half a chance, she'll come around and you'll like her."

I exhale. Somehow I doubt that's true, but arguing with him about the future is probably pointless. "Then sure, I'm always hungry."

He grins. "Great. I thought so."

Technically, I've been eating lunch at Perry's for months now, but the difference between sneaking bites of cold leftovers and eating it fresh is transformative. "This is amazing," I say around a mouthful of scalloped potatoes.

Henry sets his fork down. "I'm sorry I didn't pay

more attention. I could've helped sooner." So, probably a son of the owner perk.

I swallow. "I don't need your help, you know. My brother and I are fine on our own."

"Yeah."

"Seriously, we are."

He nods. "I know you are, but I like being able to do something." Henry has to get up a few times to answer questions and talk to various people. When he returns, I'm done eating. "Lunch shift again tomorrow?" he asks.

"I'm free for dinner tonight." I could use the money.

"We better keep you on lunch for a few days, until I'm sure you've got the hang of it. Dinner can get pretty intense, plus today's my first day. I'm a little nervous about handling things myself."

I shrug. "Okay, well, let me know."

Henry leans forward like he's going to hug me, and I jump backward without thinking about it. Evasion is my go-to reaction to physical contact from anyone but Jesse.

I'm not sure how to fix the hurt look in his eyes, so I wave awkwardly and bolt out the door. I'm outside before I realize it's almost three. I've walked over to his office, but Jesse won't be done for a few hours. I could head home now, or wait for him. I'm not sure what to do, so I take a seat on the bench in front of Jesse's new job. I'm thinking about the detective's pathetic excuse to drop my parents' case because he has his own family. What about my family, gone thanks to whoever cut those seatbelts? Why couldn't he just do his job? Why does his family matter more than mine?

"Hey, stranger." A male voice startles me.

I glance up at John. His t-shirt says, "I spend 90% of my time GAMING. The rest of my time I just waste." The way the shirt molds to his chest muscles, it looks like he spends the other ten percent of his time at the gym. Not a total waste. . .

I stand up so he's not looking down at me. "I'm not sure J will be able to handle your strict dress code over there."

He grins. "His boss is a real stickler for dressing to impress."

"How do you have your own company at the age of thirty?"

John grabs his chest like I've shot him. "Ouch. Thirty? Really?"

I can't quite keep back my smile. I was just being mean. "Fine, twenty-five."

"Try *almost* twenty-one."

"So you can't even drink yet, but you've got your own startup."

He ignores my barbed comment. "I'm headed over to get some tacos. Hungry?"

"Tacos again?" I feel like I'm always smiling around him. "Also, it's like three o'clock. You must've lost track of time testing a video game."

John looks down. "Actually. . ."

I snort, which isn't very becoming, but. . .I think a gamer nerd might forgive me. "So you're twenty years old, and you forgot to eat lunch because you were too busy sitting on a couch, playing video games. . .at work." I sigh. "J's going to be back to cutting lawns any day now, isn't he?"

"Actually, your brother fixed a big glitch this morning, and now our alien invasion game is running perfectly. So perfectly that we lost track of time."

Of course they did. I'm sure Jesse's loving it—getting paid to play.

Until their funding runs dry.

"Oh, come on. You know you want to try the tacos

that your brother liked so much he begged for them again today."

They may say food is the way to a man's heart, but it's apparently also the way to mine, and every guy in my life knows it. "Fine. I'll walk over with you, anyway."

"You coming to keep me company, or are you hungry?" His gaze rakes downward. "Because you look like you've been skipping too many meals. I'm happy to grab some extra tacos."

I just ate an enormous steak, potatoes and broccoli, and half a basket of bread, but I've got $95 in my pocket. I can afford a taco—I don't need his charity. "The first thing you should know about me—I'm always ravenous. You'll have to tell me what's good."

"It's Torchy's," he says. "All of it is good. What do you like in a taco usually?"

Texans don't mess around with their tacos. I've learned that in the time that we've been here. I pull a face. "I don't really like eggs in mine. Breakfast shouldn't come doused in salsa."

He scoffs. "You must not have had them the right way yet. Their migas taco is amazing."

"I'll take your word for it. Eggs aside, I like most any kind of meat. Beef, chicken, pork. Shredded is always better."

I try to order my own taco, but John insists. He orders three for himself, and three more for me. "So you can see which one you like best. Plus, you said you were starving." He goes on to order fifteen more tacos, to go.

"I wasn't thinking." I groan. "You're getting food for the office. I can get mine to go as well."

He shakes his head. "No rush. They're still playing, you know. To 'work out the kinks.' They won't even notice. Plus, it's a free lunch. What do they care if it's a little later in coming?"

We sit down to wait on the order. "So your startup. . .is paying a bunch of kids to sit around playing games? How can you afford that? You must've run a mean lemonade stand to raise enough startup capital."

"Harsh," he says. "But the truth is probably worse. My dad bankrolled it."

"Wow. Must be nice."

"Your dad's not well off, I take it?"

"My dad's not even alive."

"Oh, no." John frowns. "I'm so sorry."

Before I can reply, a woman shows up with our tacos. I inhale mine, they're so good.

"You liked them, then?" John asks.

"They were amazing, especially the pulled pork." I smile. "But you've probably got to get back."

He lifts one of his tacos in the air. "You eat inhumanly fast. I've got two more tacos to finish."

"Right," I say.

He takes a bite and starts to chew. I watch in silence. Awkward.

"Are you nervous Game Theory will fail?" Jesse will be out of work if it does, not that John would worry about our rent. But if his dad's rich and this is all just a lark to him, Jesse should know and plan accordingly.

"You have no idea how nervous. I'm not sure I can deal if it collapses."

"Your dad'll be mad?"

He laughs, but there's no mirth in it. "Mad is a predicable reaction, mundane even, something he'd never consider. My dad won't be disappointed, either. No, he's expecting me to fail. If I do, he'll be validated, and somehow that feels worse. He's coming by later today, to check in on our progress." John's mouth twists. "Can't wait for that meeting."

"The market's fickle," I say. "Most startups don't make it."

"Thanks for the vote of confidence," he says.

"What I mean is, your dad might just expect it because the numbers sort of lean toward, you know, new companies collapsing. But he loaned you the money, so he must have a little faith."

"Or a lot of money and no desire to argue with me."

I think about the nice office space they have and all the overpriced tacos John's buying without a second thought. Who has that much money? "I guess. Maybe."

"I wasn't going to let him fund it, you know. I had a Kickstarter, and it was doing okay."

"So why did you?"

"I quit school, and he didn't want me to."

I don't understand. "You quit school, and that made him mad. . .so he decided to give you money? You didn't want it, and kind of didn't need it, but you took it anyway?" None of this makes sense.

He grimaces. "It's more like, he knows the owner of Kickstarter and made one call. Bam, they cancelled my campaign. I was forced to make a deal with him instead. If Game Theory fails, I'll go back to school full time."

"Where were you going to college? Or did you drop out of high school?" Part of me hopes he's a high school dropout, too. Maybe he wouldn't judge me.

He snorts. "Nah, he'd have lost it over that. I'm over at Rice. And technically I didn't quite drop out. I'm taking one class a semester, to stay enrolled but make time to focus on Game Theory."

"J's been after me to apply to college."

"You should—and even better, you could apply to Rice. It's a phenomenal school."

"Which I could never afford."

"That's what financial aid is for." He ducks his head

almost shyly. "I could totally show you around. And even though college isn't totally my thing, with my dad's connections, I can introduce you to people. People who matter."

"I could never impose like that—and I doubt your friends would like me."

"Are you kidding? They'll love you," he says.

I doubt that. "Too bad there's no way I'd ever get in. When our parents died, things got rough there for a while." I look down at my hands and lower my voice. "I didn't actually graduate from high school."

"That's problematic," John says, "but it's also the point of a personal statement. If you score well on your tests, and my dad calls a few people, you could probably still get in."

"Why would your dad call anyone for me? He doesn't even know me." My voice drops to a whisper. "You barely do."

"Your brother's brain astonishes me, and if you're only half that smart, Rice would be lucky to have you. And for my dad, well, anything that makes me excited to go back, he'll do."

"I hope you're not going to start hounding me, too." Or maybe I hope he will.

"So how'd your date go last night? You were a little light on the details."

"I tried the bobotie and the peppadews."

"That's not what I meant."

Clearly. "What did you mean, then?"

John taps his hand on the table. "You're working for that guy now, and you had dinner together last night. You said it wasn't a date, but it sounds like maybe you're into him."

"Does that matter to you?" Ah, crap. Am I flirting with Jesse's boss?

"What if it does?"

"I'd say that's your problem, not mine."

John finally takes the last bite of his tacos.

I stand up. "You've got some hungry employees on your hands. I'd hate it if they all walked out on you. How would you explain that to dear old Dad?"

"I try not to explain anything to him whenever possible." John stands up, and we turn toward the door.

And that's when I see him.

He has shaved his beard, but the rest is the same. Black hair, golden skin, brown eyes so light they're practically champagne. He looks casual—he's wearing a polo shirt instead of a suit—but there's no mistaking Declan Rosenbaum for anyone else. My heart races and my hands begin to shake. I tense my muscles to run out the door, but that would attract too much attention. Is there any chance he's here by accident? Could he not have seen me?

I try to still my hands. They're trembling noticeably enough that John might worry.

Declan isn't looking at me, but what are the odds it's a coincidence?

Nil. Zip. Zilch.

He's here for me, I know it. He's sitting in a booth a few dozen feet away. I try not to speed up as I walk toward the door, but I can't help glancing over my shoulder repeatedly. At least he isn't moving.

John raises one eyebrow when I look his way. "Everything okay? You got quiet, and you're acting weird. Kinda jumpy."

I ball my hands into fists. "I'm fine. I just realized what time it is, and I've got to get home." From the corner of my eye, I can see that there's a bus coming around the corner, and no matter where it's going, I need to be on it.

"Thanks so much for lunch. Tell J I'll see him later, okay?"

I sprint toward the bus stop. I don't turn back around, sure that John will be gaping. I hope it doesn't freak him out, but honestly, it probably doesn't matter.

Things may be looking up, and Jesse and I may have new jobs, but it's not enough. We have no choice.

It's time to go.

❧ 14 ❧

EARTH

I leap onto the bus, the tremors in my hands only abating enough for me to text after I've put a few miles between me and Declan freaking Rosenbaum. I can't shake the image of his face from my mind.

HE'S HERE. I text. COME HOME ASAP.

Jesse replies. ON MY WAY.

I exit the bus and walk around our apartment complex twice, searching for anyone who might be watching. When I decide it's clear, I finally go inside from the back entrance. The good thing about having very few belongings is that I can pack everything we own in less than half an hour.

After which, I obsessively watch the clock. Where's Jesse? We need to leave. Right now.

From the time I outed myself on Terra, life has been rushing along at a hundred miles per hour. I kill Robert and he dies here. Then I'm fired. We find out Mom and Dad's seatbelts were cut. I meet my dad and brother on Terra, after barely escaping the Followers of Amun. Jesse insists I make a friend, and I open up to Henry, who randomly offers me a job. And. . .then I see him on Terra too. Jesse lands an almost unbelievably good job, and then I'm stabbed in the heart on Terra. And finally, for the last and most awful two reveals of all, I discover someone made the police drop our parents' murder investigation. . .and Declan is back.

I didn't want to risk Jesse getting caught before or creating renewed interest in our files. Now, though, I need to know what our status is in Washington. I can't hack the system, but I have another idea. Jesse taught me how to spoof domains. I check the website and then create a fake email address. The Spokane police department emails all end with spd for Spokane police department.

It takes a few false starts, but after a moment, I make the email address bethany@spd.com. Jesse will be proud that I've picked up a few things, at least.

I block my number and then dial the number for social services.

"Spokane County Department of Social Services."

"Hello. This is Bethany from Major Crimes. I need a file sent over."

"One second. I can transfer you over to our records department."

"Wait, wait. What's your name?"

"Tanya." She sounds annoyed, and from her tone and brusque demeanor, I'd guess she's underemployed. Sometimes if you let people know that you realize they're smart, they'll go above and beyond for you.

"I need a favor. I'm going to level with you, Tanya. I had a fight with the woman in records last week. She takes forever to send me everything, and I take the heat for it over here."

"Frank?"

Rats. It's a man? "Er, no. I don't know Frank."

"He's way better." The woman on the other line

clucks. "Trish is a pain in the tush for sure. What exactly do you need? If I can access it from my computer, I'll send it to you."

"That would be amazing. Thanks. I'm looking for the file on a set of boy-girl siblings who went missing. We have a possible match found."

"That's good news."

"Not exactly. They were found in a lake."

The woman croons. "Oh, no, those poor dears. That's heartbreaking. What are their names?"

"Jesse and Alora Benson." My heart leaps into my throat. Can it be this easy?

"There it is. I see their file right here under truants. Oh, I hope it's not them. Or is it better if it is?" She pauses. "I pulled up their photos. They're beautiful children. If they'd only have come back to us, we might have been able to help. Three years can make a real difference, you know?"

I feel something blocking me from speaking. Why didn't anyone we met in person have any sympathy for us? We might not have had to run. I clear my throat. "Doubtful. They were probably too far gone. Beauty often covers untold hidden issues."

"Oh my, it does say they robbed and assaulted a volunteer at their group home before they ran away."

I'm furious it was recorded like that, but I'm not really surprised. I did swipe the money, but I didn't assault anyone. "If you can email it to me directly, that would be wonderful."

"I was initiating the download to the server. Isn't that easier? I think we're supposed to, for privacy reasons."

"Our server's down today. That's why I'm calling from the lobby phone."

"I wondered why your number didn't come up. It's so frustrating that these things keep going down. Unfortunately, I'm not supposed to email files like this. The Act is pretty clear."

I suppress my frustration. I'm so close, if I can just convince her. "The children's Aunt is here," I whisper into the phone. "She's been waiting for hours already. We need the dental records to confirm, seeing as how they were found in the lake. I'd hate to make her wait until the server comes back up. Who knows when that will be?"

"I see why you didn't want to deal with Trish," the woman giggles. "She's a horrible stickler. It's not like you're asking for bank records or something. Why don't you give me your email address?"

I do.

"Alright, Bethany, it's sent. I hope it's not them, but I guess sometimes it's better to know."

"It is, thanks." As someone who's been mucking her way through life for seventeen years with no answers, it's always better to know.

I check my phone. Nothing from Jesse. Where is he? I text him again. His lack of response is making me even more jittery.

I open the file and start reading. There's a wealth of information, but it's not very well categorized. Dental records, vaccinations, and a long list of medical information on me. The prescriptions alone take up several pages, but they would have been condensable to a single line if you excluded the ones I hid under my tongue and spit out, or when I had a little more freedom, traded to other kids.

I finally reach something interesting. We lived with my aunt for two years after my parents died. Apparently she had to fill out reports on our progress for social services. At first I'm skimming, but something bothers me. She writes down all the right things, but the way she says them is odd. I can't quite pinpoint what bugs me at first. For instance, in one entry she says, "Alora loves punk rock. I find the screaming and discordant sounds disturbing. My sister certainly never encouraged that kind of thing, but there's no telling what she might have inherited."

What does she mean, *might have inherited?* Is there something I was never told about my parents? My grandparents? My father's family? A few months later, she writes, "Jesse absolutely hates any kind of green vegetable. I'm so sick of fighting with him about what we're eating. I'll frequently find that he's somehow sneaked the food into the garbage and let me believe he ate it. This kind of dishonesty is patently unacceptable. Sometimes I wonder whether my sister's empathy was a huge mistake."

Empathy? A mistake? What kind of mistake does she mean? Having kids at all? Upsetting people and somehow getting herself killed?

Or something else?

For the first time. . .I wonder whether we're biologically related to Aunt Trina. I think about how Duncan looks nothing like our Dad here, and how Jesse's my brother in both places. I shake my head. I wish for the millionth time that I understood the connection between Earth and Terra. It's not like I can use that as evidence with Jesse—especially now that he thinks my dreams are the result of some kind of repressed trauma.

I keep reading. In the last report from my Aunt, she complains about my appearance. It's nothing new, so I'm skimming. . . until something she says clicks.

"I don't even understand how anyone ever believed these were Debra's kids. She and Peter both have pale blonde hair, straight as a pin. These kids with their dark hair and curls don't even look like them, not a lick."

To be fair, my dad didn't have much hair. I always

figured our dark coloring came from his side, the Benson relatives, but obviously our aunt had some information we didn't. Adoption would explain a lot. My aunt's indifference to us, for one. The feeling I always had that our parents loved us, but weren't quite as dedicated to us as they could've been. I know many parents love their adopted children just like they love their own. I'm not trying to say they can't.

It's just, it never felt like mine did.

I remember many things from before my parents died, but I don't remember being hugged. I don't remember being told "I love you." I don't remember being rocked or sung to sleep. I was always clean, fed, and on time for school. I was taught the things I needed to learn, and I had a roof over my head, but the only one who ever fed my soul was Jesse.

He loves me and always has.

He takes care of me, and I take care of him.

But our parents? Not really.

I google adoption in the state of Washington and find out that when you're adopted, they change your birth certificate. There's a birth certificate in the file for both of us, but I wonder whether it's the original.

I decide to make another call.

"Spokane Regional Health District." The voice is chipper and young.

"Hello," I say. "I've begun to suspect that I might have been adopted. Unfortunately my parents have passed away, and my aunt won't tell me anything."

"That sounds like quite the hunt," the woman says. "I'm sorry for your loss. Was it recent?"

I hate when people ask that. They mean well, but the implication is that unless my parents died in the last year, I should be over it. As if you ever heal from losing someone you love, someone you need. "Not really," I finally say. "The thing is—"

"It's so hard," she says. "I totally get it. I mean, last year, my dog Freckles got hit by a car, and I couldn't get out of bed for like a whole week. I lost six pounds."

Six pounds in a week? That seems. . .excessive.

And if I had a dollar for every time someone compared my parents' death to the death of a beloved pet, I could open my own startup, complete with name brand tacos. It's exactly why I avoid sharing what happened to Mom and Dad.

"A car?" I finally force myself to say. "That's awful." I don't mention that my parents died from being flung out of a car two feet in front of me. The last thing I want is more awkward condolences from someone who doesn't know me, didn't know my parents, and doesn't really care. "About the records—is there any chance you might have access to the original birth certificate?"

"Hmm," she says. "Usually we do retain the original, even when it's changed. Let me check for you. Can you give me your name and date of birth?" After I do, I hear the clacking of keys on the other side of the phone. "This is curious. There's only one birth certificate on file, but another record's flagged. It's archived with the microfiche, for some reason. Hang on, let me see whether I can pull it up."

I wait, trying to avoid seeing Declan's clean-shaven face every time I close my eyes.

I check my phone again while I'm waiting. No reply, so I text Jesse. Again. I'M WORRIED. I'm definitely entering full-on panic mode.

He finally replies. LEAVING NOW. DON'T WORRY. I'M FINE.

"Okay." I hear the sound of her popping gum. "I found the file. It's not an original birth certificate. It's a petition for adoption, but it was redacted for some reason. Your parents' names are on the file, but not the names of your birth parents."

Ohmygosh ohmygosh, we were adopted. I should be more shocked—but instead it's like the answer to a question I never knew to ask.

"Hello? Did I lose you?"

Right. I have to say something. "Um, I'm here." I clear my throat. "Could you email it to me?"

"Well, we're supposed to go through a whole open records request process," she says. "I'm happy to walk you through it."

I groan. "I'm only seventeen. I'm not sure when or how I can figure that out. I don't have a printer or a scanner."

"Oh." The woman's quiet. "It sucks to lose someone. I really hope you find some answers. If you send me your address, I'll email it to you. It can be our secret."

Guilt surges through me for my unkind thoughts about Freckles and this woman in general. I'm a jerk. "Thank you so much. You really don't know how much this means to me."

I stand up and sit down a dozen times while I wait for her file. I look out the window repeatedly. When my email finally bings, I immediately open the attachment. Just like the kind woman said, the names of our birth parents have been redacted. All that's left is a black blob where they would have been.

I want to scream.

Then I notice the date on the petition. We weren't adopted until I was three years old, and Jesse was four and a half. The same time Mom ran with me on Terra.

Why don't I remember those first three years of my life?

I close my eyes and try to imagine a mother or a

father who are different than the ones who died in the accident, but I draw a blank. I'm so close to finding out the truth, but other than having my suspicions confirmed that we were adopted, this file doesn't help. Until I notice that a word near the page number of the petition has been redacted, too, probably because the name of the petitioners, my parents, was part of the label on the page number.

On every page but the second to last.

At the top in fuzzy but legible print, it reads, "Sterling Adoption Petition."

A sense of foreboding rolls over me. Good stuff rarely happens in my life, but weird stuff like this? This is more my speed.

I know what Jesse will say.

Maybe I remembered the name Sterling. Could it have worked its way into my subconscious? Maybe none of what I dream about is real. Maybe my injuries haven't been as bad as I thought and they're better the next day because of a good nights' sleep. Am I exaggerating how bad they are to myself so that I can create more evidence of a world that doesn't exist?

Maybe maybe maybe.

Maybe I'm crazy.

I pore over the social services file again, hoping something else will pop out in light of the adoption, but nothing does.

Until the last page.

It's just a requisition for a renewal of time at the group home. It's nothing I haven't seen a dozen times with various dates, but this time, a name stands out. I never thought much about the power in names. I flip back through the past forms, and sure enough, it's the same name on every form. How did I never notice this before? I guess sometimes your brain sees what it expects to see, and not what's there.

Under the line for my social worker's name, two words are printed neatly. Danica Rosenbaum. Not Declan.

But I met with Declan, a large, powerful man, dozens of times. I've seen him over and over, whenever I caused a problem or some kind of issue arose. I'll never forget the first time I met him, the day my parents died.

I still thought he wanted to help me then.

By the time he pried me away from my aunt and stuffed me into that psych hospital, and then when he released me into the group home with all the crazies and jerks. . .by then I knew. I've never seen or heard the name Danica Rosenbaum in my life.

I call social services back. "Social services," Tanya says.

"Tanya, my favorite person today."

"Who is this?"

"It's Bethany," I say. "Major crimes."

"Oh, right. Are those children. . .did they recognize them, or you know, did the records. . ." She trails off.

"They were a match, but here's the thing. There's a discrepancy in the file and their aunt's fixated on it. That happens sometimes. The human brain's a funny thing. She won't accept that they're really dead until she can make sense of this. We won't be able to get her to leave until I can tell her that I've spoken with you, and that I have some kind of explanation. The file you sent lists their social worker as Danica Rosenbaum."

"Okay," Tanya says. "Did you need to speak with her?"

I consider this briefly—processing that there *is* a Danica Rosenbaum. That's not an error, or she wouldn't offering to patch me through. "No, I don't, but I would like to confirm that the name is correct. The aunt is absolutely positive the social worker was a *man* named *Declan* Rosenbaum." Maybe it's a husband-wife team?

Tanya laughs. "No chance of that. Danica's gay, and she's been gay since long before it became cool. No husband. No brother, either. In fact, I can go one better. I've worked here at social services for twenty-two years and I can personally reassure you that there's never been a man by the name of Declan working here. Every single note logged on this case was put in by Danica herself. There's no mistake. The kids' aunt is welcome to call me if it will help. Or I'm sure Danica would be happy to reach out, too."

I should thank her. I should say something, but I can't. I'm too sick to speak. I hang up the phone, hoping as I do that I never need Tanya for information again.

How could there be no Declan?

I know his face as well as I know my parents, er, my adopted parents. Every time I close my eyes, I see it. Strong jaw, bitter eyes, wry mouth. Most importantly, if he wasn't my social worker, who was he? He took Danica's last name, so perhaps she could tell me, but something makes me believe that if she cooperated with him, calling her would only lead him to me faster.

My sense of panic redoubles. We're not safe here. We need to leave now.

When Jesse walks in the door, our duffel bags are already stacked and waiting.

He raises his eyebrows at me. "Alora?"

"Declan is here."

Jesse closes his eyes and sighs, but when he opens them I don't see panic. I don't see terror. I don't see fear.

I see sympathy.

Concern.

"I'm not crazy, Jesse. I saw him, I swear."

He walks past me and sits on the patched beanbag chair. "I believe you."

"You do? Then why are you sitting?" I pick up one of the bags. "We need to *go*."

He pats the beanbag next to him.

I shake my head. "I don't want to sit down. I want to leave, right now. We need to get out before he finds us."

"Alora, please talk to me."

I roll my eyes. "We can talk on the bus. We need to get moving. We can go to Louisiana, or maybe somewhere on the east coast. That's farther away. Actually, maybe we should go to Canada. Crossing state lines is clearly no problem. Crossing into another country might slow him down."

Jesse stands up and takes my hand. "I thought I was helping you, I really did, but now I wonder. I might have been making things worse."

I drop his hand and take a step backward. "What are you talking about?"

"The first time I figured maybe it's a coincidence that only you saw Declan. Maybe you're more observant than I am."

I square my shoulders. "Say it, Jesse."

"I think you might be schizophrenic. You might see things that aren't there. People, and other things."

Our parents put us up for adoption, and I blocked it, I guess. Our adopted parents died, and I weathered it. My aunt betrayed me and foisted us off on the system. The system evaluated me and put me in a psych hospital. They shoved pills at me, pills I never took, but eventually, they released me. At least Jesse and I were in the same place again. But then, two of the boys at the group home accosted me. I cried, and I hid, and I was horrified, but I survived. When I told adults, they ignored me. Actually it's worse than that.

They called me a liar.

But every step of the way, Jesse was there.

We held each other when Mom and Dad died. He told Aunt Trina that he had dreams of Terra too, so he could go with me to the group home. I knew that no matter what, Jesse would be there for me.

But not now.

Now he thinks this is all in my head. He thinks I made Declan up. He thinks Terra's just a dream, that it's not actually a place that exists.

He thinks I've ruined our lives.

Jesse gathers me up in his arms. "They have medication that can help. It can make things normal for you, Alora, and I'm not going anywhere. I'm right here for you. You have to believe that. I will help, and monitor, and support. Anything you need. You know I love you, right?"

"Of course I do."

"Then you have to trust me—at least talk to someone."

I shake my head. "I saw him, Jesse. Plain as day."

He pulls me tightly against him. "I know you did. I believe you."

I switch to Mandarin. "How do you explain this?"

I change to Russian. "And this? Do you think I'm speaking in gibberish? You think I'm just babbling?"

I try Tagalog. "The people I meet, the people who speak these languages, they understand me."

Jesse sighs. "I've thought about it. I know you think you're speaking other languages, and it's moderately convincing. I've seen that, but no one has ever said to me, 'Wow, how does she speak this language?'"

"How could they?" I wail. "They don't speak English —that's the only time I step in to help in the first place."

"Okay." Jesse's eyes are sad. More than anything else, that makes me desperate.

"My French teacher," I say. "She thought I was copying the answers. She accused me of cheating, my vocabulary was so extensive. Remember?"

"She did report you for cheating."

And he wonders whether that's what actually happened. Maybe I didn't really speak French. Maybe I copied the assignments. Maybe. . . maybe.

Am I nuts?

What if he's right? What if I don't even remember doing it? What if I blocked it, like our birth parents?

"We aren't running," I say. "Are we?"

He shakes his head.

"What if I say that I'll leave without you?"

Jesse's face crumples. "Would you?"

I can't even imagine a life without Jesse, a world without him by my side. Electrons orbit the nucleus. The protons in the nucleus balance the electrons in their erratic path by their weight and charge.

He's my nucleus.

And he thinks I need help.

"I think it's triggered when we start to make connections. You're afraid to be in one place, and I think that's natural. But you know I'm here for you, and you know that I love you. You trust me. I'll have good insurance by Monday. Well, maybe not good, but insurance. I think once that kicks in, it'll cover you seeing someone. We'll get you help."

I pull away and wrap my arms around my knees. "I ruined your life."

He shakes his head, and looks at me with so much love I almost can't stand it. "You *are* my life. I just want you to get through this. No one is after us. It's just you and me, doing the best we can. And this job, it's a real blessing. We've got a shot here, Alora. Now, let's unpack and do something normal. We can go see a movie. Celebrate my new job, and yours if you want to keep it. Do something that normal people do."

Do something normal. I think about seeing Declan. Calling social services about our file and our parents. Was it all in my head?

I run over to Jesse's laptop, still open on the spool. I point at the screen. "Do you see this?"

He crosses the room and looks at the file. His features fall. "I do. What is it?"

"I called and got our social services file."

He skims the pages. "Our social worker wasn't Denise —it was Danica." He taps on the keys and pulls up a website—then points at a photo—the name underneath it is Danica Rosenbaum. "I remember meeting her— that's the woman I was thinking of."

"Do you remember a Declan? A man? At all?"

Jesse shakes his head. "I met a man that one time, but I can't remember his name, and other than an impression that he was really large, I don't recall much about him."

I collapse onto a wobbly kitchen stool. "We were adopted, Jesse. I've got our birth certificate, and then a petition for adoption from when I was almost three years old."

Jesse toggles from one screen to the next, his eyes fixated on the documents. I'm relieved they're all there. I don't know what to think anymore. I don't feel sick, but if Jesse thinks I am, then I don't know any more.

Jesse looks over the fake email address I set up, then back at me. "How did you get this?"

"It's a long story," I say. "I called a lot of people today and told them a lot of things and they sent me some stuff. I was resourceful."

He clicks away on the computer and turns toward me

sharply. "Or sloppy, Alora. Haven't you heard of metadata?"

I shake my head. "I know what it is, but I didn't do anything with it, I swear. I just set up an email account and then—"

He slams his hand into the wall. "You don't do anything with it—you have to deal with the reality of it. You didn't cover your tracks. They can trace all of this to us, to Houston, if they give it half an effort."

"But you don't think anyone is after us. You think it's all in my head." Panic grips me like a vise. "And you can fix it in any case, right?"

"Maybe, but that's not the point." He swears.

"It *is* the point. If you're right, they aren't looking for us. If I'm right, we shouldn't stay in Houston long anyway. Do you remember having any other parents? I don't. And we found that out here *after* I discovered it in Terra."

"I know you want to run, but can you give me a few days?" Jesse asks. "Screw the insurance. I'll make an appointment for tomorrow, and you can talk to someone. We can pay cash. We have that much in savings, at least. You don't have to tell them everything, but talk to them about your dreams. Tell them you keep seeing someone from your past, and you don't know whether it's real. Maybe there's a test for some part of this."

I'm shaking, and I still want to bolt. It's not safe here.

But I can't leave without Jesse. He's all that matters in my life.

It's barely six-thirty, but it feels like one a.m. I'm wrung out. I walk into my room and curl up on my bed. I'm not even upset that Jesse thinks my brain may be broken. I'm not mad at him, and I don't feel betrayed, not really. In all those years of doctors shoving pills at me, it never occurred to me that something so mundane might *fix* me. But if it could? I could finally have the normal life I've always wanted.

The worst part would be the years I wasted—the pain I caused Jesse—for no reason at all. I'm mostly scared, because, as awful as it sounds. . .

I hope he's right.

❧ 15 ❧

TERRA

Someone's talking to me, saying words I don't understand, at least, not at first.

Then I recognize one of them, and I know the voice. It's a voice I've always known, since the beginning. No, wait, I only met him a few days ago.

"J," I croak. I clear my voice. "Jesse?" I sit up and rub my eyes. When I open them, I can see him, my brother. He looks relieved when he grins at me.

His smile makes me happy.

"You're okay." He leans over and squeezes my hand. I look around at a room that isn't my own. Or at least, it's not the same room Jesse said was my old room a day ago. Where am I? There are books everywhere, on shelves filling every wall. Books stacked on chests, and in some places, in piles on the floor. I'm lying on a cot in the middle of thousands of books while two people I've never seen hover over me. They're both tall, dark-skinned, and long-haired. Now that I focus on them, I realize I can't tell them apart. They look exactly the same, like mirror images of one other.

I shake my head. Maybe I'm seeing double. I shake it

again, but they're still both there. I notice small things, then. Like their brightly colored clothing and their detailed leather boots. They're Healers, presumably here because I was badly injured.

"She's awake?"

I turn my head and see someone else I recognize. Duncan Sterling turns toward me. "I'm delighted to see your eyes open."

I force a smile. "Where exactly am I?"

Duncan strides nearer and places a hand on the shoulder of each of the two identical men. They smile at him and even their smiles look the same, toothy and wide. "I'd like to introduce you to Lansing and Lincoln. They're my personal Healers. They worked with a pair of the Unit's Healers, who left a few minutes ago, to bring you back from the brink. You gave us all quite a scare there, but we're glad to have you back."

Healers *live* here and work for my dad? Bizarre. Lucky for me, though. When I reach down to my stomach, my hands feel only smooth skin. No slice wound, no bleeding hole. I look up at Lincoln and Lansing. "Are you both alright?"

"I'm Lincoln," the man on the left says. He purses his lips. "I won't lie. Healing you hurt, but we're both fine now. Passing your injuries on to three others worked. No one's badly injured anymore."

"Thank you," I say. "I'm sorry to have caused you pain." I want to ask them more questions, or send a message to Martin, but not in front of my new family. It feels wrong somehow, discussing the Healers' practices in front of outsiders. And they might refuse to answer, because now I'm an outsider, too.

Jesse tosses me a pile of clothing and takes a step toward the door. "If you feel up to it, you can get dressed and we can get out of here. I'm sure they'd like their study back."

"Oh," I say. "Yes, I'll get changed and we can leave. Of course."

The men all step out while I change into new clothes. Clothes that haven't been hacked to bits and aren't covered in blood. I notice my hair's loose, and my new clothes are a simple but well-made pair of pants and a cotton top.

I'm surprised when I exit that only Jesse's waiting for me. "Where'd they go?"

"Dad has a lot to do now, you know, in light of yesterday."

I shake my head. "I don't know. What's going on?"

"I forgot. You passed out before the messenger arrived." He sighs. "The Followers of Amun knew you'd been found, but their force finally reached their head-quarters and had time to deliberate, I guess. Their leader, Devlin Rochester, has declared war."

"This is bad, right?"

"It's not good, but it's not unexpected." He tilts his head a bit to the side. "Do you remember anything that happened after you were stabbed? Or maybe it was while you were stabbed. I'm not totally sure."

I purse my lips and try to think. Kahn was angry, and I'm sure Duncan and Jesse were upset. Did they fight?

"Nothing at all?" Jesse peers at me with a strange expression on his face.

"Not really. I was so tired at the end, instead of being able to feel things around me, everything seemed to be shaking. Things looked—" I grasp for a word to explain it. "—insubstantial, like the world wasn't really made up of objects and things, but energy, or maybe filaments of, I don't know." I shake my head. "I sound insane."

"Actually, Dad's going to want to hear this, too. He's waiting for us with food. I imagine you could eat."

Hunger pangs rip through my stomach, right on cue. "I'm starving, actually."

Jesse grins. "Predictable. Lifting uses the same energy as if you did everything yourself. So the things you Lift and fling around, it's like you carried them around, physiologically speaking. You should dramatically increase your own intake. Your body needs energy, and it'll be stronger for it." He pokes my bony arm. "Clearly you haven't been eating enough."

That explains why I'm always so hungry, and possibly my exhaustion last night. Jesse starts down the hall, and I follow.

When we walk through the door into the dining room, Duncan stands. "Walking around is a good sign. How do you feel?"

"Fine," I say.

"Can you Lift anything this morning?" Duncan looks nervous. "Or are you wiped out?"

"Oh, sure." I Lift a plate and float it over to my hands. "Why?"

"Astonishing," he says. "What has Jesse told you?"

"That we're at war. I'm sorry to hear it." Sorrier to have caused it.

"Actually, our scouts tell me that Amun's main force is almost here," Duncan says. "Apparently Devlin moved the bulk of his army to an area just south of the river as soon as he heard a rumor about you. He's been waiting there, hiding in plain sight while several mounted groups like the one that almost caught you searched."

"And they all want me dead?"

He shrugs. "It's unclear. There are rumors that Devlin's pushing for capture instead. Whether that's to discover information first, or whether he really means to spare you, is unclear."

"Wait," Jesse says. "What?"

"How do you know?" I ask.

Duncan shrugs. "Spies. Devlin has spies everywhere. Every time I do or say something that upsets anyone, or when another Unit Leader does, spies are born. They're here among us, but their hearts aren't with us. It works both ways of course, which is how I discovered that Devlin may have shifted toward planning to capture you. You should know that even if that is his plan, it's not a popular position among the Followers of Amun."

"But it's progress," Jesse says. "Right?" He sits down at the table next to Duncan and starts scooping food onto his plate, almost like nothing's wrong.

"What does it all mean?"

"It means you should eat up," Duncan says. "War is here."

Jesse smiles. "Stop being melodramatic, Dad. This has been coming for years. There were wars before Alora came, and there will be wars after we're all gone. Besides, you're made for war. You've been longing to take a swing at Devlin ever since he moved to Rochester."

Duncan swallows his eggs. "That's true. Our two factions have disagreed fundamentally for hundreds of years." He turns to me. "You're not the reason for all this, you know. You're the culmination of a prophecy that's dangled over our heads like an axe waiting to fall for as long as anyone can remember, but it's divided us all from the start."

"I'm not sure how, honestly."

"People are born looking for something to argue over, but I think it's more than that," Jesse says. "It's about women and their role on Terra."

Duncan nods. "We never viewed the coming of the

Warden as signaling destruction. It's simply the next step —and when she comes, that's the sign that Mother Terra is ready for that step. But the Followers of Amun." He takes a bite and chews.

I wait, but not very patiently.

"You should eat," Jesse says. "It's shaping up to be a busy day, and if you can Lift, you should start training."

I grab a plate and start to load it up, but I'm not letting Duncan off the hook. I plonk it down on the table and stare at him. "Amun's followers felt that women were no better than animals. We bear children, nothing more."

"They felt that keeping women under their thumb would prevent the 'end' foretold. That the Warden could be halted, and Terra kept safe."

"Safe from what?" Jesse asks. "That's what I want to know."

"People in power will always fear any shift in that power." Duncan stares out the window.

"But you're in power," I say. "And you support keeping the Warden alive."

"I'm also your father," he says. "I wonder if I'd feel the same if I weren't."

"What?" Jesse asks. "Are you kidding?"

Duncan shrugs. "I hope I would make the right decision either way, and I've always seen myself as more of a steward and a protector than an overlord."

"What about the other Unit Leaders?" Jesse asks. "What are they saying?"

"They're worried about the last line of the prophecy," he says.

"Which is?" I can't quite recall.

Duncan's eyes still gaze out the window, at the forest ahead of the city. "As Terra crumbles, the world will begin anew."

Hardly an encouraging prediction, I'll admit. I lean back in my chair. "I don't see how I can end anything."

Duncan stares pointedly at the food on my plate. Croissants, ham, eggs, toast, jam, butter, cheese. "Eat. You'll need it." He stuffs another bite in his mouth, chews, and swallows. "I realized something yesterday, as you tore through all our best warriors. You may have been raised away from us. You may not be able to throw a single decent punch. And in the end, that may not even matter."

Jesse's brow furrows. "I thought she did pretty well."

Duncan's eyebrows shoot up. "Pretty well? I've never seen anyone ascend from nothing to third in a single day. Not you, not Kahn, no one. And she had no training, not in fighting, or in Lifting, not a lick. Yes, I'd say she did pretty well."

"So you think that I'm different?" I ask. "Doomed to end the world?"

"I think that after yesterday's. . .anomaly, we should be prepared. You need training, and we need to know the extent of what you can do."

Wait, anomaly? Does he mean how well I did at the Ascension?

"Speaking of." Jesse says. "Alora, what do you remember about yesterday, right before you passed out? You said things were shaking around you?"

"I got sliced and then stabbed," I say. "It hurt pretty bad, and things got fuzzy. Yeah, it almost felt like stuff around me was wobbling."

"Before the stabbing, but after the slice, in the seconds before Stefan ran you through, do you remember doing anything?" Jesse's eyes are intense. "Because it certainly looked like you were completely drained before that."

"I was so tired that I lost control of the Bindings in

my hair. That's never happened before, not ever. I used to think Bindings were like glue," I explain. "Once applied, they just stayed. Jesse told me that's not right, but it's what I thought. I've never been *that* tired, that I couldn't hold my hair back."

"Do you remember doing anything strange?" Duncan asks. "Anything at all?"

"Like what?" I narrow my eyes at him.

"Like Lifting everything in a fifty-foot radius?" Jesse asks. "All three of the arenas, the people standing around, flagstones as big as my head? Individual blades of grass?"

I don't even understand what he's asking. "I was losing control. I can always feel the objects and people around me. I remember feeling for them, wanting to focus on something. But when I tried to focus, I couldn't. My attention just spread and spread, like butter on hot toast. The harder I pushed, the further my focus expanded until I could sense everything in the courtyard."

Jesse and Duncan share a look I don't understand.

Jesse finally asks, "Didn't you wonder why Stefan ran you through, instead of holding that sword to your throat until the count of three?"

I stand up and brace my hands on the table. "Obviously not. I figured maybe he hated me. I hacked through his friend's hamstrings. Maybe he thought I deserved it." Maybe I agree with him.

Jesse stands. "Come over here. I want to show you something."

I glance down at my food. I haven't eaten much, but I'm sure I can come back. I follow Jesse to the window and look down on the courtyard below.

It's wrecked.

The main ring where I fought every match is tilted to one side, a large crack zigging and zagging down the right side. The flagstones that ran all around it in a perfect circle have been pulled out and are scattered around in piles on the ground. The grass has been pulled up by the roots in a large, perfectly formed circle around the arena. There's a boot wedged partially underneath a rock. Discarded bags.

Is Jesse saying that somehow I did all of that? *After* all my fights? There must be some other answer. I was completely exhausted. I couldn't have Lifted a thing, or I'd surely have used my strength to keep Stefan from disemboweling me.

I walk back to the table and sit down without saying a word.

"I'm guessing you don't remember doing any of that?" Jesse asks.

"It couldn't have been me."

"Stefan didn't mean to impale you, but the entire ring tilted and his sword just went sideways."

I groan. "How could that happen? I have a lot of strength, but I know my limits. I couldn't have done that, not during the fight with Stefan. I was too drained."

"I think you may have hidden reserves you've never used." Duncan stands, his plate empty. "As I said, I have a lot to do. Evacuate the city, call in all the troops the other Unit Leaders can spare, and prepare our stores, but I've already made arrangements—"

"For Jesse to train me?" I ask.

Duncan says, "I need Jesse with me. The townsfolk love him and the nobles trust him. Besides, he's only been here a year. You need someone with a little more experience."

At the sound of boot steps in the hallway, my heart lurches. Someone with *more* experience than Jesse?

As I feared, Kahn strides through the open doorway.

TERRA

In spite of myself, my spirits lift when Kahn walks in the room. I feel giggly, like a little kid getting an extra fruit pie. I feel almost dizzy looking at him. I need someone to slap me. When I realize I'm smiling like a halfwit, I scowl immediately.

Duncan finally says, "Thank you for coming, Kahn. As I mentioned, I have a special assignment for you."

Kahn's wearing black boots that rise almost to his knee, a white linen shirt, and dark brown pants. His blond hair's tied back with a leather strap and his eyes flash as he inclines his head. "Yes, sir." Light still seems to gather around him, but I'm getting used to it.

"I'd like to introduce my daughter Alora to you. You didn't get off to the best start, but after yesterday, even you must agree that she belongs here."

"She lacks control." Kahn's kind smile belies his harsh words.

Duncan frowns. "No one could have predicted what happened yesterday."

"Which is exactly why the Warden is dangerous—we know nothing about her, or what she can do."

My scowl feels a little less forced, and I consider Lifting a plate. . .and sending it crashing right into his beautiful head.

"That's what we need to find out," Duncan says. "She may well be our biggest weapon against Devlin."

"We need to sharpen her up, for sure," Kahn says.

Jesse jumps to his feet. "Alora's proven herself to be bright, resourceful, and creative."

I love him.

"Relax," Kahn says. "I only mean that while she has a remarkable amount of power, she doesn't know how to optimally use it yet."

"Do I get a say in this?" I ask. "Because I'd prefer a different teacher."

Duncan frowns. "No one else is more qualified, other than me, and I can't be spared at the moment."

Kahn clears his throat. "Perhaps Kincaid—"

"No," Duncan says. "I want her tested and taught properly, and you're the best option."

The only way I could get out of this would be to explain the exordium to Duncan, but I fear that might have the opposite effect of the one I want. I want to grumble and moan until he changes his mind, but I settle for saying, "It's fine," in my surliest tone.

Kahn beams at me, and I catch myself staring too long at his mouth, his dimples, and the curve where his neck meets his collarbone.

I shake my head.

"Honestly," Jesse whispers. "I know you don't like him, but Kahn is smart and talented. He'll do a great job." Jesse crams his last roll in his mouth in a very ignoble manner and walks toward the door. "Father, Amanda said we need to be there by—"

"No, I know. We need to go immediately." Duncan leans in to hug me and then pauses. He straightens and pivots on his heel. Why is everything so awkward with him?

After Duncan and Jesse leave, I can't stop staring at my nearly empty plate.

"Are you finished?" Kahn asks.

"Not quite," I say. "Have you eaten?"

Kahn sits down in my father's seat. "Yes."

I take a bite and chew. I've never noticed how loud chewing is. I'm not going to be able to eat all of this while he stares at me. And if I stare at him, I'll lose focus and forget that I don't like him at all. "How about this? You let me know where to meet you, and when I'm done, I'll join you there."

"I'll wait."

Three bites later, I can't take any more. "Fine, I'm done."

He glances at my plate, but says nothing.

"Let's go." I follow him out of the room, almost jogging to keep up with his long stride. He doesn't look at me, not even a sideways glance.

But I steal plenty of looks at him.

He's tall, taller than either Jesse or Duncan. He walks with purpose, with confidence, and with gravitas. His cheekbones are high, his jaw is severe, and his features are all perfectly proportioned. All in all, if Mother Terra had to shove a soulmate at me, he's at least easy on the eyes.

Several people call out greetings as we pass into the courtyard, skirting around the rubble cleanup operation. I ignore the pangs of guilt that leaving them to clean up my mess causes, because I doubt that repairing cobblestones qualifies as the type of training Duncan has in mind.

Kahn finally turns and heads up the steps of the gray

stone building that Jesse said are the barracks for the squadron.

"We're training in there?" I ask.

"The side walls are divided into housing for the men, but there's a big room in the middle built for training purposes."

He pushes through the doorway, and I follow him into the main room. It's three stories tall with windows that open onto it from rooms on each floor.

It's divided into four equal sections. The one on my right has big black iron racks full of weights. Roland uses similar equipment to increase the size of his muscles. The area to my left is a large open space with weapons racks along the walls, interspersed between the windows. They hold weapons of every size and description: maces, clubs, sticks connected by a chain, staffs, swords, throwing stars, and knives. The sizes, weights, and styles vary widely. Near the back of the room to the right, a series of wires hang suspended in the air from huge pillars, but there are more of them, like, way more than the two we usually use. The back left has enormous boxes fixed to the ground, but I can't tell what they hold.

"Where would you like to start?" Kahn asks.

Staring at his lips is too distracting, so I keep my eyes focused on the sections in the room. The longer I'm in his presence, the more accustomed to it I become. It's like candy. The first bite is overwhelming, but by the third or fourth, it's not nearly as shocking.

"I'll be honest," I say. "I don't know what any of this is, but I'm pretty good at both balance and heights."

"Let's start with the suspended wires, then." He walks to the back right and climbs a ladder. I climb the one several feet over. He stops halfway up. "What are you doing?"

"I'm climbing. What does it look like I'm doing?"

"Why aren't you following me?"

"You want me on that wire?" I ask.

"Yes, you need to be on the same wire as me for this exercise."

That would have been helpful to know earlier. I'm almost to the top, so I climb the remaining few rungs and walk a few steps out.

"I said—"

Before Kahn can complain again, I leap to his wire.

He pinwheels his arms to keep his balance from the bouncing of the wire I caused by leaping over, and then closes his mouth with a click.

"Ready?"

"I may have misjudged your balance level. Why don't you show me what you're comfortable doing up here before we start training."

I start with my typical warm-up, running back and forth, and jumping from one wire to the next. I've never had seven separate wires of varying heights, and it's pretty fun. I feel like a monkey in the treetops. Once I'm warm, I reach my senses out and *feel* the wires. I reach to the corners of the room until I feel some dust. I Lift it over to me, and use it to make holds, until I remember my trick yesterday. I drop the dust and Bind the air in place instead when I need a handhold. So much easier! I use the spots to flip, pivot, and climb. I can sense the places I've Bound so it's easy to leave a few and use them over and over.

After a few more moments, I glance back to Kahn. "What now?" It feels nice to be competent at something already.

He snorts. "You can teach our balance class from now on. We're done here." I release my remaining Bindings, scamper down the ladder, and look at the other three sections.

"Which one looks the most foreign to you?" he asks.

"Probably the weapons," I say. "Other than the staff, I haven't done anything in that realm at all, and even my experience with a staff has been strictly for show. But the boxes are the most intriguing. What are they?" From my perch on top of the wires, I could see inside the six boxes. They hold what appear to be small metal balls, piles of shredded pieces of wood, sand, strips of cloth, mounds of feathers, and in the last one, water, I think.

"Your father wants me to test you in each at some point today. I think maybe we should keep weapons for last, in case you need some Healing after that one."

"Planning on slicing me up?" I lift one eyebrow.

Kahn's brow furrows.

Talk about mixed signals. Poor guy. One day I'm screaming at him to stay away from me, and the next I'm practically flirting with him. "I'm sorry. I may have excellent balance on top of those wires, but I'm still struggling to find equilibrium here. This exordium thing is confusing, and it's messing with my brain." I think about the redhead. "You didn't really break off your engagement after meeting me, did you?"

"Of course I did." He blinks. "Vanessa's only upset about the loss of the status marriage to me would have provided."

Looking at him, I doubt it was *only* the loss of status, but I don't bother arguing the point.

"Now that I've met you." He shrugs. "I could never marry anyone else."

Anyone *else*. I'm unprepared for the longing that pulses through me at the thought of marrying Kahn. "What would you do if I proposed to you right now?"

"I would accept, with great joy." Kahn's smile is confident. He must know how handsome he is. "Are you proposing marriage?"

I snort. "No, nothing like that. I still can't—won't—allow fate or anything else to make my decisions for me."

"Hear me out." Kahn steps closer. "That's all I'm asking."

My heart accelerates. My fingers itch to reach for him, to touch his jaw and feel the place where his hairline meets his temple.

"What if you hadn't had this shoved upon you, as you feel it was? What if you'd simply met me? Do you find me unattractive?"

I laugh.

"You do."

"Oh, come on. Of course not. No one finds you unattractive, as I presume you know."

He grins. "So if you didn't have these artificial feelings, or whatever they are, shoved upon you, you might have liked me."

I shrug.

"And you would have interacted with me without this anger and irritation."

I frown.

"I am here training you, after all."

"You challenged my father *over my very existence*."

He groans. "I knew that would come up. I did what none of the other men were brave enough to do and voiced concerns shared by many."

"Concerns about the propriety of going to war over the life of one woman."

"People are going to die, Alora. A lot of people."

I gulp.

"But I didn't know you then, not at all. None of us did. We didn't understand who you were, or what was at stake."

"Would you have come around without the exordium?"

"The other men have, nearly every one of them." Kahn begins to walk toward the boxes.

I follow.

"There have been two wars against Amun during my lifetime, although one of them was quite small. We would surely fight more with or without your existence. You feel guilt over this, over causing this war, but honestly, we've been arrayed against each other for a very long time. Maybe since the very beginning."

The beginning of Terra. I wish I knew what that meant, when that was, and what this 'end' that I'm supposed to cause might be. I bite my lip.

Kahn's eyes follow the movement and stop. His pupils dilate. His hands clench at his sides, working the muscles in his forearms. A pulse in his temple throbs.

And I want to touch it.

My hand lifts on its own. . .until I force it back down to my side. I have too much to learn to be this distracted.

"Give me a chance, give us a chance," Kahn says. "I'm not saying that you should do whatever the universe wants." He smirks. "But maybe don't *not* do something because it wants you to do it either."

That almost makes sense.

Kahn walks toward the area with the black boxes. There are also several tables near each box. Kahn leans toward the box with sand and scoops out a handful. He takes a step toward a table and dumps his handful onto the top. "Now, I know you can Lift this, but I'm more interested in what you can do with it once you have."

"What do you mean?" I ask.

His eyes flood with light, and I gasp. I've seen plenty of people whose eyes fill with a soft yellow or brown or bluish glow, but I've never seen a blue so bright that it's nearly white, not like this. He Lifts the pile of sand and spreads it out, each grain hanging suspended in front of us. He shifts the grains around in bunches until they spell out letters, clearly. The edges are completely smooth and readable. The letters say, "Alora." Then he lowers the sand into a neat pile and the light winks out of his eyes. "Can you do that?"

I focus on the sand for a moment, feeling each grain. As I do, I also feel the boxes around me. The water, the sand, the feathers. I feel each shred of wood, each metal ball. I close my eyes and pull.

"Why are you closing your eyes?" Kahn asks.

I open them. "Sorry, it's an old habit. Sometimes I have trouble focusing. Closing my eyes helps me feel instead of being distracted by what I see." I Lift the sand in front of me and form it into his name, "Kahn," just as he did with mine, but I feel like I can do more. I want to impress him, but I'm also aware that I'm not the teacher here. I release the sand into a neat pile, just as he did.

"Good. Now let's see what you can do with a larger quantity."

He stands, but before he can reach the box, I Lift every grain of sand. It flies into the air and the grains form into the words, "Kahn," "Alora," "Terra," "Jesse," and "Duncan."

He stumbles backward, his eyes wide. "Okay." He braces his hands against the table he bumped into. "Uh, good. Now drop all of that. I want to show you the point of this exercise."

I do as he asks.

"Right." His eyes brighten again, bathing me in cool light, while he Lifts a small metal ball. "This is just a tiny piece of metal. Inconsequential, right?"

I nod.

His eyes flare again and the ball flies through the air and slams into one of the tables. It doesn't go all the way through the wood, but it lodges pretty deep. "There's a rack of weapons over on the wall, but in reality, for someone who can Lift, everything around you can be a weapon."

I look at the piles of things in a new way. I Lift a dozen of the balls and fling them as fast as I can at the same table. They fly right through the wood and sink deep into the mat below. Whoops.

"Show off," Kahn says, but I can tell by his amazed smile that he's not angry. "Now, to use things like this, you need to have good control. It's downright amazing that you could Lift all that sand, but I want you to Lift it again, and we'll test your limits and control. Lifting something heavy is hard, but holding small things like this, without Binding them, requires a lot of concentration. Most members of the Unit can't even manage more than a handful of sand, so we're already deep into uncharted territory here."

I Lift the sand again and form it into hundreds of small flowers all around us.

He points at the metal balls. "These are the second hardest to manage, so add them next."

I close my eyes, but he doesn't bug me about it this time. I want to Bind the sand, but I can't do that, not if we're testing limits. I feel for the balls. There are thousands of them. I Lift them *en masse* and raise them over my head. I form them into giant words, "This is easy."

Which it isn't, not really.

Kahn laughs, but there's a nervous edge to it. He reaches over and grabs my arm. He tugs me gently toward the center of the room. "Why don't you stand over here. I'd hate to have to explain to your father how those landed on your head, if anything terrible were to happen."

"You mean, if I were to lose control?"

He glances at the sand and the balls and shudders. "I guess we keep going until you can't hold any more."

I close my eyes and sense the feathers, the wood pieces, and the fabric strips. I Lift them all, forming the pieces into decorative shapes around the pictures and words I've already created. My eyes shine so brightly that the room looks like the sun at noonday. People's faces appear in windows, their eyes wide, and almost all are fearful.

I try not to think about that.

Once I have everything in the air, I start to shift things, like a juggler. The balls leave the word formations and I wind them around and around in circles, with the fabric strips, feathers, and wood chips following through and around. I may be untrained, but I've been Lifting and hauling lots of items for years and years with Martin's troupe. I Bound fabric strips into clothing for years. Manipulating a lot of items isn't as hard as I thought it would be.

Kahn touches my arm. "Maybe we should put everything away. If you drop all of that, it'll take forever to clean up."

"But what do you do with the water?" I ask, eying the huge black box full of it.

"Water's the hardest thing to Lift. It takes time and a lot of practice because it breaks into such small droplets."

Interesting.

I carefully separate each item—starting by dumping the feathers back in their box. Next I deposit the wood chips, the metal balls, and the sand. I drop the fabric strips into their bin last.

Kahn sighs in relief.

"I'd like to try the water, now," I say.

He nods, which I take as approval.

I close my eyes and feel for the water, but I don't feel individual droplets. It feels like one big entity. I Lift it and as soon as it reaches the top of the box, it starts to slide, water pouring all over the floor.

"It's okay," Kahn says. "I'll call someone to clean it up."

"Wait." Water runs in rivulets across the floor, down under the wires, into the mats on the ground, and all over. I reach for it and suddenly I can feel the water. It wants to be together, and it wants to be alone. It wants to be separate and combined, a feeling that, thanks to being near Kahn, I also understand.

When I pull on the water as an entity, it draws back to the other droplets easily. I pull each droplet in and then Lift it all, shifting all of the moving, flowing chunks of it, and dumping them back into the box. Acceptance and individuality in the same place, for the same movement.

"That's great for today," Kahn says. "I think maybe we'd better move on to the weights."

I follow him over and watch as he puts a few small weights on a bar. "You should lie here." He points to a bench, and I lie down. He hands me the bar and our fingers brush. It feels as though the world shifts for a moment. I almost drop the bar when he pulls his hand away.

It's much heavier than he made it look, picking it up as if it was nothing.

"Now." Am I imagining it, or does his voice sound wobbly? "You need to lift the bar straight up and down. He places his hands carefully outside of mine and helps me find the right placement.

"Okay," I huff. After ten or so repetitions, I feel like my chest might burst.

He makes me do it two more times, and I can't quite

lift the last one. He has to help. Then we change positions, and I use different weights to work muscles in my arms, my back, and my legs.

It sucks.

"Can I ask something?" My legs feel like the water felt. As if, without my skin to hold them together, they'd spill out and run all over the floor.

"Sure."

"What's the point of this?"

"What do you mean?"

I gesture around at the weights. "I get why you might do this, or you know, Jesse. You could build up enough muscle to hurt someone. But me?" I squeeze my pitifully skinny arms. "This is clearly not my forte."

Kahn sits on the bench next to me. "Right now it's not, but you can improve, just as I have. In a month, or in two, you never know what your strengths may be."

My voice sounds embarrassingly vulnerable when I ask, "Do we have a month?"

His face falls.

I wonder whether he'll lie to me.

"I don't know what the future holds and neither do you. I do think that people with great power sometimes ignore the things that could save them in the end. I don't intend to let you do that."

I don't argue.

"Now that we've done all of it, it's time to exhaust you. Your dad wants me to drain your power down as low as I possibly can, to see what you can really do. So think of what we did with the sand, the steel balls, and the feathers. We're about to do the same, but with these." He gestures to the walls of weights, which weigh dramatically more than the small items. I realize after a moment that he isn't kidding.

Alright.

I close my eyes again and feel for each of the weights in the room. They're heavy, and there are a lot of them, but I think I can do it. I breathe in deeply and then Lift. They all slide off their racks and rise into the air. Once they're up, hundreds of weights of different sizes, I want to Bind them into place. I'm exhausted. My hands shake, my knees bounce, and even my lip trembles. But I don't. Instead I shift them, weaving them up and down, in and out, around and around.

Kahn stands completely still, and I wonder what he's thinking.

"You okay?" I ask.

He shakes his head, but doesn't articulate.

I slowly lower each weight back onto the rack and breathe a heavy sigh of relief when the last one is released. "What's next?"

"I have no idea," he says. "Are you still not wiped out?"

I smile. "I doubt I can do much more. I'm pretty tired."

"Good. I was getting nervous. I have a new rule. When you're tired, let's not float things up above our heads. Sound okay?"

I sit down on the weight bench. "Probably a good idea."

"How close were we to being squashed just then?"

I hold out one shaking hand. "Pretty close."

"Your hand could be shaking from physically lifting weights, though." He takes my hand with his own, his huge fingers sliding past my small ones.

The tremble in my lips, the shaking of my hands, it travels, up to my heart, my chest, and my stomach.

All of me quivers.

With anticipation.

I should pull away.

I should reaffirm that this is not what I want.

But what if I do want it?

I want him.

My hand shifts, our fingers interlacing, and he glances up at me with wonder in his eyes.

I look back down at our hands. I can't figure out the physics of it, but somehow, my small, slender fingers just fit in between his large, strong ones. His skin is rough, calloused. I think of him lying on his back on the weight bench, shifting weights up and down, up and down, and my face heats. My breathing comes faster.

I close my eyes.

I shouldn't have closed my eyes, because I'm drowning in feelings and they grow when I shut out the world. The yearning in my bones, the rhythmic pounding of my heart, and a soaring in my chest, like I could fly.

Like I could crash.

Like I don't care which happens, as long as I do something.

Kahn shifts, leaning closer. I angle toward the heat rolling off of his body, like a daisy turns toward the sunlight, like a freezing woman cups her hands toward the fire. "I—"

Kahn presses his free hand to my lips, and I want to shove it out of the way.

"I know. You don't want this. I haven't forgotten." His tone is churlish, annoyed.

I want to cover his mouth with mine and drown out his complaints forever. I want to listen to his voice in my ear for even longer.

"Duncan said you'd be hungry," a woman's voice says from the doorway. I spring away from Kahn so quickly that I fall to my backside on the floor.

"Are you alright?" Kahn leans toward me and offers his hand.

I scoot away from him like he's trying to kill me, and maybe he is, unintentionally. I stand up on my own. We each grab food from the tray and stuff our mouths in silence until it's gone. Neither of us makes eye contact. Too dangerous.

But finally, he asks, "Do you have enough strength left to practice blocks?"

"I don't know what that means."

"Throw that knife at me, right at my chest," he says.

"No way," I say.

"Trust me. Throw it as hard as you can, right here." He taps the place on his chest over his heart.

I don't want to, but he stares at me. "You can do it. Just like we practiced. Pretend it's not me. Pretend I'm a black table."

I close my eyes.

"You have to keep your eyes open. It's important for you to see what happens."

"Fine." I imagine a black table in his place. It doesn't help much, but finally, I bring my arm up to my cheek like he showed me and whip the knife through the air toward his chest. It's less than an inch from penetrating his body when it shivers as though it hit something and clatters to the ground.

Kahn pushed it back. Simple. Efficient.

"It's different than Lifting or Binding something in place. It's a small push of power that stops or slows something. You can do it, even when you're tired. Now you try."

"Do not throw a knife at me," I say.

He laughs. "We can start with a few metal balls."

I glance back at the table and lift one eyebrow.

He smiles again. "I won't throw them very hard. For someone who got stabbed yesterday without a whimper, you're a real baby today."

We spend the rest of the afternoon working on blocks, and I do improve. By the end, I'm blocking dozens of separate balls at once. I'm better with my eyes closed, which Kahn does not understand.

"I don't comprehend it, but perhaps that's okay."

"A large part of my act with the troupe took place with a blindfold."

Kahn taps his lip, thinking. "We should incorporate that into our normal training routine."

"Since I'll be teaching balance, we could start there."

He smiles at me. "Might not be a bad idea." He glances at the windows. "But right now, it's time for dinner."

"Right," I say. "Did you want to come with me, and eat back at the castle?"

The smile rolls over his face.

"I'm not asking you to spend more time with me."

His smile widens.

"I'm just offering because I wanted to show you that I appreciate your help."

His grin is almost too big for his face.

"You know what? Never mind."

"No, I'd like to come."

I should not have offered. But I'm buoyant at the prospect of more time with him. My feet practically skip over the newly repaired cobblestones.

Consider him.

That's what he asked. He wants me to make my own choices, on my own timetable, but not rule him out because the universe likes him.

Maybe it's not such a bad idea.

We aren't more than a dozen feet from the front gate when I hear the pounding of hooves. Dozens of riders are running straight up the steps toward the main gate. Kahn pulls me aside just in time and the horses run past me.

We jog toward the men who are now dismounting and trying to calm their winded horses.

"What's going on?" Kahn asks.

"They're here," the closest man says. "Close the gates!"

As I run toward the gates, I see thousands of grim-faced men climbing up the road toward the Castle. At the front, one of the scariest-looking men I've ever seen sits atop a massive black horse. His hulking muscles, black hair, and shaggy black beard would be scary enough, but his bright eyes glow with an eerie champagne light and I realize he's Lifting something. It must be something bad, too. It makes no sense because I've never seen him before, but I hate him deep down in my bones. I can sense that he's evil. I scrounge up every bit of strength I can muster and Lift the wheel to raise the drawbridge. It flies up and slams shut only a hundred feet in front of the terrifying man I assume is Devlin Rochester.

The man leading the army that has come to kill me.

"Why did you do that?" Kahn asks. "Your eyes lit up like a torch. Now he knows exactly who you are."

"He already knew I was here," I say. "He may as well know what I look like."

Because I'm not sure how I know this, but I do, deep down in my marrow, in the same place I can sense that he's evil.

I'm going to kill Devlin Rochester if it's the last thing I do.

Devlin Rochester, the head of the Followers of Amun's army, *is* Declan Rosenbaum.

Either that, or my fear of Declan, and my own mind, has caused me to dream that he is.

I stumble from my bed to the bathroom. I'm dry heaving into the toilet when Jesse appears in the doorway. He crouches down and holds my hair back. I don't want to be broken. When the dry heaves stop, I grab some toilet paper and wipe my mouth.

"What's wrong?" Jesse doesn't ask whether I'm ill. He doesn't think I have a stomach bug.

He knows it has to do with Terra—which means he believes that it's something wrong in my brain.

I want to tell him that the man who's been haunting me for years on Earth just showed up as the villain in Terra, the man who wants to capture and probably torture me. A man I unwittingly vowed to *kill on sight*.

Except, for the first time in my life, I can't bring myself to form the words, to tell my brother the truth of what I believe—or what I'm not sure that I believe. If I tell him a villain from my life here on

Earth has shown up in Terra, he'll think it's because I'm crazy.

Maybe he's right.

"I'll go see someone," I whisper.

They're the hardest words I've ever said.

Jesse doesn't smile, or grin, or smirk. He pulls me against him and hugs me tightly to his chest. "It's going to be okay. I'm here for you. Always." He strokes my hair with one hand. "You know, I've been thinking about what you said. That I'm your anchor."

He has?

"It's appropriate," he says. "A ship is made to sail the seas, to travel, to move, to explore. But sometimes it needs to stop, to refuel, to be repaired, to be improved."

I need to be repaired. I've never felt more broken.

"And when that's happening, when the ship stops sailing and exploring, they drop an anchor. It doesn't keep the ship from moving or floating or *being*, but it keeps it from drifting, it keeps the ship safe."

Jesse's right. He is my anchor, in every way.

"Then when the ship's ready, the anchor lifts with it, and sticks around, ready to keep the ship steady whenever it needs to be still again."

Our life has been one storm after another, but Jesse has always been there to keep me steady while I refuel, repair, and recharge. I think about that during my shower, and afterward I feel much better.

I sit down in front of a plate of eggs and toast and take my first bite.

Jesse clears his throat. "I found someone for you to talk to, someone who has amazing reviews online. He's actually a specialist in schizophrenia."

Am I supposed to be excited about that? "When?"

"He said he'll make time for the initial screening right away. He says it's excellent that you're open to the idea and willing to meet with him. We don't want to lose any momentum."

Because loony people don't usually want to consider that they might be crazy. Ugh. That certainly fits.

I force myself to go, and I don't go alone. Jesse tells John he'll be a few minutes late this morning—which I'm sure made a stellar impression on his second day—and he goes with me to the Medical Center, where we wait for almost half an hour. I glance at my watch. 9:20. Depending on how long this takes, I may miss work entirely. I text Henry. FAMILY DRAMA. MAY BE LATE.

He texts back immediately. OKAY. LET ME KNOW.

Ten seconds later, the door opens, and I walk away from Jesse, leaving him to wait for me while a doctor evaluates the inner workings of my twisted brain. Jesse and I agreed I should tell my story as it happened, with only one exception. I won't admit that I'm still a minor. From Jesse's Internet research, it seems like being a minor might trigger some kind of reporting requirements.

I lay out my life as clearly as I can. I've never had a single normal dream, not in seventeen, er, eighteen, years. I always wake up in Terra when I go to sleep here. On Terra, I have telekinetic powers. My mom left my dad when I was three, and recently we discovered that my brother and I were adopted when I was three and Jesse was four and a half in real life.

No, neither of us recall anything about our birth parents. My aunt turned us over to the state when our adoptive parents died, claiming I was crazy. Social services found me to be stable, although possibly delusional, and sent me to a group home. I was bullied and abused there, and eventually we both ran. Our social worker pursued me, and we've been on the run ever since. I was too afraid to talk to anyone until now, because we were still minors. Now that we aren't, and I've seen this social worker again, my brother wanted me to be evaluated.

I also don't mention speaking and understanding every language I've encountered or miraculously healing from injuries on Earth while I'm in Terra.

That seems like asking for trouble.

Dr. Agour asks questions now and then, especially about people and places I've mentioned, but mostly he leans back in his chair and stares at me calmly while I speak.

Once I've told him everything, I stop.

He still says nothing.

"So, am I crazy? Do I have schizophrenia?"

He frowns. "First of all, schizophrenic people are not *crazy*. They suffer from an illness. Would you say someone with the flu was crazy for lying in bed? Would you believe they should feel guilty about taking medicine to counteract the side effects of fighting that very real medical illness?"

Uh, no. "I guess not."

"This is the same. Crazy should only be used to describe impulses that are uncontrolled, unsafe, and unhealthy. Schizophrenic people suffer from an illness as real and as debilitating as the flu. Thanks to modern diagnosis and new treatments, in many instances, it's as treatable as the flu as well."

"Okay," I say. "Sorry."

"It's alright—society has not been fair, or kind, to people dealing with mental health issues, mostly because as humans, we fear what we do not understand."

No one knows that better than me.

"Now that we have that issue laid out, front and

center, I can tell you that it is my professional opinion that you do not suffer from schizophrenia. You don't exhibit signs of disorganized speech, catatonic behavior, affective flattening, alogia, or avolition. I understand your concern that these dreams of Terra are a delusion. They may in fact be a delusion, but schizophrenia almost never presents in very young children, and your dreams began when you were quite young indeed. We have no real evidence that you're hallucinating either. You may merely be seeing men who fit the description of this, justifiably, terrifying figure from your past. While that may indicate that you suffer from a mild and isolated paranoia, I'd say the root of your problem probably lies in something to do with your sleep patterns. I also recommend that you find a qualified psychologist and work through a lot of the childhood trauma that still persists in causing you understandable fear and anxiety."

"Sleep patterns?" I bite my lip. "What does that mean?"

"I'm going to order a sleep study. Sleep specialists will monitor your body and brain signals while you sleep, and they can determine what patterns you're following, REM or otherwise. They can identify whether you suffer from sleep paralysis."

My eyebrows climb my face. "I'm never stuck in place. I can always move."

"If you experience sleep paralysis, you might not even realize you're asleep. You may think you're awake, or. . .on another world."

Like Terra. "Okay."

"You're amenable to a sleep study, then?"

I nod.

"I'll have my secretary work with you to set up a time. They're usually booked out for a week or two, but I'll request that they get you in sooner rather than later.

Once we have those results, we'll know whether to put you in touch with a neurologist, or whether we need additional tests run."

"Can you explain this to my brother?" I ask.

He smiles. "It's hard for the loved ones. They want to support you, and sometimes knowing how to do that is difficult. I'll be sure to explain everything to him. But one of the critical points is this: you have experienced a lot of significant trauma that is very, very real. You seem to place a lot of importance on whether your dreams are 'real' or not, but that's not actually as relevant as how they are impacting your life here on Earth."

Tears roll freely down my face. Dr. Agour waits until I've dried my cheeks to call Jesse into his office.

As relieved as I was, Jesse looks even more reassured. "Yes, a sleep study. That makes sense."

I text Henry to let him know I'll be there on time. When Jesse and I sit down on the bus, he bumps me with his knee.

"I'm sorry."

I shake my head. "You're trying to help because you love me."

We ride the rest of the way in silence, but when we're a few miles away, I remember I have some M&Ms in my purse. I pull them out and hand them to Jesse. He grins widely at me. Jesse never misses an M&M, unless we're on the bus. The shaking and lurching around makes tossing candy in the air and catching it in your mouth extra tricky. He likes the challenge.

He tears the top off and starts tossing them in the air. The other people on the bus scowl at us whenever he misses and M&Ms hit the ground, but Jesse still gets most of them in his mouth.

When we reach La Centerra, we both climb off the bus. I walk with Jesse over to his office since I have ten minutes to spare. Just before he goes inside, I say, "I'm sorry, J."

"For what?"

"Everything. Making your life suck. Ruining things over and over. I didn't mean to mess anything up for you. Not then and not now. Not ever."

He puts his arm around me. "If I could pick any person in the entire world—" he pauses and smiles, "or even anyone I've heard about on Terra, I'd still pick you for a sister. Every single time, without hesitation. I'm sorry I put you through that today."

"I'm glad you did, and I hope this sleep study is helpful. Maybe we'll finally get some answers," I say.

He shakes his head. "I'm not sure that we even need a sleep study." He runs a hand through his hair, leaving it standing on end. "It can't explain your speedy healing, or the languages. The more I think about things, the more I realize that while I can't understand what you were saying, the people you spoke to did respond to you—I've watched you go back and forth. I just lost sight for a little bit, probably because I'm so tired of running. But if you really saw Declan." He sighs. "I don't know what to think. He's not a social worker, so if he's following us around, maybe it has to do with the seatbelts." Jesse steps a bit closer and drops his voice. "Maybe we should run. The things I've seen—and what you told me the detective said—being afraid of whatever or whoever hurt our parents and got the investigation shut down, that isn't paranoia. That's justifiable fear."

I should tell him that I saw Declan in my dream, and that Terra's in the middle of a war. I should tell him yes, let's run, but. . .

I just convinced him that I'm not mentally deranged. If I tell him an Earth villain has turned up on Terra, well, it will seem like mighty convenient timing. I'm terrified that Declan will catch us and haul us back to Washington. I'm afraid Devlin will kill or capture me in Terra. Both of those things are near the top of my MOST HORRIBLE THINGS list.

But I'm more afraid of losing Jesse.

I can't survive without him in either place. Things between us are getting strained, and I want to shore that up before I insist on leaving again. Maybe Jesse will see Declan, too. Then he'd believe me for sure.

For the first time in my entire life, I choose *not* to tell my brother about something I fear. I choose to let him live his life and not destroy it again. I choose to be brave and to trust his judgment.

"I know you love me, J, and I love you, too. We're a set. No Jesse without Alora, no Alora without Jesse."

"Let's go see a few movies tonight after work," he says.

We always sneak into a second movie after we pay for the first. It's not about the second movie. It's about pretending, even for just an hour or two, that our life is normal. That the riskiest part of our existence is sneaking into a movie for which we haven't paid. Once we got confused and ended up watching this movie about all these old women squabbling over a vase. It was one of my fondest memories—laughing at all the terrible dialogue and amateur acting. We'd have been upset that we paid for a movie that bad, if we'd paid for it.

"I'd like that." I grin.

He hugs me and walks into the office building. I watch until I can't see him anymore. Only then do I head over to Perry's for the lunch shift. Tips are even better today, and I stay for late hits, so it's already almost four when I walk out the door. I decide to wait on the bench outside and meet Jesse here instead of heading home.

"If you aren't careful, they're going to start charging you rent for this bench," John says.

I glance up and smile. He sits down next to me.

"You are *really* late for lunch today if you're only now getting it. Like, your staff might file a claim for hostile working conditions."

"Don't give your brother any ideas. He looks like a rabble-rouser, a natural leader of men, but remember. I took a chance on him when no one else would."

"And he's late to work on the second day." I scrunch up my nose. "Sorry, that was my fault."

He angles his head. "Is everything okay?"

"I just haven't been sleeping well lately. Nightmares. I'm supposed to get a sleep study. Apparently their solution to me not sleeping well is to have me sleep in an unfamiliar place with a lot of wires and whatnot poking out of my body."

He snorts. "Science. I swear, half the time their solution is worse than the problem."

"And the other half of the time, they're guessing."

"Exactly. Well, I hope you get some answers. What do you dream about? Your parents?"

I shake my head. "It's mostly the same dream over and over. I'm in another place, and I'm running from my past." That seems vague enough, and plausible without giving too much away. Jesse would be proud.

"My mom had bad dreams," John says.

"Did they stop? Or does she still have them?"

He slumps on the bench next to me. "I guess you could say they stopped. She had them for a long time, and finally my dad committed her. While she was receiving treatment, she died."

A chill runs down my spine. That story sounds close enough to my own that it makes me uneasy. When I look at John, though, the raw emotion in his face eases my anxiety. I think about what Dr. Agour said. When someone in your family suffers, the loved ones don't know what to do. They suffer, too.

I reach over and take his hand in mine without think-ing. Our fingers interlace, and since I barely know him, it should feel weird, but it doesn't.

It just feels right.

And unlike Terra, I chose this. My feelings are entirely my own.

The buzzing from my phone jolts me out of my daze. "Did you come out here to do something?"

He straightens, but doesn't let go of my hand. "I did. I need to run to Best Buy for some supplies. Want to come with me?"

I pull out my phone and notice it's nearly five o'clock. ALMOST DONE. EAT AND THEN MOVIE?

"That actually sounds kind of nice." Normal. I haven't done much normal in my life. "But sadly, I can't today."

John glances at Perry's. "Another hot date?" I may be imagining it, but he seems annoyed.

"Nah." I stand up, letting go of his hand in the process. "J said he's nearly done for the day. We didn't get to celebrate his new job yet. We thought we'd go get dinner and catch a movie."

"I take it that, as the boss, I'm not invited?"

He wants to come? Surprisingly, I'd like to have him there, but not tonight. Jesse and I have had a weird enough couple of days. We need some time alone to find our equilibrium. Also, we need to talk about what we should do. If I really am paranoid, we should stay. But if I'm not, if Terra's real, and a man is impersonating a social worker to hunt us down, he might have murdered our parents. He could be after us right now, and not to haul us back to Washington.

John can't hear all the things we need to discuss.

"Sorry, but this is invite only, party of two. Next time, for sure."

A tall man with dark hair walks past me and my heart races until I realize it's not Declan. When John heads for his car, I suppress an urge to hide in the bushes while I wait for Jesse. When my big brother finally comes down, it's closer to five-thirty.

We walk toward the bus stop, but my steps speed up incrementally until we're practically jogging.

"Whoa, there. You seem jumpy."

"I saw Declan yesterday, in this shopping center. Coming back here and sitting around for an hour and a half wasn't good for my mental health."

"I think it was," he says. "If it really was Declan, and he knew you were here, wouldn't he have caught you by now? You've been here all day."

I want to believe him, but I can't help biting my lip and looking over my shoulder, from the time we reach the bus stop until we hop off at the movie theater. I insist on using my tip cash to pay for nachos, a piece of pizza for each of us, and Icees. Then for good measure, I order a large popcorn, too. We head in to watch the newest movie by that guy who left Saturday Night Live. It's just as dumb as every other movie he's ever made, but that's the point, I think.

We have a fun time tossing popcorn into the air to try and catch it. Of course Jesse's tosses all go right into his mouth while mine scatters all over the ground.

We duck into a second movie about a cataclysmic earthquake as soon as the ridiculous comedy ends. We have to wait a bit for the previews to start, but it gives us a chance to chat.

"I'm going to dig into this Declan character," he says. "See what I can find out about him. Maybe you should call Danica and ask her if she has any relatives who might have filled in for her or something."

I sigh, but I don't argue. By the time the movie ends, it's twenty minutes until midnight and we're both exhausted. "No work tomorrow, though, right?"

"True," he says. "I've only been working a normal job for two days, and I'm already looking forward to sleeping in on Saturday. Pathetic."

We sit through the credits and let everyone else filter out so we don't have to wait in a line just to shuffle out of the room. Plus we have fifteen more minutes until the last bus, so there's no rush. "You do like the job, though, right?"

"I love it." It's dark, but even in the low light, I know he's smiling.

When we stand up to leave, only three other people are left in the theater. It's still so dark, I can barely make out the steps in front of me, much less what the three people on the front row look like, but when I walk past them, I glance over.

And freeze.

I claw frantically at Jesse's hand. Jesse may have only met him once, but I can tell from the look on his face that I'm not being paranoid.

It's him.

"Declan Rosenbaum." My voice is flat, emotionless. But inside, inside I'm reeling. Terror, hatred, and the tiniest bit of relief that I haven't been imagining him.

He smiles, but his eyes are resolved. The other two men with him stand up, and I spare a glance for each of them. One is taller, even, than the massive Declan. He's wearing a black jacket and dark blue jeans. In September. In Houston. The other man is short, but wide, like a moveable brick wall. He even has a blocky face. The reddish hair cropped close to his head doesn't help.

"You came with goons? Strange that Washington's social services would send you three, and on a Friday night, no less." Jesse sounds flippant, but the wobble in his voice belies his confidence. "You need three grown men to bring in two truant teenagers?"

"We aren't here to bring you in," Declan says. "That was never the goal."

"Then why are you here?" I ask.

"Why don't you follow us outside, and we'll tell you all about it while we take a little drive," the guy in the black jacket says.

"I'd rather not," Jesse says, "but thanks for the offer."

The blocky guy grabs Jesse's arm. "We aren't offering, kid, we're telling."

"Easy," I say. "We'll go with you. No reason to rip his arm off." I glance at Jesse and then back at Declan, but I think Jesse understands.

He shakes his arm free and begins to walk down the last few steps toward the exit. The men allow me to walk ahead with Jesse, but the second our feet touch the ground floor, we sprint to the left and out the exit that takes us behind the theater. We've had to run before, when someone noticed we snuck into a movie.

It was a pretty good plan. We should've escaped. It was only three minutes until midnight, and we'd have just made the bus, too.

Except for one thing.

Declan is telekinetic. Not just on Terra, but here on Earth.

His power is weak, nothing like mine there, but I'm not accustomed to watching for it here, and I have no powers on Earth to counteract his. I don't turn back until Jesse cries out. Declan's eyes are still glowing, and I realize that he knocked my brother to the ground.

His bodyguards are closing in.

"This is going to be fun." The blocky man rubs his meaty hands together.

"Remember, your directive has changed," Declan says. "The girl is our target now, not him."

I don't know whether to turn around and try to free Jesse, or to run for help.

As if he senses my indecision, Jesse yells, "Alora, run!"

I sprint about ten steps before an unseen force yanks on my leg. I sprawl face first onto the concrete. We were idiots for running out the back where no one could see or hear us.

I struggle, but my leg won't budge. I can't sense the Binding, but I know it's there. Declan reaches my side, leans over, and grabs the back of my shirt, releasing the Binding and hauling me to my feet. "I don't know why I bother bringing those idiots along at all when I always have to do everything myself."

He spins me around, his enormous hand digging into my back, and shoves me toward Jesse. He pushes me down, and I cling to my big brother as though somehow he's less helpless than I am.

"Grief didn't work when your parents died. Terror from your sister's attacks at the group home didn't crack you either. Each time, it was like, with the two of you to protect each other, you weren't quite desperate enough." Declan's eyes are bright, almost mad.

What's he saying? *He* was behind my parents' deaths? And the group home?

"We hoped that the fear and trouble from running away might Wake your brother." Declan hisses. "But then when it didn't help, we went to round you up again. . .and you disappeared." He swears under his breath. "A year and a half down the drain before we located you again." Declan circles us slowly, tapping his lip with his finger. "Please try to remember that we made every effort to do this in a gentler way before we wound up here. It's not like we went straight to extreme measures. The problem is, you feel stronger together, like you can take on the world. To Wake, you must feel powerless. You can't have any options at all. Utter despair and terror are the only things that work."

I look up at him. "What are you talking about?"

He laughs bitterly. "I thought you knew."

My breath hitches. "You're Devlin Rochester."

"Precisely." He peers at me closely. "My source was correct. You *are* her. I can't recall you at all, of course, since men don't dream of Terra, but she assures me you're the Warden."

"Who?" I ask. "Who assures you?"

He tsks at me. "A magician never reveals his secrets. Or is it a journalist that never reveals his source? Either way, I can't tell you how I know. I just do."

"You Lift here?" Jesse's eyes are wide. "On Earth? It's all real?"

"Oh, I'm much stronger on Terra, and even that is a fraction of what's coming once we get things squared away." He eyes me again, his eyes tracking up and then back down.

Jesse pushes to his feet. "What do you want from us?"

Devlin turns toward him, as if just remembering he's there. "I don't need anything from you. You're just leverage. I'll admit, you were our target at first, but that's all changed now that we know the truth of who your sister is." He rubs his hands together.

"What does that even mean?" Jesse asks.

"I'm getting ahead of myself. We've been patient, but it's time to Wake you up. No more playing around."

"Wake me up?" I ask. "I'm wide awake."

"No. You aren't asleep, but you aren't Awake," he says. "We're wasting time with idle chit chat." He pulls out a gun and shoots Jesse in the foot. It happens so quickly that I can't quite process what happened.

Jesse falls back to the concrete, blood slowly forming a circle around him. He screams and screams, hunched over his foot. My heart breaks in two. I crouch down next to him, frantic to do something, but I have no idea what to do.

"No? Not enough?" Devlin aims his gun at Jesse again, this time at his chest.

I leap in front of it. "No, please, please don't shoot. I'll do anything."

"Just do it already." Devlin lowers the gun and grabs my shoulder. "Wake up!"

Tears stream down my face. I can't look away from the blood gushing out of Jesse's foot. Will he ever walk right again? How bad was the damage? How will I get him to the hospital? "I have no idea what you're talking about. I'll do it, anything, just tell me what to do!"

"That's the problem with the Isis pansies." He swears. "If you don't tell someone who they really are, how can you get away with acting superior and holier than thou? Isn't lying just as bad as any of the other sins in this world?"

My mind spins senselessly. I want to wake up and discover that it's all a terrible nightmare, my very first one. He keeps telling me to wake up, and I've never wanted to listen so badly in my life.

"Perhaps we should try another angle," the man in the black coat says. "Maybe we should focus on her. Perhaps injury to her brother isn't enough of a threat to her personally. Did any of the other children in the orphanage ever succeed in doing any . . . specific damage?"

Devlin looks at me, lying on the ground with my arm around Jesse, and then back at the man in the black coat.

He's quiet for a moment, but then he nods. "She'll hate us, but I'm not sure that can be avoided at this point."

I don't know what he intends until the blocky man grabs me by my shoulders and drags me to the ground. He holds my arms and back flat against the ground while the man in the black coat looms over me, his hands on the button on his jeans.

Jesse moans. "Stop." He draws up to a sitting position, his eyes filled with a helpless rage. "Stop right now!"

The man in the black coat doesn't listen. His pants have dropped down to his knees and he leans over me. I lift one leg and kick at him, but he dodges me easily. "Sometimes my job isn't so bad. Not so bad at all. You're nice to look at, and I like young ladies."

Bright blue light floods the parking lot and the man flies backward, his head cracking into the concrete.

"Bravo," Devlin says, "but your idea worked on the wrong sibling, Phillip. Even so, I'll take any progress."

The blocky man releases me and steps back.

Jesse crawls toward me, dazed. "What just happened?"

"You Lifted him off me," I say, "just like I've always described. You're telekinetic, J. I think that's what they're talking about when they say they want me to Wake up. They want me to access my powers here, on Earth."

"Try, Alora. Please."

Devlin's listening with interest. But I've tried thousands and thousands of times to use my powers. Of course I have. I've done everything the same way I do it in Terra, only here, nothing happens.

Devlin pulls his gun back out. "I worried this might be the only way."

"Don't shoot me," I say. "I'll try harder."

"The problem, princess, is that I think you already *have* tried your best."

"I can do more," I say.

"Go ahead, then."

I look at Devlin. He has a nicely shaped face, commanding champagne eyes, nice hair, and a powerful build, especially for his age. He's gorgeous for an older man, if I'm being impartial.

And I've never wanted to hurt anyone in my life as badly as I want to hurt him.

I focus on the world around me. The concrete beneath my fingers, sticky with Jesse's blood. Devlin, the blocky man, Jesse, and Phillip's slumped form are obscured by shadows, but they're all visible.

But I can't sense them. I try, but it's like nothing is there, not like I can feel things around me on Terra. I focus on Devlin's head and will it to Lift from his body, but nothing happens.

"We've wasted years already. We're out of time." Devlin motions to the blocky man, who approaches us. "Besides. If they don't already know, Isis will know who you are any day."

Jesse's eyes flare again, and Devlin's gun flies away from his hand. Devlin laughs. "You've been Awake for ten seconds, son. You're no match for me. If I want to kill you, I don't need a firearm to do it." Devlin's eyes shine with golden light and the gun flies right back into his hand. "I use a gun because it's easier for law enforcement to explain the injury. That makes cleaning up the official reports less messy. It amuses me that humans have created such ways to kill, in the absence of the powers God gave us. Powers that were taken to shift the course of humanity, to bring peace, allegedly, and look what we've done without them. We removed the claws from the monsters, but the monsters still have teeth. No one can save the wolf from himself."

I'm beginning to think Devlin's insane.

Jesse's eyes flare again, and Devlin's gun zips through the air and into Jesse's hand. "I don't care how effective it is, as long as it works." Jesse fires the gun at Devlin's head.

The gun kicks as the bullet flies out, almost knocking the firearm from Jesse's hand, but I think Jesse's aim was true.

Only, the bullet doesn't ever connect with its intended target.

It stops and then drops to the ground. Jesse fires off three more shots, and Devlin smiles at him the entire time. Clink, plink, clink. All three bullets fall, harmless, to the asphalt.

"Go ahead," Devlin says.

The blocky man walks up behind us, grabs Jesse by the shoulders, lifts him up and bashes his head against the wall. Jesse slumps down to the pavement, blood oozing through his hair and down his neck. His eyes aren't tracking anymore.

I stand transfixed, unable to move, unable to process anything that's happening. Everything around me, the night sky, the stars, the monsters who came with Devlin, the man himself, the concrete beneath me, it all falls away. My focus narrows to the one person in the universe whom I really care about. My anchor in a dark ocean.

Jesse's body spasms at first, and then slowly goes still.

My world narrows again, to a tiny pinpoint, to Jesse's face, blood marring his beautiful nose, his big blue eyes staring blankly at nothing. Then, just as quickly, the world snaps back into focus and I see and feel *everything*.

Thousands of tons of concrete. Cars, so many cars for this time of night. Dumpsters filled with garbage a dozen feet behind me. Two disgusting men staring at me intently, and the heartbeat of my brother.

It stutters. I sense it in a way I never have before.

Maybe I can take his injury on myself. Maybe I can Heal him.

I lean over and feel the bump on his head, slick with blood. It's the size of a plum, and I feel for it, for the injury, but his heart is barely beating, and I don't know what I'm doing. His heart pumps in a staccato rhythm and then stutters and then beats again.

One last time.

I close my eyes and imagine my own head swelling up and his healing, but nothing happens. I imagine his heart beating and nothing happens. I take his face in my hands and try to force him to see me, but his eyes are empty. Is his soul already gone? I focus on his heart and squeeze, and it moves. I repeat that over and over, but it just makes blood evacuate faster from the hole created by the bump on his head.

My soul is shredded, my mind shattered. My heart —explodes.

When I look around, Declan is the first thing I see. Declan, who killed Jesse just to Wake me up. Fury floods my entire body, every cell of my being writhing with a rage so intense I don't know where it can possibly go.

Declan won't just die. He will suffer. He will *writhe*.

I Lift him off the ground. He shoves against me pitifully, like a puppy pawing at my shoe. I laugh. The sound that emerges should frighten me, but I'm beyond that. I Lift him a few feet into the air, hovering over me. I shove his arms and legs apart, as far apart as I can.

"Have you heard the phrase 'drawn and quartered'?" I ask. I don't wait for an answer, since he's screaming and barely conscious. "It's an old punishment. I thought it was barbaric when I studied it in history, but I think I've gained a new appreciation for its purpose."

I focus on his hand. "Do you have any idea what you stole from me?" I snap the bone of the smallest finger on his left hand. Then I Lift his ring finger, and snap it too. His screaming is entirely incoherent, which bothers me. I release him for a moment. "You killed my brother. You will pay for that, and I want you aware of why."

He thrashes around in the air. "I had no choice. If you didn't Wake, hundreds of thousands of people would have died. It's in the prophecy. You loved your brother and I commend you for it, but the world needs you. This is bigger than any one person."

Except he's wrong. It's not bigger than one person. The world and all its occupants can *burn*. What has the world ever done for me? I'll raze it all to the ground, now that the only person I've ever loved is gone. Actually, forget making him suffer. Every second Declan lives feels like an affront to justice, like a luxury he doesn't deserve.

I snap every bone left in his hands, and every bone in his feet, and I smile as Declan's body contorts soundlessly.

"He wouldn't have wanted this to happen," Declan moans. "What would your brother want you to become?"

I stop, caught by his words. Jesse wouldn't want me to become a monster like this man I'm torturing. What would he tell me to do, if he were still alive?

A sharp blow hits me on the side of my head.

Splitting pain radiates outward from it.

I forgot about the blocky man. How could I forget about Declan's goon? I try to think around the drilling feeling inside my skull and realize through the throbbing that my face is being dragged across the ground. I didn't Bind Declan in place, so he's no longer hanging in the air. Where did he go? I force my head up from the ground and look upward at my assailant. Instead of the blocky man, I'm being dragged along the concrete by a shaggy brown bear, his *paw* wrapped around my ankle.

No time to think further, and I can barely lift my head, much less search for Declan.

Concrete surrounds me. The dumpsters, the cars. My hands shake, and the ground around me begins to vibrate. From the corner of my eye, I see Declan, collapsed in a heap on the ground. His broken hands and feet won't hold his weight, so he's slithering away from me on his belly as quickly as he can. Fitting, actually. Writhing, wriggling, like the snake that he is.

I Lift the bear-man away from me and slam him against the wall. At the same time, I reach for everything around me. The concrete, the building, the dumpsters, all of it. I crawl over to my brother, and pull him onto my lap. I cradle his head in my arms, and then I tear the world apart, piece by piece.

Chunks of concrete, light poles, I pulverize it all and hurl every last bit of it at the monsters who destroyed me, piling the debris up so high that it reaches the same level as the top of the theater.

When I'm sure there's no way anyone could have survived, I stop. Everything I've Lifted and haven't used falls to the earth. I lean over my brother's body, draw it close, curl around it, and close my eyes, ready to leave this world, too. No point in staying here when my heart has already stopped beating.

Except I can't just do nothing. It's not in me to quit.

I close my eyes. I feel my brother's body slowly, quietly, calmly, until I can feel his heart, his lungs, his stomach. I gently reach for his heart and squeeze. I squeeze it again and again, until I can feel the little blood that remains pumping through his veins. I'm still doing that when the ambulance arrives.

The woman who hops out of the back of the ambulance looks at me, and then takes in the rubble and the piles of concrete. Luckily, she can't see the three dead bodies. "What happened here?" she asks.

"His heart," I say. "It stopped. Can you help him?" I feign CPR.

She nods. To her credit, she jumps to work without any more questions, which is good, because I'm light-headed. I slump backward as spots dance in front of my eyes. I can't seem to remain conscious, so I hope what I've done is enough.

I fear it isn't.

❧ 18 ❧

TERRA

Kahn didn't eat dinner with us last night, because we didn't eat dinner together at all. Once the siege began, troops were required at all times to man the walls and defend against incursions by the thousands of Amun fighters who overran the evacuated city. Jesse brought food and we ate as we walked along the top of the wall. Sterling Castle itself and the surrounding courtyard was well built, with two-thirds of the circumference built right on the edge of the top of a very steep hill. As a result, protecting those areas uses few resources. In order to reach the top of the wall overlooking the drop-off, a man would need to climb up hundreds of feet of rock, and then scale the sheer face of a fifty-foot wall. They might Lift someone, so occasional guards are posted, but they wouldn't make easy inroads.

The remaining one-third of the wall shelters against Sterling City below. Maintaining that wall requires constant effort. Devlin's men haven't launched a full-scale assault yet, but every attempt has been focused on that segment. So far, Devlin's testing the edge of our defenses like a snake flicking its tongue.

We're in the dining room going over the long-term strategy with all the Unit Leaders. "The problem is, we didn't have enough time." Duncan slams his hand down on the table, and I watch as my eggs and biscuit jump into the air.

"We did what we could," Jesse says. "At least we evacuated the city. That had to be our focus."

"I hate that we didn't clear the city of all the supplies." Duncan begins pacing. "Everything we left, every chicken, every bag of grain, goes straight into our enemy's belly."

"I doubt that will make a difference, though, surely," I say.

Jesse, Kahn, and Duncan look sharply in my direction, and several of the others cover their mouths to keep from laughing.

Kahn says, "Most wars are won or lost through the soldiers' bellies."

I raise my eyebrows, but say nothing else. Clearly everyone here thinks I'm an idiot. And when it comes to warfare, they're probably right.

"Flynn and Stefan, you'll cover the daytime on the North Wall," Duncan says. "Pratt will cover the night, and I'll assist him as needed. Adaniel, you have the East Wall by day, and Francis, you have it by night. Seth will cover the West by day, Quincey by night. On the South Wall, I want Beren by day, Nathaniel by night. Jesse, you're in charge of the front gate. Kahn, you and Alora will fill in anywhere that needs help or where the team needs a break. As you all know, we did manage to bring our entire army inside these walls. That means we have thirteen thousand men at our disposal. Devlin is surrounding us with almost twenty thousand. We believe he will hold off on a full attack until his reinforcements arrive."

"Don't we have more troops coming?" Kahn asks. "Ours should arrive first, since they don't have as far to travel, which would put us in a hammer and anvil situation, hopefully."

"We should have troops on the way," Duncan says, "but the surrounding cities are all dealing with the integration of the refugees from Sterling. The other Unit Leaders want to keep enough men to protect their own fortifications, and I can't fault them for that. As you know, several of the Isis castles are farther from our capital than most of Amun's outlying castles. Sterling Castle and Rochester Castle are both centrally located and not divided from one another by much distance."

"Our plan is to what, then?" Stefan asks. "Just hold on and hope more of our troops arrive than theirs? What will the troops do when they do arrive?"

Jesse snorts. "Did you hear Kahn? Have you ever seen a hammer hit an anvil?"

"When our troops arrive, we'll attack, then?" Stefan asks. "How will we coordinate that?"

Duncan raises one eyebrow. "Pigeons, unless you have a better idea."

Stefan stands. "I do. Conway Castle will send troops soon, but we should strike now, when Amun's followers aren't expecting it. Bring this battle to them immediately."

"And in so doing, throw away our biggest advantage," Kahn says. "We can whittle away more of their troops every day through arrow slits and from behind the safety of our walls. We can pick them off in consistent numbers while not losing any of our own men. We may not have cleared all the supplies, but we have enough for a prolonged siege and we hold the position of power right now, even outnumbered by more than seven thousand troops. You think we should throw that advantage away?

Fling our gates open and just rush toward them with our swords drawn?"

Stefan sits back down and mumbles. "I hate doing nothing."

"It's not in our nature to sit," Duncan says. "But sometimes we all have to do things that are not in our nature." He glances toward Jesse, who has laid his head down on the table.

"Are you alright, son?"

"I'm just tired," Jesse says.

My head snaps toward him immediately. "Are you warm?" I reach out my hand and touch his forehead.

It's hot.

I want to break down and sob right here.

I close my eyes and think back to when I was only six years old. My mom was the one constant in my life. She worked hard, and I was frequently left to entertain myself, but she loved me, and she was there for me. Always. Until one day, she spiked a fever. She became progressively hotter over the next two days until on the third day, she died. Just like that.

Gone.

I force myself to look my brother in the eye. He can't have the Wasting. He can't. No one knows what causes it, and nothing can be done to stop it. Once you heat up, you die.

Simple.

Inexorable.

Unstoppable.

Except I'm older now, and I won't accept it.

I stand up. No one meets my eyes, not even Duncan. "Jesse and I need to see every Healer you have. Send them to his room." I turn to Kahn. "I'll meet you at the front gate in an hour."

No one objects as Jesse and I walk out of the meeting.

When we reach the hall, I ask, "Any chance this is a joke? You just stood too long in front of the fire and thought it would be a good way to get out of gate duty? Because I will totally trade with you. I'll take all your shifts."

Jesse smiles, but it's half-hearted. When we reach his room, Lansing and Lincoln are already there.

"Oh good," I say. "You came quick. Jesse's hot."

Lansing and Lincoln look at each other and then glance at Jesse. They exchange a knowing glance and ice runs through my veins.

"Lie down for us, Jesse, and we'll conduct an examination."

Jesse lies down on his bed and Lansing stands near his head, with Lincoln near his legs. Lansing places his hands on Jesse's head. Lincoln places his hands over Jesse's shins. They both close their eyes, but the light shines through anyway. They're delving him.

They both step away at the same time. Lincoln looks at Lansing and then they look at me. After only a moment, they each drop their eyes. "Maybe it's best if we wait for the other Healers."

"It's the Wasting," Jesse says. "Pretending it isn't won't change anything. It's only going to get worse."

I can't help thinking about the little boy, Joshua, whose father wouldn't see what was right in front of him. Even so, with that memory fresh in my mind, I can't help myself. "There has to be something we can do, even if it is—" I gulp. "—the Wasting. Someone must have survived it at some point in the last thousand years, or there must be something we can try. Anything."

The brothers' faces are grim. "In several thousand years of records, no one has ever halted a confirmed case of the Wasting. If a patient exhibits a high fever, he or she dies."

I think about their room full of books. I believe that they've combed through years and years of research, but that doesn't mean they know everything. I can't give up. "Someone has to be the first. What's the leading theory?"

Jesse stands up and walks over to me. He doesn't say a word. He just reaches out and hugs me tight. "It's going to be okay."

I can't prevent my tears. "How? How will this be okay?"

"Dad will keep you safe, and maybe that's why we needed to find you now. Now you two won't be alone. . .when I go."

I shake my head so hard that Jesse pulls away. "No. I refuse to believe it."

Two other Healers arrive then, evaluate him, and come to the same conclusion. And then two more.

When I find myself sobbing on Jesse's shoulder, I realize I've placed him in the horrible situation of having to comfort me, instead of being able to grieve himself. I take a few jerky breaths and force myself to stop crying. We have a war to fight, and a very bad man to kill. I can't sit in here and cry for three days while thirteen thousand men fight a war for me.

"I'm sorry," I tell Jesse. "I will come up with something, I promise. I haven't given up, but I'll back off for now."

He smiles. "I'm not gone yet, and I have work to do."

"No way." I point at his bed. "You need to rest."

"It doesn't help."

I know he's right; he's living on borrowed time already. I don't object when he follows me out and walks toward the gate to discuss fortifications with the guards on duty. I'm still watching him, trying to get myself together, when Kahn finds me. "Are you ready to take a tour of the perimeter?"

"Sure," I say.

"I'm sorry." He doesn't say anything else, and I'm glad.

I'm holding on by a thread as it is. "Thanks."

I struggle to keep up with him as we head for the North Wall, the side that faces the city. The side that's under attack. I'm short of breath by the time we reach the top.

Smoke wafts out of many of the chimneys in the evacuated city. Devlin's army certainly didn't waste any time making themselves right at home. I fume at their presumption, at the violation of all those people's homes, the use of their private possessions, but there's nothing I can do, so I try to let it go. I'm letting go of *everything* lately. I clench my fists.

Kahn points to the men weaving together a ladder. "See there?"

I nod.

"Once they're done with that one, and a few dozen more, they'll go up at the same time. It's harder for us to fight off simultaneous attacks."

"What will we do?"

Kahn gestures behind us, to the metal fire pits spaced every fifteen feet or so along the perimeter. "First, hot tar. It usually incapacitates or kills the men climbing up the ladder." He grabs an arrow from one of the racks lining the back wall of the walkway. "A flaming arrow will destroy the ladder entirely. Anyone dumb enough to climb it after it's been doused in tar will burn to death, too. Sometimes we wait, hoping to wipe out a few more with the same effort. It only works with very green soldiers."

What a depressing thought.

A few dozen feet down I see men climbing the wall without a ladder. "What's going on there?" I ask.

He walks toward them. He points at the man standing at the bottom of the wall. "He's Binding hand-holds, and painting them, one at a time, so that everyone can see them. He's a pretty powerful Lifter, judging by the size of his Bindings."

The few times I've taken someone's life, it has made me sick. Not once in seventeen years have I ever *wanted* to mortally harm someone. But I look at that man below and I want it—I want to end his life, so his men can't follow him up and fight *my* men, kill *my* men.

"What should we do?" I ask.

Kahn shrugs. "We can't burn Bindings, or eliminate them either. We usually station a few men to pick off anyone brave enough to climb up until they quit, and our archers try to pick off the one making them—they disappear if he dies. But they're mostly practicing right now, making sure we're staying at full force. Wearing us out for the real attack to come."

Wearing us down slowly, with constant little fires, so we won't be strong when the real attack comes.

Like the Wasting is doing to Jesse right now.

Except here, today, I can do something. I can fight back against this. I focus on the man Binding and painting, and I Lift him out. . .and drop him. The man's eyes turn toward me with horror. He can see that I'm a woman, the light spilling from my eyes giving away that I'm the one who sent him off.

He counters me, Lifting himself enough that his descent is slow.

I lean farther out over the wall and I Lift a few rocks. Just as Kahn taught me, I pretend he's a black table, and I fling the rocks at him. I assume he'll block them, as we learned yesterday, since he's good at Bindings and slowing his own fall.

He doesn't.

He gasps and falls to the ground, bleeding from the holes I created with my rocks. The painted Bindings collapse.

I fall back, shaking uncontrollably. "What did I do?"

"What was your plan when you flung rocks at him?" Kahn asks. "Didn't you do exactly as you intended?"

"Why didn't he block them?" I try to dispel the image of the man, collapsed, bleeding out from my actions.

Kahn takes my shoulders in his hands. "This isn't a game, Alora. Those men out there plan to kill every single one of us, and they're all here because they want to kill, or capture and torture, *you*. They'll fight the rest of us, but only because we want to keep you safe. Whatever your father thinks about Devlin's plans, the rank and file with Amun want you dead. Each one of those men has some amount of strength. That man was probably great at Bindings, which is why he was here, trying to breach our wall. Since he didn't employ them when you attacked, he was probably terrible at blocks. Most people have both talents and weaknesses. You've eliminated one of their best Binders. That's good for us. You might have saved dozens of lives. That's exactly what we've been tasked to do, by the way. Our goal is to get their numbers down any way we can, with minimal risk to our soldiers."

"It's what you'll be doing?"

Kahn nods.

"It's awful to know you've killed someone." I think about Robert. And now this nameless man.

"I said I'll be doing it. . .I didn't say I'd sleep great afterward."

I follow Kahn for the next few hours, helping people on the various walls and even lending a hand to Jesse at the gate. I try to remember what Kahn said, that every one of them is here to kill me, but I cringe every time one of them dies. The Followers of Amun may mistreat women, and they may want to kill me, but they're still people. People who won't ever wake up again, thanks to us.

"You hate it," Jesse says softly.

I frown. "Hate it?" That he's dying? Of course I do.

"Warfare." He clasps his hands behind his back. "I can tell. It's killing you slowly, just to watch."

"I did a little more than watch." I tell him. Besides, warfare isn't killing me as fast as the Wasting is killing him.

"This is my first war too, but I've heard it helps to look at it like a game. Dad said that if you pretend it's a training exercise, that it's not real, that you can do what you need to do and it doesn't hurt so badly."

His advice isn't too far from Kahn's, about pretending I'm hurling balls at a table.

Neither trick helps much.

Yelling on the east side of the North Wall has us running up to see what's happening. There aren't dozens of ladders this time—there are over a hundred. Men climb the ladders like ants evacuating a ruined anthill, rung over rung, pouring onto the wall. Amun soldiers are mowing down the Isis men on the top of the battlement. I close my eyes and feel for each ladder. I try to forget that people are on them, living people. I inhale and exhale once, and think about my men standing at the top, dying as these attackers close in. I owe my protection to those men. I yank on the ladders, and they all pitch forward at once, men flying to their deaths from every last one.

I glance around and see the results of the last attack. Seven of our men dead. The man closest to me is part of my new squadron. I learned this afternoon that he hates carrots, and he picks them out of his stew. Now he's dead, his eyes glazed over.

This isn't a game, and I can't hide from it. These men are dying for me, and I won't stand back and participate a little here and a little there. Not anymore.

"I need a box of those metal balls," I tell Kahn. "Can someone bring them to us?" I look out over the hundreds of Amun troops milling around below. "I think it's time we evened up the odds."

Kahn narrows his eyes at me, but he orders several men to return with as many of the balls as they can bring—and they do it quickly.

A few moments later, I ask the archers to take their positions and cover me. Once they're in place, I Lift several hundred balls at once. They're small, the size of a grape or maybe even smaller. I close my eyes and feel for the men below us. I feel their heartbeats, their breathing. I feel them shifting back and forth. For a moment, my resolve weakens. These are *people*, like me, like Kahn, like Jesse.

My brother, who's Wasting.

Life is short, and it's not guaranteed. All we have are our decisions.

And there's nothing I can do to stop my brother's death, but I can defend the men standing with me, the men who did nothing to provoke these attackers other than shelter me from harm. I *must* do whatever I can to protect them. So I send the balls over the wall and they hover for one beat, then two. Amun soldiers walk toward the wall, checking out the latest disturbance. More men emerge from the houses. They all want to know what's happening. Once I can sense enough targets for each and every one of the small steel projectiles, I fling them straight at the hearts of the soldiers below. A few dozen manage to block.

The rest of the soldiers drop immediately, all at once, silently, except for the unharmed men around them.

Blood pours from the holes in their chest cavities. The Healers might save a few, but not many. By the time I line up for another strike, Amun soldiers are fleeing their positions as quickly as they can. My second volley only kills a few dozen men. The rest have taken cover.

"That was brilliant," Kahn says. "Come with me."

Before word spreads to the other sections, I'm able to get off two quick volleys in three more areas. Thanks to my ability to sense the soldiers, I know that I've killed over a thousand men with my efforts. Unfortunately, now that I'm done, I feel ill.

Really ill.

Not from Lifting.

But because the reality of what I've done sinks into my soul. I rush over to a fire pit and bend over double behind it, retching. These men are someone's Jesse and someone's Duncan. Their families will grieve, and it will be all my fault, and not only because I propelled the projectiles through their chests, but *because I exist at all*. Because I'm threatening their world with destruction and they want to stop it.

I stand up and wipe my mouth a little too soon. I bend over again, still heaving, but this time there's nothing left in my stomach.

Kahn's glance is full of empathy and understanding. "For every single man you killed, one of my friends will live."

"I *hate* this."

He nods. "We didn't pick this fight."

He's right, but he's also wrong. There's something we could do to end it right now. Before I came, there wasn't a war. It's easy for Kahn to blame the Followers of Amun, but they only really object to one person.

Me.

A few moments later, men with food circulate. They offer me a hunk of bread and cheese, and a slab of ham. I take it. I force myself to eat, because if I don't eat, I can't help. I need to help, even if I'll never recover from the price of that aid.

After lunch, I'm notified that the army has prepared a battering ram. They're lining up to bring it against the front gate. I look at Jesse. Sweat pours freely down his forehead.

"I have an idea, Jesse."

He looks at me gratefully.

"Ask your men to step back."

"We need them there, to brace the gate."

"Give me a minute," I say.

I climb up to the highest point behind the gate, the guard lookout post, and I glance over. The men are lining up to bring the ram against the gate. I don't have much time. I locate the nearest vats of tar and Lift the two closest ones. I swing them out over the battering ram and pour the tar over the top of it, coating most of the men, and the entire wooden tree trunk. Kahn orders his archers to fire flaming arrows.

Jesse waves at me when I pass. "Thanks."

"I'm always here." Which only reminds me that he won't be.

Unfortunately, Devlin's soldiers quickly figure out that any time they congregate in large groups, my little balls appear. Maybe that's okay. "We're almost out of projectiles," Kahn says. "I've ordered the blacksmiths to shift all their efforts into making more."

I snort. "I wouldn't have imagined my contribution to

this war would be flinging tiny metal blobs, but I think we've done alright with them."

"You certainly have."

"You're too modest," I say. "You've thrown at least a hundred."

"Maybe not quite." He smiles. "But I'm trying to do my part. If you keep going like you are now, no one will even need me. Perhaps they'll remember me as your trainer."

I sock him in the arm. "Or they could remember you as the finest commander, after Duncan, of course."

"Why don't you call him Dad?" he asks.

I shrug. "My mom took me and hid me a long time ago, to prevent all this, I suppose." I gesture at the army encamped just outside the gate. "Or at least to delay it. I don't even remember having a father, so I guess it feels weird thinking of him like that."

"He's going to need you," Kahn says.

"When they decide to attack in full force?" I ask.

"Then too," Kahn says, "but that's not what I mean." He doesn't clarify, but understanding dawns.

Jesse.

Less than an hour later, Devlin inexplicably brings his entire force to bear. All at once, everyone's calling for us, and I don't know where to go.

"Maximum damage," Kahn says. He orders the men to bring as many of the metal spheres as they can find, and then runs up the steps to the North Wall, near the gate. I follow him up, but he stops and sends me back down. "I can only handle a few dozen at a time, but so can Jesse, Duncan, and Pratt. They've all come to rein-force me along this side. You take the northwest. Think you can handle that?"

I change directions. "If there aren't enough spheres, what do we use?"

"Arrowheads. Rocks. Anything you can find," Kahn says.

The troops clear a wide path for me as I walk up to the northwest steps alone. At first I think they're happy to see me, proud that I'm here to help, but then I notice the twist of their lips, the hunch of their shoulders, and the slant in their eyes.

They're afraid, but not of the attack.

They're afraid of me.

Several boxes of metal balls are waiting for me when I arrive. I Lift about two hundred and notice that I'm straining. That's odd. Yesterday I Lifted far more, and then Lifted hundreds and hundreds of weights. How can I be tiring already?

It's probably nothing. I hold the balls and focus on the ocean of men standing in front of me. I close my eyes so I can feel the men climbing the ladders, scrambling up the Bindings. Then I let them loose. Hundreds of men fall. I do the same thing three more times. Before I can start a fourth, a runner comes with a message. "They need you on the East Wall."

I frown at him. The East Wall stands above the sheer cliff. How could they need me there? I run down the steps, leaving the archers to manage without me. Several men break away to bring the nearly empty crates with all the remaining metal balls along.

By the time I reach the East Wall, it's almost overrun. Men in the blood red livery of Rochester Castle swarm the top of the wall, a few spilling down below. Men with swords hack away at one another in a bloody melee that's so much worse than a puncture wound to the heart.

I keep my eyes open this time, focusing on small batches on men with blood red coats. Since I'm not sending the balls so far away, it's much easier. I fling the same three or four dozen balls over and over, conserving my resources, but more men pour over the second I clear away the last. Adaniel, eyes alight, is fighting three invaders to my right. I dispatch them and call for him.

"Can you cover me? I need to reach the top of the wall to force the bulk back down."

He nods and jogs to my side. I'm lucky he's good with a sword. Two or three other men join him, and together they manage to fight our way upward, dragging me and my crates toward the top of the wall.

When I finally reach the overlook, I see hundreds of painted Bindings the men below are climbing up. My hands tremble. Sweat rolls down my brow, but I know what I need to do. They'd have figured out by now that I'm killing people in batches—with the balls. They'd be sheltering the men who made the Bindings—but not far away. The farther from the Bindings, the more power it draws.

I squint and search, spreading my senses out until I find it. A tent on the edge of the city, full of a dozen men, sitting in a circle. I line up the projectiles, and I fling them right through the tent walls—killing the men all at once. The Bindings disappear, and so many soldiers fall, each man screaming. The same thing that horrified me just this morning now brings me a sense of profound relief. Once I've eliminated the Bindings the soldiers of Amun painstakingly created, I Lift fifty or so balls at a time, flinging them as hard as I can at the soldiers who have climbed up.

Until I run out.

With the help of my troops, and a dozen or so metal projectiles, we go after the two hundred or so men who broke through before my arrival, preparing to clear the breach of the East Wall. Now that their reinforcements and way of retreat have been cut off, the soldiers yield their weapons quickly—great, prisoners.

Now we'll have even more mouths to feed. Won't Duncan be pleased. . .

Kahn calls me back to the North Wall next, and I want to sit down and cry. "I don't know if I can Lift any more," I say.

"I hope you can," he says. "We're almost overrun."

Again. When will it stop?

I drag in a ragged breath and follow him, climbing the stairs so slowly that Kahn takes pity on me. I'm not sure I quite believed that Lifting was the same as physical activity in terms of its physical drain on the body until today. Kahn slings me over his shoulder and carries me to the top. When I see the ocean of men before me, despair overwhelms me. I turn on my heel, but that action shows me the circle of brave Unit Leaders, standing in front of column after column of Isis men congregated here.

I have to try something, anything, or they'll all be at risk.

"Looks like his reinforcements have arrived," Duncan says.

"Ours haven't?" I ask, as if I don't already know the answer.

Kahn shakes his head.

I sigh. "I need every arrowhead, every rock, and every piece of rubble you can find."

Men scramble away and within a few moments, begin to reappear with crates, loaded with rocks, pebbles and misshapen lumps of metal in every shape and size. I'm pleased to see rings, pendants, and earrings scattered into the pile. At least the men understand the importance of what we're doing here.

"Clear some room," I say.

Duncan, Jesse, and Kahn's eyes bore into me. Everyone is counting on me. Everyone needs me.

I close my eyes and feel for the men, thousands upon

thousands, stretching down to the bottom of the city and beyond for almost a mile. I bring my focus in closer and feel for the rocks and metal bits in the bins. I'm so tired. The idea of Lifting it all makes me want to lie down and sob. But it's my exhaustion. . .versus the lives of all our men. It's not even a contest.

I open my eyes and look at the faces of the people I care about. I haven't known them long, but Duncan, Kahn, and my brother matter to me, more than anything. I inhale and exhale, and then I Lift as much as I can. It's only a few dozen rocks. I release them. Even exhausted, I can do more.

I have to do more.

I focus on the contents of every single crate, all eleven that have been brought. I think of my fear, my sorrow, and the injustice of the world we've all been placed into. I channel my rage at the fact that Jesse's Wasting and my inability to help. I focus on the fact that this is something I *can* do. I can Lift, I can rend, and I can save all these other soldiers, the men of Isis, the men who may be afraid of me but are still standing behind me.

I reach down deep, deep inside, and I *pull*.

The world around me begins to shake. The walls vibrate, the gate, and the soil below it. It feels exactly like it did during the Ascension, before I blacked out. Only this time, I don't have that luxury. I can't check out, I can't give in, it's not only my success on the line.

It's so much more.

That's when Jesse places his hand on my arm and the world shakes a little less. Duncan places his hand on my other arm. Only the contents of the boxes are shaking now. Finally, heat from Kahn stepping in close behind me warms my back. He reaches out his hand and places it on my shoulder and a surge of strength pulses through me, almost as if their presence grounds me.

I take a deep breath and Lift the contents of all eleven boxes. Thousands of projectiles ranging in size from a tiny pebble to my fist.

"Perhaps one crate at a time," Jesse says.

"This is the end for me. This will wipe me out," I say. "It needs to count."

I don't have the strength to identify individual targets, not this time. Matching up my assaults with specific targets may be what has left me this drained. So for now, I Lift the mass of improvised weapons higher and then launch toward the men nearest to the front gate. Although a few, a small few, block the attack, the rest of my projectiles find marks.

Once I've released the last one, I collapse and darkness swallows me whole.

❧ 19 ❧

EARTH

When I open my eyes, everything is white. Four snowy walls, a smooth, pristine ceiling. A single bed with a single pillow, covered in bright white sheets. Even the blanket folded across the bottom of the bed has no color. The small table near the bed, and the door on the opposite side of the room from the bed, are also painted white. My billowy nightgown, that I certainly didn't put on myself, is white cotton. The porcelain toilet near my bed is also snowy white, and I really need to use it, but I don't.

Because there's one thing in this room that isn't white.

A black camera dangles from the ceiling, its eye poised to spy on me no matter where I move. But worse than the endless white, and the camera, and the enclosed space, is the blank hole where knowledge of what happened to my brother would be. I open my mouth to shout at whomever is behind that camera. I want to demand answers to why I'm here, where this is, and where Jesse is.

For a moment, I wonder whether perhaps last night

290

was my first real dream. Perhaps Jesse's still alive. Maybe I had a complete mental break, and now I'm an inpatient.

Please, God, if there is a God, please let me be institutionalized.

Because if I am, maybe Jesse's still alive.

As I sit, holding my pee in for so long that my kidneys ache, glaring at the black camera, I consider how bad things are that my best case scenario is insanity. Finally, I can't hold it anymore. I take the white table and wedge it underneath the door handle, blocking the locked door, I hope. I toss the neatly folded blanket over the lens of the black camera, and finally, I pee.

I've barely stood up when the door flies open, the small white table clattering across the shiny white tiles of the pristine floor. So much for that idea.

A man dressed entirely in camouflaged fatigues enters the room, both his hands wrapped around a big black gun. He has closely cropped dark hair and eyes so dark they almost look black. His gun is trained on the space right between my eyes. "Put your hands in the air."

I don't comply. If I'm nuts, that's a tranq gun and I don't care whether he shoots me. If I'm not insane, well, shooting me might be doing me a favor. Unless Jesse miraculously survived. Maybe they resuscitated him.

"Turn and face the wall. Now."

I do not turn. An awareness I'm accustomed to feeling only on Terra steals over me. The taut, stressed contours of the man's body, the hard plastic of the table, the cold metal of the gun. I feel them here, on Earth, just as I always have on Terra.

If Terra's real, and if I can Lift here on Earth, then I'm not crazy. The idea threatens to break me. Because that means. . . "Who are you?"

He lifts the gun slightly and repeats his command. "Turn and face the wall."

"Why? What have I done?" I'm pretty sure I killed a few men, but I need to hear him confirm that.

"I have orders. Turn and face the wall, kid. I don't want to do it, but I'll shoot you in the head if I have to." I focus on the gun. It doesn't have darts in it, it has bullets. I feel them, cold, hard, full of powder. I could Lift the gun, Bind him in place, and walk out the door, but I have no idea what's on the other side.

I need answers, especially now that it seems unlikely I'm in a psych ward. Unless America has changed dramatically, there's not a single hospital where they rush in with guns and threaten to shoot patients.

This is a holding cell, and I'm the enemy.

"You think I'm afraid of being shot? I'm only here because someone who gives you orders wants something from me. Tell me where Jesse is, or better yet, bring him to me, and I'll tell you whatever you want to know."

The man touches his finger to his ear, walks to the toilet and flushes it, and then backs out of the room, closing the door behind him.

"I would have flushed that," I say to the camera. "If you hadn't rushed in before I had the chance."

I'm not sure how long I sit on the foot of the bed waiting, but eventually the door opens again. A tall man with dark blond hair and icy blue eyes enters, and he's not wearing khaki fatigues. He's wearing jeans and a deep blue polo shirt.

The haircut's different, but I know the face, and here, even here on Earth, he *practically glows*.

"Kahn?"

His eyes move up to meet mine slowly, and his entire body freezes, his nostrils flaring, and I know—I'm glowing for him, too.

Bizarre. Yeah, I'm aware.

Kahn's face. Kahn's body. Kahn's voice.

He doesn't ask how I know his name, which means he must know about Terra. Unsurprisingly. I mean, last night I destroyed the back of a movie theater and then passed out right after the medics helped me into an ambulance.

I ignore the glow and the weird cosmic pull, and I suppress the overwhelming desire I have to rush across the room and wrap my arms around his waist and press my lips against his. It's easier to do, since it's not my first exordium experience. "Why am I here? And what do you want?"

Kahn looks as if he's fighting his way through a fog.

Oh, boy, I know that feeling.

He crosses the room and gestures at the bed. "Okay if I sit?"

I nod.

"I'm with a group called the Followers of Isis. We're the good guys, I promise. It looks like you've already had some pretty extensive dealings with Amun. I thought I might be able to answer some questions for you."

"You're Isis?" On Earth as well as Terra, and he was clearly chosen because someone knows we're friendly on Terra. They're trying to manipulate me. They should know better than that—don't attempt to maneuver a kid who's been in the system. Seeing through that kind of BS is simpler than singing the ABCs.

He nods. "We clean up a lot of Amun's messes, and we were happy to discover that you survived last night." He doesn't mention Jesse. "I'd like to answer all your questions, and then I'm hoping you can help us, too."

"What do you want?" I ask. "Why am I locked up?"

"We aren't in the habit of detaining people, but when we found you last night. . .well, we need answers. A lot of answers."

I stand up and put my hands on my hips. It's hard to look tough in a white nightie. "You're the good guys? You can see where I was confused, what with the peeing on camera and the gun to my head."

"I'm sorry about all that. There was a misunderstanding up the line that we're working to clear up."

"Overcharging someone for coffee is a misunderstanding. Washing a red shirt with all your white clothes, that's a mistake. They're similar. If you misunderstand or make a mistake, it's no big deal."

Kahn swallows.

"A man in fatigues pointing a gun at my head and yelling for me to face the wall is not a misunderstanding." My fists clench, and I'm tempted to slam him against the wall. But I still need information. Information I'm sick of waiting to get.

"I'm so sorry about everything, Alora. Really, we all are. We're the good guys, I swear."

He used my name—Alora. Which means he probably knows I'm this stupid Warden. Now I just need to figure out what they plan to do about it. "The good guys don't have to *say* they're the good guys. They're out there saving people and doing good things. You're locking me in a room and threatening me."

"You must know me on Terra. Do you think I'm really so different here?"

He's doing it again, trying to manipulate me into trusting him because of how he treats me on Terra—and I have no way to know whether people really *are* the same in both places. But Jesse was the same. I'm the same. Devlin sure seems to be the same. So from my extensive sampling of three. . .

I know it's a ploy, and I don't trust him, but when I look at him I forget all of that.

His eyes are soft, his lips slightly parted. He's just as gorgeous here as he is there. He's just as fit, as clean cut, and as well spoken. Without meaning to, I sway toward him. He inhales quickly, and I want to reach for him. I want to touch his jaw, his shoulder, his arm.

I want him to touch me, too.

Clearly some infuriating force is still trying to hijack my feelings.

And these so-called *good guys* will take advantage of whatever force is at play, and that angers me most of all. Yet, I still want to believe him. Only my deep-seated distrust and skepticism of everyone and everything, honed from every single important event in my entire life, prevents it.

And the gun to the head. That didn't help.

"Where's my brother?"

"We found you both behind the movie theater. We came by ambulance because that's easier to explain to the authorities. We even brought a Healer." A muscle in Kahn's jaw twitches. "But in spite of our best efforts, it was too late to save Jesse."

"No," I say. "I don't believe you."

Kahn looks at his shoes. "We thought you might say that." He gestures at the camera. The door opens and a man dressed in a white lab coat wheels a stretcher through the door.

"No." I leap to my feet. I close my eyes tightly, willing this away, but when I reopen them, nothing has changed. "No, no, no." I shake my head. "The ambulance came. You said there was a Healer. You must have saved him."

Kahn reaches for my hand.

I jump away. "That's not my brother. It can't be."

Kahn stands and walks behind the stretcher. "I'm going to give you a little while. When you want me to come back inside, call for me."

The man in the lab coat follows Kahn out. I'm not sure how long I sit on the bed, staring at the stretcher that holds a body covered with a white sheet. Eventually,

I take the three steps that separate us and peel back the fabric.

It's Jesse, and it isn't.

It looks like him, and it doesn't.

I can't quite tell why it's not him, but he just feels wrong. I'm shaking my head, and I can't seem to stop. I start to shake, my hands first, and then my arms, and finally my entire body. I fall back on the bed and curl into a fetal position, my eyes still locked on my brother. He can't be gone, he can't. Because the world is all *wrong* without him.

Once, when we were really young, we had a garden. Mom, er, Debra—I have no idea how to think of her anymore—loved strawberries, and Jesse and I were barely old enough to help her pick them. We had two raised planter boxes full of strawberry plants, so we picked a big bowl of them almost every day for weeks. But sometimes when you grabbed a big, red, perfect berry, it collapsed in your hands. It looked fine, perfectly normal, but when your fingers closed around it—it was actually nothing but slimy seeds and strawberry skin. The snails, you see, would hollow the berry out. Everything good, everything that mattered, was gone. I'm just like that.

Nothing but seeds and skin.

I can talk and move and curl up on my side, and I look perfectly fine.

But inside there's nothing left.

I'm a hollow shell. At the slightest touch, I'll collapse.

I've never been in more desperate need of repair and refueling, but my anchor is gone. A ship without an anchor drifts. It crashes against the rocks or it's lost at sea and capsized.

Sobs wrack my body. I curl more tightly inward, my arms wrapping around my legs until I take up the least space possible. "You can't be gone, J. You can't. I can't survive it."

Eventually, my tears run dry. I have no idea how that could happen, but I guess a body can only make so many. I'm sure if I drink a glass of water, they'll come pouring back out. But something occurs to me then, once sobs no longer wrack my body.

On Terra, Jesse's Wasting.

Which means he's still alive.

I have two days until that's no longer the case.

No one in Terra ever gets ill. No one gets colds, or the flu, or a stomach bug. Other than cuts, scrapes, or other injuries, no one's body malfunctions. No one dies of old age. You die in battle, or you Waste, and that's it.

Suddenly it hits me. Jesse died here, and now he's Wasting there. Wasting is what happens in Terra when your body dies on Earth. It must be. How did I not see it before? It's like the puzzle Jesse said we could piece together, if only we saw enough parts of the bigger picture.

Somehow, Terra's a warped reflection of Earth. It must be, but how can I change that? And what does it mean that Jesse's still alive there? A desperate need drives me. I look at Jesse's body, a body that's still alive on Terra. Can I bring him over to Earth somehow?

Can I save him?

I think about the prophecy. I'm the Warden, or so they say. I'm supposed to end everything or begin it all. It's so unclear, but if anyone could change the Wasting, if anyone could bring someone from Terra to Earth, shouldn't it be me? I have more power than any Lifter. I'm the only female who can Lift.

And now I can Lift here on Earth—even more than I can on Terra.

But what if saving Jesse. . .destroys everything? What if it's the catalyst of this ending?

I look at my brother, and I realize that I don't care. No one on Earth has ever cared about us. Why should I care about any of them?

I'll burn the world down to bring him back, if that's what it takes.

And I won't even regret it.

I glance up at the camera. Isis should have the answers I need. I think about what they know about me already. They know I'm on Terra, but clearly Kahn clearly doesn't have memories of me there. Maybe they *don't* know that I'm the Warden or that I can Lift here.

If they find out, they might keep me in this box forever.

What answers could Kahn want from me? I haven't Lifted around him, and he hasn't asked me to. Declan, or Devlin, or whoever he was, could Lift here. I'm positive I can too, but can Kahn? Can the Followers of Isis? Declan said something about them being unwilling to do what it takes.

"I'm ready to talk."

After a few moments, Kahn steps through the door again. He glances at Jesse, whose body is now lying uncovered. His eyes shift from the body to me and back again, but ultimately he says nothing. He crosses the room and sits down beside me.

It's a struggle, as always, to ignore the powerful pull between his body and mine. I want to giggle and scoot next to him and kiss him on the mouth. With my brother's dead body a few feet away. I couldn't possibly hate the exordium and destiny more than I do in this moment. What kind of twisted fate would make me want to kiss someone while my brother's lying dead next to me?

"What do the authorities believe happened?" I ask, because it's an answer I can process right now.

"That's a good question. We have men and women placed within essentially all of the critical organizations. They doctor reports with the police, rubber stamp claims with insurance, and prepare appropriate releases for the press. In this case, I believe it was listed as a terrorist attack the police detected early and prevented from causing any significant harm. That sort of thing disappears quickly when you control the bureaucracy. But that doesn't mean that we don't need to know what actually happened."

And now we're back to what he needs from me.

"The men who attacked you were Amun operatives. You may have worked this out already, but all the men on Terra have telekinetic powers, while only a few key individuals on Earth do—always male."

I swear under my breath.

"I agree that it's not fair—I'm simply telling you how things work. Each person on Terra has a body here on Earth—males and females alike."

"I figured that out, yeah." Like two minutes ago, but he doesn't need to know that.

"Terra's quite small, which is alright because it houses only the humans who have the abilities of Lifting and Healing."

I don't understand. "What do you mean, it *houses* them?"

Kahn blinks. "Terra's a prison, basically."

I splutter. "Wait, a what?"

"I'm sorry. I'm making a mess of this. I don't usually introduce people to any of this, and typically it happens —I should start over."

"Who does introduce people?" And why didn't they come to talk to me? "Why are you here?" As if I don't know. They rushed him in here to try and lower my guard. Good guys? Yeah right.

"I should start at the beginning, really." His eyes search mine for something, possibly agreement.

"I'll try and be patient," I say. I should be giddy—after seventeen and a half years, I'm getting some answers. *Finally.* The cost has been too high, but with enough information, maybe I can fix this. Maybe I can make things right again.

So I close my mouth and resolve to keep it shut.

"You clearly have dreams of Terra."

I nod.

"We've been split into two groups for thousands of years. The Followers of Isis—that's the group I've joined—believe we shouldn't attempt to use our powers on Earth, whereas the Followers of Amun think we should."

"Why wouldn't w—" I catch myself, barely in time "—you—use your powers, if you have them?"

"That's the catch, I suppose. On Earth our powers are stronger than in the linked prison world, but acquiring them is only achieved by paying a steep price. We can't use them naturally when we're born—a byproduct of the existence of Terra in the first place. Its entire purpose, really."

"You said it's a prison, but I don't understand."

"The names, Isis and Amun." Kahn frowns. "Thousands of years ago, Amun, whom you may have heard referred to as Ra, an ancient Egyptian God, led a vast group of people. No one dared oppose him."

None of this is a surprise to me—I'm no expert, but when people on Terra kept using the names Isis and Amun, I looked them up. Obsessively, when I had access to a library.

I don't argue, but he still pauses to convince me. "It's confusing, and it sounds far-fetched, I know, but so does the concept that humans should be able to telekinetically Lift things. Right?"

Not really. "Sure."

"And this Amun-Ra, we don't really know who he was or how he came to be. For a while he was worshipped as two separate entities. Then he was worshipped only as one. Some scholars say Amun was Ra's father. Some say they were the same. Some say that neither existed and that the pharaohs made them up for political reasons—priests and all that—and that they were combined for the same reason. Some believe Amun-Ra was at one time a human. Others argue that he was always a God. Most of the Egyptian pharaohs claimed to be his physical offspring."

I read that much myself.

"And somehow, his enemy, Isis—"

"I read Isis was his *wife*," I say.

Kahn's mouth drops open. "You've researched—"

"Of course I did. Wouldn't you?"

"I guess I would." Kahn's eyes stare into mine, their icy-blue depths flecked with silver. "Well, apparently Isis, his wife, his enemy, whatever she was to him, somehow created a prison world that binds our powers on Earth, and she named it Terra. People think she either killed or bound Amun to create the prison. The result is that unless something traumatic or terrifying happens to us on Earth, each human born will pass from birth to death without ever knowing we have powers at all."

"Wait. Are you saying every single human on Earth has some kind of power?"

"All the males, anyway. Not all of them are Lifters or Healers, and their strengths vary widely. But every human on earth would have some kind of power, had Terra not been created. Bear with me for a moment. I'll get to that part."

I don't get it. At all.

"Think of all the men and women and children you see on Terra. Every mother who is on Terra—all her children will be born there, on Terra, too. Every single person on Terra is either someone who can Lift or Heal, or someone who can have a child who can Lift or Heal."

Children just appearing in their mother's bellies. The Naming, the Wasting. It all begins to make a bizarre sort of sense. "Terra mirrors Earth, then."

"In everything, yes." Kahn looks at his hands. "I wish I could dream of it to experience life there—but I suppose I should be happy that I have powers instead of dreams."

"Because the women can dream of Terra—but we can't Lift or Heal, here or there."

Kahn's brow furrows, and his voice drops to a whisper. "I know you know me there—I hope that I'm kind to you."

Poor guy. He knows he's stuck with a mirror image walking around on another world, but he has no control over what he says or does. I mean—he does—it's still him. But. This is confusing. "You have been kind to me—helped me, even."

He exhales. "I'm glad."

"So the women, they can all dream of Terra?"

He shakes his head. "It's like the men, sort of. Our strength varies, and so too does the attenuation of the women to Terra. Some may only have a dream once or twice in their lifetimes. Some dream of it regularly."

"Are there any women who *always* dream of Terra? Any females who experience every waking second there?"

His jaw drops.

"Because every single time I go to sleep. . ."

"That can't be right," he says. "Because you must sleep here for, what? Eight or so hours? You'd only be able to witness eight or so hours of waking time on Terra."

"I speak every language," I say. "Can you explain that one?"

Kahn's eyes widen. "It must be something to do with being the Warden. We believe you're responsible for ruling Terra—for its upkeep and everything else. I'm not sure how that could be possible, but if anyone can defy the laws of space and time. . ." He shrugs. "I can't explain it, but I'm in awe."

Fan-freaking-tastic. I'm an even bigger weirdo than I realized.

Kahn stares at me for a moment and then shivers. "I guess I should explain the rest?"

"Go ahead."

"The process of gaining access to men's powers on Earth is commonly called 'Waking.' Typically, the greater the powers, the more difficult it is to gain access to them. Isis leadership believes no one should ever be Woken on purpose, but Amun disagrees. They believe that whatever damage is done to the individual in pursuit of unlocking their power is worth it in the end. They forcibly Wake all their members, as well as those members' male children."

I turn to face the camera. I wonder who else is watching. "So that's what they wanted to do to my brother?"

"It's likely. What can you tell us about Amun? What happened last night?" His voice drops to the barest whisper. "What we don't know is whether you've been Woken here."

Is he helping me? Is he sharing information he shouldn't? Or is this yet another manipulation?

"You think *I* can Lift here?"

"Can't you?" He Lifts a pen from his pocket and flings it through the air toward me.

I could block it. I could bat it out of the way easily. I

could even seize it and flip it around and impale him with it.

But I don't.

I let it wham into my forehead and fall to the ground with a clatter.

"Ouch." I clap my palm against my head, where the beginning of a splitting headache is now forming. "Why'd you do that?"

"I'm sorry," he says. "I momentarily lost control." But he looks pointedly at the camera. "We can't say for sure, but we believe Amun orchestrated the long sequence of horrible events that happened to you and your brother with the express purpose of trying to Wake Jesse."

"How did they even know who we were?"

"Your parents are known in our circles on Earth. When they had a son, they considered fostering him out, to prevent Amun from doing just what they did. We all wanted to protect your brother, to prevent him from having to undergo something like, well, like what took place last night. As I mentioned, the stronger the power, the harder it is to Awaken."

The pieces click into place. "My parents put us up for adoption and had the records redacted to hide us." I come by my paranoia and desire to run honestly, I guess. "Except Amun found us anyway, and they orchestrated the car crash. Only, it didn't work."

"We feel awful about your adoptive parents' deaths. They were good people, and they had no idea what risk they were taking. They knew nothing about Amun or Isis or Terra."

"Even their deaths didn't Wake Jesse." Or me.

I close my eyes and think about that day, the day my whole world tilted on its axis for the first time.

The first time I remember it happening, anyway.

Why don't I remember my birth parents? Why didn't

Jesse? "How old were we when it happened? The adoption I mean."

"You were three. Jesse was four."

But. . ."If my parents were only worried about Jesse, why did they give me up, too?" I don't ask whether I was broken.

"According to your file, you and Jesse always had a special bond, far beyond the normal sibling connection. When they took him to his new family, the two of you clung to one another. After they pried you apart and took you home, you both refused to eat. With no advance planning, and in separate locations, you behaved the same way, refusing all food. You'd spit out anything they shoved at you, or scream so much you puked up anything forced into you. After a week, your parents feared that neither of you would survive if they kept you apart. Even then, at such a young age, it was both of you or neither."

"Why don't I remember any of that? Or my birth parents?"

"We have people who specialize in easing transitions, Healers who are adept with things like that."

I scowl at him. "Why didn't they make me forget Jesse?"

"They tried." He sighs. "It didn't take."

Because Jesse has always been my anchor—and I've been his.

And now he's gone, ripped away from me.

A tear rolls down my cheek.

"Our files end with you running from a group home, but I'm guessing the Followers of Amun didn't give up."

I shake my head. "No, they didn't."

"What happened last night?" Kahn's eyes are intent, his shoulders rigid. This is the question he's been working up to asking me.

They want to know whether I've been Woken. As

much as I'd love to trust Kahn, as drawn to him as I am, even here, I can't risk it.

The only person I've ever trusted is lying on a stretcher right now.

"Jesse Woke last night." I grit my teeth and force the next words out. "When one of them planned to rape me, but it was too late."

"What happened, exactly?" Kahn shifts on the edge of the bed, clearly uncomfortable. "If you don't mind telling me."

Of course I mind, but to have a hope of escaping, I need him to believe me, and the best lies wrap around the truth. "Jesse attacked them, but one of the men hit him in the head. He must've pulled everything down in the same instant, because that's the last thing I remember."

"That's all you remember? The two men we found under the rubble were some of Amun's top agents."

"Wait, two?"

Kahn glances at the camera. "We've never seen damage like we saw in that alley. Two full-grown men crushed by hundreds of pounds of concrete. Chunks ripped from the ground and tossed around like confetti. Dumpsters full of trash crumpled up a hundred feet away. We need to know what happened and who exactly was present."

"How many bodies did you find?" I barely grind the next words out. "Not including my brother's."

Kahn's brow furrows. "Two."

"Who were they?" I need to know.

"One man controls the elemental form of water—and he specializes in ice. His name is Phillip Sangrini. The other man turns into a bear. His name is Dmitri Volki."

Ice powers and man-bears? It's like a cartoon, a very bad cartoon. "We'll have to come back to that—

elemental form? A bear?" I pause and refocus. "What about Devlin Rochester? Or maybe you call him Declan Rosenbaum. I don't know what his real name is. He posed as our social worker."

Kahn's eyebrows rise. "Devlin Rochester's body was not found. He's the leader of the Telekinetic Branch of the Followers of Amun."

Huh?

"Wait, was he present last night?"

I nod.

"His name is Devlin Rochester on Earth—I've never heard of him using the alias Declan Rosenbaum."

He must save that for when he's being a freaking creeper who follows and harasses little girls. I leap to my feet. "You didn't find his body?"

"We did not. He's a very powerful telekinetic, Alora, maybe the strongest on Earth, but if he did what we witnessed last night, his power is growing. I have no idea how or why, but it's nothing good."

I know Devlin's power isn't growing—I did what they're worried he did. Jesse thought I was paranoid, and I tried to trust better and look where that got me. Instead of fighting it this time, I lean in. Let them think whatever they want about Devlin. I don't owe them anything.

"We want to help you, Alora." Kahn stands up, too. "You don't have to be alone anymore. I know we never should have put you in a cell, but we didn't know what had happened or how that damage occurred. Can I take you to a hotel? Or anywhere you think you'll be safe? Tell me what you need."

"I'm not sure I want help."

"Devlin's still out there, and you're surely his top priority. You may not be Awake, but as you learned last night, they see that as a challenge."

"If I didn't Wake when they killed my brother, nothing will work."

Kahn holds my gaze for a moment before sighing heavily. "I'm not the enemy, Alora. I think you'll eventually see that."

Maybe.

"You seemed interested in the bear man and the water elemental."

I am, but compared to getting out of here and figuring out how to try and save Jesse—it's not my top priority.

Kahn sits down again. "One of the most valuable things I can offer you is knowledge."

"I won't stop you from sharing." I fold my arms, rumpling the dumb nightgown they put me in.

"There have always been four main powers on Earth. All humans were born with one of them, in varying styles and strengths. The telekinetic branch included the macro power of Lifting and the micro power of Healing. Elementals control the elements of earth, water, wind, and fire. Renders and Reapers have the power to change into animals that are either prey or predator. Assimilators are very rare and a little confusing. They take strength from other living things and inspired the legends of vampires. Think of them as power vampires."

In spite of myself, I'm avidly listening. It's as if my whole life has been spent inside a lockbox. . .and he's dangling the key.

"Each group had related subcategories, of course, and there were leaders of all the groups. Ra was an Assimilator. Power passes from woman to child, you see, which meant that Ra, as badly as he might want to—"

"He couldn't pass his power along." That's why all the children born to women on Terra. . .are born in Terra. "All those little telekinetic children are born in prison."

Kahn nods. "Yes." He clears his throat. "And it was all thanks to the women that Ra was defeated and the powers were locked away. Under Isis's direction, the women came to a consensus: the power imbalance was a problem. They sacrificed their powers to create a prison for everyone else. They named the prison T.E.R.R.A. Telekinetics, Elementals, Renders and Reapers, and Assimilators."

"Thousands of years ago, they named it Terra? They didn't even have English."

Kahn laughs. "You're supposed to be an orphan—no formal schooling."

"You shouldn't conflate uneducated with dumb."

"Fair point," Kahn says. "They had a different name— many names in fact. But we came up with the English name based on the names we arrived upon for the component parts."

"But on Terra, they say Terra."

"Do they?" Kahn lifts his eyebrows, and I realize he's right. On Terra, they speak Terran. My brain simply translates it into English, the way I translate everything.

I need a nap. My brain hurts. "So it's a mirror of Earth." I tap my lip. "But there are only Telekinetics. What about the rest, the other three categories?"

"They're imprisoned too, but they were segregated. Think of them like cells. The Terra you know imprisons Telekinetics. For someone with the ability to shift into an animal form, their prison world is full of animal shifters."

"But if you die on Earth?"

"You die on Terra, but that takes time for some reason. Something about an energy lag or a soul residue— we aren't sure. No records about that really make sense. There's a couple day lag. They have a name for it, but I can't remember what."

The Wasting. "And if you die on Terra?"

He scratches his chin. "You die on Earth, too, only much quicker. A few minutes later, as I understand it. Massive heart attack, usually."

I think of Robert, whom I almost certainly did kill. I shudder.

"It's unfortunate—like we all need *more* ways to die, right?" He shakes his head. "The creation of the prison cost the women their powers, eliminating all their abilities in either place. In exchange for their sacrifice, the women can see into the prison worlds and make sense of what happens there, no matter what native tongue they speak on Earth. They're Terra's keepers, sort of. Some of the men were very angry, and they quickly found a. . . loophole."

"The Followers of Amun," I say.

He nods. "They were furious at the defeat of their leader and the loss of their powers. In their brutality, in attempting to exact their revenge, they discovered that powers *can* be unleashed here on Earth, with much smaller capacity, and only after a huge trauma. They began to Wake everyone they could. The attacks were. . .brutal."

"The Followers of Isis worked to stop them."

"And the attacks only firmed the resolve of Isis to oppose them. Amun still wants to destroy Terra and bring their powers back to Earth fully."

"They think the Warden can accomplish it. They think I can destroy Terra."

"I don't know whether you can, but they believe it, yes. They also believe you can resurrect Amun-Ra somehow."

"Excuse me?"

"The prophecies about the destruction of Terra almost always reference his return."

A terrifying sense of unease slides down my spine.

"I'm sure it's not possible," Kahn says. "But Amun has justified their brutality in Waking members for millennia because it was the only way for them to maintain their power and influence. They think you can bring an end to all of the suffering and augment their power at the same time. That makes you a high priority."

"What if I run?"

He shrugs. "We won't stop you. Isis believes in agency, the power to make choices for yourself, but I should warn you. If you Wake." He swallows. "We can't risk you tearing down the prison walls. Or bringing back some psychotic God-man."

So much for Kahn's alleged misunderstanding. Ignoring the pen he flung at my head may have been the most important thing I've ever done in my life.

Because.

"If I Wake Up, you'll kill me."

20

EARTH

The bad news is that the good guys really should kill me before I can muck up their precious prison system.

The good news is that Isis has more scruples than I do, and they don't know I'm Awake.

Which gives me a little bit of wiggle room.

I learned how to make do with very little at an early age.

And when I think about it, I don't even blame them for wanting to kill me. I mean, of course they want to prevent all the bad guys on Earth from having a load of powers with which to muck about hurting people. The thought of a bunch of telekinetics, even more powerful than the ones on Terra, wandering around free?

It's horrifying.

Plus three more worlds' worth of monsters? Perish the thought.

But some of these folks already have powers here, and the Followers of Amun are already hunting.

For me.

I do feel a bit like a fox that has been released for

some kind of wacky hunt. Which way do I go? On Terra, Devlin allegedly wants to capture me, even though Amun as a whole wants me dead. And here, apparently the Followers of Amun want me alive to unravel the prison, and the Followers of Isis want me dead so it won't fall apart. It's a good thing that Kahn and his buddies can't send messages from Earth to Terra, or Duncan might strangle me himself.

"I'm sure it wouldn't come to that," Kahn says. "But if you Wake, we'd definitely need to keep a very close eye on you. Isis has a vested interest in keeping Earth as it is —with very few superhuman villains lurking around."

"I definitely don't want a bunch of lunatics freed from prison."

"We'd love to keep an eye on you," he says. "Even if you don't want our help. I doubt Amun will be content to give up on you—and they want you Awake."

"I need to deal with Jesse." I look pointedly at his body—hoping he won't realize that I have no intention of accepting that he's gone.

"Of course you do." He exhales slowly. "We're happy to pay for the funeral expenses, and I can send him to any funeral home you'd like."

A funeral home. I try not to completely freak out at the thought. Jesse's still alive on Terra—I remind myself over and over and over. "Sure, thanks."

"You can go with the body, if you'd like. Or not."

That's my ticket out of here. "I'd like that," I say. "To stay with him, I mean." What I really want is to get out of here so I can interrogate Devlin and develop a plan to save Jesse. Then I'll kill Devlin, of course.

In precisely that order.

I'm pretty sure the second I'm free, Devlin will come for me. I just need to get away from my magically delicious goody two-shoes soulmate and his band of seditious babysitters. Kahn stands up waves toward someone—who passes a box into the room.

"We have clothing for you," he says. "It's not yours, but we thought it might be better—"

"Than a white nightie?" I take the box from him. "What about that?" I glare at the camera.

Kahn tosses the white blanket over it—just like I did before the guy shoved the gun in my face. "Sorry about that."

I lift one eyebrow.

"Seriously, I am sorry."

A split second later, without any warning, men rush into the room. Three, four, six, then eight men in fatigues surround me, all of them holding guns. One places the cold hard muzzle directly against my forehead, clearly prepared to blow my brains out.

"What is happening?" Kahn asks. "This wasn't cleared. Who sent you?"

"Stand down, Brantley," the man with the gun to my forehead says. "We don't answer to you."

Kahn's eyes light up and the man is flung backward against the wall. His gun flies to Kahn's hand. "You may not answer to me, but you don't point firearms at anyone in my custody without someone explaining why."

Two of them swivel around and point their weapons at Kahn, and another man steps to the left and places his gun where the first soldier's was before, flush with the center of my forehead. "We've been told to eliminate the prisoner," the new soldier with the gun to my head says.

"And anyone who tries to stop us." The tall soldier pointing his weapon at Kahn steps closer, his gun now aimed directly at him. "Are you trying to stop us?"

"From killing her?" Kahn asks.

The soldier nods.

"Yes. I am."

In that split second, I can act—I can Block or Lift or defend, and I ought to do it. Kahn's doing nothing but trying to spare me—defending me.

But if I save him, they'll know who I am, and they'll all be after me. And part of me thinks this is another test —like the pen flung at my head.

So I gamble.

And I do nothing.

The soldier with his gun pressed against Kahn's forehead fires. At my soulmate. Ending him, forever.

My heart skips a beat. . .and then I realize he fired a blank.

Kahn's fine.

The soldiers glance from Kahn to me and back again.

"See? I told you she's not Awake," Kahn says. "She's fine." He offers the gun he stole to the first soldier, who takes it with a scowl.

They all march back out the door.

"Why don't you get changed?" Kahn opens his mouth and closes it again. Then he steps closer, and freezes. "I really am sorry, for all this. We had to make sure you weren't Awake before letting you go. The hearse won't be here for a few hours, so if you want to leave now—you can. If you'd like to wait and go with your brother's body, that's fine too."

By the time I change into a pair of jeans that are a little too large, and a plain blue t-shirt they've provided, I've decided. I have very little time, and I can't waste it. I need to get to Devlin, find out what he knows, and then make him pay. "Can you just give me the phone number on the funeral home? I can talk to them on the phone about the arrangements?" I glance at Jesse's body as if it makes me nervous. "I think that would be simpler."

"Of course," Kahn says.

"Where are we, exactly?"

Kahn leads me out the door, around the corner. . .and into the hallway of a regular-looking house. My white-washed cell turns out to be in the center of a normal, suburban home in Cypress, not too far from Katy. I suppose with all the various and sundry monsters running around, keeping padded rooms in nondescript locations around town isn't such a bad idea.

"I can drive you wherever you need to go," Kahn says.

"Where are you going to allow me to go?" I ask. "I mean, the Followers of Amun are after me—and now you guys know about me, too. What exactly am I allowed to do?"

"You can go about your life," he says. "That's our hope."

"How would I possibly do that?" I frown. "My brother's gone, and monsters are hunting me."

"Your brother." Kahn's face falls. "You can't know how sorry I am, truly. You can hold a memorial service for friends and any family you may want to invite. We can make sure you're safe from social services, etc. We really are quite good at dealing with. . .the bureaucracy. And let us worry about keeping the Followers of Amun away. Now that we know who and where you are, Devlin can't bother you anymore."

I do hope he's wrong.

Kahn gives me a ride to the closest bus stop—and when I get out and sit on the bench, he insists on giving me a few hundred dollars. "I'm not sure what bills you may have, but I know that losing your brother will make paying them hard. Isis is happy to help," he says. "And of course, I'm happy to help, too. With anything." He presses a piece of paper into my hand as well.

"What's that?"

"It's my phone number. If you need help, I want you to call me personally."

Call Isis? Yeah, right. But Kahn's eyes are steady and kind. The connection that I feel to him—he must feel it too. It's bizarre. It's unexplainable. I shouldn't trust him, yet I find that I do. "If I had been Awake, would you really have let them shoot me?"

He sits down next to me on the bench. "Alora, every single gun in that room was filled with blanks."

If I'd had the presence of mind to feel for it, I might have figured that out. But there aren't guns on Terra, so I've never sensed bullets before. I'm sick of never having any training or skill. I'm sick of being the idiot who can only half use her own power. I clench my fists in my lap.

"I've said it before, and I'll say it again. Some of the Followers of Isis might be a little overzealous or even misguided, but I'm telling you. We won't kill you for Waking if that happens. I'd never let it happen." His eyes are wide and his expression earnest.

Like he could stop them. He couldn't even keep them from making me pee with a camera in my room.

"You'll take care of me because of your convictions?" Why did I ask that? I shouldn't be hoping that he says no. I'm an idiot.

It's a warm day—every day in Houston is warm, pretty much—but I find myself inching closer to him, not sliding away to encourage the breeze.

"Of course, my beliefs, but also. . ." He shakes his head. "It doesn't matter."

"What if it matters to me?"

He's just as tall and just as broad-shouldered here on Earth. His hair is much shorter, but still perfect—a dozen shades of golden blond. His hand rests next to mine on the concrete bench and I feel almost compelled to reach for him. Which is exactly why I can't. Stupid fate, trying to shove us together.

"You—I—it's not only my convictions." His voice is

low and rough. His eyes rise to mine. "It's also. . ." He clears his throat. "I can't explain what it is, actually. But even though we've just met, you're important to me. Does that sound bonkers?"

"It's the exordium," I blurt out. "That's all. We felt it on Terra, too." Having never dreamed of Terra, he may not know what that is. "It's like this weird—"

Kahn frowns. "The exordium is the pull that two people on Terra feel when they've fallen in love on Earth. It was created, or so the legends say, so that it would be easier, when children were formed, for the Naming to show the child's father and mother at once."

But that means. . .

"Since we're not on Terra, whatever I feel for you can't possibly be the exordium."

And when I met Kahn on Terra, I'd never met him here. So that couldn't have been. . . My mouth goes dry. My stomach tumbles round and round.

"You're saying that on Terra, you feel, what? Drawn to me? Like you'd burn down a building and dance on the ashes, if only it meant you could kiss me?"

How could he have so perfectly named how I feel right now?

He must be feeling it too.

"You've never even been to Terra. How do you know what the exordium is and isn't?" But of course he knows. I'm just arguing to argue. What he says makes perfect sense. Of course they'd need something to pull the same people together on Terra whenever possible, to help family units form there too, and to keep the children safe.

"I only know what I've been told." Kahn's voice is low and rough again. His eyes meet mine and a thrill runs up my spine.

"If this isn't the exordium, if it's not. . .then what *is* it?"

The corner of Kahn's mouth turns up in a wicked, wicked smile. "So you do feel the same?"

I shrug. "I don't know. I mean, I don't want to burn any buildings or anything."

His laugh is one of the most beautiful sounds I've ever heard. "But you know what I mean."

I look up at him, and his head lowers, slowly, his lips approaching mine. I could no sooner stop him than I could breathe underwater, or swim through the sky. His lips are a hair's breath away when. . .

A bus pulls up in front of us. I start as I hear the discordant hiss of the air release on the doors. "That's my bus," I whisper.

"Forget the bus." Kahn's eyes are on my lips.

My heart is in my throat, and I want to kiss him. Badly. But I have very little time. I leap to my feet. How could I have forgotten about Jesse? I've got to get information, and then I have to do whatever it takes to save—or avenge—him, or possibly both.

For a brief moment, I consider asking Kahn to help me. Part of me desperately wants to unfold my innermost desires to him—to trust that he'll help me based entirely on how I feel about him. It would be so nice to share my desperate idea to save Jesse and ask for his help.

But I don't know him.

And I can't trust him.

Nothing matters as much as saving Jesse for as long as it might be an option.

So I turn around instead, and I climb on the bus. I'm so distracted by watching him standing at the bus stop, forlornly waving, that I almost don't notice the men following me.

Almost.

Clearly Isis can't just let me go. I knew they'd send bodyguards. But they look a little bit like spies. . .and I actually don't need their help.

Because I want Devlin to find me.

I think about what I know of Terra—that it's a prison for anyone on Earth with telekinetic powers. It keeps their powers trapped, and the downside is that anyone there can die in more than one way—battle or injury on Terra, and of course the whole slew of normal things here.

As a prison, if Jesse is here, and he dies, he'd die there. Wasting. Which is exactly what's happened. But, he's still alive for a few more days. . .so obviously there's more to it. He must be alive in both places. If he dies there, Jesse would have a heart attack sometime later on Earth? Or at the same time?

These are the kinds of questions I need to find answers for—and exactly what I plan to torture out of Devlin, just before I kill him.

The bus jolts and whirs down the road, hitting every pothole, and bumping into the curb now and then. But eventually, I reach my destination.

I've been riding these buses for a while now, and I've gotten to know the stops in this area reasonably well, thankfully. I hop off the bus. . .and jog as quickly as I can around the corner, and down the block. The gray Honda Civic that's been following me races around the corner too. Two men are in the car, the driver quite tall and thin, the passenger muscly and short. Both of them are wearing sunglasses.

I duck into the CVS pharmacy on the corner, hoping to lose them. I stroll as casually as I can toward the back door. When no one's looking, I duck through the "Staff Only" door and into their break room. There's always another exit, and I finally find it. I race through, and jog around to the dumpsters. I find a big rock, big enough, I hope, to knock a man out.

I could easily Bind the men in place, or knock them out by Lifting something, but then Isis would know I'm Awake. Unless I'm willing to kill them, which I can't bring myself to do, I have to do this old school. I crouch down behind the dumpsters and wait. Sure enough, the short, brawny man zips out the back door and looks around. I pull back a little more and reach out with my senses. He's walking toward me. I wait until he walks past, and then I jump up and clock him on the back of the head with the rock.

He's supposed to go down in a heap. That's what happens in the movies.

Instead, he turns around, cursing in a steady stream, and puts one hand over the back of his neck. "What is wrong with you?" I notice a gun at his side. "I'm here to keep you safe. Why are you hitting me?"

So much for keeping anyone from knowing. I Lift the gun and turn it on him.

I'm surprised to see it's a weird gun, and it has darts in it. "Tranqs?" I ask.

"Holy sh—"

I dart him before he can finish his sentence. He collapses in the heap I was hoping for that first time around.

And it happens just in time for his partner to come flying out the back door. I dart him, and he goes down, too. I hit them both with a second dart, just to be safe.

Because once they wake up, in spite of Kahn's reassurances, I'm guessing that all of Isis will be shooting to kill.

This isn't a very well thought out plan.

I've never been so anxious on my way to work in my entire life. Even on the day I thought Declan, er, Devlin was coming for me. But this time, I hope he is. Because soon enough, Kahn and his men will be.

And I need to reach Devlin first.

It's almost three o'clock when I reach Perry's and walk inside. I find Henry in the back office. He jumps off the chair when he sees me.

"Alora! Where have you been? Do you have any idea how much crap I've gotten for you just disappearing?"

So much for Henry being worried about me.

"Umm, I'm sorry I missed work today."

He drops his voice to a whisper, which seems a little late. No one in the restaurant missed him yelling my name. "No, I mean, forget all that." He looks back and forth and then turns back toward me. "It's not safe."

I know it's not safe, but how does clueless Henry know? It occurs to me then, the stupid thing I should have thought about earlier. *Henry is on Terra*. His mom must have powers, and she's a woman. So when she met me. . . and she disliked me unreasonably. . .she probably knew who I was.

She probably recognized me, maybe as the woman who defeated her son in the Ascension. Ugh.

"Who do your parents work for, Henry?"

I saw Declan a few hours later, on the very day I met her.

Henry shakes his head. "We've always worked with Isis. I swear I had no idea who you were. I just liked you, okay? I still do. My mom, though, she was mad. Apparently you beat me in some kind of fight on Terra, and she was angry. She called someone she knew with Amun. She thought they'd take care of you."

"Your *mom* turned me in?"

Henry sputters. "I had no idea, I swear."

I stumble backward, my butt hitting the wall. Everyone I thought was a friend is somehow involved.

The only good news is that I've got a way to reach Devlin.

"Where's your mom now? I need to call someone with the Followers of Amun."

He shakes his head. "She's in a holding cell. Isis is upset, to put it lightly. They said if Amun had managed to Wake the Warden because of her, well. . .they're pissed." Henry's mouth shuts with a click.

"I need a number for Amun, Henry."

He sits back down. "I can't give you something I don't have, and I'm pretty sure Isis wants to keep you away from them for a reason. I need to call and tell them you're here, or I'll wind up in a cell, too." His eyes are round and full of regret.

"Grow a backbone, Henry. Help me like you said you would." I plead with my eyes. "Don't call anyone."

He shakes his head again, and I realize that John was right. Henry really isn't housebroken—he's a big old puppy.

I groan, but I pull out the dart gun again and shoot Henry, too. I still have no way of reaching Devlin, and now I'm standing in Perry's Steakhouse with the owner's son passed out on the floor at my feet. I grab his cell phone, flip location services off, put it on airplane mode, and walk back outside. I haven't gone three steps when John comes running down the sidewalk. "Alice, wait. Your brother never showed up today. I called his cell a few times and he never answered. Is he okay?"

His eager, concerned face, and his normal assumptions, that Jesse's home sick or at the hospital, stab at something inside of me. Which is why I burst into tears. Without paying any attention to the people walking to shops who are staring, he steps toward me and pulls me into a hug. For some reason, that makes me cry harder.

He leads me over to the bench where I usually sit and

lets me cry on his shoulder until the tears dry up. "He was murdered last night, John. He's dead." Saying the words shatters something inside me.

And for the first time, it feels true. I've been running on fumes, hoping against hope that I can do something Earth-shattering, or I guess, Terra-shattering, to save him. But now that I've said the words, how could I possibly?

You can't reverse dead.

My brother, my everything, the only person I love, is *gone*. Forever.

"I'm—" His face falls. "—I'm so sorry, I don't even know what to say."

I should tell him it's okay, but even I can't force out a lie that big. The people passing us turn to stare, and I realize I'm sitting here like a Thanksgiving turkey, waiting for Isis and Amun to find me. I've botched everything so badly I don't see a way out. Jesse's gone, and all I want to do is find the man who killed him, torture him for information, and kill him too. But instead, it looks like I'll either end up back in a cell or with a hole in my head before I can do anything useful.

I lean back against the bench and close my eyes.

"Is there anything I can do for you?" John asks. "Anything at all? Are you. . ." he bites his lip, "hungry, or anything?"

I haven't thought about food since yesterday, which means it's probably a good idea. "Uh, not really. But I ought to eat."

"Where do you want to go?"

I shake my head. "I don't know. Not here. Not something close."

"My car's behind the office. I can take you anywhere you want."

I stand up and follow him without saying a word.

John opens the passenger side door of a red BMW Z4. Not exactly something that will blend in, but I need to get somewhere to regroup and formulate a better plan.

"What sounds edible?" he asks.

I notice he doesn't say 'good,' as though he knows there's nothing in the world that could approach 'good' right now.

I shake my head. "Honestly, I don't even care. I just had to get away from there."

"At the risk of sounding creepy, I can pick up takeout and we can eat at my place. There won't be anyone around to stare at you. Or I can take you home. Wherever you want to go."

John's the opposite of creepy, and my place is out, so. "Any kind of food is fine, and your place sounds good if you don't mind." I swallow. "I feel terrible. You hardly know me."

"Stop."

He doesn't ask me questions, although he must have a million. He doesn't even speak. He drives through Chick-Fil-A, of all places. His car looks absurd sandwiched between two minivans. He orders five orders of chicken nuggets, and several large French fries.

"I bet you haven't eaten in a while," he says. "And if I remember right, you don't eat like a bird."

The nicest non-compliment I've ever had. In spite of everything, I smile. John's a good guy. I hope he's not too upset when I die in the near future.

I don't know where I expect him to live, but an older house in a small midtown neighborhood isn't it. He opens the garage door on the little white house with the touch of a button and parks his flashy car in the garage. When he grabs the bag of food, I follow him inside, numb.

"Not what you expected?" he asks.

"I didn't know what to expect."

"My mom inherited quite a lot of money, and when she passed, it all came to me, in trust of course. My grandmother's the trustee, and she told me she thought I should take an interest in investing some of it. I bought this house and the one next door. I live here and rent out that blue one." The blue house next door looked exactly like this one when we pulled up.

"Seems like a good idea," I say.

He groans. "Don't be so sure. These houses are both pretty old, and everything keeps breaking. I have to contact my grandma every time I want a disbursement until I turn twenty-five, so if the repairs exceed the rent, I usually just put them off or figure out how to take care of them myself. It eats up way too much free time, but the family that lives next door is really sweet, and their little girl is adorable."

My heart aches, thinking about a normal family with a little girl they love. Why couldn't I have been born into a life like that?

John walks into the kitchen and sets the bag down on a simple oak table. The kitchen's small, with terra cotta tile floors and tiled counters. But the appliances all match, and the furniture looks almost too new for the room. I pull out one of the spindle-backed chairs and slide up to the table. I start eating then, just to have something to do. Before I realize what I'm doing, I've inhaled all the food.

All five orders of nuggets.

And fries.

I flog my brain for other ways to locate Devlin. I have Henry's cell phone. Maybe I can find something there, but I doubt it. I lay my head down on the table, frustrated and confused. I don't know what to do or how to proceed. And I'm running out of time.

Without meaning to, I almost fall asleep.

I jerk awake and gasp. John walks into the kitchen. "Everything okay? You look tired. I have a guest room. You're welcome to take a nap."

I shake my head. "I can't sleep, I can't."

He pulls up a chair and sits next to me. "Why? Bad dreams?"

I shake my head. I can't exactly explain that as soon as I go to sleep, since I won't remember a single thing that I currently know, I'll have to watch my brother die. Again. I don't think I can bear it. "You wouldn't believe me if I told you."

"Try me," he says.

I sigh. "It's complicated and it makes no sense."

"Your brother was murdered yesterday," John says. "I don't mean to pry, but I expect complications."

"It's not just that."

"Because you dream about Terra?" He raises one eyebrow.

I Lift him and slam him up against the wall, which knocks a picture to the ground.

"Take it easy." He's surprisingly unconcerned for someone I might kill any second.

"Who are you?" I ask. "And which side are you on?"

"I'm a friend, Alora. I swear it. I'm not with Amun *or* Isis, but I've known about you and your brother for years. In fact, I started looking for you because I was angry about how much time Devlin Rochester was spending looking for you. Maybe I was even a little jealous. At first I wanted to find you to show him that I could, to prove my value." He grunts. "But then I got to know you both, and I felt awful. You didn't deserve any of the horrible things he was doing to you. I really just want to help you. That's the absolute truth."

I lower him to the ground, shove him into a chair, and bind his hands and feet behind him.

"Talk. Why did you care what Devlin Rochester did? How did you even know who he was or what he wanted? And most of all, why should I believe you aren't one of the Followers of Amun?"

"For starters, Devlin Rochester is my father."

21

EARTH

I want to rip his head from his shoulders. I want to pull his cute little house apart and shred the bits into potpourri. A pile of John-scented chunks sounds about right. I've been wracking my brain over how to find Devlin Rochester and his son was busy hiring my brother and posing as my friend.

I'm a chump.

"Give me one good reason why I shouldn't mail your head to your father with an invitation to his own funeral?"

John's eyes are clear, calm, and unafraid. "Just one? Alright, how about this. I want him dead as much as you do."

My eyes widen. "Why would you want your own father dead? He's bankrolling your stupid start-up company. He's the reason you can sit around all day playing video games. He probably paid for that red sports car, too."

"My dad killed my mom. I didn't like him much before, but I've hated him every day since her death."

I recall him mentioning that his mom had bad dreams. "She dreamt of Terra."

He shrugs. "Well, Erra, really."

"Huh?"

"She was an elemental, not a telekinetic. They call their world, er, prison place Erra."

"Are you serious?"

"Not the point," he says. "So yes, she dreamed of it, just like you."

"But your dad obviously knew it was a real place."

He nods. "He did. He and my mom married young, and she was so excited that he was interested in her. The Followers of Amun Woke my dad when he was only eleven, and he hated them for it, for years and years." He gulps. "Mom hated them too—they met at an Isis meeting. But then one day, he just decided to join the enemy."

I shake my head. "That makes no sense."

"He joined after he read their prophecy about you, Alora."

I want to know if it's the same prophecy. I want to know why Amun wants to kill me on Terra, but here they're the ones who want me to live.

"No." I slam his chair into the ground. "You don't get to use some stupid prophecy to lure me. My dad abandoned my brother and me, and even when our new parents died, he never showed up. I know he's alive, because he's alive on Terra. Even so, I don't hate him. I'd punch him in the jaw, but I wouldn't kill him. Why should I believe you haven't just lured me in as a favor to your dad? Maybe you're just killing time until he arrives."

"Check my phone."

I follow John's eyes to the latest iPhone on the counter.

"Go ahead. Use my face to get into it. If I had texted him, there'll be some kind of history."

Unless he deleted it, but I haven't noticed him even glance at his phone since meeting me on that bench.

"Look, Alora, my dad was a pretty important guy with Isis for a long time, and my parents seemed happy enough. Eventually, he got promoted and promoted and he had access to the oldest records they have. At the end of the day, he didn't agree that they should kill the Warden. He thought when she came, it was a sign that the prison *should* crumble, like it was a sort of training wheels scenario, where we could have developed enough to rule benevolently, and do better than we did long ago. When he switched sides and joined Amun, Dad had some issues with forcing kids Awake, but he got over those." John grits his teeth and looks at the wall.

"Are you okay?" He looks so convincingly broken.

"The leadership insisted that I be Woken as a condition of his membership approval."

He looks upset, but what if it's just a manipulation? "Get to the part about your mom."

"Mom lost it when he joined the Followers of Amun. Her father worked for them and she hated them all the way down to her bone marrow. No prophecy would change her feelings. The bad blood goes back decades. She freaked out and left him. When he pursued her, she tried to kill him. I know that makes my mom sound bad, but the way Amun treats women sometimes, well, she couldn't bear the thought of going back to someone who would be working for them, even though my dad swore he'd protect her. . ."

"Why not simply divorce him? That happens every day."

"You'd think, right? My dad's not conventional, I guess. He wouldn't allow it—he had her committed, using her dreams as his excuse. When she sent a letter, threatening to end it all, he should have gone to get her. He should have let her out and allowed her to move on. Only, the Followers of Amun saw it as weakness that he couldn't control his wife. He needed to Wake his son, and get his woman under control. Or maybe he just wanted to prove he was ruthless enough to do whatever it took. Either way, he wouldn't let her go."

"Oh, no," I say.

John closes his eyes. "I was only ten when my mom committed suicide. Too young to do anything about it or even really understand why. I only realized it was Dad's fault a few years ago, when I found her letter. I vowed to make him pay for what he did to our family."

I've spent most of my life listening to people lie in some way, shape, or form. I've gotten pretty good at spotting baloney. His words ring with truth, authenticity, and pain. His anger seems real enough, too.

I release the Binding on his hands and feet, and he slumps forward in the chair.

"Your dad ruined my life. He tried to Wake Jesse over and over and it destroyed us. No matter how many times we ran, he always followed. And then, when nothing else worked. . ." I watch him for a moment to make sure that John is really listening. "He killed my brother to Wake me."

"I am so, so sorry. But I'm not surprised. He's a zealot, and. . .he thinks you're the Warden, doesn't he?"

"He does—everyone does, here and on Terra." I've seen that prophecy, but not this one. "Do you have the prophecy? The one that changed your dad's mind? You said it's not the same as the one on Terra?"

He shrugs. "I don't have it, but I've seen it and Dad's recited it before. I could probably write most of it down. I'm not sure if that'll help or hurt, if I'm off on some things."

"It can't hurt." I sure hope that's true.

He grabs a piece of paper and starts writing. Finally, he hands it to me. "That's as close as I can remember."

As with women it began, with the warden it ends. She who can bridge the divide will rend the prison walls, rescuing the wartorn. They will fall one at a time, all four walls, until the world is whole again. The bindings will shake, and if she fails, will be ripped apart. The storm will rage against her and will require a great sacrifice, but none can stand against her wrath. Salvation comes from her hand, and with the rod she shall be healed.

Only she can choose. Only she can restore. Only she can redeem. But she won't do it alone.

Bridge the divide? Rend the prison walls, rescuing the war torn?

Rescuing.

That's what I need to do—rescue Jesse. "You said you're an elemental?"

John's eyes widen and he nods.

"What can you do, then?"

"Everyone gets the power their mother has, with hardly any exceptions," he says. "Mom was a fire elemental, and so. . ." He holds out his hand, palm up, and flattens his fingers quickly, and a tiny flame dances in the air above his hand. A moment later he closes his hand and it winks out.

Whoa. Crazy. "Okay, so you can start fires anywhere?"

He shrugs. "I can put them out, too."

"But you can't Lift."

He shakes his head. "Nope. Sorry."

"Which means you're not even present on Terra." I bite my lip. "Your dad is, but you're not."

"Correct. My mom would have had a Naming thingy on Erra, and she would have known she'd named me John here, and called me that there. But no father on Erra would have felt the same. I'd either be raised by her husband, if she has one, or by a single mom. Pretty terrible, huh?"

It is sad, but I can't worry about that right now. I've got to either figure out how to save Jesse. . .or if I can't. . .

"Amun thinks that once you're born, the prison world will crumble no matter what you do. They think your appearance signals the end. Or at least, Dad's positive it's true. The one line I know for sure is 'bridge the divide and rescue the wartorn.' Dad's obsessed with you being the only person who can bring people back over from Terra to Earth." His eyes are wide and concerned when he says, "Without you, Dad thinks every single one of us with powers will die when our mirror dies as Terra crumbles."

"I'm some kind of a savior, then? I thought Amun only wants me because if I collapse the worlds, their powers here magnify and they won't need to Wake anyone else."

"That's true, too. They do think that once the prisons are gone, everyone will have more power. We aren't sure whether the women will get theirs back or not."

"Kahn said all the women on Earth gave up their powers millennia ago to form the prison world."

John's eyes flash. "You know Kahn?"

I step back and bump into the cabinet behind me. "How do you know him?"

"We went to school together. I've known him for ages. He's with Isis, though, and they want you dead."

I shake my head. "Only if I Wake."

"Which you have." He leans against the chair back. "Wait, you met him, and he didn't figure it out?" He whistles.

"They pushed and pushed."

His smile nearly splits his face in half. "I bet they did. You're an impressive lady."

I raise one eyebrow. "Life has taught me not to trust anyone."

"You're smart to have learned that lesson, but eventually one of them will convince the others that they need to destroy you while they still can, before you can bridge the worlds. They think if the worlds don't come together, Terra will continue onward."

"Um." I bite my lip. "I kept it from Kahn, but I might have Lifted in front of one of their men who was tailing me."

John frowns. "Did he see you?"

I nod.

He swears. "Well."

A wave of exhaustion rolls over me, and I sit down and rest my head on my arms. I want to curl up into a ball and cry for a month, but I can't. I need John's help, and I'm running out of time. "I need to find your dad." So I can take one last stab at learning anything that might save Jesse. . .and kill him before Isis kills me if I can't save him.

"You need a nap. You look like you're about to collapse."

I shake my head. "I can't go to sleep. I'm not ready yet."

"What are you thinking? Have you seen Jesse's body? Are you absolutely sure he's dead?" John asks.

He's too smart for his own good. I imagine bringing Jesse's energy over—would it go to his corpse? Would I be inadvertently creating some sort of undead version of Jesse? I shudder. No way—surely not. "I've seen it." I gulp. "And here's the honest truth. I don't want to live in a world without my brother, John. I can't do it."

He covers his face with his hands, and I can barely hear his next words. "You're planning to kill my dad, and then let Isis kill you, aren't you?"

John figured out my original plan. Surely Kahn will have figured it out, too, or he will the second he finds out that I can Lift. If John helps, I can do it. I can get my revenge, and pass from this world. Jesse and I will be together—heaven or hell or whatever comes next. The threat of prison destruction will be averted. It's what Jesse would want. It's the right thing to do.

But.

Maybe I can bring Jesse back. Maybe he doesn't have to be gone, not really. Maybe I have a second chance at doing things right and saving his life. It might unleash monsters on Earth. It might burn the world down.

I'm not sure whether I care.

"Jesse's Wasting."

His mouth drops open. "You're wondering whether he might survive. . .if you bring the worlds together."

I wanted to tell Kahn, badly. The universe kept shoving him at me, and some glowing feeling I can't understand told me to trust him, but I didn't.

And yet somehow, in spite of everything, I do trust John.

"Yes, that's exactly what I'm hoping." I look at my fingers—the torn cuticles. The jagged nails. The dirt underneath each and every one. I'm no princess. I'm no savior.

I'm just me.

"Do you think it's crazy? Would I be dooming the world if I try?"

John shrugs. "The world sucks. You don't owe it a thing."

I blink back tears, but it doesn't work. They stream down my face. "You really think so?"

He walks toward me slowly.

I run into his arms, wrapping my hands around his

waist. His arms tighten around me and for the first time in a very long time, I feel safe. I feel supported.

I don't feel alone.

In the circle of John's arms, by my own choice, for no reason other than that I choose to trust him, I think about my time in Terra. Knowing it was created with the power of all the women stuck there, the whole world must be molecularly different than Earth.

Which jogs a memory.

"I've only felt it twice," I say, "but when I get really tired on Terra, like so tired I can't think straight, and so drained I can't Lift another thing, the world blurs. It almost. . .vibrates."

"Vibrates? Like how?"

"I don't know how to explain it, but it's like everything around me buzzes. The last time it happened, my dad, my brother, and Kahn reached out and steadied me. It let me focus enough to Lift and launch several thousand projectiles, something I definitely didn't have the strength to do. I'm not sure where that power came from. It almost felt like I pulled that strength from the rocks in the wall, or the dirt beneath me, from Terra itself. I wonder if the entire world is constructed from the same power we use to Lift."

John's face scrunches up. "I know that Terra and Earth aren't the same, but I was taught that our strength comes from within us—we literally can only use the power we have inside."

It sounds an awful lot like what Kahn said about Lifting—but I definitely used power that I didn't have inside. "I wonder whether it has to do with being the Warden, or the bridge, or whatever I am. Maybe unlike anyone else, I can see beneath the construct."

"But how can you test that theory?"

"I can't, right? Because when I go to Terra, I forget

everything I know here. It's like I'm blindfolded." Surely that's some part of the prison walls, I guess, but then an idea strikes me. If I want to create a bridge, ever, I'll have to tear off the blindfold. I'll need to be able to *see* Earth *from* Terra. I think that's the entire point.

"I think I may need to take a nap after all."

"You're going to try bringing the worlds together." John groans. "Have you really thought this through? This might save your brother." He pauses. "Or it might destroy. . .everything."

When I hear the words, *this might save your brother*, I stop listening. Because to me, that's all that matters.

"I don't remember Earth when I'm on Terra." I tap my lip. "That's the riddle I need to solve before I take a nap."

"Not at all? Nothing?"

"The only times I've even had a hint of anything from Earth all involve Jesse. I'm pretty sure the first time I met him, the familiarity I felt was because I know him on Earth." I think about the way I felt, the strange trust I had in him. "I'm already motivated on Terra, desperate really, to save him from the Wasting. All I need is to get one good message through to myself." I laugh. "I need to Wake on Terra."

"How can you do that?" John looks confused. "You said you forget everything."

Actually, that's not entirely correct. One puzzle from Earth has plagued me on Terra my entire life. In fact, it's one of the only things that kept me sane on this end, because it helped me believe that I wasn't crazy and that Terra was real. "I have an idea, but I doubt you're going to like it much."

John sighs. "What?"

"In fact, you may want to step out for a minute."

He lifts one eyebrow. "Why?"

I pull a butter knife out of the drawer and click the gas burner on his stovetop to high. "Because I'm about to send myself a message."

"How?"

"By burning it into my arm."

My arm screams like someone's holding a branding iron against it. I shove the sleeve of my nightgown upward to see the edge of a burn, and a bad one at that. Maybe what I did at the end wasn't enough. Maybe Devlin's forces broke through. But if so, why am I still alive? Or did Devlin actually want me alive? My brain's moving too slowly, and my head's pounding too loudly against the inside of my skull.

"You're awake." Jesse's slumped in a chair next to my bed. "You okay?"

"What are you doing here?" I sit up and press my hand to his forehead. I could roast a chicken on it. "You should be in bed yourself."

"It won't make a difference. We've been over this." He straightens, and then tilts his head. "Hey, what's wrong with your arm?"

"I'm not sure. I thought you might know. Did something happen to it on the wall yesterday?" I don't say, 'after I passed out.' I figure he knows that's when I mean.

"The Healers have been in here several times. I'm not

sure how they could have missed Healing anything." Jesse wipes the sweat from his forehead with his sleeve. "Our reports show that you killed more than a thousand troops with Kahn on those initial cycles, and almost five hundred on the west side of the North Wall. Then, in that final volley, you took out more than two thousand soldiers in a single pass. No wonder you collapsed. I've never seen anything like it. It scared Devlin half to death, and his entire force fell back. They're regrouping below the city."

"Was Dad happy with the reprieve?"

Jesse smiles. "We all were."

"My murder of thousands of people brought you all joy. How lovely."

"They wanted to kill my sister and our people, so yes, it was lovely. But that's not why I'm smiling."

"Why are you smiling?" I'd do most anything to see him smile right now. Every time could be his last.

"You called Duncan 'Dad.'"

I scowl. "Don't be silly."

"He's going to need you, and you'll need him. He's a really good man, and he loves you. He was a wonderful father to me."

I sit up. "Stop saying was. He *is* your dad. And I told you, we're going to figure this out." I reach out to take his hand and my forearm brushes against the bed. Pain blossoms across my skin, and I cringe.

Jesse flips my arm over.

Only then do I realize it's not a normal injury. This wasn't a burn from a hot pan, or even a hearth fire. It wasn't sliced as someone dragged me away from the wall. It wasn't a graze from a careless blade. No, the pain is from *words* that have been *burned* into my forearm. Clear, bright, purposeful words. It's a message.

"What is that?" Jesse asks.

I look at him, and then I look back at my arm. "My burn?"

"I mean, it almost looks like they're symbols or something."

I tilt my head. "They're words. You're the future lord of Sterling Castle. Are you saying you don't know how to read?"

Jesse rolls his eyes. "I can't read gibberish, even if it looks like somewhat meaningful gibberish."

I glance at my burns again. The symbols make sense to me, but now that he points it out, they aren't from the Terran alphabet I learned as a child. I read them aloud. "It says, 'You've always known Jesse. To save him, *remember*. Embrace the dissonance.'"

"I heard my name. The rest. . .huh?"

What language was I speaking? I say the words aloud again, this time in Terran.

"Okay, that makes no sense, but at least you're using real words. What's dissonance? And what does it mean, *remember*? Remember what?"

Who would have sent me that message? And what does the dissonance mean? I wrack my brain. I've been finding injuries I can't explain all my life. I have no idea who or what causes the injuries, but I think back on them. A broken arm, several small cuts, a split lip, a broken wrist, bruises frequently, but nothing like this. This message is new, and for some reason, it's in a language Jesse can't understand. . .but I can.

My brother slumps in his chair, his skin pale and clammy, his hands shaking, but he's taking care of me. He's dying, and he's still at my side.

Someone thinks I can save him, but I have to decode this puzzle to have the slightest chance of success.

Who would send me a message? "Were you here with me all night?"

"No one has been in or out, other than you and me. Well, a maid changed you last night, but you didn't seem to be in distress. I doubt she could've burned you. I only stood outside for a few minutes."

I raise my eyebrows, and he squirms. "She's been here her whole life. You needed fresh clothing, and I wasn't about to do it." He grins at me weakly.

"If she didn't do this while you stood outside, and no one else did, then where did it come from?"

He shrugs. "But clearly we need to get you to a Healer."

That would cause too many questions. I pull the sleeve back down. "Let's leave it for now. I need to think about it—and maybe the throbbing in my arm will help me focus."

Jesse steps closer and puts his hand on my non-burned wrist. "It looks bad. No one can fix me, but the Healers could take care of that."

"Please, Jesse. For now, can you let it go?"

After a moment, he releases my arm. "Are you hungry?"

I change clothes, wincing when the fabric of my nightshirt rubs against my arm again, but I grit my teeth and slide another long-sleeved shirt over my head. I'd like to go sleeveless, but I can't risk it. What if someone else sees the symbols? How would I even begin to explain what the mysterious injuries mean?

Jesse shuffles down the hall ahead of me. He should be resting, not sitting up all night. Not following me to the dining room to make sure I eat. "You need to conserve your strength. Give me time to figure something out for you."

He stops walking and turns to face me. "You are my strength. Dad's my strength. My goals, my family, and my job keep me strong. If I only have a day left, I won't spend it lying in bed, tossing and turning alone. If helping the people I love shortens my life a little, at least I lived every minute of the time I had."

I choke back tears, because they won't help him, and they won't help me.

Kahn and Duncan are already eating when we reach the dining room, along with Stefan, Seth, and Beren. The day shift must be about to relieve the night. Stefan doesn't like me very well, and I'm guessing he's one of the ones who remember that I'm the reason for this war.

Every single one of them stands when Jesse and I enter, and then, as though they practiced it, they bow.

Duncan smiles. "You bought us precious time last night, my dear. We're all very grateful."

Kahn grins and waves to the seats across from him. "Hungry?"

"Yes," I say. "I really am." I don't even cringe when I reach for food and my sleeve brushes my burn. I'm kind of proud of myself.

"It's good to see you up again," Kahn says. "What you did last night was nothing short of miraculous, especially with how tired you were beforehand. I was worried you were already wiped out."

I was. I had nothing left when they called me to the front.

"Was it just me?" Stefan asks, "Or did it feel like the entire wall shook when those projectiles flew?"

"I didn't feel any shaking," Jesse says, "but it felt like something was off in the world around me. I thought you might need support."

"You were right," I say. "I was losing it. Without you and Dad and Kahn, I couldn't have done it."

My dad's smile is even goofier than Jesse's was when I glance his way. I have got to remember not to call him Dad.

"Why did you step near, Kahn?" Duncan asks. "I did it because Jesse did. Nothing felt off to me."

"The moment felt. . .dissonant to me," Kahn says.

My jaw drops. "Excuse me?"

Jesse frowns at him, and then glances my direction.

"You know, like when you're standing in between two rooms, and you hear different music coming from both. Perhaps someone's playing the piano in one and the harp in the other, and you're standing in just the right spot to hear both tunes, but they don't harmonize." He shrugs. "They're dissonant."

I had no idea what that word meant. Can it be a coincidence that he's using it right now? I stare at Kahn.

"Is everything okay?" His eyes are soft—pleading with me to let him provide support. The glowing is back with a vengeance.

I turn away. "I'm fine." I stand abruptly, needing to think about things. "I'm going to check on the North Wall. I want to confirm everything looks alright."

Jesse grabs my hand. "Wait. I'm coming."

Duncan clears his throat. "I need your advice on something here. Alora will be fine."

I nod. "I'll be back to check on you in an hour." Jesse squeezes my hand, but after a moment, he lets me go.

Kahn stands up and follows me out.

"I don't need an escort."

He raises his eyebrows questioningly. "You don't want me to come?"

He did just help me unravel a piece of the puzzle. Maybe I need him around.

Or maybe I just want him around.

I force my eyes away from his face. "Do what you want."

"I thought I'd show you what the blacksmiths have done. After last night, they all volunteered to work through the night. They've made ten thousand barbed metal shards. They're as lightweight as they could make them, but still provide the width to pierce a heart and kill quickly. I think they knew it might make the difference between our survival and our demise."

"It couldn't have been that close," I say. "You're all trained fighters."

"Before you turned the force back, our scouts reported that Devlin's force was nearly forty thousand strong. Our soldiers would have been demolished. Unfortunately, they're regrouping. They've been working on methods to counteract your attacks."

"I'm not sure why anyone's grateful to me, since the entire attack's my fault in the first place."

Kahn stops walking and turns a few feet to his left. He pulls me into an alcove, probably so no one will overhear our conversation. But my heart races like he's pulling me to the side to be alone with me. To press himself against me. To touch my face. To run his hand down the side of my body and press his palm against my hip. I inhale deeply to dispel my feverish thoughts.

Focus, Alora. Stop letting the stupid exordium melt your brain!

Kahn releases my hand and leans against the stone. "You're the subject of a prophecy. This attack is no more your fault than the rising and setting of the sun. Anyone who blames you for it, or any other issues that misguided idiots around you cause, is a fool."

"I can't change the prophecy," I say. "And I can't be other than I am." I look at my feet. "But I've been thinking about this." I look up into his eyes.

His gaze doesn't waver.

"If I surrender, no one else has to die."

Kahn's jaw tightens. "They'll kill you."

"Maybe they should."

Kahn slams his hand against the stone above my head and slowly lowers his face to mine, almost as if he can shield me from all attackers. "I won't allow it."

I should be furious that he wants to dictate my actions. I should slap the possessive look off his face. I should shove past him and march back to the main path.

I don't do any of those things, and I'm surprisingly not mad. In fact, there's no fury inside me at all.

Mostly I feel melty and tingly and warm. I'd love it if he kept lowering his head. . .and lowering it. And lowering it. Until our lips finally touched. If I feel this way having him near, how will I feel when we kiss?

"You won't allow it?" I don't smile, but my eyes slant upward, toward his.

"No. And I'm your commander, so you have to listen."

"You would've handed me over the day we met."

"I was an idiot." Kahn brings his other hand up against the wall, effectively surrounding me with his body.

Something in my belly flutters. Heat spreads from my chest into the rest of my body, and I inhale and exhale quickly to try and snap out of it. I can't waste time here, ogling Kahn, no matter how wonderful it feels.

I have a brother to save and a war to win. "Jesse," I manage to whisper. Like the name is a shield. Like it'll protect me from all the things I feel when I'm too close to Kahn.

His brow furrows. "What?"

"My brother. He's Wasting."

When Kahn frowns, when the corners of his perfect lips turn downward, my fingers itch to touch them. To see whether, with my touch, they'd curl up into a smile. I want to repair everything wrong in his life. "You can't possibly blame yourself for that. No one knows the cause. It happens every day."

He doesn't point out that it can't be stopped, because everyone already knows. "I'm cursed. It probably is my fault, somehow."

Kahn's head dips incrementally closer. In spite of my resolve not to be distracted, my heart hammers inside my chest. I long to close the space between us. "My parents both died of the Wasting on the same day. Do you think that was my fault? I was eight years old."

I gasp. "Of course not. I'm so sorry."

"It took me years to learn something, and I want you to listen to what I learned. Not everything that happens to us is our fault—some things are out of our control. You've done everything you can to make things better, to help, and to learn from your mistakes. That's all anyone can do."

I open my mouth to thank him, but the words don't emerge. Kahn's face is too close, his lips only inches from mine. His eyes widen, noticing my eyes on his mouth, and he smiles. He's always been almost painfully handsome. His jaw and his nose—the slopes, the angles—they're like an angel from a painting. His eyes are like ice, but alive. They're silver and blue and white all rolled together. His hair shines like the sun—and his lips. Full, wide, and mischievous. Strong.

I could have walked away. I could have thumbed my nose at fate and destiny and Mother Terra.

But when Kahn smiles, it's just for me. It's the most beautiful thing I've ever seen.

And it's too much.

As if he can sense the dissolution of my resolve, his head dips lower still. One of his hands drops from the cool stone to cup my face. He angles my mouth upward, gently, and his other arm reaches behind my back to pull my body flush against his.

I melt against him, his lips barely brushing against

mine, and he groans, deep in the back of his throat. My hands take hold of the collar of his shirt, like I've imagined doing dozens of times, and pull him down.

More. I need more.

Kahn knows exactly what to do without being told. His lips press harder, his hands clasp tighter, and the fluttering in my belly transforms into a thrill that spirals throughout my entire body. The world melts away.

Until I hear a voice, as if from far away.

"Unit Leader? Excuse me, but there's a disturbance at the front gate."

I pull back so fast I knock my head against the stone. The soldier standing behind Kahn looks at the ground. When he glances up at me, his eyes are round as saucers.

Kahn growls. Honest to goodness, he sounds like a feral wolf. "Tell Jesse. He's in charge of the gate."

The words penetrate our brains at the same time. Obviously Jesse isn't up to handling the gate, not now. Kahn closes his eyes, pained at his slip, and turns to follow the soldier. I follow close on his heels. We reach the front of the enclosure just in time to see it. A piece of parchment, curled into a roll, floating ten feet in the air, about a dozen paces from the gate.

I reach out and tear it away from whomever Lifted it over. There isn't much resistance. I bring it over the gate and drop it into Kahn's outstretched hands.

He starts to unroll it, but I reach out a hand to stop him. "Shouldn't we take this to my dad?"

"Yes." He lets it go, and it curls back up. He shakes his head like a dog after a bath. "I'm not thinking straight right now."

His half-smile is. . .the smile of a co-conspirator. I'm in on it—it's a smile for *us*, and that thought nearly breaks my brain.

He takes my hand before turning to walk back to the

castle, and I don't even stop him. I'm done fighting it, whatever this is. When we pass the alcove we just left, my heart thudding a little too fast, Kahn spins me into the small sheltered enclosure again, and this time he backs into the wall. I slide my hands against the stone on either side of Kahn's massive body. I don't have time to notice much else before Kahn's full, eager lips press against mine.

Stone and war and soldiers and Terra and armies all fall away. Nothing is wrong, and everything is right. And the only things holding me inside my skin are the points where his body touches mine. My mouth, my hip, and my cheek where his hands rest. My mind, for once, is blessedly blank, and my heart is full. His arms drop and then circle my waist, and I pull him even closer, his lips soft but insistent.

Without warning, he moves me backward, only an inch or two. He breathes the words against my mouth, almost like he's saying a prayer. "I have no idea what this scroll says. I don't know what will happen in the next hour, much less tomorrow, next week, or next year. But I needed to do that again while I still could."

I tighten my arms around his waist, meaning to pull his lips back down, but I bump my arm against his side and the pain that flares as a result brings me back to the present. I have a riddle to puzzle out, and not much time left in which to do it.

"I'm sorry I fought it for so long."

"So long?" His grin is all masculine pride. "Those three days felt like forever, but I would have waited as long as it took. You're worth any wait."

❧ 23 ❧

TERRA

I step away from Kahn, his words still warming my heart, and we walk quickly back to the castle side by side.

Stefan and the others have left, but Duncan's still in the dining hall talking to some men I haven't yet met. They all turn our way when we enter the room. Duncan nods at them. "We can work this out later. I need to speak to Kahn and Alora." The men file from the room, but several of them glance at me thoughtfully before they turn the corner.

"There's been a message from the Followers of Amun." Kahn hands the scroll to Duncan.

Dad unrolls it and reads aloud.

Felicitations, Donny.

Who'd have thought, twenty years ago, that we'd be here now, squabbling over your little girl? I'll admit that until recently, it never even occurred to me that your wife and daughter might have survived the "accident."

Well done.

For old times' sake, I'm offering you a deal. You'll have heard reports by now that I received a second wave of reinforcements early this morning. I now command almost sixty thousand troops. That really was quite a trick last night, but unless your little princess can repeat it—about thirty times in a single hour —I'm guessing our next attack will succeed. When we do, I'll order my men to kill every man they reach, and we won't stop until we've neutralized your daughter.

And don't hold out hopes for reinforcements. You see, my first move was to approach your Unit Leaders, the ones you left to their own strongholds. I had a discussion with them about their future, and they agree that Alora's care should be handed over to someone who isn't blinded by familial affection. They won't be sending you more troops—not now, not ever.

If you care at all about the people you command, spare us all the misery and send your daughter out to me instead. The ending will be the same for her either way, but you'll have so much less blood on your hands—and a life in which to appreciate that fact. I'll spare you and all your men for old times' sake.

You have one hour to consider my very reasonable offer.

Devlin

Duncan crumples the parchment into a ball in his hand. He stares out the window without uttering a single word.

"I thought you heard Devlin wanted to spare me," I say. "Didn't someone say that?"

"Neutralize is a polite word for kill," Kahn says.

"I know that." Duncan starts pacing. "I won't send my daughter to him to be butchered, but what's the alternative? We'll all die. He's right. An army that large will roll over us. How did he get so many men here so quickly?"

"Do you really think he flipped the others?" Kahn's eyes spark, and the muscle in his jaw jerks.

"What's going on?" Jesse walks in. "I heard a lot of yelling."

No one speaks. None of us want to tell Jesse that it

looks like both of Duncan's kids will be dead by tomorrow.

I sit down at the table and pick up an apple. "You should eat something. We don't know much about the Wasting, but going without sustenance can't help."

Jesse looks at each one of us and frowns, but he dutifully leans toward the dining table and grabs a grape. Then he tosses it into the air and catches it in his mouth.

The motion looks so familiar.

Remember.

Something inside my brain shifts, and I see him do that same movement, but in another place, with something else. Something red. Something green. Not a grape. Then more images, more sounds, and more smells flicker and then flash. A barrage of sensation tries to squeeze into my brain from a crack in a doorway that leads somewhere else entirely. It's uncomfortable and it feels *wrong*. I want to slam the door shut and keep my brain right side up.

But that discomfort. . .

Remember.

Could it be dissonance? Could this have something to do with saving Jesse? Instead of slamming it shut, I lean in. I focus on the non-grapes Jesse threw.

As he walked down the sidewalk.

As he sat in a small room.

As he stood by a park bench.

I shove it farther open, and the pain, oh, the pain. I clutch at my head. Sharp, stabbing agony accompanies every new image, every new event. The memories aren't of Jesse, and yet, they are. He's wearing strange clothes, and his hair is cut way too short, but it's him.

And then, as abruptly as the door cracked, it slams shut, and the memories slip away.

Remember.

Remember.

Remember.

I slide down into a chair and close my eyes. I pick just one memory of which I saw a glimpse. The first one that surfaced. It may have hurt, but it wasn't well formed. It wasn't sharp.

For some reason, I feel like it needs to be clear.

It was Jesse, but it wasn't Jesse.

I focus on the details. Not-Jesse tosses up a yellow, stone-looking thing. It lands in his mouth, and he crunches it with pleasure. He smiles at me. He shakes some other little stones out of a yellow bag that says "M&M" on it, but not in Terran. In another language, a language I inexplicably know. The one seared into the flesh of my arm. The not-Jesse holds his hand out to me, and I shake my head.

"You know I'm terrible at that," I say.

It's my voice, but it's not me saying it. It's Jesse, but not quite. Then, like I'm pulling on a piece of cord, trying to work out a knot, I feel a tugging. Another memory comes directly after that one. Jesse, who's not quite Jesse, says, "You can just put them in your mouth you know. Not everyone can be as amazing as me."

I squeeze my hands more tightly over my ears. A buzzing sound comes from all around me. It grows and grows and grows until I can't hear anything else, and then there's a tremendous pop that knocks me back against the chair. I rub my eyes and clutch at my head because it feels full of cotton, and while the buzzing has lessened, it's wider, broader, more massive.

Will it ever go away?

Will I ever turn right-side up again?

When I open my eyes, Kahn, Duncan, and Jesse peer down at me. I'm looking at the same room and the same people as a moment ago, but they're all different, too.

Especially Jesse.

I know him so well. He's Jesse, and he's not-Jesse, but they're the same. He's beloved, he's my rock, he's my favorite person in all the world. And that's when it hits me that not-Jesse. . .is gone. He was torn from me by evil people, by the same person who's threatening to eliminate every person standing with me in this castle.

Devlin Rochester.

The man who wants to harm every person who has defended what is right and true and good. Not-Jesse is gone, and as a result, Jesse is Wasting.

But now I know how to save him.

I feel it all around me. In my exhaustion, my depression, and my despair, I finally feel the edges of the world we're all trapped inside. The gentle humming surrounding me has always been here, but I've never noticed it, never listened for it. I've tuned it out my entire life. The dissonance, the noise at the edges of my consciousness when I was beyond tired, *that's* the true nature of Terra.

Nothing in this world is real except the people. Everything else is composed of threads and strings, cords and cables of energy, pure energy, forced into the forms that surround me. Rocks, food, furniture, even animals, every bit of matter here is a construct.

A construct I can now access and utilize, now that I see it.

I turn toward my dad. "I know how to fix this, all of it."

He looks confused, but he nods. "What will you do?" He doesn't argue or question my proclamation. He simply believes, and he's willing to do whatever I ask.

I won't let him down.

I'm sure he thinks I'm going to hand myself over to

Devlin, because before this happened, I was leaning toward that. I would have insisted on it, in fact.

"I'm going to end this war. It isn't fair to either side."

"You can't give up," Kahn says. "Devlin may have more troops than we do, but he hasn't seen what you can do, and we have contingencies in place. Your dad even has an evacuation plan, if it comes to that. And we hold the upper hand in terms of fortifications and terrain."

I shake my head. "Which is exactly why we can't run. You all know that as well as I do. And with odds as long as they are, we need a different angle. We need leverage."

Kahn looks as if I've punched him.

"Don't worry." I smile. "I've found it."

Now that I understand Terra, and I understand myself, I can end Devlin and as many of his men as I need, before the war even starts. I can wrap them in cords of energy and pull. I can fire projectiles at each of them, one by one, or hundreds upon hundreds until they yield. I won't run out of energy, because it's literally *all around me*.

Except that's not the solution to everything, not yet.

I turn to my darling brother, the bedrock of my life. "I need you to come with me, Jesse. Can you do that?"

Jesse nods. "Yes." Simple. He trusts me entirely.

Kahn says, "I'm coming, too."

I frown, because I'm not sure what to do with Kahn. "If you come with us, you should know. We won't be returning."

Kahn shrugs. "So be it."

I turn and hug my dad for the first, and possibly the last, time. When I pull back, a tear rolls down his face. He doesn't understand, but he trusts me, too. "It's going to be okay, Dad, I swear."

"You won't be coming back."

I shrug. "I can't explain my plan right now. You won't

understand. But I promise you'd agree if I could make it something you'd get."

"Should I come?"

I shake my head. "Devlin needs to think I'm surrendering."

His forehead wrinkles as his eyebrows rise. "But. . .you aren't surrendering?"

I am in a way, but not to Devlin, which is what Dad's asking. "No."

My dad hugs me one more time, and then he hugs Jesse, but not too hard. I can't blame him. Jesse's gray face and sweat-soaked brow don't inspire confidence.

I really can't wait any longer.

We leave the room and make it down the hall before Jesse stumbles and almost falls.

"I'm glad you're coming," I tell Kahn. "I'm going to need a hand."

Kahn and I each step underneath one of Jesse's arms. Together, we walk out of the castle proper, through the courtyard, and to the front wall. Once the guards lower the drawbridge, we walk through the gate, and down the steps. Several dozen men follow us through with crates, as I requested, but once they place them on the ground behind me, they practically sprint back into the courtyard.

I stop a few dozen paces in front of the drawbridge, which is already rising behind us.

I call out. "Devlin!"

Silence.

"Devlin! I'm here to respond to your offer. Come out and face me."

We wait.

Seconds turn into minutes, and then those minutes pile up.

Sweat pours down Jesse's face where he sags against

Kahn. I'm about to apply some pressure—I'm not sure how much time Jesse has—when Devlin appears. The ranks of soldiers shift as he walks toward us. He looks very small from this far away, but it's definitely him. Here on Terra, Devlin has longer hair, pulled back into a knot, but his eyes and his mouth and everything else are the same—he's every bit as imposing.

"Duncan sent you." Devlin rubs the bristle on his chin. "I'm surprised. It was the right move, which he so rarely makes."

"Are you planning to kill me?" I ask. "That's what my father believes."

Devlin steps back, his brows drawn in confusion. "Why would I kill you? You can't fulfill that prophecy until you know everything. I doubt you've even seen the original. I think I have the only copy."

"Why are you the only one who has it?"

"I trained with your father, you know. I courted your mother before she ever clapped eyes on him. This exordium thing is infuriating. You can't fight it, you can't do anything about it. You might have been my child, had things gone differently, had the laws not been what they are."

I shudder at that thought.

"You don't like me, and that's okay. You don't have to like me as long as you fulfill your purpose."

I'm getting sick of people telling me what I need to do, and if I hear the word prophecy one more time. . .

"Go ahead, then. Tell me."

Devlin opens his mouth to talk, but Jesse cries out at the same time. "Alora!"

I turn back to look at him, but he's lying slack, and Kahn lowers him gently to the ground.

"What's going on, Kahn?"

He shakes his head. "I don't know. I think he passed out."

I rush to Jesse's side, feeling for a pulse. I can't find one, so I reach out with another sense. I close my eyes again and feel for his heartbeat. I've done this before, and it didn't go well, but this time it's different. This time, Jesse's different. It's faint, but his heart still beats. On Earth, I felt his physical body and his heart. Here, I feel his consciousness, but it's surrounded by energy filaments, like a spider's web that holds together the pieces of who he is.

I open my eyes and look up at Kahn, and then I turn to face Devlin. He glances at Jesse with pity.

"Your brother's not doing well. I'd say he has an hour left at most."

I reach out with my newfound senses for Devlin, a bundle of red thoughts and black feelings. His spiderweb of energy looks and feels different than Jesse's, different than Kahn's. I push beyond, to the mass of people behind Devlin, many of them holding weapons pointed in my direction. I feel my father's men standing behind the gate. I feel the strands of power, spun together to make the drawbridge and the moat. I pull on the energy around Devlin and I realize that I can unwind him as easily as the bushes or blades of grass beside his boot. I could pull him apart in pieces and the world would be rid of him, once and for all.

I want to do it, but something distracts me.

Jesse's filaments are unwinding on their own. That's the Wasting—a slow unwinding of someone's filaments, the energy signature that holds them together, that makes them who and what they are. It takes time, but it begins to unravel once the person dies on Earth, and then. . . they're gone. Forever.

Which means I'm all out of time.

I take a deep breath and step back. I place one hand on Kahn and one on Jesse. "This might be scary. Try to hang on."

I turn back toward Devlin and I Lift all ten thousand of the barbed metal shafts the blacksmiths worked through the night to manufacture. I think of the nails, the bed frames, everything that went into these, and I realize that they wasted their time, because everything here is pure energy. All the objects were a lie holding me back. I Lift a piece of rock from the ground and slowly remold it into a metal shaft. I feel the smile on my lips, but Kahn's watching, and his expression isn't a smile.

His eyes widen with fear, and his jaw drops. "What did you do?"

I shake my head. "No time to explain."

I cast about for the lives of the soldiers. I can't thoroughly search the intentions of every one of them, but I can sense which are dark and which are light. I can sense which tangles of thought and combinations of feelings are good and which are dark and twisty. I isolate the bad ones easily, and suddenly I'm ready.

Devlin's eyes fill with fear when he looks at the ten thousand projectiles I've Lifted. The more I probe at him, the less I understand. While his intentions are dark, those strands are entwined with light ones. He's not entirely evil, but he'll try to stop me, and I won't let a half-light and half-dark man prevent me from saving my brother.

"Wait." Devlin jogs toward me, his hands out. "You don't understand what you're doing."

"Oh, I think I do." I hurl those shafts at every dark man in front of me and feel them pierce almost every heart. I hurl a dozen of them at Devlin to be safe.

He blocks them all.

I gnash my teeth, but I don't have time to deal with him right now.

It's time for me to go back to Earth, but not by sleeping. Not this time.

I need to go back wide awake.

When I try to tug backward, when I try to fall away from this place, everything on Terra resists. I crouch down and pull Jesse over against my chest, close to my heart. I pull his bundle of light thoughts, good intentions, and shining light against me, and then for the first time ever, instead of going to sleep, I intentionally *shift* away from Terra. At first, I feel as though I've merely stepped away from a room. I see the people that surrounded me, gasping at the empty space where I used to be. Everyone's face fills with shock, fear, and confusion when I disappear.

Everyone except Kahn.

He sees me, even here, on an invisible pathway leading away from Terra.

Now that I'm not standing next to him, I see that a bright, pulsing light fills Kahn, a light I couldn't possibly contain myself. I don't want to leave him, so I tug on the filaments that are Kahn, but it feels like pulling on a semi-truck, or a dumpster full of concrete. Reluctantly, I release him, because Earth beckons.

I let myself go and fall backward. I realize that I've done this a million times without being aware of the journey. Every night when I go to sleep, I travel the same path. My mind knows what to do, but this time, there's something dragging against me, a resistance that increases as I move toward Earth.

It must be Kahn, fighting my plan to take Jesse.

But when I glance back, it's clear that Kahn's following me—on his own. He isn't pulling on me, or even connected to me.

So what's the difficulty? I look around, but everywhere I look, there's only blank space. Empty nothingness. Except for my arms. In my arms, I'm carrying Jesse. His soul in my arms weighs an eternity and pulls like a mountain. Bringing him along feels like trying to contain the ocean. He's trying to collapse, his filaments and threads dissolving into raw energy.

I know I ought to let his energy flow into me like it keeps trying to do, but *I can't*.

He's dead on Earth. If this energy dissipates, Jesse's gone, so I funnel more energy into him from my core, and I brace myself.

The farther I travel, the harder it becomes to bring Jesse along. His filaments curl and twist. His thoughts and feelings tug and writhe. I wrap the energy from myself around him like a cocoon to shelter him, and I shove harder. I don't care what it takes. I can do it. As Earth draws near, Kahn veers off. I try calling to him, but my voice doesn't work here. Also, the resistance changes and I forget Kahn entirely as I face a new challenge.

Jesse's body bucks and kicks and I shake with the effort of funneling enough energy into him to keep him from dissolving. My muscles contract painfully, my skin melts and reforms. I pull harder and my own filaments strain, my body beginning to unwind as I span the last bit of space separating me from Earth. In the end, I need more energy—I need more power. So I reach out into the void and I *pull*.

Like drinking a milkshake, the energy responds to my demand. Lights on Earth, lights all around me, *flicker* in response to my tugging, but they don't blink out. And then finally, I reach my destination. I'm back home. On Earth.

I'm terrified to look down into my arms, not sure what I'll see.

But when I finally do, it's Jesse. He looks fine, normal
even. His hair is long, but it's shiny and smooth and just
as it was on Terra.

I sigh and collapse, releasing Jesse, and open my eyes.
I close my eyes and reopen them—but nothing changes.
I've done it.

Jesse lies next to me, smack in the middle of John's
king-size bed.

❦ 24 ❦

EARTH

John appears in the doorway, bleary-eyed in his superhero pajama pants. His eyes widen when he sees Jesse. I place my hand on Jesse's sleeping forehead and breathe a sigh of relief. He doesn't feel hot to the touch anymore, either. I make a shushing sound with one finger and climb down from the bed.

I'm surprised to find that I'm still wearing my Terran knee-high black boots, tight black pants, and linen shirt. John and I tiptoe out and pull the door shut. Before I've even taken two steps, John pulls me against him, and I relax into his arms.

"You're safe. I was going crazy, worried that you'd die on Terra. That you weren't coming back."

"I'm safe."

"I'm glad." John's eyes spark, and I realize he likes me. Not in a general flirting, casual way. There's real concern in his eyes. My lips part and his eyes shift toward them.

Too many things in my life right now, too much going on. And Kahn. What do I feel for him? I pull back, and John releases me immediately.

"What happened?" John settles on the corner of a chair.

I sit down on the edge of his plaid sofa. Plaid? Really?

"Terra still stands?"

I nod.

"And you saved Jesse." John beams. "That's amazing. You were able to come back and drag someone with you." He shakes his head. "My dad would be beside himself right now if he knew."

"Actually, something strange happened at the end there."

"At the end?" John smiles. "Every single part of this has been strange."

True. "But someone. . .sort of followed me back." I scrunch my nose.

"Who?"

"Someone you know." I cough into my hand. "Kahn."

"What?" John scowls. "Then where is he?"

I shrug. "He kind of. . .peeled off when we got close. Maybe his soul from Terra went to his real body? I'm not sure. I didn't bring him, he just sort of tagged along."

"No way. He can't do that. Only you can go back and forth."

"How do you know that? It doesn't say that in the prophecy."

He shrugs. "It's in the stories."

"What stories?" I groan. "I'm so tired of knowing nothing."

"I grew up with bedtime stories, except mine were about the Blessed, the people born with powers in the beginning of time. Unfortunately, the Blessed didn't honor their abilities and used them instead to get what they wanted. As you know, the women came to see that it had to be stopped. People with powers couldn't simply control everyone and everything."

"Except that kind of happens, even without powers involved."

"True enough. Although a lot of the people in power you know about do have abilities. They just aren't open about them anymore, because our powers are hard to access and they're weakened. As you know, these Blessed people set up Terra, intending to free the world from the rule of the less ethical among them. Only the bridge could bring the Blessed back to the Earth, and only if she deemed them worthy."

"I don't know any stories, but I didn't bring Kahn. I tried, actually, but I couldn't shift him at all. He followed me entirely on his own."

John's eyebrows draw together. "So you did try to bring him back."

I explain everything that happened, as quickly and clearly as I can. Although, I don't mention that Kahn kissed me. I'm trying to figure out why I left that out when there's a knock at the door.

John freezes.

Then he stands up and walks toward the door. A second knock pounds before he reaches it. He turns to me and motions for his bedroom. If this is Amun, or Isis for that matter, I don't know why I'd be safer in his bedroom, but I go.

I glance at the clock in the family room on my way. It's showing the time as 3:07. Based on the pitch black window, I'm guessing it's a.m.

A third knock bangs, more insistent than the last two. John yells, "Coming. Geez, it's the middle of the night. Give me a minute."

I'm ducking into the bedroom when the door opens. The voice of the person who walks through sends chills down my spine. "I needed to make sure you're okay. The Warden just unleashed an insane amount of power in

Terra, killing nearly ten thousand people. You didn't answer your phone."

"Dad, I'm not even *on* Terra. Remember?"

"Erra and Terra are connected. You know that." Devlin Rochester stands not twenty feet away, pulling his son into a stiff embrace.

I should stay hidden in the bedroom. I should wait for John to get rid of him, but I'm suddenly drowning in a fury so great that it engulfs me. I regret killing those men over the past few days, men forced by Devlin to attack my father's castle. I regret each projectile that ended a life. I feel sick about them, actually. But today? I don't regret killing the men I did before I left. They were dark, twisted, and evil, every single one.

My only regret from tonight is not killing the man who managed to destroy half of my brother's soul. I should have diverted more of those shafts his way.

I shouldn't have left Terra until I pulled him apart, one wriggly filament at a time.

"Declan Rosenbaum," I say.

John turns sharply in my direction, shaking his head furiously, but it's too late. I know Devlin recognized my voice, just as Moriarty would know Holmes' voice anywhere, anytime.

"So you do answer to your fake name." My nostrils flare. "I wondered."

"What're you doing here?" His smile isn't even icy. It looks almost genuine. "I've been looking for you everywhere, and you were hiding right under my nose?" Devlin's smile grows until it stretches from ear to ear. He turns toward his son. "I didn't give you enough credit, clearly."

"You're telling me you didn't know Jesse was working for me?" John asks.

His father scoffs. "Of course I knew. I just didn't realize she had figured out. . ."

Devlin looks from his son's pajama bottoms and no shirt, to where I'm standing in the doorway to his bedroom. "Wait, you didn't capture her for me." He frowns. "You're conspiring *with* her *against* me."

John squares his shoulders. "You've always been a terrible father. Are you really surprised?"

"That you turned out to have a backbone after all?" Devlin asks. "Yes, I am. You were always too much like your mother."

"I hope that's true," John says.

Devlin rolls his eyes. "You want to be like your mother? A woman so weak that when things became complicated, she shattered?"

"Better than someone who kills people in the name of a stupid, vague prophecy," I say.

"You killed ten thousand people in a split second tonight," Devlin says. "How do you justify that?"

"I only killed wicked souls," I say. "Every single person I ended had dark thoughts and evil intentions. John's just and good. I would never kill him."

"You can't see his soul on Terra. Can you see it here?"

I scowl.

"I thought not. You don't know a thing about him, not really." He glances at his son, and then turns back to face me. "Would you like him quite as much if he were ugly? If his face was pockmarked and his hair thinning?"

My scowl deepens.

"Life's not as simple as you want it to be. You killed men with evil intentions *on Terra.* How do you know what kind of people they are here?"

"People are the same," I say. "My brother was good here, and he was good there. Henry was weak here, so he's weak on Terra." Even as I say it, I realize I'm not sure it's true. I didn't know Devlin or Henry on Terra, not really. My nostrils flare and I double down. It must be right. It feels right, anyway. "It stands to reason that if they're evil there, they're evil here."

"You're unbearably naive."

The door behind me cracks open, and Jesse pokes his head out, awakened by the shouting.

"Go back, please. I'll explain later, I swear," I whisper. He ducks back into the room, but it's too late.

I expect surprise. I expect Devlin to freak out and start screaming, or yelling, or ranting. I do not expect the fear that floods his eyes to the brim. I don't expect terror to cause his hands to shake, or his breathing to become shallow and rapid.

"What have you done?" He backs away from me, as if I could infect him with a deadly virus. "He's dead."

I shrug. "You killed him here. He was dying there too, until I brought him over. Now he's fine. The fever's gone."

He stumbles backward, toward the entryway. "You've shattered the walls. You'll kill us all. Isis was right."

"You're one to talk," I say. "You've been killing people right and left."

"I didn't want to kill Jesse," Devlin says. "I tried everything I could think of before it came to that. We knew the Warden would be the hardest person on Earth to Wake. The prophecy says so. It's close to impossible to bring out power that strong. In fact, if you didn't have a brother you loved dearly, if you didn't have someone you loved without question, if I hadn't done all the other awful things to you, leaving you only one person in the world to care for, I probably couldn't have Woken you *at all*. Jesse was a necessary sacrifice."

I step toward him, still gripped by an all-consuming rage. "You obviously don't understand the word 'sacrifice.' It means to surrender something that matters to you, or to offer something of yourself, something *that's yours to give*. What you did wasn't a sacrifice. *It was theft!* You stole my brother from me, and wrenched his life away from him. You gave up nothing."

"I'm sorry about that." He pleads with me then, his hands out in front of him, clasped together in supplication. "I'll apologize every single day, and I'll sacrifice something myself, anything you want, but you must listen to me now. You don't understand what you've done. By removing an inmate, by bringing Jesse here to Earth, you cracked the prison walls wide open. If you don't converge our worlds soon, everyone there, every single person on Terra will die. It'll make your massacre tonight look like a water gun attack compared to. . .a tsunami!"

I shake my head. He can't be right. When I left, everything looked fine. "Why should I believe a single thing you say?"

"I don't lie," he says.

"Oh don't you, *Declan Rosenbaum?*"

The whites of his eyes flash at me, and I revel in his horror. "I'm not lying now. Everything I've done has been because I've had no other choice."

"Is that why you killed Mom?" John asks. "You had no choice? You couldn't have rescued her?"

Devlin turns to his son, his face stricken, his hands at his side. "I didn't kill your mother. Why would you even think that? I did every single thing I could to help her."

"You helped her right into suicide, after ignoring her when she begged for help."

"She didn't commit suicide." Devlin's voice drops to a whisper. "You've always blamed me for her death, but it's time you learned the truth. Amun required that I Wake you as a test of loyalty before I could defect from Isis. They wanted me to prove that I truly believed as they did. I tried several things to accomplish it, but they didn't work. Your mother grew increasingly upset about my attempts, so I sent her to stay with her sister."

John shakes his head. "No, you checked her into an institution. I saw the stationery on the letters she wrote. It was a place in Arizona called the Citadel. I looked it up. They specialize in the treatment of mentally unstable patients. It's an inpatient psychiatric hospital."

"No, son. I don't know whether there's a psych hospital by that name, but Aunt Gertrude was older. She lived in an Assisted Living center known as the Citadel."

John shakes his head. "She sent that note, saying she couldn't take any more. She said she'd end it if you didn't."

"I didn't want to lose your mother. I called her and promised I'd pack our things and head back by the end of the week. If Amun wouldn't take me, I'd return to Isis and redouble my efforts to alter their path."

"Mom died," John says flatly, but his voice isn't as firm, isn't as sure. The rage is leeching away. "She committed suicide."

"She died, yes," Devlin says gently. "She Wasted on Erra, and then had a heart attack here. She didn't take her own life. I told you she had a heart attack, remember?"

John shakes his head, and so do I.

"No," John says. "It was your fault."

"His story makes no sense," I say. "People die here and then Waste on Terra. Not the other way around."

"You know so little—it's like you're peering through a peephole without having ever seen the actual room. We don't have time to argue this right now," Devlin says. "But I can show you later, any time or by any method you want, that I didn't institutionalize her. I tried to help her."

"I don't believe you," John says.

I look him in the eye and make a decision. "Neither do I."

I Lift Devlin, and walk down the hall, shoving him into the recliner. I Bind his arms and legs, and when I'm convinced he can't move, I sit down on the sofa. John perches on the ottoman.

"Is this really necessary?" Devlin asks. "Have I threatened you in any way?"

"You must be asking whether you've threatened me today, because I think telling your henchman to rape me was threatening. And I definitely consider shooting my brother in the foot—" I choke. I inhale a new breath. "—and then *killing him* to be *threatening*!"

John's hands tighten into fists, and I realize he didn't know any details about his dad's methods that night. Poor John. This must be awful for him. I step between John and Devlin. "Stop defending yourself, and tell me what I need to know."

"You're the Warden and you've accelerated things, but it's not your fault the prison is coming down. You've just sped up the process. The Followers of Isis didn't understand that, because they hadn't studied the proper translation of the original prophecy." I release the Bindings on his hand and Lift a pen and paper from the kitchen.

"Write down the original prophecy, then."

"That's not the whole story," he says. "It's not everything you need to know."

"It's a good start," I say. "You can fill me in on the rest after I've seen it. I'm sure you know the original prophecy by heart."

He starts writing. I wait until he's done before I try to read it. He slides the paper over to me and I Bind his hand again before picking it up.

With the women it began, with the birth of the Warden it will end. She who can bridge the divide will rend the prison walls, rescuing the wartorn. They will fall, one after another, each in turn. The Telekinetics, the Elementals, the Renders and Reapers, and the Assimilators. In time, the prison walls will disintegrate until the world becomes whole again. The Earth will come unbound, and if the Warden fails, will be ripped apart. The storm will rage against her, but with a great sacrifice, and with the strength of her balance, all will fall and be remade. None can stand against her wrath, and none can endure without her compassion. Salvation comes from her hand, but at the end of all things, the world will only be healed when she is reunited with the OathMaker and the mistake is undone, the crime forgiven.

Only she can choose. Only she can restore. Only she can forgive. But she can't do it alone.

Once I've finished reading, I hand it to John. "You were pretty close. Nice work."

"I missed a few key details," John says.

"What's your plan?" Devlin asks.

"I've already enacted my plan. Except for one small thing."

"What?" he asks.

I Lift a kitchen knife from a block in John's kitchen and float it over to press against Devlin's throat. "Killing you. See, there's this thing they call a sacrifice. You thought you'd made one. It's time for you to actually do it."

I feel him push back against me, but it's the pitiful pressure of a single wave against the incoming tide.

"Wait," he cries. "You still don't understand. You can't bring your brother here and then do nothing more."

"I think you're done telling me what I can and can't do." I Lift every single thing in the room, the light from my eyes flooding the room with light. "You have no power over me, Devlin Rochester. None!"

His eyes are so wide the whites are showing, but he doesn't give up. "The prison walls are coming down with or without you. Your job isn't to dismantle Terra or to abandon it either. It began unraveling the second you were born. It's why people, like John's mother, have Wasted on Erra even when they were fine on Earth. Terra's falling apart in all its iterations, and the people caught onboard are dying like rats on a sinking ship. Your choice isn't to dismantle the prison or to walk away. It's whether to save them, or leave them all there to die." His eyes are desperate.

Devlin lies so often that I can't believe a word he says. I press the knife harder.

"Wait," John says.

I do feel for John. I know better than anyone that there's light entwined in the darkness of Devlin's soul. If he were my dad, I'd hesitate, too.

But he isn't my dad.

"I warned you." My hands tremble. "I was upfront about what I planned to do from the first moment."

He bites his lip and waves his phone at me. "Alora, I looked it up. There's a Citadel that's an assisted living, just like he said. If he really didn't kill my mom. . .maybe I was wrong." John looks at me with tortured eyes, and I soften.

I release everything I've Lifted, rearranging the room carefully, and walk toward him. "He may be telling the truth," I say, "but we have no way to know that."

"My dad's complicated, but he has never lied to me outright. What if what he says *is* true?"

"What if it is?" I ask. "We can deal with that without him."

He puts his hand on mine. "We can deal with him

after we figure out what's happening on Terra. He knows more than anyone. He's dedicated his life to researching this. Don't kill him while we might yet need him."

I wrench my hand away, and it takes every bit of my self-control not to slap John with it. "He killed my parents, he ruined my life. He forced me into a group home where things. . .*bad* things happened to me. And all of that, I might forgive. But John," my voice breaks. "In case you've forgotten, he killed Jesse in front of me."

"He did those things because he thought he had to Wake you. I don't know whether he's right, but he thought he was. That matters, doesn't it? His intent?"

"Once the bowl is shattered, it doesn't really matter why you broke it."

"You're the Warden, Alora, and what he did was awful, but your brother's right back there." John gestures to his bedroom.

"We don't know if he's the same. We don't know if he'll survive the transition. And even if he does, he won't remember *me here* or anything from Earth." A tear streaks down my face and rage makes me tremble. "Devlin doesn't get a pass because I ran across broken glass to try and clean up the mess he made. He must pay."

"If you kill him, aren't you as bad as he is?" His words are a slap in the face.

I collapse onto the sofa, but I think about it, and honestly. . .

I don't know.

In the end, I realize that I don't care. Even if I become like Devlin, dark and light twisted together, it doesn't matter, because I can't forgive or forget what he did. I can't allow his actions, his ruthlessness, and his careless disregard for shredding the lives of people around him to continue.

"I'm not saying he did the right thing," John says,

"but if he's right, if Terra's falling apart, if my mom's death was collateral damage, that means he's trying to save the lives of what? A hundred thousand people?"

"More like three hundred thousand," Devlin says. "On Terra alone."

"Shut up!" I Bind his mouth and watch him struggle to speak.

"I'm not saying he's a good person," John says earnestly, ignoring his dad. "I'm just saying he had some justification for tormenting you, not that it excuses what he did to you or Jesse."

I feel profoundly betrayed.

I blink several times, wondering if I'm actually having my first real nightmare. Maybe now that I've left Terra for good, I'm dreaming. It's too bizarre, John pleading for his awful father's life. I reach out with my senses, the same ones I used in Terra, but I can't sense them here, the strands that wind together to form John's soul. I can't feel his motivations, his thoughts, or his desires.

I don't care what Devlin thinks of me, but I realize that I do care what John thinks. "I can't believe—"

Devlin's eyes roll back in his head and he begins to writhe against the Bindings.

"It's happening," John says. "Terra—like he said. There must be something wrong."

So what. Let him die. At least then it's not my fault.

"It's not just him," John says. "If Dad's dying, if he's right, everyone on Terra will be seizing just like this as it crumbles."

What if that's really happening? I don't even think about it any further. I plummet downward, toward Terra. The pathway's easy to find this time, and there's no resistance as I rocket back.

When I arrive, appearing in the precise spot I left not that long ago, I'm standing in the midst of chaos. People sit in bunches all around me, some of them leaning against one another, some alone. All of them are sweating profusely. Many of them look confused, dazed even. Every face is filled with despair or downcast or panicked. The trees and the buildings have begun to unravel. In the blink of an eye, a tree goes from its normal form to a flickering mess and then back again. Or it disappears in a flash of pure light. It's happening everywhere I look. The ground, the walls, the buildings. Flashing, flickering, pulsing, twisting.

Devlin was right. Terra's in its death throes.

I hope he's right and it's not my fault for bringing Jesse home. Because if he's wrong about that, then maybe he and I aren't so different after all.

I close my eyes and feel for the people around me. There are so many, stretching on and on and on. Hundreds of thousands. Have they already started dying?

The icy tendrils of guilt drag me downward.

Is Duncan alive? What about Martin? I focus on the souls I know. I find Duncan and Martin both still pulsing. I feed energy into them and breathe a sigh of relief as they seem to lighten. I seek for the rest of my family, the troupe. They're all there, flickering, but lit up. I feed them the energy from their own wagons.

That's when I realize that Devlin was right about something else.

I can't bolster everyone. I need to get them to Earth before they're extinguished forever.

But I don't have enough power to bring three hundred thousand people back with me.

I pull Martin toward me. I pull Duncan. I pull my troupe and the Unit. I start selecting souls who are nearest to me. I realize I can only bring, maybe, a thousand. I look around panicked. So many will die, because saving Jesse sped this up. Thanks to my selfish maneuver, we're out of time.

He will blame himself if he ever finds out.

Which means that if he survives the transition, he'll never forgive me.

I can't think about that. Not now. I focus on saving all I can—what else can I do?

But how can I possibly choose?

I gather up as many souls as possible, and I pull. They zing along with me, shrinking down to sparks of light like fireflies, darting and flashing all around me. I step back from Terra and they follow, and it's hard. Harder than ripping Jesse free. Harder than anything I've ever done. I'm not sure I can even make it with everyone I gathered.

Except now I see something I didn't before. I don't personally have the power to do what's necessary. It would end me to even try. I'd burn up on the return.

But I'm surrounded with vast, unfathomable power.

I step back down to Terra, my gathered fireflies following me eagerly. I touch the ground under my feet and *pull* and it floods into me, from the rocks, from the trees, from the being and matter of Terra. I slurp the world around me up like a Slurpee, drawing people like flickering lights into a swarm that swirls and darts and dips in every direction. The power I need swells inside me as I gather, and when I think I can't take a single speck more, the stream just keeps on flowing. I'm so full of energy that I may burst into a million tiny lights. My skin stretches tight, my eyes burn.

And still I don't stop.

The swarm of souls around me grows and grows, flowing into me as I consume the ground beneath their feet and the buildings in which they're cowering. I suck them down, and they join the darting, flickering, flying masses. They're scared, angry, and hurt, but I push onward. It takes hours, it takes a millisecond.

I lose track of anything but the power, the pull, and the pain.

The unfathomable pain.

Finally, when I have gathered every last soul, I cast just one back, and I begin the voyage home. I see one thing as I leave Terra forever. Devlin, Lord of Rochester Castle. He salutes me from where he stands alone on a single flagstone.

He was right. He spoke the truth.

He is dark and light entwined, but I will not bring him back. I will not spare his life. He owes me for the death of my parents, for the life of my brother, for the memories of Jesse's that I can't ever restore, and for the years of my life he ruined.

I'm calling in the debt.

And I'm not looking back.

I cast off, blasting away from the ruins of Terra as quickly as possible. The closer I grow, the harder it becomes, much as the trip with Jesse became more and more difficult.

Although I want to quit, I want to let go, I pull those thousands upon thousands of souls along with me, every last one. I move quickly through the darkness, my entire being quivering with the immeasurable strain. I burn through the power I siphoned as I drag the lights back to Earth. This time, like Kahn, the lights I'm dragging with me veer off, presumably returning to their own bodies. Each departure lightens my load, and I'm glad, because I'm almost out of energy.

I'm so close, but I'm nearly empty, coasting on fumes.

I slam back into Earth, the ground shaking as I reconnect in the family room of John's modest home. His lamps, his furniture, everything in the apartment shakes.

I'm not imagining it—the world around me really is cracking, as though Houston's being wracked by its first earthquake. Once the tremors stop, I collapse. It takes every ounce of strength I have left, but I look up, into Devlin's eyes, and I smile. It's not a smile full of joy, but it's a smile full of satisfaction.

He knows.

He knows I've saved everyone but him, and he doesn't even look angry. He looks relieved. I feel him shove at my Bindings, but my power's spent, and I can't stop him. I know he can probably come over and kill me, and there's nothing I can do to stop him. He breaks free, but instead of coming for me, he stumbles over to his son.

"John." He grabs for his boots, but John lifts him up and hugs him. "I'm sorry, John. I'm sorry that I did everything wrong. That I got it all backward."

Devlin begins to spasm again—as though he improved with my return to Terra. . .and now that he's stuck, he's back to convulsing.

I feared this man for years, and as I grew, that fear turned into hate. I've hated every decision he's made. I hated how he destroyed my life, and how he brought an army against me in Terra that would have destroyed all my family and friends.

I hated every fiber of his being when he murdered my brother.

I shouldn't feel bad about leaving him to his death. After the thousands of men I killed back on Terra, even before being able to see their intentions and the state of their souls, I shouldn't feel so much guilt over this one. This blackened man, this horrible, misguided, person.

Except we *become* our actions.

I hate Devlin because of the choices he made, even though he thought he was doing the right thing. His intentions don't excuse what he's done. . .just as my intentions won't excuse my choices, not now that I know the truth.

Who am I to decide whether Devlin was justified or whether he can be redeemed? I'm not God. I'm not all-knowing—not even close. I may not be able to forgive him, but I can at least keep my soul clean, keep my tiny light as bright as it can possibly be.

I don't want to make the journey again.

I want to let him die, because he deserves to pay. But I fling myself back toward Terra anyway. When I arrive, I grab Devlin's salt and pepper soul, unsure how I can possibly make the return trip. I'm a juiced orange. I'm a cloth that's been wrung dry. I won't make it back alone, much less dragging someone with me. After he shrinks down, into a not-so-sparkly firefly, all that's left of Terra is the single flagstone I left him to die on. It flickers and shifts, but it's there. I suck it up, a mere teaspoon of power compared to the fire hose I drank from before.

I use that drip to take us both back home. It's enough, but only just.

When we arrive, I collapse in a heap. Exhaustion tugs at me and I drift toward it. This time, I know I won't wake up on Terra. I'll never wake up there again, because it's gone.

I don't mind. Not at all.

I'm looking forward to having a normal dream for once. I let myself go, imagining puffy clouds and unicorns with wings, and myself as the princess of all of them, with Jesse at my side, keeping me safe, keeping me sane, and making fun of every stupid thing my non-Terra-shackled brain can cook up.

When I finally fall asleep, I'm smiling.

EPILOGUE

Ra

The world is darkness. It has been darkness. It will be darkness. I haven't seen light in so long that I forget its shape, its texture, its feeling. I forget the joy it brings.

Until, finally, after an unimaginably long time. . .a single crack splits open.

And one small ray of energy shines through.

It wakes me from my drowsy half-sleep with its painful, piercingly sharp intrusion. Joy pulses through my core from the pain—because even pain is *feeling* and it's been so long since I felt anything at all. My body craves the energy like it craves life itself. I slurp down the single ray and I hunger, *I long* for more. But that one sip portends great things. A single crack is a beacon—a warning—it's the hope I've been waiting to see.

The time has finally come.

The Warden has been reborn. My prison walls are

weakening. The world beckons. I want to break free now —to fly—to soar—to consume—to destroy. I have so many debts to repay.

But it's not yet time.

Soon.

Very, very soon.

Ah, Sekhmet. As I wake, the sting of your betrayal lashes me again, as deeply as it did the first time. I've loved no other as I loved you, so no one else could hurt me as you did.

But I forgive you.

For Amun-Ra is no monster. No, Amun-Ra is a God.

You'll understand this time. Once you hear me out, once you *see*, you'll accept and repent and return and I will welcome you back into my arms with the mercy and generosity I've always shown you. Together we'll set things right. Together we'll rule them all.

Together, we'll Bind the world.

The energy from that tiny shaft of light fades, and exhaustion tugs me back downward with heavy hands. Sleep. Darkness. Peace, for now. I use the tiny burst of energy to break the lock on one inconsequential door. I can't free myself, not yet. But I can free one of my acolytes, my lowest lieutenant.

It's enough.

I allow the prison walls to pull me down, because I know my time is short now. My sentence is nearly served. My darling daughter, Sekhmet, you'll come for me.

The world will tremble and obey and worship us once again. Very, very soon now.

ACKNOWLEDGMENTS

First and foremost, I need to thank my editor, Carrie Harris. She went above and beyond, at an inconvenient time. I love her. Like, love love love her. (Did you get that? Blink blink blink?)

Peter Sentfleben is an amazing editor too, and he helped me turn a formless mess into what you read. If you think it's still a mess, that's probably his fault, too. Also, his skills with blurbs are unparalleled. THANK YOU for saving me.

My husband and kids are UNFAILINGLY supportive. I mean, they could not BE more supportive. Every time I whined, moaned, groaned, and gave up, they would cajole, compliment, encourage, and generally buoy me up in every way. This book is ONLY out in the world because of them. (Except for maybe Sammy, who would far prefer if I quit writing and spent more time squeezing him. Actually, I could get behind that most days, too.)

And for my ARC team. You guys know that in the finalization of this book, there were some miserable hiccups. I love your support, your long-suffering patience and your cheerleading. You are my best and most wonderful fans and I love you.

My cover artist Lara—you are a wizard and a friend. No one is more patient. No one is more understanding. I trust you with the most important thing for my baby—its face. Thank you for never letting me down. I admire your vision and appreciate your tireless support.

And I can't forget my readers, past, current, future. At the end of the day, I go through every step of this process for YOU. Thank you for loving Alora and Jesse and the whole crew. Thank you for cheering and crying and laughing with them, just like I do.

Bridget loves her husband (every day) and all five of her kids (most days). She's a lawyer, but does as little legal work as possible. She has three goofy horses, one very busy dog and one very tiny fluffy one, one spoiled barn cat, two lion's head rabbits, and more chickens than she cares to admit. She makes cookies too often, and believes they should be their own food group. In a (possibly misguided attempt) to level the scales between consumption and exertion, she kick boxes every day. So if you don't like her books, her kids, or her cookies, maybe don't tell her in person.

Yuck! What's for Dinner?